Pretty Little Liars

VOLUMES 3 AND 4

BOOKS BY SARA SHEPARD

Pretty Little Liars
Flawless
Perfect
Unbelievable
Wicked
Killer
Heartless
Wanted
Twisted
Ruthless
Stunning
Burned
Crushed
Deadly
Toxic

Pretty Little Secrets
Ali's Pretty Little Lies

The Perfectionists

The Lying Game
Never Have I Ever
Two Truths and a Lie
Hide and Seek
Cross My Heart, Hope to Die
Seven Minutes in Heaven

The First Lie (a digital original novella)
True Lies (a digital original novella)

Pretty Little Liars

VOLUME 3

PERFECT

VOLUME 4

UNBELIEVABLE

SARA SHEPARD

HARPER TEEN

An Imprint of HarperCollinsPublishers

Produced by Alloy Entertainment
1700 Broadway, New York, NY 10019

ISBN 978-0-06-232293-7

Typography by Amy Trombat

14 15 16 17 18 CG/RRDH 10 9 8 7 6 5 4 3 2

First edition, 2014

CONTENTS

PERFECT

To ALI

Look and you will find it—what is unsought will go undetected.

—SOPHOCLES

KEEP YOUR FRIENDS CLOSE . . .

Have you ever had a friend turn on you? Just totally transform from someone you thought you knew into someone . . . else? I'm not talking your boyfriend from nursery school who grows up and gets gawky and ugly and zitty, or your friend from camp whom you've got nothing to say to when she comes to visit you over Christmas break, or even a girl in your clique who suddenly breaks away and turns goth or into one of those granola Outward Bound kids. No. I'm talking about your soul mate. The girl you know everything about. Who knows everything about you. One day she turns around and is a completely different person.

Well, it happens. It happened in Rosewood.

"Watch it, Aria. Your face is going to freeze like that." Spencer Hastings unwrapped an orange Popsicle and slid it into her mouth. She was referring to the squinty-eyed drunk-pirate face her best friend, Aria Montgomery, was making as she tried to get her Sony Handycam to focus.

"You sound like my mom, Spence." Emily Fields laughed, adjusting her T-shirt, which had a picture of a baby chicken in goggles on it and said, INSTANT SWIM CHICK! JUST ADD WATER! Her friends had forbidden Emily from wearing her goofy swimming T-shirts—"Instant Swim Dork! Just add loser!" Alison DiLaurentis had joked when Emily walked in.

"Your mom says that too?" Hanna Marin asked, throwing away her green-stained Popsicle stick. Hanna always ate faster than anyone else. *"Your face will freeze that way,"* she mimicked.

Alison looked Hanna up and down and cackled. "Your mom should've warned you that your *butt* would freeze that way."

Hanna's face fell as she pulled down her pink-and-white striped T-shirt—she'd borrowed it from Ali, and it kept riding up, revealing a white strip of her stomach. Alison tapped Hanna's shin with her flip-flop. "Just joking."

It was a Friday night in May near the end of seventh grade, and best friends Alison, Hanna, Spencer, Aria, and Emily were gathered in Spencer's family's plushly decorated family room, with the Popsicle box, a big bottle of cherry vanilla Diet Dr Pepper, and their cell phones splayed out on the coffee table. A month ago, Ali had come to school with a brand-new LG flip phone, and the others had rushed out to buy their own that very day. They all had pink leather holsters to match Ali's, too—well, all except for Aria, whose holster was made of pink mohair. She'd knitted it herself.

Aria moved the camera's lever back and forth to zoom in and out. "And anyway, my face isn't going to freeze like this. I'm concentrating on setting up this shot. This is for posterity. For when we become famous."

"Well, we all know *I'm* going to get famous." Alison thrust back her shoulders and turned her head to the side, revealing her swanlike neck.

"Why are you going to be famous?" Spencer challenged, sounding bitchier than she probably meant to.

"I'm going to have my own show. I'll be a smarter, cuter Paris Hilton."

Spencer snorted. But Emily pursed her pale lips, considering, and Hanna nodded, truly believing. This was *Ali*. She wouldn't stay here in Rosewood, Pennsylvania, for long. Sure, Rosewood was glamorous by most standards—all its residents looked like walk-on models for a *Town & Country* photo shoot—but they all knew Ali was destined for greater things.

She'd plucked them out of oblivion a year and a half ago to be her best friends. With Ali by their sides, they had become *the* girls of Rosewood Day, the private school they attended. They had such power now—to deem who was cool and who wasn't, to throw the best parties, to nab the best seats in study hall, to run for student office and win by an overwhelming number of votes. Well, that last one only applied to Spencer. Aside from a few twists and turns—and accidentally blinding Jenna Cavanaugh, which they tried their hardest not to think about—their lives had transformed from passable to perfect.

"How about we film a talk show?" Aria suggested. She considered herself the friends' official filmmaker—one of the many things she wanted to be when she grew up was the next Jean-Luc Godard, some abstract French director. "Ali, you're famous. And Spencer, you're the interviewer."

"I'll be the makeup girl," Hanna volunteered, rooting through her backpack to find her polka-dotted vinyl makeup bag.

"I'll do hair." Emily pushed her reddish-blond bob behind her ears and rushed to Ali's side. "You have gorgeous hair, *chérie*," she said to Ali in a faux-French accent.

Ali slid her Popsicle out of her mouth. "Doesn't *chérie* mean *girlfriend*?"

The others were quick to laugh, but Emily paled. "No, that's *petite amie*." Lately, Em was sensitive when Ali made jokes at her expense. She never used to be.

"Okay," Aria said, making sure the camera was level. "You guys ready?"

Spencer flopped on the couch and placed a rhinestone tiara left over from a New Year's party on her head. She'd been carrying the crown around all night.

"You can't wear that," Ali snapped.

"Why not?" Spencer adjusted the crown so it was straight.

"Because. If anything, *I'm* the princess."

"Why do *you* always get to be the princess?" Spencer muttered under her breath. A nervous ripple swept through the others. Spencer and Ali weren't getting along, and no one knew why.

Ali's cell phone let out a bleat. She reached down, flipped it open, and tilted it away so no one else could see. "Sweet." Her fingers flew across the keypad as she typed a text.

"Who are you writing to?" Emily's voice sounded eggshell-thin and small.

"Can't tell. Sorry." Ali didn't look up.

"You can't tell?" Spencer was irate. "What do you mean you can't tell?"

Ali glanced up. "Sorry, *princess*. You don't have to know *everything*." Ali closed her phone and set it on the leather couch. "Don't start filming yet, Aria. I have to pee." She dashed out of Spencer's family room toward the hall bathroom, plopping her Popsicle stick in the trash as she went.

Once they heard the bathroom door close, Spencer was the first to speak. "Don't you just want to *kill* her sometimes?"

The others flinched. They never bad-mouthed Ali. It was as blasphemous as burning the Rosewood Day official flag on school property, or admitting that Johnny

Depp really wasn't *that* cute—that he was actually kind of old and creepy.

Of course, on the inside, they felt a little differently. This spring, Ali hadn't been around as much. She'd gotten closer with the high school girls on her JV field hockey squad and never invited Aria, Emily, Spencer, or Hanna to join them at lunch or come with them to the King James Mall.

And Ali had begun to keep secrets. Secret texts, secret phone calls, secret giggles about things she wouldn't tell them. Sometimes they'd see Ali's screen name online, but when they tried to IM her, she wouldn't respond. They'd bared their souls to Ali—telling her things they hadn't told the others, things they didn't want *anyone* to know—and they expected her to reciprocate. Hadn't Ali made them all promise a year ago, after the horrible thing with Jenna happened, that they would tell one another everything, absolutely *everything*, until the end of time?

The girls hated to think of what eighth grade would be like if things kept going like this. But it didn't mean they hated *Ali*.

Aria wound a piece of long, dark hair around her fingers and laughed nervously. "Kill her because she's so cute, maybe." She hit the camera's power switch, turning it on.

"And because she wears a size zero," Hanna added.

"That's what I meant." Spencer glanced at Ali's phone,

which was wedged between two couch cushions. "Want to read her texts?"

"I do," Hanna whispered.

Emily stood up from her perch on the couch's arm. "I don't know. . . ." She started inching away from Ali's phone, as if just being close to it incriminated her.

Spencer scooped up Ali's cell. She looked curiously at the blank screen. "C'mon. Don't you want to know who texted her?"

"It was probably just Katy," Emily whispered, referring to one of Ali's hockey friends. "You should put it down, Spence."

Aria took the camera off the tripod and walked toward Spencer. "Let's do it."

They gathered around. Spencer opened the phone and pushed a button. "It's locked."

"Do you know her password?" Aria asked, still filming.

"Try her birthday," Hanna whispered. She took the phone from Spencer and punched in the digits. The screen didn't change. "What do I do now?"

They heard Ali's voice before they saw her. "What are you guys doing?"

Spencer dropped Ali's phone back onto the couch. Hanna stepped back so abruptly, she banged her shin against the coffee table.

Ali stomped through the door to the family room, her eyebrows knitted together. "Were you looking at my phone?"

"Of course not!" Hanna cried.

"We were," Emily admitted, sitting on the couch, then standing up again. Aria shot her a look and then hid behind the camera lens.

But Ali was no longer paying attention. Spencer's older sister, Melissa, a senior in high school, burst into the Hastings' kitchen from the garage. A takeout bag from Otto, a restaurant near the Hastings' neighborhood, hung from her wrists. Her adorable boyfriend, Ian, was with her. Ali stood up straighter. Spencer smoothed her dirty-blond hair and straightened her tiara.

Ian stepped into the family room. "Hey, girls."

"Hi," Spencer said in a loud voice. "How are you, Ian?"

"I'm cool." Ian smiled at Spencer. "Cute crown."

"Thanks!" Spencer fluttered her coal-black eyelashes.

Ali rolled her eyes. "Be a little more obvious," she sing-songed under her breath.

But it was hard not to crush on Ian. He had curly blond hair, perfect white teeth, and stunning blue eyes, and none of them could forget the recent soccer game where he'd changed his shirt midquarter and, for five glorious seconds, they'd gotten a full-on view of his naked chest. It was almost universally believed that his gorgeousness was wasted on Melissa, who was totally prudish and acted way too much like Mrs. Hastings, Spencer's mother.

Ian plopped down on the edge of the couch near Ali. "So, what are you girls doing?"

"Oh, not much," Aria said, adjusting the camera's focus. "Making a film."

"A film?" Ian looked amused. "Can I be in it?"

"Of course," Spencer said quickly. She plopped down on the other side of him.

Ian grinned into the camera. "So what are my lines?"

"It's a talk show," Spencer explained. She glanced at Ali, gauging her reaction, but Ali didn't respond. "I'm the host. You and Ali are my guests. I'll do you first."

Ali let out a sarcastic snort and Spencer's cheeks flamed as pink as her Ralph Lauren T-shirt. Ian let the reference pass by. "Okay. Interview away."

Spencer sat up straighter on the couch, crossing her muscular legs just like a talk show host. She picked up the pink microphone from Hanna's karaoke machine and held it under her chin. "Welcome to the Spencer Hastings show. For my first question—"

"Ask him who his favorite teacher at Rosewood is," Aria called out.

Ali perked up. Her blue eyes glittered. "That's a good question for you, Aria. You should ask him if he wants to *hook up* with any of his teachers. In vacant parking lots."

Aria's mouth fell open. Hanna and Emily, who were standing off to the side near the credenza, exchanged a confused glance.

"All my teachers are dogs," Ian said slowly, not getting whatever was happening.

"Ian, can you *please* help me?" Melissa made a clattering noise in the kitchen.

"One sec," Ian called out.

"*Ian.*" Melissa sounded annoyed.

"I got one." Spencer tossed her long blond hair behind her ears. She was loving that Ian was paying more attention to them than to Melissa. "What would your ultimate graduation gift be?"

"*Ian,*" Melissa called through her teeth, and Spencer glanced at her sister through the wide French doors to the kitchen. The light from the fridge cast a shadow across her face. "I. Need. Help."

"Easy," Ian answered, ignoring her. "I'd want a base-jumping lesson."

"Base-jumping?" Aria called. "What's that?"

"Parachuting from the top of a building," Ian explained.

As Ian told a story about Hunter Queenan, one of his friends who had base-jumped, the girls leaned forward eagerly. Aria focused the camera on Ian's jaw, which looked hewn out of stone. Her eyes flickered for a moment to Ali. She was sitting next to Ian, staring off into space. Was Ali *bored*? She probably had better things to do—that text was probably about plans with her glamorous older friends.

Aria glanced again at Ali's cell phone, which was resting on the cushion of the couch next to her arm. What was she hiding from them? What was she up to?

Don't you sometimes want to kill her? Spencer's question floated through Aria's brain as Ian rambled on. Deep down, she knew they all felt that way. It might be better if Ali were just . . . gone, instead of leaving them behind.

"So Hunter said he got the most amazing rush when he base-jumped," Ian concluded. "Better than anything. Including sex."

"Ian," Melissa warned.

"That sounds incredible." Spencer looked to Ali on the other side of Ian. "Doesn't it?"

"Yes." Ali looked sleepy, almost like she was in a trance. "Incredible."

The rest of the week had been a blur: final exams, planning parties, more get-togethers, and more tension. And then, on the evening of the last day of seventh grade, Ali went missing. Just like that. One minute she was there, the next . . . gone.

The police scoured Rosewood for clues. They questioned the four girls separately, asking if Ali had been acting strangely or if anything unusual had happened recently. They all thought long and hard. The night she disappeared had been strange—she'd been hypnotizing them and had run out of the barn after she and Spencer had a stupid fight about the blinds and just . . . *never came back*. But had there been other strange nights? They considered the night they tried to read Ali's texts, but not for very long—after Ian and Melissa left, Ali had snapped out of her funk. They'd had a dance contest and played with Hanna's karaoke machine. The mystery texts on Ali's phone had been forgotten.

Next, the cops asked if they thought anyone close to Ali might have wanted to hurt her. Hanna, Aria, and Emily all thought of the same thing: *Don't you sometimes want to kill her?* Spencer had snarled. But no. She'd been kidding. Hadn't she?

"Nobody wanted to hurt Ali," Emily said, pushing the worry out of her mind.

"Absolutely not," Aria answered too, in her own separate interview, darting her eyes away from the burly cop sitting next to her on the porch swing.

"I don't think so," Hanna said in her interview, fiddling with the pale blue string bracelet Ali had made for them after Jenna's accident. "Ali wasn't that close with many people. Only us. And we all loved her to death."

Sure, Spencer seemed angry with Ali. But really, deep down, weren't they all? Ali was perfect—beautiful, smart, sexy, irresistible—and she was ditching them. Maybe they did hate her for it. But that didn't mean any of them wanted her gone.

It's amazing what you don't see, though. Even when it's right in front of your eyes.

1

SPENCER'S HARD WORK PAYS OFF

Spencer Hastings should have been sleeping at six-thirty on Monday morning. Instead, she was sitting in a therapist's blue-and-green waiting room, feeling a little like she was trapped inside an aquarium. Her older sister, Melissa, was sitting on an emerald-colored chair opposite her. Melissa looked up from her *Principles of Emerging Markets* textbook—she was in an MBA program at the University of Pennsylvania—and gave Spencer a motherly smile.

"I've felt so much *clearer* since I started seeing Dr. Evans," purred Melissa, whose appointment was right after Spencer's. "You're going to love her. She's incredible."

Of course she's incredible, Spencer thought nastily. Melissa would find anyone willing to listen to her for a whole uninterrupted hour amazing.

"But she might come on a little strong for you, Spence," Melissa warned, slapping her book closed. "She's going to tell you things about yourself you don't want to hear."

Spencer shifted her weight. "I'm not six. I can take criticism."

Melissa gave Spencer a tiny eyebrow-raise, clearly indicating that she wasn't so sure. Spencer hid behind her *Philadelphia* magazine, wondering again why she was here. Spencer's mother, Veronica, had booked her an appointment with a therapist—*Melissa's* therapist—after Spencer's old friend Alison DiLaurentis had been found dead and Toby Cavanaugh committed suicide. Spencer suspected the appointment was also meant to sort through why Spencer had hooked up with Melissa's boyfriend, Wren. Spencer was doing fine though. Really. And wasn't going to her worst enemy's therapist like going to an ugly girl's plastic surgeon? Spencer feared she'd probably come out of her very first shrink session with the mental-health equivalent of hideously lopsided fake boobs.

Just then, the office door swung open, and a petite blond woman wearing tortoiseshell glasses, a black tunic, and black pants poked her head out.

"Spencer?" the woman said. "I'm Dr. Evans. Come in."

Spencer strode into Dr. Evans's office, which was spare and bright and thankfully nothing like the waiting room. It contained a black leather couch and a gray suede chair. A large desk held a phone, a stack of manila folders, a chrome gooseneck lamp, and one of those weighted drinking-bird toys that Mr. Craft, the earth science teacher, loved. Dr. Evans settled into the suede chair and gestured for Spencer to sit on the couch.

"So," Dr. Evans said, once they were comfy, "I've heard a lot about you."

Spencer wrinkled her nose and glanced toward the waiting room. "From Melissa, I guess?"

"From your mom." Dr. Evans opened to the first page of a red notebook. "She says that you've had some turmoil in your life, especially lately."

Spencer fixed her gaze on the end table next to the couch. It held a candy dish, a box of Kleenex—of *course*—and one of those pegboard IQ games, the kind where you jumped the pegs over one another until there was only one peg remaining. There used to be one of those in the DiLaurentis family den; she and Ali had solved it together, meaning they were both geniuses. "I think I'm coping," she muttered. "I'm not, like, suicidal."

"A close friend died. A neighbor, too. That must be hard."

Spencer let her head rest on the back of the couch and looked up. It looked like the bumpily plastered ceiling had acne. She probably needed to talk to someone—it wasn't like she could talk to her family about Ali, Toby, or the terrifying notes she'd been getting from the evil stalker who was known simply as A. And her old friends—they'd been avoiding her ever since she'd admitted that Toby had known all along that they'd blinded his stepsister, Jenna—a secret she'd kept from them for three long years.

But three weeks had gone by since Toby's suicide, and almost a month had passed since the workers unearthed Ali's body. Spencer was coping better with all of it, mostly, because A had vanished. She hadn't received a note since before Foxy, Rosewood's big charity benefit. At first, A's silence made Spencer feel edgy—perhaps it was the calm before the hurricane—but as more time passed, she began to relax. Her manicured nails dislodged themselves from the heels of her hands. She started sleeping with her desk light off again. She'd received an A+ on her latest calc test and an A on her Plato's *Republic* paper. Her breakup with Wren—who had dumped her for Melissa, who had in turn dumped him—didn't sting so much anymore, and her family had reverted back into everyday obliviousness. Even Melissa's presence—she was staying with the family while a small army renovated her town house in Philly—was mostly tolerable.

Maybe the nightmare was over.

Spencer wiggled her toes inside her knee-high buff-colored kidskin boots. Even if she felt comfortable enough with Dr. Evans to tell her about A, it was a moot point. Why bring A up if A was gone?

"It is hard, but Alison has been missing for years. I've moved on," Spencer finally said. Maybe Dr. Evans would realize Spencer wasn't going to talk and end their session early.

Dr. Evans wrote something in her notebook. Spencer

wondered what. "I've also heard you and your sister were having some boyfriend issues."

Spencer bristled. She could only imagine Melissa's extremely slanted version of the Wren debacle—it probably involved Spencer eating whipped cream off Wren's bare stomach in Melissa's bed while her sister watched helplessly from the window. "It wasn't really a big deal," she muttered.

Dr. Evans lowered her shoulders and gave Spencer the same *you're not fooling me* look her mother used. "He was your sister's boyfriend first, wasn't he? And you dated him behind her back?"

Spencer clenched her teeth. "Look, I know it was wrong, okay? I don't need another lecture."

Dr. Evans stared at her. "I'm not going to lecture you. Perhaps . . ." She put a finger to her cheek. "Perhaps you had your reasons."

Spencer's eyes widened. Were her ears working correctly—was Dr. Evans seriously suggesting that Spencer wasn't 100 percent to blame? Perhaps $175 an hour wasn't a blasphemous price to pay for therapy, after all.

"Do you and your sister ever spend time together?" Dr. Evans asked after a pause.

Spencer reached into the candy dish for a Hershey's Kiss. She pulled off the silver wrapper in one long curl, flattened the foil in her palm, and popped the kiss in her mouth. "Never. Unless we're with our parents—but it's not like Melissa talks to *me*. All she does is brag to my parents about her accomplishments and her insanely boring town house renovations." Spencer looked squarely at Dr. Evans. "I guess you know my parents bought her a town house in Old City simply because she graduated from college."

"I did." Dr. Evans stretched her arms into the air and two silver bangle bracelets slid to her elbow. "Fascinating stuff."

And then she winked.

Spencer felt like her heart was going to burst out of her chest. Apparently Dr. Evans didn't care about the merits of sisal versus jute either. *Yes.*

They talked a while longer, Spencer enjoying it more and more, and then Dr. Evans motioned to the Salvador Dalí melting-clocks clock that hung above her desk to indicate that their time was up. Spencer said good-bye and opened the office door, rubbing her head as if the therapist had cracked it open and tinkered around in her brain. That actually hadn't been as torturous as she'd thought it would be.

She shut the therapist's office door and turned around. To her surprise, her mother was sitting in a pale-green wing chair next to Melissa, reading a *Main Line* style magazine.

"Mom." Spencer frowned. "What are you doing here?"

Veronica Hastings looked like she'd come straight from the family's riding stables. She was wearing a white

Petit Bateau T-shirt, skinny jeans, and her beat-up riding boots. There was even a little bit of hay in her hair. "I have news," she announced.

Both Mrs. Hastings and Melissa had very serious looks on their faces. Spencer's insides started to whirl. Someone had died. Someone—Ali's killer—had killed again. Perhaps A was back. *Please, no,* she thought.

"I got a call from Mr. McAdam," Mrs. Hastings said, standing up. Mr. McAdam was Spencer's AP economics teacher. "He wanted to talk about some essays you wrote a few weeks ago." She took a step closer, the scent of her Chanel No. 5 perfume tickling Spencer's nose. "Spence, he wants to nominate one of them for a Golden Orchid."

Spencer stepped back. "A Golden *Orchid*?"

The Golden Orchid was *the* most prestigious essay contest in the country, the high school essay equivalent of an Oscar. If she won, *People* and *Time* would do a feature story on her. Yale, Harvard, and Stanford would beg her to enroll. Spencer had followed the successes of Golden Orchid winners the way other people followed celebrities. The Golden Orchid winner of 1998 was now managing editor of a very famous fashion magazine. The winner from 1994 had become a congressman at 28.

"That's right." Her mother broke into a dazzling smile.

"Oh my God." Spencer felt faint. But not from excitement—from dread. The essays she'd turned in hadn't been hers—they were Melissa's. Spencer had been in a rush to finish the assignment, and A had suggested she "borrow" Melissa's old work. So much had gone on in the past few weeks, it had slipped her mind.

Spencer winced. Mr. McAdam—or Squidward, as everyone called him—had loved Melissa when she was his student. How could he not remember Melissa's essays, especially if they were *that* good?

Her mother grabbed Spencer's arm and she flinched—her mother's hands were always corpse-cold. "We're so proud of you, Spence!"

Spencer couldn't control the muscles around her mouth. She had to come clean with this before she got in too deep. "Mom, I can't—"

But Mrs. Hastings wasn't listening. "I've already called Jordana at the *Philadelphia Sentinel*. Remember Jordana? She used to take riding lessons at the stables? Anyway, she's thrilled. No one from this area has ever been nominated. She wants to write an article about you!"

Spencer blinked. Everyone read the *Philadelphia Sentinel* newspaper.

"The interview and photo shoot are all scheduled," Mrs. Hastings breezed on, picking up her giant saffron-colored Tod's satchel and jingling her car keys. "Wednesday before school. They'll provide a stylist. I'm sure Uri will come to give you a blowout."

Spencer was afraid to make eye contact with her mom, so she stared at the waiting-room reading material—an assortment of *New Yorker*s and *Economist*s, and a big book of fairy tales that was teetering on top of a Dubble Bubble tub of Legos. She couldn't tell her mom about the stolen paper—not now. And it wasn't as if she was going to *win* the Golden Orchid, anyway. Hundreds of people were nominated, from the best high schools all over the country. She probably wouldn't even make it past the first cut.

"That sounds great," Spencer sputtered.

Her mom pranced out the door. Spencer lingered a moment longer, transfixed by the wolf on the cover of the fairy tale book. She'd had the same one when she was little. The wolf was dressed up in a negligee and bonnet, leering at a blond, naïve Red Riding Hood. It used to give Spencer nightmares.

Melissa cleared her throat. When Spencer looked up, her sister was staring.

"Congrats, Spence," Melissa said evenly. "The Golden Orchid. That's huge."

"Thanks," Spencer blurted. There was an eerily familiar expression on Melissa's face. And then Spencer realized: Melissa looked exactly like the big bad wolf.

2

JUST ANOTHER SEXUALLY CHARGED DAY IN AP ENGLISH

Aria Montgomery sat down in English class on Monday morning, just as the air outside the open widow started to smell like rain. The PA crackled, and everyone in the class looked at the little speaker on the ceiling.

"Hello, students! This is Spencer Hastings, your junior class vice president!" Spencer's voice rang out clear and loud. She sounded perky and assured, as if she'd taken a course in Announcements 101. "I want to remind everyone that the Rosewood Day Hammerheads are swimming against the Drury Academy Eels tomorrow. It's the biggest meet of the season, so let's all show some spirit and come out and support the team!" There was a pause. "Yeah!"

Some of the class snickered. Aria felt an uneasy chill. Despite everything that had happened—Alison's murder, Toby's suicide, A—Spencer was the president or VP of every club around. But to Aria, Spencer's spiritedness sounded . . . fake. She had seen a side of Spencer others hadn't. Spencer had known for years that Ali had threatened Toby Cavanaugh to keep him quiet about Jenna's accident, and Aria couldn't forgive her for keeping such a dangerous secret from the rest of them.

"Okay, class," Ezra Fitz, Aria's AP English teacher, said. He resumed writing on the board, printing *The Scarlet Letter* in his angular handwriting, and then he underlined it four times.

"In Nathaniel Hawthorne's masterpiece, Hester Prynne cheats on her husband, and her town forces her to wear a big, red, shameful *A* on her chest as a reminder of what she's done." Mr. Fitz turned from the board and pushed his square glasses up the bridge of his sloped nose. "Can anyone think of other stories that have the same falling-from-grace theme? About people who are ridiculed or cast out for their mistakes?"

Noel Kahn raised his hand and his chain-link Rolex watch slid down his wrist. "How about that episode of *The Real World* when the housemates voted for the psycho girl to leave?"

The class laughed, and Mr. Fitz looked perplexed. "Guys, this is supposed to be an AP class." Mr. Fitz turned to Aria's row. "Aria? How about you? Thoughts?"

Aria paused. Her life was a good example. Not long ago, she and her family had been living harmoniously in Iceland, Alison hadn't been officially dead, and A hadn't existed. But then, in a horrible unraveling of events that started six weeks ago, Aria had moved back to preppy Rosewood, Ali's body had been discovered under the concrete slab behind her old house, and A had outed the Montgomery family's biggest secret: that Aria's father, Byron, had cheated on her mother, Ella, with one of his students, Meredith. The news hit Ella hard and she promptly threw Byron out. Finding out that Aria had kept Byron's secret from her for three years hadn't helped Ella much either. Mother-daughter relations hadn't been too warm and fuzzy since.

Of course, it could have been worse. Aria hadn't gotten any texts from A in the last three weeks. Although Byron was now allegedly living with Meredith, at least Ella had begun speaking to Aria again. And Rosewood hadn't been invaded by aliens yet, although after all the weird things that had happened in this town, Aria wouldn't have been surprised if that were next.

"Aria?" Mr. Fitz goaded. "Any ideas?"

Mason Byers came to Aria's rescue. "What about Adam and Eve and that snake?"

"Great," Mr. Fitz said absentmindedly. His eyes rested on Aria for another second before looking away. Aria felt a warm, prickly rush. She had hooked up with Mr. Fitz— Ezra—at Snooker's, a college bar, before either of them knew he would be her new AP English teacher. He was the one who'd ended it, and afterward, Aria had learned he had a girlfriend in New York. But she didn't hold a grudge. Things were going well with her new boyfriend, Sean Ackard, who was kind and sweet and also happened to be gorgeous.

Besides, Ezra was the best English teacher Aria had ever had. In the month since school had started, he'd assigned four amazing books and staged a skit based on Edward Albee's "The Sandbox." Soon, the class was going to do a *Desperate Housewives*-style interpretation of *Medea,* the Greek play where a mother murders her children. Ezra wanted them to think unconventionally, and unconventional was Aria's forte. Now, instead of calling her Finland, her classmate Noel Kahn had given Aria a new nickname, Brownnoser. It felt good to be excited about school again, though, and at times she almost forgot things with Ezra had ever been complicated.

Until Ezra threw her a crooked smile, of course. Then she couldn't help but feel fluttery. Just a little.

Hanna Marin, who sat right in front of Aria, raised her hand. "How about that book where two girls are best friends, but then, all of a sudden, one of the best friends turns *evil* and steals the other one's boyfriend?"

Ezra scratched his head. "I'm sorry . . . I don't think I've read that book."

Aria clenched her fists. *She* knew what Hanna meant. "For the last *time,* Hanna, I didn't steal Sean from you! You guys were already. Broken. Up!"

The class rippled with laughter. Hanna's shoulders became rigid. "Someone's a little self-centered," she murmured to Aria without turning around. "Who said I was talking about *you*?"

But Aria knew she was. When Aria had returned from Iceland, she'd been stunned to see that Hanna had morphed from Ali's chubby, awkward lackey to a thin, beautiful, designer-clothes-wearing goddess. It seemed like Hanna had everything she'd ever wanted: she and her best friend, Mona Vanderwaal—also a transformed dork—ruled the school, and Hanna had even nabbed Sean Ackard, the boy she'd pined over since sixth grade. Aria had only gone for Sean after hearing that Hanna had dumped him. But she quickly found out it had been the other way around.

Aria had hoped she and her old friends might reunite, especially since they'd all received notes from A. Yet, they weren't even speaking—things were right back to where they'd been during those awkward, worried weeks after Ali's disappearance. Aria hadn't even told them about what A had done to her family. The only ex–best friend Aria was still sort of friendly with was Emily Fields—but their conversations had mostly consisted of Emily blubbering about how guilty she felt about Toby's death, until Aria had finally insisted that it wasn't her fault.

"Well, anyway," Ezra said, putting copies of *The Scarlet Letter* at the front of each row to pass back, "I want everyone to read chapters one through five this week, and you have a three-page essay on any themes you see at the beginning of the book due on Friday. Okay?"

Everyone groaned and started to talk. Aria slid her book into her yak-fur bag. Hanna reached down to pick her purse off the floor. Aria touched Hanna's thin, pale arm. "Look, I'm sorry. I really am."

Hanna yanked her arm away, pressed her lips together, and wordlessly stuffed *The Scarlet Letter* into her purse. It kept jamming, and she let out a frustrated grunt.

Classical music tinkled through the loudspeaker, indicating the period was over. Hanna shot up from her seat as if it were on fire. Aria rose slowly, shoving her pen and notebook into her purse and heading for the door.

"Aria."

She turned. Ezra was leaning against his oak desk, his tattered caramel leather briefcase pressed to his hip. "Everything okay?" he asked.

"Sorry about all that," she said. "Hanna and I have some issues. It won't happen again."

"No problem." Ezra set his mug of chai down. "Is everything *else* okay?"

Aria bit her lip and considered telling him what was going on. But why? For all she knew, Ezra was as sleazy as her father. If he really did have a girlfriend in New York, then he'd cheated on her when he'd hooked up with Aria.

"Everything's fine," she managed.

"Good. You're doing a great job in class." He smiled, showing his two adorably overlapping bottom teeth.

"Yeah, I'm enjoying myself," she said, taking a step

toward the door. But as she did, she stumbled over her super-high stack-heeled boots, careening into Ezra's desk. Ezra grabbed her waist and pulled her upright . . . and into him. His body felt warm and safe, and he smelled good, like chili powder, cigarettes, and old books.

Aria moved away quickly. "Are you okay?" Ezra asked.

"Yeah." She busied herself by straightening her school blazer. "Sorry."

"It's okay," Ezra answered, jamming his hands in his jacket pockets. "So . . . see you."

"Yeah. See you."

Aria walked out of the classroom, her breathing fast and shallow. Maybe she was nuts, but she was pretty sure Ezra had held her for a second longer than he needed to. And she was certain she'd liked it.

3

THERE'S NO SUCH
THING AS BAD PRESS

During their free period Monday afternoon, Hanna Marin and her best friend, Mona Vanderwaal, were sitting in the corner booth of Steam, Rosewood Day's coffee bar, doing what they did best: ripping on people who weren't as fabulous as they were.

Mona poked Hanna with one end of her chocolate-dipped biscotti. To Mona, food was more like a prop, less like something to eat. "Jennifer Feldman's got some logs, doesn't she?"

"Poor girl." Hanna mock-pouted. *Logs* was Mona's shorthand term for tree-trunk legs: solid and unshapely thighs and calves with no tapering from knees to ankles.

"And her feet look like overstuffed sausage casings in those heels!" Mona cawed.

Hanna snickered, watching as Jennifer, who was on the diving team, hung up a poster on the far wall that read,

SWIM MEET TOMORROW! ROSEWOOD DAY HAMMERHEADS VS. DRURY ACADEMY EELS! Her ankles *were* hideously thick. "That's what girls with fat ankles get when they try to wear Louboutins," Hanna sighed. She and Mona were the thin-ankled sylphs Christian Louboutin shoes were meant for, obviously.

Mona took a big sip of her Americano and pulled out her Gucci wallet diary from her eggplant-colored Botkier purse. Hanna nodded approvingly. They had other things to do besides criticize people today, like plan not one but two parties: one for the two of them, and the second for the rest of Rosewood Day's elite.

"First things first." Mona uncapped her pen. "The Frenniversary. What should we do tonight? Shopping? Massages? Dinner?"

"All of that," Hanna answered. "And we definitely have to hit Otter." Otter was a new high-end boutique at the mall.

"I'm *loving* Otter," Mona agreed.

"Where should we have dinner?" Hanna asked.

"Rive Gauche, of course," Mona said loudly, talking over the groaning coffee grinder.

"You're right. They'll definitely give us wine."

"Should we invite boys?" Mona's blue eyes gleamed. "Eric Kahn keeps calling me. Maybe Noel could come for you?"

Hanna frowned. Despite being cute, incredibly rich and part of the über-sexy clan of Kahn brothers, Noel wasn't really her type. "No boys," she decided. "Although that's very cool about Eric."

"This is going to be a fabulous Frenniversary." Mona grinned so broadly that her dimples showed. "Can you believe this is our *third*?"

Hanna smiled. Their Frenniversary marked the day Hanna and Mona had talked on the phone for three and a half hours—the obvious indicator that they were best friends. Although they'd known each other since kindergarten, they'd never really spoken before cheer-leading tryouts a few weeks before the first day of eighth grade. By then, Ali had been missing for two months and Hanna's old friends had become really distant, so she'd decided to give Mona a chance. It was worth it—Mona was funny, sarcastic, and, despite her thing for animal backpacks and Razor scooters, she secretly devoured *Vogue* and *Teen Vogue* as ravenously as Hanna did. Within weeks, they'd decided to be best friends and transform themselves into the most popular girls at school. And look: Now they had.

"Now for the bigger plans," Mona said, flipping another page of her notebook. *"Sweet seventeen,"* she sang to the MTV *My Super Sweet Sixteen* melody.

"It's going to rock," Hanna gushed. Mona's birth-day was this Saturday, and she had almost all the party details in place. She was going to have it at the Hollis Planetarium, where there were telescopes in every room—even the bathrooms. She'd booked a DJ, caterers, and a trapeze school—so guests could swing over the dance floor—as well as a videographer, who would film the party and simultaneously webcast it onto a Jumbotron screen. Mona had carefully instructed guests to wear formal dress only on the invites. If someone turned up in jeans or Juicy sweats, security would not-so-politely turn them away.

"So I was thinking," Mona said, stuffing a napkin into her empty paper coffee cup. "It's a little last-minute, but I'm going to have a court."

"A court?" Hanna raised a perfectly plucked eyebrow.

"It's an excuse to get that fabulous Zac Posen dress you keep frothing over at Saks—the fitting is tomorrow. And we'll wear tiaras and make the boys bow down to us."

Hanna stifled a giggle. "We're not going to do an opening dance number, are we?" She and Mona had been on Julia Rubenstein's party court last year, and Julia had made them do a dance routine with a bunch of D-list male models. Hanna's dance partner smelled like garlic and had immediately asked her if she wanted to join him in the coatroom. She'd spent the rest of the party running away from him.

Mona scoffed, breaking her biscotti into smaller pieces. "Would I do something as lame as that?"

"Of course not." Hanna rested her chin in her hands. "So I'm the only girl in the court, right?"

Mona rolled her eyes. *"Obviously."*

Hanna shrugged. "I mean, I don't know who else you could pick."

"We just need to get you a date." Mona placed the tiniest piece of biscotti in her mouth.

"I don't want to take anyone from Rosewood Day," Hanna said quickly. "Maybe I'll ask someone from Hollis. And I'll bring more than one date." Her eyes lit up. "I could have a whole load of guys carry me around all night, like Cleopatra."

Mona gave her a high five. "*Now* you're talking."

Hanna chewed on the end of her straw. "I wonder if Sean will come."

"Don't know." Mona raised an eyebrow. "You're over him, right?"

"Of course." Hanna pushed her auburn hair over her shoulder. Bitterness still flickered inside her whenever she thought about how Sean had dumped her for way-too-tall, I'm-a-kiss-ass-English-student-and-think-I'm-hot-shit-because-I-lived-in-Europe Aria Montgomery, but whatever. It was Sean's loss. Now that boys knew she was available, Hanna's BlackBerry inbox was beeping with potential dates every few minutes.

"Good," Mona said. "Because you're *way* too hot for him, Han."

"I know," Hanna quipped, and they touched palms lightly in another high five. Hanna sat back, feeling a warm, reassuring whoosh of well-being. It was hard to believe that things had been shaky between her and Mona a month ago. Imagine, Mona thinking that Hanna wanted to be friends with Aria, Emily, and Spencer instead of her!

Okay, so Hanna *had* been keeping things from Mona, although she'd confessed most of it: her occasional purges, the trouble with her dad, her two arrests, the fact that she'd stripped for Sean at Noel Kahn's party and he'd rejected her. She'd downplayed everything, worried Mona would disown her for such horrible secrets, but Mona had taken it all in stride. She said every diva got in trouble once in a while, and Hanna decided she'd just overreacted. So what if she wasn't with Sean anymore? So what if she hadn't spoken to her father since Foxy? So what if she was still volunteering at Mr. Ackard's burn clinic to atone for wrecking his car? So what if her two worst enemies, Naomi Zeigler and Riley Wolfe, knew she had a bingeing problem and had spread rumors about her around the school? She and Mona were still tight, and A had stopped stalking her.

Kids began filtering out of the coffee bar, which meant that free period was about to end. As Hanna and Mona swaggered through the exit, Hanna realized they were approaching Naomi and Riley, who had been hiding behind the giant swirling Frappuccino machine. Hanna set her jaw and tried to hold her head high.

"*Baaaarf,*" Naomi hissed into Hanna's ear as she passed.

"*Yaaaaak,*" Riley taunted right behind her.

"Don't listen to them, Han," Mona said loudly.

"They're just pissed because you can fit into those Rich and Skinny jeans at Otter and they can't."

"It's cool," Hanna said breezily, sticking her nose into the air. "There's that, and at least I don't have inverted nipples."

Naomi's mouth got very small and tense. "That was because of the *bra* I was wearing," she said through clenched teeth. Hanna had seen Naomi's inverted nipples when they were changing for gym the week before. Maybe it *was* just from the weird bra she had on, but hey—all's fair in love and the war to be popular.

Hanna glanced over her shoulder and shot Naomi and Riley a haughty, condescending look. She felt like a queen snubbing two grubby little wenches. And it gave Hanna great satisfaction to see that Mona was giving them the exact same look. That was what best friends were for, after all.

4

NO WONDER EMILY'S
MOM IS SO STRICT

Emily Fields never had practice the day before a meet, so she came straight home after school and noticed three new items sitting on the limestone kitchen island. There were two new blue Sammy swim towels for Emily and her sister Carolyn, just in time for their big meet against Drury tomorrow . . . and there was also a paperback book titled *It's Not Fair: What to Do When You Lose Your Boyfriend*. A Post-it note was affixed to the cover: *Emily: Thought you might find this useful. I'll be back at 6. —Mom.*

Emily absentmindedly flipped through the pages. Not long after Alison's body had been found, Emily's mother had started surprising her with little cheer-me-ups, like a book called *1001 Things to Make You Smile*, a big set of Prismacolor colored pencils, and a walrus puppet, because Emily used to be obsessed with walruses when she was younger. After Toby's suicide, however, her mother had merely given Emily a bunch of self-help books. Mrs. Fields seemed to think Toby's death was harder for Emily than Ali's—probably because she thought Toby had been Emily's boyfriend.

Emily sank into a white kitchen chair and shut her eyes. Boyfriend or not, Toby's death *did* haunt her. Every night, as she was looking at herself in the mirror while brushing her teeth, she thought she saw Toby standing behind her. She couldn't stop going over that fateful night when he'd taken her to Foxy. Emily had told Toby that she'd been in love with Alison, and Toby had admitted he was glad Ali was dead. Emily had immediately assumed Toby was Ali's killer and had threatened to call the cops. But by the time she realized just how wrong she was, it was too late.

Emily listened to the small settling sounds of her empty house. She stood up, picked up the cordless phone on the counter and dialed a number. Maya answered in one ring.

"Carolyn's at Topher's," Emily said in a low voice. "My mom's at a PTA meeting. We have a whole hour."

"The creek?" Maya whispered.

"Yep."

"Six minutes," Maya declared. "Time me."

It took Emily two minutes to slip out the back door, sprint across her vast, slippery lawn, and dive into the woods to the secluded little creek. Alongside the water was a smooth, flat rock, perfect for two girls to sit on. She and Maya had discovered the secret creek spot two weeks ago, and they'd been hiding away here as much as they possibly could.

In five minutes and forty-five seconds, Maya emerged through the trees. She looked adorable as usual, in her plain white T-shirt, pale pink miniskirt, and red suede Puma sneakers. Even though it was October, it was almost eighty degrees out. She had pulled her hair back from her face, showing off her flawless, caramel-colored skin.

"Hey," Maya cried, a little out of breath. "Under six minutes?"

"Barely," Emily teased.

They both plopped down on the rock. For a second, neither of them spoke. It was so much quieter back here in the woods than by the street. Emily tried not to think about how she had run from Toby through these very woods a few weeks ago. Instead, she concentrated on the way the water sparkled over the rocks and how the trees were just starting to turn orange at the tips. She had a superstition about the big tree she could just make out at the edge of her backyard: if its leaves turned yellow in the fall, she would have a good school year. If they turned red, she wouldn't. But this year, the leaves were orange— did that mean so-so? Emily had all sorts of superstitions. She thought the world was fraught with signs. Nothing was random.

"I missed you," Maya whispered in Emily's ear. "I didn't see you at school today."

A shiver passed through Emily as Maya's lips grazed her earlobe. She shifted her position on the rock, moving closer to Maya. "I know. I kept looking for you."

"Did you survive your bio lab?" Maya asked, curling her pinkie around Emily's.

"Uh-huh." Emily slid her fingers up Maya's arm. "How was your history test?"

Maya wrinkled her nose and shook her head.

"Does this make it better?" Emily pecked Maya on the lips.

"You'll have to try harder than that to make it better," Maya said seductively, lowering her green-yellow catlike eyes and reaching for Emily.

They had decided to try this: sitting together, hanging out whenever they could, touching, kissing. As much as Emily tried to edit Maya from her life, she couldn't. Maya was wonderful, nothing like Em's last boyfriend, Ben—nothing, in fact, like any boy she'd ever gone out with. There was something so comforting about being here at the creek side by side. They weren't just *together*— they were also best friends. This was how coupledom should feel.

When they pulled away, Maya slid off a sneaker and dipped her toe into the creek. "So we moved back into our house yesterday."

Emily drew in her breath. After the workers had found Ali's body in Maya's new backyard, the St. Germains had moved to a hotel to escape the media. "Is it . . . weird?"

"It's okay." Maya shrugged. "Oh, but get this. There's a stalker on the loose."

"*What?*"

"Yeah, a neighbor was telling my mom about it this morning. Someone's running around through people's yards, peeping into windows."

Emily's stomach began to hurt. This, too, reminded her of Toby: back when they were in sixth grade, he was the creepy kid who peeked into everyone's windows, especially Ali's. "Guy? Girl?"

Maya shook her head. "I don't know." She blew her curly bangs up into the air. "This town, I swear to God. Weirdest place on earth."

"You must miss California," Emily said softly, pausing to watch a bunch of birds lift off from a nearby oak tree.

"Not at all, actually." Maya touched Emily's wrist. "There are no Emilys in California."

Emily leaned forward and kissed Maya softly on her lips. They held their lips together for five long seconds. She kissed Maya's earlobe. Then Maya kissed her bottom lip. They pulled away and smiled, the afternoon sun making pretty patterns on their cheeks. Maya kissed Emily's nose, then her temples, then her neck. Emily shut her eyes, and Maya kissed her eyelids. She took a deep breath. Maya ran her delicate fingers along the edge of Emily's jaw; it felt like a million butterflies flapping their wings against her skin. As much as she'd been trying to convince herself that being with Maya was wrong, it was the only thing that felt right.

Maya pulled away. "So, I have a proposal for you."

Emily smirked. "A proposal. Sounds *serious*."

Maya pulled her hands into her sleeves. "How about we make things more open?"

"Open?" Emily repeated.

"Yeah." Maya ran her finger up and down the length of Emily's arm, giving her goose bumps. Emily could smell Maya's banana gum, a smell she now found intoxicating. "Meaning we hang out *inside* your house. We hang out at school. We . . . I don't know. I know you're not ready to be, like, *out* with this, Em, but it's hard spending all our time on this rock. What's going to happen when it gets cold?"

"We'll come out here in snowsuits," Emily quipped.

"I'm serious."

Emily watched as a stiff wind made the tree branches knock together. The air suddenly smelled like burning leaves. She couldn't invite Maya inside her house because her mother had already made it clear that she didn't want Emily to be friends with Maya . . . for terrible, almost-definitely racist reasons. But it wasn't like Emily was going to tell *Maya* that. And as for the other thing, coming out— no. She closed her eyes and thought of the picture A had texted her a while ago—the one of Emily and Maya kissing in the photo booth at Noel Kahn's party. She winced. She wasn't ready for people to know.

"I'm sorry I'm slow," Emily said. "But this is what I'm comfortable with right now."

Maya sighed. "Okay," she said in an Eeyore-ish voice. "I'll just have to deal."

Emily stared into the water. Two silvery fish swam tightly together. Whenever one turned, the other turned too. They were like those needy couples who made out in the hallway and practically stopped breathing when they were separated. It made her a little sad to realize she and Maya could *never* be one of those couples.

"So," Maya said, "nervous about your swim meet tomorrow?"

"Nervous?" Emily frowned.

"Everyone's going to be there."

Emily shrugged. She'd competed in much bigger swimming events than this—there had been camera crews at nationals last year. "I'm not worried."

"You're braver than I am." Maya shoved her sneaker back onto her foot.

But Emily wasn't so sure about that. Maya seemed brave about everything—she ignored the rules that said you had to wear the Rosewood Day uniform and showed up in her white denim jacket every day. She smoked pot out her bedroom window while her parents were at the store. She said hi to kids she didn't know. In that way, she was just like Ali—totally fearless. Which was probably why Emily had fallen for both of them.

And Maya was brave about this—who she was, what

she wanted, and who she wanted to be with. She didn't care if people found out. Maya wanted to be with Emily, and nothing was going to stop her. Maybe someday Emily would be as brave as Maya. But if it was up to her, that would be someday far, far away.

5

ARIA'S ALL FOR
LITERARY REENACTMENTS

Aria perched on the back bumper of Sean's Audi, skimming through her favorite Jean-Paul Sartre play, *No Exit*. It was Monday after school, and Sean said he would give her a ride home after he grabbed something from the soccer coach's office . . . only he was taking an awfully long-ass time. As she flipped to Act II, a group of nearly identical blond, long-legged, Coach-bag-toting Typical Rosewood Girls strode into the student parking lot and gave Aria a suspicious once-over. Apparently Aria's platform boots and gray knitted earflap hat indicated she was *surely* up to something nefarious.

Aria sighed. She was trying her hardest to adjust to Rosewood again, but it wasn't easy. She still felt like a punked-out, faux-leather-wearing, free-thinking Bratz doll in a sea of Pretty Princess of Preppyland Barbies.

"You shouldn't sit on the bumper like that," said a

voice behind her, making Aria jump. "Bad for the suspension."

Aria swiveled around. Ezra stood a few feet away. His brown hair was standing up in messy peaks and his blazer was even more rumpled than it had been this morning. "I thought you literary types were hopeless when it came to cars," she joked.

"I'm full of surprises." Ezra shot her a seductive smile. He reached into his worn leather briefcase. "Actually, I have something for you. It's an essay about *The Scarlet Letter*, questioning whether adultery is sometimes permissible."

Aria took the photocopied pages from him. "I don't think adultery is permissible or forgivable," she said softly. *"Ever."*

"Ever is a long time," Ezra murmured. He was standing so close, Aria could see the dark-blue flecks in his light-blue eyes.

"Aria?" Sean was right next to her.

"Hey!" Aria cried, startled. She jumped away from Ezra as if he were loaded with electricity. "You . . . you all done?"

"Yep," Sean said.

Ezra stepped forward. "Hey, Sean is it? I'm Ez—I mean, Mr. Fitz, the new AP English teacher."

Sean shook his hand. "I just take regular English. I'm Aria's boyfriend."

A flicker of something—disappointment, maybe—passed

over Ezra's face. "Cool," he stumbled. "You play soccer, right? Congrats on your win last week."

"That's right," Sean said modestly. "We have a good team this year."

"Cool," Ezra said again. "Very cool."

Aria felt like she should explain to Ezra why she and Sean were together. Sure, he was a Typical Rosewood Boy, but he was really much deeper. Aria stopped herself. She didn't owe Ezra any explanations. He was her *teacher*.

"We should go," she said abruptly, taking Sean's arm. She wanted to get out of here before either of them embarrassed her. What if Sean made a grammatical error? What if Ezra blurted that they'd hooked up? No one at Rosewood knew about that. No one, that was, except for A.

Aria slid into the passenger seat of Sean's tidy, pine-smelling Audi, feeling itchy. She longed for a few private minutes to collect herself, but Sean slumped into the driver's seat right next to her and pecked her on the cheek. "I missed you today," he said.

"Me too," Aria answered automatically, her voice tight in her throat. As she peeked through her side window, she saw Ezra in the teacher's lot, climbing into his beat-up, old-school VW Bug. He had added a new sticker to the bumper—ECOLOGY HAPPENS—and it looked like he'd washed the car over the weekend. Not that she was obsessively checking or anything.

As Sean waited for other students to back out in front of him, he rubbed his cleanly shaven jaw and fiddled with the collar of his fitted Penguin polo. If Sean and Ezra had been types of poetry, Sean would have been a haiku—neat, simple, beautiful. Ezra would have been one of William Burroughs's messy fever dreams. "Want to hang out later?" Sean asked. "Go out to dinner? Hang with Ella?"

"Let's go out," Aria decided. It was so sweet how Sean liked to spend time with Ella and Aria. The three of them had even watched Ella's Truffaut DVD collection together—in spite of the fact that Sean said he really didn't understand French films.

"One of these days you'll have to meet my family." Sean finally pulled out of the Rosewood lot behind an Acura SUV.

"I know, I know," Aria said. She felt nervous about meeting Sean's family—she'd heard they were wildly rich and super-perfect. "Soon."

"Well, Coach wants the soccer team to go to that big swim meet tomorrow for school support. You're going to watch Emily, right?"

"Sure," Aria answered.

"Well, maybe Wednesday, then? Dinner?"

"Maybe."

As they pulled onto the wooded road that paralleled Rosewood Day, Aria's Treo chimed. She pulled it out nervously—her knee-jerk response whenever she got a text was that it would be A, even though A seemed to be gone. The new text, however, was from an unfamiliar

484 number. A's notes always came up "unavailable." She clicked READ.

> Aria: We need to talk. Can we meet outside the Hollis art building today at 4:30? I'll be on campus waiting for Meredith to finish teaching. I'd love for us to chat. —Your dad, Byron

Aria stared at the screen in disgust. It was disturbing on so many levels. One, her dad had a cell phone now? For years, he'd shunned them, saying they gave you brain cancer. Two, he'd *texted* her—what was next, a MySpace page?

And three . . . the letter itself. Especially the qualifying *Your dad* at the end. Did he think she'd forgotten who he was?

"You all right?" Sean took his eyes off the winding, narrow road for a moment.

Aria read Sean Byron's text. "Can you believe it?" she asked when she finished. "It sounds like he just needs someone to occupy him while he waits for that skank to finish teaching her class."

"What are you going to do?"

"*Not go.*" Aria shuddered, thinking of the times she'd seen Meredith and her father together. In seventh grade, she and Ali had caught them kissing in her dad's car, and then a few weeks ago, she and her younger brother, Mike, had happened upon them at the Victory Brewery. Meredith had told Aria that she and Byron were in love, but how was that *possible*? "Meredith is a homewrecker. She's worse than Hester Prynne!"

"Who?"

"Hester Prynne. She's the main character in *The Scarlet Letter*—we're reading it for English. It's about this woman who commits adultery and the town shuns her. I think Rosewood should shun Meredith. Rosewood needs a town scaffold—to humiliate her."

"How about that pillory thing at the fairgrounds?" Sean suggested, slowing down as they passed a cyclist. "You know that wooden contraption with the holes you can stick your head and arms through? They lock you up in it and you just hang there. We always used to get our pictures taken in that thing."

"*Perfect*," Aria practically shouted. "And Meredith deserves to have 'husband-stealer' branded on her forehead. Just stitching a red letter *A* to her dress would be too subtle."

Sean laughed. "It sounds like you're *really* into *The Scarlet Letter*."

"I don't know. I've only read eight pages." Aria grew silent, getting an idea. "Actually, wait. Drop me off at Hollis."

Sean gave her a sidelong glance. "You're going to meet him?"

"Not exactly." She smiled devilishly.

"Ohhhhkay . . ." Sean drove a few blocks through

the Hollis section of town, which was filled with brick and stone buildings, old bronze statues of the college founders, and tons of shabby-chic students on bicycles. It seemed like it was permanently fall at Hollis—the colorful cascading leaves looked perfect here. As Sean pulled into a two-hour parking spot on campus, he looked worried. "You're not going to do anything illegal, are you?"

"Nah." Aria gave him a quick kiss. "Don't wait. I can walk home from here."

Squaring her shoulders, she marched into the Arts Building's main entrance. Her father's text flashed before her eyes. *I'm on campus waiting for Meredith to finish teaching.* Meredith had told Aria herself that she taught studio art at Hollis. She slid by a security guard, who was supposed to be checking IDs but was instead watching a Yankees game on his portable TV. Her nerves felt jangled and snappy, as if they were ungrounded wires.

There were only three studio classrooms in the building that were big enough for a painting class, which Aria knew, because she'd attended Saturday art school at Hollis for years. Today, only one room was in use, so it had to be the one. Aria burst noisily through the doors of the classroom and was immediately assaulted by the smell of turpentine and unwashed clothes. Twelve art students with easels set up in a circle swiveled around to stare at her. The only person who didn't move was the wrinkly, hairless, completely naked old drawing model in the center of the room. He stuck his bandy little chest out, kept his hands on his hips, and didn't even blink. Aria had to give him an A for effort.

She spied Meredith perched on a table by the far window. There was her long, luscious brown hair. There was the pink spiderweb tattoo on her wrist. Meredith looked strong and confident, and there was an irritating, healthy pink flush to her cheeks.

"Aria?" Meredith called across the drafty, cavernous room. "This is a surprise."

Aria looked around. All of the students had their brushes and paints within easy reach of their canvases. She marched over to the student closest to her, snatched a large, fan-shaped brush, swiped it in a puddle of red paint, and strode over to Meredith, dribbling paint as she went. Before anyone could do anything, Aria painted a large, messy *A* on the left breast of Meredith's delicate, cotton eyelet sundress.

"Now everyone will know what you've done," Aria snarled.

Giving Meredith no time to react, she whirled around and strode out of the room. When she got out onto Hollis's green lawn again, she started gleefully, crazily laughing. It wasn't a "husband-stealer" brand across her forehead, but it might as well have been. *There, Meredith. Take that.*

6

SIBLING RIVALRY'S
A HARD HABIT TO BREAK

Monday afternoon at field hockey practice, Spencer pulled ahead of her teammates on their warm-up lap around the field. It had been an unseasonably warm day and the girls were all a little slower than usual. Kirsten Cullen pumped her arms to catch up. "I heard about the Golden Orchid," Kirsten said breathlessly, readjusting her blond ponytail. "That's awesome."

"Thanks." Spencer ducked her head. It was amazing how fast the news had spread at Rosewood Day—her mother had only told her six hours ago. At least ten people had come up to talk to her about it since then.

"I heard John Mayer won a Golden Orchid when he was in high school," Kirsten continued. "It was, like, an essay for AP music theory."

"Huh." Spencer was pretty sure John Mayer hadn't won it—she knew every winner from the past fifteen years.

"I bet you'll win," Kirsten said. "And then you'll be on TV! Can I come with you for your debut on the *Today* show?"

Spencer shrugged. "It's a really cutthroat competition."

"Shut up." Kirsten slapped her on the shoulder. "You're always so modest."

Spencer clenched her teeth. As much as she'd been trying to downplay this Golden Orchid thing, everyone's reaction had been the same—*You'll definitely win it. Get ready for your close-up!*—and it was making her crazy. She had nervously organized and reorganized the money in her wallet so many times today that one of her twenties had split right down the center.

Coach McCready blew the whistle and yelled, "Crossovers!" The team immediately turned and began running sideways. They looked like dressage competitors at the Devon Horse Show. "You hear about the Rosewood Stalker?" Kirsten asked, huffing a little—crossovers were harder than they looked. "It was all over the news last night."

"Yeah," Spencer mumbled.

"He's in your neighborhood. Hanging out in the woods."

Spencer dodged a divot in the dry grass. "It's probably just some loser," she huffed. But Spencer couldn't help but think of A. How many times had A texted her about something that it seemed *no one* could have seen? Now she looked out into the trees, almost certain she'd see a shadowy figure. But there was no one.

They started running normally again, passing the Rosewood Day duck pond, the sculpture garden, and the cornfields. When they looped toward the bleachers, Kirsten squinted and pointed toward the low metal benches that held the girls' hockey equipment. "Is that your *sister*?"

Spencer flinched. Melissa was standing next to Ian Thomas, their new assistant coach. It was the very same Ian Thomas Melissa had dated when Spencer was in seventh grade—*and* the same Ian Thomas who had kissed Spencer in her driveway years ago.

They finished their loop and Spencer came to a halt in front of Melissa and Ian. Her sister had changed into an outfit that was nearly identical to what their mother had been wearing earlier: stovepipe jeans, white tee, and an expensive Dior watch. She even wore Chanel No. 5, just like Mom. *Such a good little clone,* Spencer thought. "What are you doing here?" she demanded, out of breath.

Melissa leaned her elbow on one of the Gatorade jugs resting on the bench, her antique gold charm bracelet tinkling against her wrist. "What, a big sister can't watch her little sister play?" But then her saccharine smile faded, and she snaked an arm around Ian's waist. "It also helps that my boyfriend's the coach."

Spencer wrinkled her nose. She'd always suspected

Melissa had never gotten over Ian. They'd broken up shortly after graduation. Ian was still as cute as ever, with his blond, wavy hair, beautifully proportioned body, and lazy, arrogant smile. "Well, good for you," Spencer answered, wanting out of this conversation. The less she spoke to Melissa, the better—at least until the Golden Orchid thing was over. If only the judges would hurry the hell up and knock Spencer's plagiarized paper out of the running.

She reached for her gear bag, pulled out her shin guards, and fastened one around her left shin. Then she fastened the other around her right. Then she unfastened both, refastening them much tighter. She pulled up her socks and then pulled them down again. Repeat, repeat, repeat.

"Someone's awfully OCD today," Melissa teased. She turned to Ian. "Oh, did you hear the big Spencer news? She won the Golden Orchid. The *Philadelphia Sentinel* is coming over to interview her this week."

"I didn't win," Spencer barked quickly. "I was only nominated."

"Oh, I'm sure you *will* win," Melissa simpered, in a way Spencer couldn't quite read. When her sister gave Spencer a wink, she felt a pinch of terror. *Did she know?*

Ian let out a whistle. "A Golden Orchid? Damn! You Hastings sisters—smart, beautiful, *and* athletic. You should see the way Spence tears up the field, Mel. She plays a mean center."

Melissa pursed her shiny lips, thinking. "Remember when Coach had me play center because Zoe had mono?" she chirped to Ian. "I scored two goals. In *one* quarter."

Spencer gritted her teeth. She'd known Melissa couldn't be charitable for long. Yet again, Melissa had turned something completely innocent into a competition. Spencer scrolled through the long list in her head for an appropriate fake-nice insult but then decided to screw it. This wasn't the time to pick a fight with Melissa. "I'm sure it rocked, Mel," she conceded. "I bet you're a way better center than I am."

Her sister froze. The little gremlin that Spencer was certain lived inside Melissa's head was confused. Clearly it hadn't expected Spencer to say something nice.

Spencer smiled at her sister and then at Ian. He held her gaze for a moment and then gave her a little conspiratorial wink.

Spencer's insides flipped. She *still* got gooey when Ian looked at her. Even three years later, Spencer remembered every single detail about their kiss. Ian had been wearing a soft gray Nike T-shirt, green army shorts, and brown Merrills. He smelled like cut grass and cinnamon gum. One second, Spencer was giving him a good-bye peck on his cheek—she'd gone out to flirt, nothing more. The next second, he was pressing her up against the side of his car. Spencer had been so surprised, she'd kept her eyes open.

Ian blew the whistle, breaking Spencer out of her thoughts. She jogged back to her team, and Ian followed. "All right, guys." Ian clapped his hands. The team surrounded him, taking in Ian's golden face longingly. "Please don't hate me, but we're going to do Indian sprints, crouching drills, and hill running today. Coach's orders."

Everyone, including Spencer, groaned. "I told you not to hate me!" Ian cried.

"Can't we do something else?" Kirsten whined.

"Just think how much butt you're going to kick for our game against Pritchard Prep," Ian said. "And how about this? If we get through the entire drill, I'll take you guys to Merlin after practice tomorrow."

The hockey team whooped. Merlin was famous for its low-calorie chocolate ice cream that tasted better than the full-fat stuff.

As Spencer leaned over the bench to fasten her shin guards—*again*—she felt Ian standing above her. When she glanced up at him, he was smiling. "For the record," Ian said in a low voice, shadowing his face from her teammates, "you play center better than your sister does. No question about it."

"Thanks." Spencer smiled. Her nose tickled with the smell of cut grass and Ian's Neutrogena sunscreen. Her heart pitter-pattered. "That means a lot."

"And I meant the other stuff, too." The left corner of Ian's mouth pulled up into a half-smile.

Spencer felt a faint, trembling thrill. Did he mean the "smart" and "beautiful" stuff? She glanced across the field to where Melissa was standing. Her sister leaned over her BlackBerry, not paying a bit of attention.

Good.

7

NOTHING LIKE AN
OLD-FASHIONED INTERROGATION

Monday evening, Hanna parked her Prius in her side driveway and hopped out. All she had to do was change clothes, and then she was off to meet Mona for their dinner. Showing up in her Rosewood Day blazer and pleated skirt would be an insult to the institution of Frenniversaries. She had to get out of these long sleeves—she'd been sweating all day. Hanna had spritzed herself with her Evian mineral water spray bottle about a hundred times on the drive home, but she still felt overheated.

When she rounded the corner, she noticed her mother's champagne-colored Lexus next to the garage and stopped short. What was her mom doing home? Ms. Marin usually worked über-long hours at McManus & Tate, her Philadelphia advertising firm. She often didn't get back until after 10 P.M.

Then Hanna noticed the four other cars, stuffed one after the other against the garage: the silver Mercedes coupe was definitely Spencer's, the white Volvo Emily's, and the clunky green Subaru Aria's. The last car was a white Ford with the words ROSEWOOD POLICE DEPARTMENT emblazoned on the side.

What the hell?

"Hanna."

Hanna's mother stood on the side porch. She still had on her sleek black pantsuit and high snakeskin heels.

"What's going on?" Hanna demanded, annoyed. "Why are my old friends here?"

"I tried calling you. You didn't pick up," her mother said. "Officer Wilden wanted to ask you girls some questions about Alison. They're out back."

Hanna pulled her BlackBerry out of her pocket. Sure enough, she had three missed calls, all from her mom.

Her mother turned. Hanna followed her into the house and through the kitchen. She paused by the granite-topped telephone table. "Do I have any messages?"

"Yes, one." Hanna's heart leapt, but then her mother added, "Mr. Ackard. They're doing some reorganization at the burn clinic, and they won't need your help anymore."

Hanna blinked. That was a nice surprise. "Anyone . . . else?"

The corners of Ms. Marin's eyes turned down, understanding. "No." She gently touched Hanna's arm. "I'm sorry, Han. He hasn't called."

Despite Hanna's otherwise back-to-perfect life, the silence from her father made her ache. How could he so easily cut Hanna out of his life? Didn't he realize she'd had a very good reason to ditch their dinner and go to Foxy? Didn't he know he shouldn't have invited his fiancée, Isabel, and her perfect daughter, Kate, to *their* special weekend? But then, Hanna's father would be marrying plain, squirrelly Isabel soon—and Kate would officially be his stepdaughter. Maybe he hadn't called Hanna back because Hanna was one daughter too many.

Whatever, Hanna told herself, taking off her blazer and straightening her sheer pink Rebecca Taylor camisole. Kate was a prissy bitch—if her father chose Kate over her, then they deserved each other.

When she looked through the French doors to the back porch, Spencer, Aria, and Emily were indeed sitting around the giant teak patio table, the light from the stained-glass window sparkling against their cheeks. Officer Wilden, the newest member of Rosewood's police force *and* Ms. Marin's newest boyfriend, stood near the Weber grill.

It was surreal to see her three ex–best friends here. The last time they'd sat on Hanna's back porch had been at the end of seventh grade—and Hanna had been the dorkiest and ugliest of the group. But now, Emily's shoulders had broadened and her hair had a slight greenish tint. Spencer looked stressed and constipated. And Aria was a zombie, with her black hair and pale skin. If Hanna was a couture Proenza Schouler, then Aria was a pilly, ill-fitting sweatshirt dress from the Target line.

Hanna took a deep breath and pushed through the French doors. Wilden turned around. There was a serious look on his face. The tiniest bit of a black tattoo peeked out from under the collar of his cop uniform. It still amazed Hanna that Wilden, a former Rosewood Day badass, had gone into law enforcement. "Hanna. Have a seat."

Hanna scraped a chair back from the table and slumped down next to Spencer. "Is this going to take long?" She examined her pink diamond-encrusted Dior watch. "I'm late for something."

"Not if we get started," Wilden looked around at all of them. Spencer stared at her fingernails, Aria chomped on her gum with her eyes freakishly closed, and Emily fixated on the citronella candle in the middle of the table, like she was about to cry.

"First thing," Wilden said. "Someone has leaked a homemade video of you girls to the press." He glanced at Aria. "It was one of the videos you gave the Rosewood PD years ago. So you might see it on TV—all the news channels got it. We're looking for whoever leaked it—and they'll be punished. I wanted to let you girls know first."

"Which video is it?" Aria asked.

"Something about text messages?" he answered.

Hanna sat back, trying to remember which video it could be—there were so many. Aria used to be obsessive about videotaping them. Hanna had always tried her hardest to duck out of every shot, because for her, the camera added not ten pounds but *twenty*.

Wilden cracked his knuckles and fiddled with a phallic-looking pepper grinder that sat in the center of the table. Some pepper spilled on the tablecloth, and the air immediately smelled spicy. "The other thing I want to talk about is Alison herself. We have reason to believe that Alison's killer might be someone *from* Rosewood. Someone who possibly still lives here today . . . and that person may still be dangerous."

Everyone drew in a breath.

"We're looking at everything with a fresh eye," Wilden went on, rising from the table and strolling around with his hands clasped behind his back. He'd probably seen someone on *CSI* do that and thought it was cool. "We're trying to reconstruct Alison's life right before she went missing. We want to start with the people who knew her best."

Just then, Hanna's BlackBerry buzzed. She pulled it out of her purse. Mona.

"Mon," Hanna answered quietly, getting up from her chair and wandering to the far side of the porch by her mother's rosebushes. "I'm going to be a couple minutes late."

"Bitch," Mona teased. "That sucks. I'm already at our table at Rive Gauche."

"Hanna," Wilden called gruffly. "Can you please call whoever that is back?"

At the same time, Aria sneezed. "Bless you," Emily said.

"Where are you?" Mona sounded suspicious. "Are you with someone?"

"I'm at home," Hanna answered. "And I'm with Emily, Aria, Spencer, and Off—"

"You're with your *old friends*?" Mona interrupted.

"They were here when I got home," Hanna protested.

"Let me get this straight." Mona's voice rose higher. "You invited your old friends to your *house*. On the night of our Frenniversary."

"I didn't *invite* them." Hanna laughed. It was still hard to believe Mona could feel threatened by her old friends. "I was just—"

"You know what?" Mona cut her off. "Forget it. The Frenniversary is cancelled."

"Mona, don't be—" Then she stopped. Wilden was next to her.

He plucked the phone from her hand and snapped it shut. "We're discussing a murder," he said in a low voice. "Your social life can wait."

Hanna glared at him behind his back. How dare Wilden hang up her phone! Just because he was dating her mom didn't mean he could get all dadlike on her. She stormed back to the table, trying to calm down. Mona was the queen of overreacting, but she couldn't ice Hanna out for long. Most of their fights only lasted a few hours, tops.

"Okay," Wilden said when Hanna sat back down. "I received something interesting a few weeks ago that I think we should talk about." He pulled his notepad out. "Your friend, Toby Cavanaugh? He wrote a suicide note."

"W-we know," Spencer stuttered. "His sister let us read part of it."

"So you know it mentioned Alison." Wilden flipped back through his notebook. "Toby wrote, *'I promised Alison DiLaurentis I'd keep a secret for her if she kept a secret for me.'*" His olive-colored eyes scanned each of them. "What was Alison's secret?"

Hanna slumped down in her seat. *We were the ones who blinded Jenna.* That was the secret Toby had kept for Ali. Hanna and her friends hadn't realized Toby knew that—until Spencer spilled the beans three weeks ago.

Spencer blurted out, "We don't know. Ali didn't tell any of us."

Wilden's brow crinkled. He leaned over the patio table. "Hanna, a while ago you thought Toby *killed* Alison."

Hanna shrugged impassively. She'd gone to Wilden during the time they'd thought Toby was A and Ali's killer. "Well . . . Toby didn't like Ali."

"Actually, he *did* like Ali, but Ali didn't like him back," Spencer clarified. "He used to spy on her all the time. But I'm not sure if that had anything to do with his secret."

Emily made a small whimper. Hanna eyed her

suspiciously. All Emily talked about lately was how guilty she felt about Toby. What if she wanted to tell Wilden that they were responsible for his death—*and* Jenna's accident? Hanna might have taken the rap for The Jenna Thing weeks ago when she had nothing to live for, but there was no way in hell she would confess now. Her life was finally back to normal, and she was in no mood to be known as one of The Psycho Blinders, or whatever they'd inevitably be called on TV.

Wilden flipped a few pages on his pad. "Well, everyone think about it. Moving on . . . let's talk about the night Alison went missing. Spencer, it says here that right before she disappeared, Ali tried to hypnotize you. The two of you fought, she ran out of the barn, you ran after her, but you couldn't find her. Right?"

Spencer stiffened. "Um. Yeah. That's right."

"You have *no* idea where she went?"

Spencer shrugged. "Sorry."

Hanna tried to remember the night Ali vanished. One minute, Ali was hypnotizing them; the next, she was gone. Hanna really felt like Ali had put her in a trance: as Ali counted down from one hundred, the vanilla candle wafting pungently through the barn, Hanna had felt heavy and sleepy, the popcorn and Doritos she'd eaten earlier roiling uncomfortably in her stomach. Spooky images began to flicker in front of her eyes: Ali and the others ran through a dense jungle. Large, man-eating plants surrounded them. One plant snapped its jaws and grabbed

Ali's leg. When Hanna had snapped out of it, Spencer was standing in the doorway of the barn, looking worried . . . and Ali was gone.

Wilden continued to stroll around the porch. He picked up a Southwest-style ceramic pot and turned it over, like he was checking for a price tag. Nosy bastard. "I need you girls to remember all you can. Think about what was happening around the time Alison disappeared. Did she have a boyfriend? Any new friends?"

"She had a boyfriend," Aria offered. "Matt Doolittle. He moved away." As she sat back, her T-shirt slid off her shoulder, revealing a lacy, fire engine red bra strap. Slut.

"She was hanging out with these older field hockey girls," Emily volunteered.

Wilden looked at his notes. "Right. Katy Houghton and Violet Keyes. I got them. How about Alison's behavior. Was she acting strangely?"

They fell silent. *Yes, she was,* Hanna thought. She thought of one memory straightaway. On a blustery spring day, a few weeks before Ali disappeared, her dad had taken them both to a Phillies game. Ali was jittery the whole night, as if she'd downed packs and packs of Skittles. She kept checking her cell phone for texts and had seemed livid that her inbox was empty. During the seventh inning stretch, when they sneaked to the balcony to ogle a group of cute boys sitting in one of the skyboxes, Hanna noticed Ali's hands trembling. "Are you okay?" Hanna asked. Ali smiled at her. "I'm just cold," she explained.

But was that suspicious enough to bring up? It seemed like nothing, but it was hard to know what the police were looking for.

"She seemed okay," Spencer said slowly.

Wilden looked at Spencer dead-on. "You know, my older sister was a lot like Alison. She was the leader of her clique, too. Whatever my sister said, her friends did. *Anything.* And they kept all kinds of secrets for her. Is that how it worked for you guys?"

Hanna curled up her toes, suddenly irritated at where this conversation was going.

"I don't know," Emily mumbled. "Maybe."

Wilden glanced down at the vibrating cell phone clipped to his holster. "Excuse me." He ducked toward the garage, pulling his phone from his belt.

As soon as he was out of earshot, Emily let out a pent-up breath. "Guys, we have to tell him."

Hanna narrowed her eyes. "Tell him *what*?"

Emily held up her hands. "Jenna is blind. We did that."

Hanna shook her head. "Count me out. And anyway, Jenna's fine. Seriously. Have you noticed those Gucci sunglasses she wears? You have to get on, like, a year-long waiting list for a pair of those—they're harder to score than a Birkin bag."

Aria gaped at Hanna. "What *solar system* are you from? Who cares about Gucci sunglasses?"

"Well, obviously not someone like *you*," Hanna spat.

Aria tensed her jaw and leaned back. "What is *that* supposed to mean?"

"I think you know," Hanna snarled.

"Guys," Spencer warned.

Aria sighed and turned to face the side yard. Hanna glared at her pointy chin and ski-slope nose. Even Aria's profile wasn't as pretty as hers.

"We should tell him about Jenna," Emily goaded. "And A. The police should handle this. We're in over our heads."

"We're not telling him anything, and that's final," Hanna hissed.

"Yeah, I don't know, Emily," Spencer said slowly, poking her car keys through one of the tabletop's wide slats. "That's a big decision. It affects all our lives."

"We've talked about this before," Aria agreed. "Besides, A is gone, right?"

"I'll leave you all out of it," Emily protested, crossing her arms over her chest. "But I'm telling him. I think it's the right thing to do."

Aria's cell phone chirped and everyone jumped. Then Spencer's Sidekick vibrated, wriggling toward the edge of the table. Hanna's BlackBerry, which she'd shoved back into her purse, let out a muffled chime. And Emily's little Nokia made that old-school telephone ring sound.

The last time the girls' phones all rang at once had been outside Ali's memorial service. Hanna had the same feeling she'd had the first time her father had taken her on the Tilt-a-Whirl at the Rosewood County Fair when she was five—that of dizzying nausea. Aria opened her phone. Then Emily, then Spencer. "Oh God," Emily whispered.

Hanna didn't even bother reaching for her BlackBerry; instead, she leaned over Spencer's Sidekick.

You really thought I was gone? Puh-lease. I've been watching you this whole time. In fact, I might be watching you right now. And girls—if you tell ANYONE about me, you'll be sorry. —A

Hanna's heart throbbed. She heard footsteps and turned around. Wilden was back.

He shoved his cell phone into his holster. Then he looked at the girls and raised an eyebrow. "Did I miss something?"

Had. He. Ever.

8

IT'S ALWAYS GOOD TO *READ* THE BOOK BEFORE STEALING FROM IT

About a half hour later, Aria pulled up to her fifties-modern brown box of a house. She cradled her Treo to her chin, waiting for Emily's voice-mail message to finish. At the beep, she said, "Em, it's Aria. If you're really considering telling Wilden, please call me. A's capable of . . . of more than you think."

She hit END, feeling anxious. She couldn't imagine what dark secret of Emily's A might out if she talked to the police, but Aria knew from experience that A would do it.

Sighing, she unlocked her front door and clomped up the stairs, passing her parents' bedroom. The door was ajar. Inside, her parents' bed was neatly made—or was it only Ella's bed now? Ella had draped it with the bright salmon batik-print quilt that she loved and Byron despised. She'd piled all the pillows up on her side. The bed felt like a metaphor for divorce.

Aria dropped her books and aimlessly wandered back downstairs into the den, A's threat spinning around in her head like the centrifuge they'd used in today's biology lab. A was *still here*. And, according to Wilden, so was Ali's killer. *A* could be Ali's killer, worming her way into all of their lives. What if Wilden was right— what if Ali's killer wanted to hurt someone else? What if Ali's killer wasn't only Ali's enemy, but Aria's, Hanna's, Emily's, and Spencer's, too? Did that mean one of them was . . . next?

The den was dark except for the flickering TV. When Aria saw a hand curled over the edge of the tweedy love seat, she jumped. Then Mike's familiar face appeared.

"You're just in time." Mike pointed to the TV screen. *"Coming up, a never-before-seen home video of Alison DiLaurentis shot the week before she was murdered,"* he said in his best Moviefone-announcer impersonation.

Aria's stomach tightened. This was the leaked video Wilden had been talking about. Years ago, Aria had thrown herself into filmmaking, documenting everything she could, from snails in the backyard to her best friends. The movies were generally short, and Aria often tried to make them arty and poignant, focusing on Hanna's nostril, or the zipper on Ali's hoodie, or Spencer's fidgety fingers. When Ali went missing, Aria turned her video collection over to the police. The cops combed through them but had found no clues about where Ali could have gone. Aria still had the originals on her laptop, although she hadn't looked through them in a long, long time.

Aria flopped down on the love seat. When a Mercedes commercial ended and the news came back on, Aria and Mike sat up straighter. "Yesterday, an anonymous source sent us this clip of Alison DiLaurentis," the anchorman announced. "It offers a look at how chillingly innocent her life was just days before she was murdered. Let's watch."

The clip opened with a fumbling shot of Spencer's leather living room couch. "And because she wears a size zero," Hanna said offscreen. The camera panned to a younger-looking Spencer, who had on a pink polo and capri-length pajama pants. Her blond hair cascaded around her shoulders, and she wore a sparkly rhinestone crown on her head.

"She looks hot in that crown," Mike said enthusiastically, tearing open a large bag of Doritos.

"*Shhh,*" Aria hissed.

Spencer pointed at Ali's LG phone on the couch. "Want to read her texts?"

"I do!" Hanna whispered, ducking out of the shot. Then the camera swung to Emily, who looked nearly the same as she did today—same reddish-blond hair, same oversize swimming T-shirt, same pleasant-but-worried expression. Aria suddenly remembered this night—before they'd turned on the camera, Ali had gotten a text message and hadn't told them whom it was from. Everyone had been annoyed.

The camera showed Spencer holding Ali's phone. "It's locked." There was a blurry shot of the phone's screen.

"Do you know her password?" Aria heard her own voice ask.

"Damn! That's you!" Mike whooped.

"Try her birthday," Hanna suggested.

The camera showed Hanna's chubby hands reaching in and taking the phone from Spencer.

Mike wrinkled his nose and turned to Aria. "Is this what girls do when they're alone? I thought I was going to see pillow fights. Girls in panties. *Kissing.*"

"We were in seventh grade," Aria snapped. "That's just gross."

"There's nothing wrong with seventh-grade girls in their panties," Mike said in a small voice.

"What are you guys doing?" Ali's voice called. Then her face appeared on-screen, and Aria's eyes brimmed with tears. That heart-shaped face, those luminous dark blue eyes, that wide mouth—it was *haunting.*

"Were you looking at my phone?" Ali demanded, her hands on her hips.

"Of course not!" Hanna cried. Spencer staggered backward, clutching her head to keep her crown on.

Mike shoved a handful of Doritos into his mouth. "Can I be your love slave, princess Spencer?" he said in falsetto.

"I don't think she goes out with prepubescent boys who still sleep with their blankies," Aria snapped.

"Hey!" Mike squeaked. "It's not a blankie! It's my lucky lacrosse jersey!"

"That's even worse," Aria said.

Ali floated on-screen again, looking alive and vibrant and carefree. How could Ali be dead? *Murdered?*

Then Spencer's older sister, Melissa, and her boyfriend, Ian, walked past the camera. "Hey, girls," Ian said.

"Hi," Spencer greeted him loudly.

Aria smirked at the TV. She'd forgotten how they all lusted over Ian. He was one of the people they would prank-call sometimes—along with Jenna Cavanaugh before they hurt her, Noel Kahn because he was cute, and Andrew Campbell because Spencer found him annoying. For Ian, they took turns pretending they were girls from 1-800-Sexy-Coeds.

The camera caught Ali rolling her eyes at Spencer. Then Spencer scowled at Ali behind her back. *Typical,* Aria thought. The night Ali disappeared, Aria hadn't been hypnotized, and she'd listened to Ali and Spencer fight. When they ran out of the barn, Aria waited a minute or two, then followed. Aria called their names. But she couldn't catch up with them. She went back inside, wondering if Ali and Spencer had just ditched the rest of them, staging the whole thing so they could run off to a cooler party. But eventually Spencer burst back inside. She looked so *lost,* as if she was in a trance.

On-screen, Ian plopped down on the couch next to Ali. "So, what are you girls doing?"

"Oh, not much," Aria said from behind the camera. "Making a film."

"A film?" Ian asked. "Can I be in it?"

"Of course," Spencer said, taking a seat next to him. "It's a talk show. I'm the host. You and Ali are my guests. I'll do you first."

The camera panned off the couch and focused on Ali's closed phone, which was next to Ali's hand on the couch. It got closer and closer until the phone's tiny LED screen took up the whole picture. To this day, Aria didn't know who had texted Ali that night.

"Ask him who his favorite teacher at Rosewood is," Aria's younger, slightly higher voice called out from behind the camera.

Ali chuckled and looked straight into the lens. "That's a good question for you, Aria. You should ask him if he wants to *hook up* with any of his teachers. In vacant parking lots."

Aria gasped, and heard her younger self gasp on-screen, too. Ali had really *said* that? In front of *all* of them?

And then the clip was over.

Mike turned to her. There were neon-orange Dorito crumbs around his mouth. "What did she mean about hooking up with teachers? It seemed like she was only talking to you."

A dry rasp escaped Aria's mouth. A had told Ella that Aria had known about Byron's affair all these years, but Mike still didn't know. He'd be so disappointed in her.

Mike stood up. "Whatever." Aria could tell he was trying to be all unaffected and casual, but he bumbled out of the room, knocking over a framed, signed photo of Lou Reed—Byron's rock star hero, and one of the few Byron artifacts Ella hadn't removed. She heard him stomp up to his bedroom and slam the door hard.

Aria put her head in her hands. This was the three-thousandth instance she wished she were back in Reykjavík, hiking to a glacier, riding her Icelandic pony, Gilda, along a dried-up volcano bed, or even eating whale blubber, which everyone in Iceland seemed to adore.

She shut off the TV, and the house became eerily silent. When she heard a rustling at the door, she jumped. In the hall, she saw her mother, lugging in several large canvas shopping bags from Rosewood's organic market.

Ella noticed Aria and smiled wearily. "Hey, sweetie." Since she'd kicked Byron out, Ella seemed more disheveled than usual. Her black gauzy tunic was baggier than ever, her wide-leg silk pants had a tahini stain on the thigh, and her long, brownish-black hair sat in a rat's nest at the crown of her head.

"Let me help." Aria took a bunch of bags from Ella's arms. They walked into the kitchen together, hefted the bags onto the island, and started unpacking.

"How was your day?" Ella murmured.

Then Aria remembered. "Oh my God, you'll never believe what I did," she exclaimed, feeling a surge of giddiness. Ella glanced at her before putting the organic peanut butter away. "I went down to Hollis. Because I was looking for . . . you know. *Her.*" Aria didn't want to say Meredith's name. "She was teaching an art class, so I ran inside, grabbed a paintbrush, and painted a scarlet *A* across her chest. You know, like that woman in *The Scarlet Letter?* It was awesome."

Ella paused, holding a bag of whole-wheat pasta midair. She looked nauseated.

"She didn't know what hit her," Aria went on. "And then I said, 'Now everyone will know what you've done.'" She grinned and spread her arms out. *Taa-daa!*

Ella's eyes darted back and forth, processing this. "Do you realize that Hester Prynne is supposed to be a *sympathetic* character?"

Aria frowned. She was only on page eight. "I did it for you," Aria explained quietly. "For revenge."

"Revenge?" Ella's voice shook. "Thanks. That makes me look really sane. Like I'm really handling this well. This is hard enough for me as it is. Don't you realize you've made her look like . . . like a martyr?"

Aria took a step toward Ella. She hadn't considered that. "I'm sorry. . . ."

Then Ella crumpled against the counter and started to sob. Aria stood motionless. Her limbs felt like Sculpey clay straight out of the oven, all hardened and useless. She couldn't fathom what her mom was going through, and she'd gone and made it worse.

Outside their kitchen window, a hummingbird landed on the replica of a whale penis Mike had bought at Reyk-javík's phallological museum. In any other circumstance, Aria would've pointed it out–hummingbirds were rare here, especially ones that landed on fake whale penises– but not today.

"I can't even look at you right now," Ella finally stammered.

Aria put her hand to her chest, as if her mother had speared her with one of her Wüsthof knives. "I'm *sorry*. I wanted Meredith to pay for what she's done." When Ella didn't answer, the searing, acidic feeling in Aria's stomach grew stronger. "Maybe I should get out of here for a while then, if you can't stand the sight of me."

She paused, waiting for Ella to jump in and say, *No, that's not what I want*. But Ella stayed quiet. "Yes, maybe that's a good idea," she agreed quietly.

"Oh." Aria's shoulders sank and her chin trembled. "Then I . . . I won't come home from school tomorrow." She didn't have any idea where she'd go, but that didn't matter right now. All that mattered was doing the one thing that would make her mom happy.

9

EVERYONE, A BIG ROUND OF APPLAUSE FOR SPENCER HASTINGS!

On Tuesday afternoon, while most of the Rosewood Day junior class ate lunch, Spencer sat on top of the conference table in the yearbook room. Eight blinking Mac G5 computers, a whole bunch of long-lensed Nikon cameras, six eager sophomore and freshman girls, and a nerdy, slightly effeminate freshman boy surrounded her.

She tapped the covers of the past few Rosewood Day yearbooks. Each year, the books were named *The Mule* due to some apocryphal, inside joke from the 1920s that even the school's oldest teachers had long forgotten. "In this year's *Mule*, I think we should try to capture a slice of what Rosewood Day students are like."

Her yearbook staff diligently wrote down *slice of life* in their spiral-bound notebooks.

"Like . . . maybe we could do some quickie interviews with random students," Spencer went on. "Or ask people what's on their favorite iPod playlist, and then publish it in boxes next to their photos. And how are the still lifes going?" Last meeting, they had planned to ask a couple kids to empty the contents of their bags to document what Rosewood Day girls and guys were carrying around.

"I got great photos of the stuff in Brett Weaver's soccer bag and Mona Vanderwaal's purse," said Brenna Richardson.

"Fantastic," Spencer said. "Keep up the good work."

Spencer closed her leaf green leather-bound journal and dismissed her staff. Once they were gone, she grabbed her black fabric Kate Spade bag and pulled out her Sidekick.

There it was. The note from A. She kept hoping it wouldn't be there.

As she slid the phone back into her bag, her fingers grazed against something in the inside pocket: Officer Wilden's business card. Wilden wasn't the first cop to ask Spencer about the night Ali went missing, but he was the only one who'd ever sounded so . . . suspicious.

The memory of that night was both crystal clear and incredibly muddled. She remembered a glut of emotions: excitement over getting the barn for their sleepover, annoyance that Melissa was there, giddiness that Ian was. Their kiss had been a couple weeks before that. But then Ali started talking about how Melissa and Ian made the cutest couple and Spencer's emotions swung again. Ali had already threatened to tell Melissa about the kiss. Once

Ian and Melissa left, Ali tried to hypnotize them, and she and Spencer got in a fight. Ali left, Spencer ran after her, and then . . . *nothing*. But what she never told the cops—or her family, or her friends—was that sometimes when she thought about that night, it felt like there was a black hole in the middle of it. That something had happened which she couldn't remember.

Suddenly, a vision flashed in front of Spencer's eyes. *Ali laughing nastily and turning away.*

Spencer stopped in the middle of the packed hallway and someone ran into her back.

"Will you move?" the girl behind her whined. "Some of us have to get to class."

Spencer took a tentative step forward. Whatever she had just remembered had quickly disappeared, but it felt like there had been an earthquake. She looked around for shattered glass and scattering students, certain the rest of the world had felt it, too, but everything looked completely normal. A few steps away, Naomi Zeigler inspected her reflection in her mini locker mirror. Two freshmen by the Teacher of the Year plaque laughed at the pointy Satan beard and horns drawn over Mr. Craft's smiling photo. The windows that faced the commons weren't the tiniest bit cracked, and none of the vases in the Pottery III display case had fallen over. What was the vision Spencer had just seen? Why did she feel so . . . slithery?

She slipped into her AP econ classroom and slumped

down at her desk, which was right next to a very large portrait of a scowling J. P. Morgan. Once the rest of the class filed in and everyone sat down, Squidward strode to the front of the room. "Before today's video, I have an announcement." He looked at Spencer. Her stomach swirled. She didn't want everyone looking at her right now.

"For her first essay assignment, Spencer Hastings made a very eloquent, convincing argument on the invisible-hand theory," Squidward proclaimed, stroking his tie, which had Benjamin Franklin's C-note portrait stamped all over it. "And, as you may have heard, I have nominated her for a Golden Orchid award."

Squidward began to applaud, and the rest of the class followed. It lasted an intolerable fifteen seconds.

"But I have another surprise," Squidward continued. "I just got off the phone with a member of the judges' panel, and Spencer, you've made the finals."

The class burst into applause again. Someone at the back even wolf-whistled. Spencer sat very still. For a moment, she lost all vision completely. She tried to paste a smile on her face.

Andrew Campbell, who sat next to her, tapped her on the shoulder. "Nice job."

Spencer looked over. She and Andrew had hardly spoken since she'd been the world's worst Foxy date and ditched him at the dance. Mostly, he'd been giving her dirty looks. "Thanks," she croaked, once she found her voice.

"You must have really worked hard on it, huh? Did you use extra sources?"

"Uh-huh." Spencer frantically pulled out all the loose handouts from her econ folder and started straightening them. She smoothed out any bent-down corners and folds and tried to organize them by date. Melissa's paper was actually the only outside source Spencer had used. When she'd tried to do the necessary research for the essay, even Wikipedia's simple definition of *invisible hand* had completely perplexed her. The first few sentences of her sister's essay were clear enough—*The great Scottish economist Adam Smith's invisible-hand concept can be summed up very easily, whether it's describing the markets of the nineteenth century or those of the twenty-first: you might think people are doing things to help you, but in reality, everyone is only out for themselves.* But when she read the rest of the essay, her brain got as foggy as her family's eucalyptus steam room.

"What kind of sources?" Andrew continued. "Books? Magazine articles?" When she looked over again, he seemed to have a smirk on his face, and Spencer felt dizzy. Did he *know*?

"Like the . . . like the books McAdam suggested on his list," she fumbled.

"Ah. Well, congratulations. I hope you win."

"Thanks," she answered, deciding Andrew couldn't know. He was just jealous. Spencer and Andrew were ranked number one and number two, respectively, in the class and were constantly shifting positions. Andrew probably monitored Spencer's every achievement like a stockbroker watches the Dow Jones Industrial Average ticker. Spencer went back to straightening her folder, although it wasn't making her feel any better.

As Squidward dimmed the lights and the video—*Microeconomics and the Consumer*, with cheesy, upbeat music—came on, Spencer's Sidekick vibrated in her bag. Slowly, she reached in and pulled it out. Her phone had one new text.

> Spence: I know what you did. But I won't tell if you do EXACTLY what I say. Wanna know what happens if you don't? Go to Emily's swim meet . . . and you'll see. —A

Someone next to Spencer cleared his throat. She looked over, and there was Andrew, staring right at her. His eyes glowed against the flickering light of the movie. Spencer turned to face forward, but she could still feel Andrew watching her in the darkness.

10

SOMEONE DIDN'T LISTEN

During the break at the Rosewood Day–Drury Academy swim meet, Emily opened her team locker and pulled down the straps of her Speedo Fastskin racing suit. This year, the Rosewood Day swim team had splurged on full-body, drag-free, Olympian-caliber swimsuits. They'd had to special-order them, and they'd just arrived in time for today's meet. The suits tapered to the ankles, clung to every inch of skin, and showed every bulge, reminding Emily of the photo in her bio textbook of a boa constrictor digesting a mouse. Emily grinned at Lanie Iler, her teammate. "I'm so happy to be getting out of this thing."

She was also happy she'd decided to tell Officer Wilden about A. Last night, after Emily returned home from Hanna's house, she'd called and arranged to meet Wilden at the Rosewood police station later tonight. Emily didn't care what the others said or thought about

A's threat—with the police involved, they could put this drama behind them forever.

"You're so lucky you're done," Lanie responded. Emily had already swum—and won—all of her events; now the only thing she had left to do was cheer along with the zillions of other Rosewood students who had showed up for the meet. She could hear the cheerleaders screaming from the locker room and hoped they wouldn't slip on the natatorium's wet tiled floor—Tracey Reid had taken a spill before the first event.

"Hey, girls." Coach Lauren strode down their aisle of lockers. Today, as usual, Lauren was wearing one of her inspirational swimming T-shirts: TOP TEN REASONS I SWIM. (Number five: BECAUSE I CAN EAT 5,000 CALORIES AND NOT FEEL GUILTY.) She clapped a hand on Emily's shoulder. "Great job, Em. Pulling ahead in the medley relay like that? Fantastic!"

"Thanks." Emily blushed.

Lauren leaned over the chipped red bench in the middle of the aisle. "There's a local recruiter from the University of Arizona here," she said in a low voice, only to Emily. "She asked if she could speak to you during the second half. That okay?"

Emily's eyes widened. "Of course!" The University of Arizona was one of the best swimming schools in the country.

"Great. You guys can talk in my office, if you want." Lauren gave Emily another smile. She disappeared toward the hall that led to the natatorium, and Emily followed. She passed her sister Carolyn, who was coming from the other direction.

"Carolyn, guess what!" Emily bounced up and down. "A University of Arizona recruiter wants to talk to me! If I went there and you went to Stanford, we'd be close!" Carolyn was graduating this year and had already been recruited by Stanford's swim team.

Carolyn glanced at Emily and disappeared into a bathroom stall, shutting the door behind her with a slam. Emily backed away, feeling stunned. What just happened? She and her sister weren't super-close, but she'd expected a *little* more enthusiasm than that.

As Emily walked toward the hall that led to the pool, Gemma Curran's face peeped at her from the showers. When Emily met her eyes, Gemma snapped the curtain closed. And as she walked by the sinks, Amanda Williamson was whispering to Jade Smythe. When Emily met their eyes in the mirror, their mouths made small, startled *O*'s. Emily felt goose bumps rise to the surface of her skin. What was going on?

"God, it seems like even *more* people are here now!" Lanie murmured, walking into the natatorium behind Emily. And she was right: the stands seemed more packed than during the first half. The band, set up near the diving well, was playing a fight song, and the foamy gray Hammerhead mascot had joined the cheerleaders in front of the stands. Everyone was in the stands—the popular

kids, the soccer boys, the drama club girls, even her teachers. Spencer Hastings sat next to Kirsten Cullen. Maya
was up there, typing furiously into her cell phone, and
Hanna Marin sat near her, all alone and gazing out into
the crowd. And there were Emily's parents, dressed up
in their blue-and-white Rosewood Swimming sweatshirts
decorated with GO EMILY and GO CAROLYN buttons. Emily
tried to wave to them, but they were too busy studying
a piece of paper, probably the heat sheet. Actually, a lot
of people were looking at the heat sheet. Mr. Shay, the
geezerish biology teacher who always watched practice
because he'd been a swimmer about a thousand years
ago, held a copy about three inches from his face. The
heat sheet wasn't *that* interesting—it just listed the order
of events.

James Freed stepped in Emily's path. His mouth
stretched into a broad grin. *"Hey,* Emily," he said leeringly.
"I had no idea."

Emily frowned. "No idea . . . what?"

Aria's brother, Mike, sauntered up next to James. "Hi,
Emily."

Mona Vanderwaal came up behind the two boys.
"Stop bothering her, you two." She turned to Emily.
"Ignore them. I want to invite you to something." She
dug through her giant butterscotch suede satchel and
handed Emily a white envelope. Emily turned it over in
her hands. Whatever this was, Mona had scented it with
something expensive. Emily glanced up, confused.

"I'm having a birthday party on Saturday," Mona explained, twisting a long piece of white-blond hair around her fingers. "Maybe I'll see you?"

"You should *totally* come," Mike agreed, widening his eyes.

"I . . ." Emily stammered. But before she could say anything more, the band struck up another fight song and Mona skipped away.

Emily looked at the invite again. What on earth was *that* all about? She wasn't the type of girl who got hand-delivered invitations from Mona Vanderwaal. And she certainly wasn't the type who got salacious looks from boys.

Suddenly, something across the pool caught her eye. It was a piece of paper taped to the wall. It hadn't been there before halftime. And it looked familiar. Like a photo.

She squinted. Her heart dropped to her knees. It *was* a photo . . . of two people kissing in a photo booth. In *Noel Kahn's* photo booth.

"Oh my God." Emily ran across the natatorium, sliding twice on the wet pool deck.

"Emily!" Aria ran toward her from the side entrance, her suede platform boots clomping against the tile and her blue-black hair flapping wildly all over her face. "I'm sorry I'm late, but can we talk?"

Emily didn't answer Aria. Someone had placed a Xerox of the kissing photo next to the big marker board that listed who was swimming in what race. Her whole team would see it. But would they know it was her?

She tore the Xerox off the wall. On the bottom, in big black letters, it said, LOOK WHAT EMILY FIELDS HAS BEEN PRACTICING WHEN SHE'S NOT IN THE POOL!

Well, that cleared *that* up.

Aria leaned over and examined the photo. "Is that . . . you?"

Emily's chin trembled. She crumpled up the paper in her hands, but when she looked around, she saw another copy sitting on top of someone's gear bag, a fold already down the center. She grabbed it and crumpled it up, too.

Then she saw another copy lying on the ground near the tub of kickboards. And another one . . . in Coach Lauren's hands. Lauren looked from the picture to Emily, from Emily to the picture. "Emily?" she said quietly.

"This can't be happening," Emily whispered, raking her hand through her wet hair. She glanced over at the wire-mesh wastebasket near Lauren's office. There were at least ten discarded pictures of her kissing Maya at the bottom. Someone had thrown a half-drunk can of Sunkist on top. The liquid had oozed out, coloring their faces orange. There were more near the water fountains. And taped up to the racing lane storage wheel. Her teammates, who were all filtering out from the locker rooms, gave her uneasy looks. Her ex-boyfriend, Ben, smirked at her, as if to say, *Your little lesbo experiment isn't so fun now, huh?*

Aria picked up a copy that had seemingly fluttered down from the ceiling. She squinted and pursed her shiny, strawberry-red lips together. "So what? You're kissing someone." Her eyes widened. *"Oh."*

Emily let out a helpless *eep.*

"Did A do this?" Aria whispered.

Emily looked around frantically. "Did you see who was giving these out?" But Aria shook her head. Emily unzipped the pouch to her swim bag and found her cell phone. There was a text. Of course there was a text.

Emily, sweetie, I know you're all about tit for tat, so when you made plans to out me, I decided to out you too. Kisses! —A

"Damn," Aria whispered, reading the text over Emily's shoulder.

A sickening thought suddenly hit Emily. Her parents. That paper they were looking at—it wasn't the heat sheet. *It was the photo.* She glanced over at the stands. Sure enough, her parents were staring at her. They looked like they were about to cry, their faces red and nostrils flared.

"I have to get out of here." Emily searched for the nearest exit.

"No way." Aria grabbed Emily's wrist and spun her around. "This is nothing to be ashamed of. If someone says something, screw 'em."

Emily sniffed. People might *call* Aria weird, but she

was normal. She had a boyfriend. She would never know what this felt like.

"Emily, this is our opportunity!" Aria protested. "A is probably *here*." She looked menacingly into the bleachers.

Emily peeked over at the stands again. Her parents still wore the same angry and hurt expressions. Maya's spot was now empty. Emily scanned the length of the stands for her, but Maya was gone.

A *was* probably up there. And Emily wished she was brave enough to climb up into the bleachers and shake everyone until someone confessed. But she couldn't.

"I . . . I'm sorry," Emily said abruptly, and ran for the locker room. She passed the hundred or so people who now knew what she was really like, trampling over copies of her and Maya on the way.

11

EVEN HIGH-TECH SECURITY DOESN'T PROTECT YOU FROM EVERYTHING

Moments later, Aria pushed through the fogged-up double doors of Rosewood Day's natatorium and joined Spencer and Hanna, who were talking quietly by the vending machines. "Poor Emily," Hanna whispered to Spencer. "Did you know about . . . this?"

Spencer shook her head. "No idea."

"Remember when we snuck into the Kahns' pool when they were on vacation and went skinny-dipping?" Hanna murmured. "Remember all the times we changed in dressing rooms together? I never felt weird."

"Me neither," Aria piped up, ducking out of the way so a freshman boy could get a soda out of the Coke machine.

"Do you think she thought any of us were cute?" Hanna widened her eyes. "But I was so fat back then," she added, sounding a little disappointed.

"A passed around those flyers," Aria said to Hanna and Spencer. She pointed toward the pool. "A might be here."

They all peered into the natatorium. Competitors stood on the blocks, waiting. The hammerhead shark mascot paraded up and down the length of the pool. The stands were still packed. "What are we supposed to do about it?" Hanna asked, narrowing her eyes. "Stop the meet?"

"We shouldn't do anything." Spencer zipped up her khaki Burberry anorak to her chin. "If we look for A, A might get mad . . . and do something worse."

"A. Is. Here!" Aria repeated. "This might be our big chance!"

Spencer looked at the crowd of kids in the lobby. "I . . . I have to go." With that, she darted through the revolving doors and sprinted across the parking lot.

Aria turned to Hanna. "Spencer ran out of here like *she* was A," she half-joked.

"I heard she's a finalist in some big essay contest." Hanna pulled out her Chanel compact and began dabbing at her chin. "You know she gets manic when she's competing. She's probably going home to study."

"True," Aria said quietly. Maybe Spencer was right— maybe A *would* do something worse if they searched the stands.

Suddenly, someone whipped her hood off her head from behind. Aria swirled around. "Mike," she gasped. *"God."*

Her brother grinned. "Did you get a photo of the lesbo action?" He pretended to lick the picture of Emily and Maya. "Can you get me Emily's digits?"

"Absolutely not." She surveyed her brother. His STX lacrosse cap smashed down his blue-black hair, and he was wearing his blue-and-white Rosewood Day Varsity lacrosse windbreaker. She hadn't seen him since last night.

"So." Mike put his hands on his hips. "I hear you got kicked out of the house."

"I wasn't kicked out," Aria said defensively. "I just thought it would be better if I stayed away for a while."

"And you're moving into Sean's?"

"Yeah," Aria answered. After Ella had told Aria to leave, Aria had called Sean in hysterics. She hadn't been fishing for an invitation—but Sean had offered, saying it wouldn't be any trouble at all.

Hanna's jaw dropped. "You're *moving* to Sean's? As in, his house?"

"Hanna, not by choice," Aria said quickly. "It's an emergency."

Hanna cut her eyes away. "Whatever. I don't care. You're going to hate it. Everybody knows that staying with your boyfriend's parents is relationship suicide." She whirled around, pushing through the crowd toward the front door.

"Hanna!" Aria protested, but Hanna didn't turn around. She glared at Mike. "Did you *have* to mention that when she was standing here? Do you have no tact at all?"

Mike shrugged. "Sorry, I don't speak PMS." He pulled out a PowerBar from his pocket and started to eat it, not bothering to offer Aria any. "You going to Mona's party?"

Aria stuck out her lip. "Not sure. I haven't thought about it."

"Are you *depressed* or something?" Mike asked, his mouth full.

Aria didn't have to think about it too hard. "Kind of. I mean . . . Dad left. How do *you* feel?"

Mike's face changed from being open and jokey to hardened and guarded. He let the paper fall to his side. "So, last night I asked Mom some questions. She told me Dad was seeing that girl before we went to Iceland. And that you knew."

Aria put the ends of her hair in her mouth and stared at the blue recycling can in the corner. Someone had drawn a cartoonish pair of boobs on the lid. "Yeah."

"So why didn't you tell *me* about it?"

Aria glanced at him. "Byron told me not to."

Mike took a violent bite of PowerBar. "It was okay, though, to tell Alison DiLaurentis. And it's okay for her to say it in a video that's *all over the news*."

"Mike . . ." Aria started. "I didn't *tell* her. She was with me when it happened."

"Whatever," Mike grunted, colliding with the shark

mascot as he pushed angrily through the natatorium's double doors. Aria considered going after him but didn't. She was reminded, suddenly, of the time in Reykjavík when she was supposed to baby-sit Mike but had gone off to the Blue Lagoon geothermal spa with her boyfriend, Hallbjorn, instead. When she returned, smelling like sulfur and covered in curative salt, she'd discovered that Mike had set half the backyard's wood trellis on fire. Aria had gotten in deep trouble for it—and really, it *had* been her fault. She'd noticed Mike eagerly eyeing the kitchen matches before she left for the lagoon. She could have stopped him. She probably could have stopped Byron, too.

"So this one's yours," Sean said, leading Aria down his mahogany-floored, immaculately clean hallway to a large, white bedroom. It had a bay window with a window seat, gauzy white curtains, and a white bouquet of flowers on the end table.

"I love it." The room looked like the Parisian boutique hotel room her family stayed in the time her father was interviewed on Parisian television for being an expert on gnomes. "You sure it's okay for me to stay?"

"Of course." Sean gave her a demure kiss on the cheek. "I'll let you get settled."

Aria looked out the window at the pinkish, late-Tuesday sky and couldn't help comparing this view to hers at home. The Ackards' estate was nestled in the deep woods and surrounded by at least ten acres of untouched land. The nearest property, a castlelike monolith with medieval-style turrets, was at least three football fields away. Aria's house was in a lovely but rickety neighborhood close to the college. The only thing she could see of her neighbors' yard was their unfortunate collection of birdbaths, stone animals, and lawn jockeys.

"Everything okay with the room?" Mrs. Ackard, Sean's stepmother, asked as Aria drifted downstairs into the kitchen.

"It's great," Aria said. "Thank you so much."

Mrs. Ackard gave her a sweet smile in return. She was blond, a bit pudgy, with inquisitive blue eyes and a mouth that looked like it was smiling even when she wasn't. When Aria closed her eyes and pictured a mom, Mrs. Ackard was pretty much what she imagined. Sean had told her that before she married his dad she'd worked as a magazine editor in Philadelphia, but now she was a full-time housewife, keeping the Ackards' monstrous house looking photo-shoot ready at all times. The apples in the wooden bowl on the island were unbruised, the magazines in the living room rack all faced the same direction, and the tassels on the giant Oriental rug were even, as if they'd just been combed.

"I'm making mushroom ravioli," Mrs. Ackard said, inviting Aria to come over and smell a pot of sauce. "Sean said you're a vegetarian."

"I am," Aria answered softly. "But you didn't have to do that for me."

"It's no trouble," Mrs. Ackard said warmly. There were also scalloped potatoes, a tomato salad, and a loaf of the hearty, gourmet seven-grain bread from Fresh Fields that Ella always scoffed at, saying anyone who paid $10.99 for some flour and water ought to have his head examined.

Mrs. Ackard pulled the wooden spoon out of the pot and rested it on the counter. "You were good friends with Alison DiLaurentis, weren't you? I saw that video of you girls on the news."

Aria ducked her head. "That's right." A lump grew in her throat. Seeing Ali so alive in that video had brought Aria's grief to the surface all over again.

To Aria's surprise, Mrs. Ackard wrapped her arm around her shoulder and gave her a little squeeze. "I'm so sorry," she murmured. "I can't imagine what that's like."

Tears prickled at Aria's eyes. It felt good to be nestled in a mom's arms, even if she wasn't *her* mom.

Sean sat next to Aria at dinner, and *everything* was the antithesis of how it went at Aria's house. The Ackards put their napkins on their laps, there was no television news droning in the background, and Mr. Ackard, who was rangy and balding but had a charismatic smile, didn't read the newspaper at the table. The younger Ackard twins, Colin and Aidan, kept their elbows off the table and didn't poke each other with their forks—Aria could only imagine what atrocities Mike would commit if *he* had a twin.

"Thank you," Aria said as Mrs. Ackard poured more milk in her glass, even though Byron and Ella had always said milk contained synthetic hormones and caused cancer. Aria had told Ezra about her parents' ban on milk the evening she'd spent at his apartment a few weeks ago. Ezra had laughed, saying his family had their freak-show granola moments, too.

Aria laid down her fork. How had *Ezra* crept into her peaceful dinnertime thoughts? She quickly eyed Sean, who was chewing a forkful of potatoes. She leaned over and touched his wrist. He smiled.

"Sean tells us you're taking AP classes, Aria," Mr. Ackard said, spearing a carrot.

Aria shrugged. "Just English and AP studio art."

"English lit was my major in college," Mrs. Ackard said enthusiastically. "What are you reading right now?"

"The Scarlet Letter."

"I love that book!" Mrs. Ackard cried, taking a small sip of red wine. "It really shows how restrictive the Puritan society used to be. Poor Hester Prynne."

Aria chewed on the inside of her cheek. If only Aria had talked to Mrs. Ackard *before* she branded Meredith.

"The Scarlet Letter." Mr. Ackard put his finger to his lips. "They made that into a movie, didn't they?"

"Uh-huh," Sean said. "With Demi Moore."

"The one where the man falls in love with a younger girl, right?" Mr. Ackard added. "So scandalous."

Aria drew in her breath. She felt like everyone was looking at her, but in reality, only Sean was. His eyes were wide and drawn down, mortified. *I'm sorry,* his expression said. "No, David," Mrs. Ackard said quietly, in a voice that indicated she had some idea of Aria's situation. "That's *Lolita.*"

"Oh. Right." Mr. Ackard shrugged, apparently not realizing his faux pas. "I get them all mixed up."

After dinner, Sean and the twins went upstairs to do their homework, and Aria followed. Her guest room was quiet and inviting. Some time between dinner and now, Mrs. Ackard had put a box of Kleenex and a vase of lavender on her nightstand. The flowers' grandmotherly smell filled the room. Aria flopped on her bed, switched on the local news for company, and opened Gmail on her laptop. There was one new note. The name of the sender was a series of garbled letters and numbers. Aria felt her heart stop as she double-clicked it open.

Aria: Don't you think Sean should know about that extra-credit work you did with a certain English teacher? Real relationships are built on truth, after all. —A

Just then, the central heating shut off, making Aria sit up straighter. Outside, a twig snapped. Then another. *Someone was watching.*

She crept to the window and peered out. The pine trees cast lumpy shadows across the tennis court. A security camera perched on the edge of the house slowly swiveled from right to left. There was a flicker of light, then nothing.

When she looked back into her room, something on the news caught her eye. *New stalker sighting*, the banner at the bottom of the screen said. "We've received news that a few people have seen the Rosewood Stalker," said a reporter, as Aria turned up the volume. "Stand by for details."

There was an image of a police car in front of a behemoth of a house with castlelike turrets. Aria turned to the window again—there they were. And sure enough, a blue police siren was now flashing against the far-off pines.

She stepped into the hall. Sean's door was shut; Bloc Party drifted out. "Sean?" She pushed his bedroom door open. His books were strewn all over his desk, but his desk chair was empty. There was an indentation on his perfectly made bed where his body had been. His window was open, and a chilly breeze blew in, making the curtains dance like ghosts.

Aria didn't know what else to do, so she went back to her computer. That's when she saw a new e-mail.

P.S. I may be a bitch, but I'm not a murderer. Here's a clue for the clueless: someone wanted something of Ali's. The killer is closer than you think. —A

12

AH, COURT LIFE

Tuesday evening, Hanna strolled down the main concourse at the King James Mall, puzzling over her BlackBerry. She'd sent Mona a text asking *R we still meeting 4 my dress fitting?* but she hadn't received a response.

Mona was probably still annoyed at her because of the Frenniversary thing, but whatever. Hanna had tried to explain why her old friends had been at her house, but Mona had interrupted her before she could even start, declaring in her frostiest voice, "I saw you and your besties on the news. Congrats on your big TV debut." Then she hung up. So sure she was pissed, but Hanna knew Mona couldn't stay mad for long. If she did, who would be her BFF?

Hanna passed Rive Gauche, the mall brasserie where they were supposed to have their Frenniversary dinner yesterday. It was a copy of Balthazar in New York, which was a copy of zillions of cafés in Paris. She caught sight of a group of girls at Hanna's and Mona's favorite banquette. One of the girls was Naomi. The next was Riley. And the girl next to her was . . . Mona.

Hanna did a double take. What was Mona doing with . . . *them*?

Even though the lights in Rive Gauche were dim and romantic, Mona was wearing her pink-tinted aviators. Naomi, Riley, Kelly Hamilton, and Nicole Hudson—Naomi and Riley's bitchy sophomore toadies—surrounded her, and a big, uneaten plate of fries sat in the middle of the table. Mona appeared to be telling a story, waving her hands around animatedly and widening her big, blue eyes. She came to a punch line, and the others hooted.

Hanna squared her shoulders. She strode through the café's antique brown door. Naomi was the first to notice her. Naomi nudged Kelly, and they whispered together.

"What are you girls doing here?" she demanded, standing over Riley and Naomi.

Mona leaned forward on her elbows. "Well, isn't this a surprise? I didn't know if you still wanted to be on the court, since you're so busy with your old friends." She flicked her hair over her shoulder and took a sip of Diet Coke.

Hanna rolled her eyes and settled on the end of the dark red banquette bench. "Of course I still want to be on your court, drama whore."

Mona gave her a bland smile. "'Kay, tubbykins."

"Bitch," Hanna shot back.

"Slut," Mona said. Hanna giggled . . . and so did Naomi, Riley, and the others. Sometimes she and Mona got in mock-fights like this, although normally they didn't have an audience.

Mona twirled a piece of pale blond hair around her finger. "Anyway, I decided the more, the merrier. Small courts are boring. I want this party to be over-the-top."

"We're *so* excited," Naomi gushed. "I can't wait to try on the Zac Posen dress Mona picked out for us."

Hanna shot them a taut smile. This really didn't make any sense. Everyone at Rosewood knew Riley and Naomi had been talking about Hanna behind her back. And wasn't it just last year that Mona had vowed she'd despise Naomi forever after Naomi gossiped that Mona had gotten skin grafts? Hanna had fake-friended Naomi for that—she'd pretended she and Mona were in a fight, won Naomi's confidence, then pilfered a cheesy love letter Naomi had written to Mason Byers from Naomi's notebook. Hanna posted the letter anonymously on Rosewood Day's intranet the very next day, everyone laughed, and all was right again.

All at once, Hanna had an epiphany. Of course! Mona was fake-friending! It *completely* made sense. She felt a little better, realizing what was going on, but she still wanted confirmation. She eyed Mona. "Hey, Mon, can I talk to you for a sec? Alone?"

"Can't right now, Han." Mona looked at her Movado

watch. "We're late for our fitting. C'mon."

With that, Mona strolled out of the restaurant, her three-inch heels clacking against the shiny walnut floor. The others followed. Hanna reached over to grab her enormous Gucci purse, but the zipper had come undone and the entire contents spilled under the table. All her makeup, her wallet, her vitamins, the Hydroxycut she'd stolen ages ago from GNC but was a little too scared to take . . . everything. Hanna scrambled to pick it all up, her eyes on Mona and the others as they snaked away. She knelt down, feverishly trying to stuff everything into her bag as quickly as possible.

"Hanna Marin?"

Hanna jumped. Above her was a familiar, tall, floppy-haired waiter. "It's Lucas," he reminded her, fiddling with the cuff on his white button-down, the Rive Gauche uniform. "You probably don't recognize me because I look so French in this outfit."

"Oh," Hanna said wearily. "Hey." She'd known Lucas Beattie forever. In seventh grade, he'd been popular—and, bizarrely, for a second, he'd liked Hanna. Word had gotten around that Lucas was going to send Hanna a red heart-shaped box of candy on the schoolwide Candy Day. A boy sending you a heart-shaped box of candy meant *love,* so Hanna got really excited.

But then, a few days before Candy Day, something changed. Lucas was suddenly a dork. His friends started to ignore him, girls began to laugh at him, and a rampant rumor that he was a hermaphrodite swirled. Hanna couldn't believe her luck, but she secretly wondered if he'd gone from popular to a loser all because he'd decided to like *her*. Even if she was Ali D's friend, she was still a fat, dorky, clumsy loser. When he sent her the candy, Hanna hid it in her locker and didn't thank him.

"What's up?" Hanna asked blandly. Lucas had pretty much stayed a loser.

"Not much," Lucas responded eagerly. "What's up with you?"

Hanna rolled her eyes. She hadn't meant to start a conversation. "I have to go," she said, looking toward the courtyard. "My friends are waiting for me."

"Actually . . ." Lucas followed her toward the exit, "your friends forgot to pay the bill." He whipped out a leather booklet. "Unless, um, you were getting it this time."

"Oh." Hanna cleared her throat. Nice of Mona to mention it. "No problem."

Lucas swiped her AmEx and gave her the bill to sign, and Hanna strode out of Rive Gauche without adding a tip—or telling Lucas good-bye. The more she thought about it, she was excited that Naomi and Riley were part of Mona's court. Around Rosewood, party court girls competed over who could get the birthday girl the most glamorous gift. A day pass to the Blue Springs Spa or a Prada gift card didn't cut it, either—the winning gift had to be totally over the top. Julia Rubenstein's best friend had hired male strippers to perform at an after-party for a select few—and they'd been *hot* strippers, not muscle-heads. And Sarah Davies had convinced her dad to hire Beyoncé to sing "Happy Birthday" to the girl-of-honor. Thankfully, Naomi and Riley were about as creative as the newborn panda at the Philadelphia Zoo. Hanna could out-glam them on her worst day.

She heard her BlackBerry humming in her bag and pulled it out. There were two messages in her mailbox. The first, from Mona, had come in six minutes ago.

> Where R U, bee-yotch? If you're any later, the tailor's going to get pissed. —Mon

But the second text, which had arrived two minutes later, was from a blocked number. That could only be one person.

> Dear Hanna, We may not be friends, but we have the same enemies. So here are two tips: One of your old friends is hiding something from you. Something big. And Mona? She's not your friend, either. So watch your back. —A

13

HELLO, MY NAME IS EMILY.
AND I'M GAY.

That night at 7:17 Emily pulled into her driveway. After she'd run out of the natatorium, she'd walked around the Rosewood Bird Sanctuary for hours. The busily chirping sparrows, happy little ducks, and tame parakeets soothed her. It was a good place to escape from reality . . . and a certain incriminating photo.

Every light in the house was on, including the one in the bedroom that Emily and Carolyn shared. How would she explain the photo to her family? She wanted to say that kissing Maya in that picture had been a joke, that someone was playing a prank on her. *Ha ha, kissing girls is gross!*

But it wasn't true, and it made her heart ache.

The house smelled warm and inviting, like a mixture of coffee and potpourri. Her mother had turned on the hallway Hummel figurines cabinet. Little figurines of a boy milking a cow and a lederhosen-clad girl pushing a wheelbarrow slowly rotated. Emily made her way down the floral wallpapered hallway toward the living room. Both her parents were sitting on the flowered couch. An older woman sat on the love seat.

Her mother gave her a watery smile. "Well, hello, Emily."

Emily blinked a few times. "Um, hi . . ." She looked from her parents to the stranger on the love seat.

"You want to come in?" her mother asked. "We have someone here to see you."

The older woman, who was wearing high-waisted black slacks and a mint-green blazer, stood and offered her hand. "I'm Edith." She grinned. "It's so nice to meet you, Emily. Why don't you sit down?"

Emily's father bustled into the dining room and dragged another chair over for her. She sat down tentatively, feeling jumpy. It was the same feeling she used to get when her old friends played the Pillow Game—one person walked around the living room blindfolded, and, at a random moment, the others bombarded her with pillows. Emily didn't like playing—she hated those tense moments right before they started smacking her—but she always played anyway, because Ali loved it.

"I'm from a program called Tree Tops," Edith said. "Your parents told me about your problem."

The bones in Emily's butt pressed into the bare wood of the dining room chair. "Problem?" Her stomach sank. She had a feeling she knew what *problem* meant.

"Of course it's a problem." Her mother's voice was choked. "That picture—with that girl we *forbade* you to see—has it happened more than once?"

Emily nervously touched the scar on her left palm that she'd gotten when Carolyn accidentally speared her with the gardening shears. She'd grown up striving to be as obedient and well behaved as possible, and she couldn't lie to her parents—at least not well. "It's happened more than once, I guess," she mumbled.

Her mother let out a small, pained whimper.

Edith pursed her wrinkly, fuchsia-lined lips. She had an old-lady mothball smell. "What you're feeling, it's not permanent. It's a sickness, Emily. But we at Tree Tops can cure you. We've rehabilitated many ex-gays since the program began."

Emily barked out a laugh. "Ex . . . *gays*?" The world started to spin, then recede. Emily's parents looked at her self-righteously, their hands wrapped around their coffee cups.

"Your interest in young women isn't genetic or scientific, but environmental," Edith explained. "With counseling, we'll help you dismiss your . . . urges, shall we say."

Emily gripped the arms of her chair. "That sounds . . . *weird*."

"Emily!" scolded her mother—she'd taught her children never to disrespect adults. But Emily was too bewildered to be embarrassed.

"It's not weird," Edith chirped. "Don't worry if you don't understand it all now. Many of our new recruits don't." She looked at Emily's parents. "We have a *superb* track record of rehabilitation in the greater Philadelphia area."

Emily wanted to throw up. *Rehabilitation?* She searched her parents' faces, but they gave her nothing. She glanced out to the street. *If the next car that passes is white, this isn't happening,* she thought. *If it's red, it is.* A car swept past. Sure enough, it was red.

Edith placed her coffee cup on its saucer. "We're going to have a peer mentor come talk to you. Someone who experienced the program firsthand. She's a senior at Rosewood Senior High, and her name's Becka. She's very nice. You'll just talk. And after that, we'll discuss you joining the program properly. Okay?"

Emily looked at her parents. "I don't have time to talk to anybody," she insisted. "I have swimming in the mornings and after school, and then I have homework."

Her mother smiled tensely. "You'll make time. What about lunch tomorrow?"

Edith nodded. "I'm sure that would be fine."

Emily rubbed her throbbing head. She already hated Becka, and she hadn't even met her. "Fine," she agreed. "Tell her to meet me at Lorence chapel." There was no way Emily was talking with Little Miss Tree Tops in the cafeteria. School was going to be brutal enough tomorrow as it was.

Edith brushed her hands together and stood up. "I'll make all the arrangements."

Emily stood against the foyer wall as her parents handed Edith her coat and thanked her for coming. Edith navigated down the Fieldses' stone path to her car. When Emily's parents turned back to her, they had weary, sober looks on their faces.

"Mom, Dad . . ." Emily started.

Her mother whirled around. "That Maya girl has a few tricks up her sleeve, huh?"

Emily backed up. "Maya didn't pass that picture around."

Mrs. Fields eyed Emily carefully, then sat down on the couch and put her head in her hands. "Emily, what are we going to do *now*?"

"What do you mean, *we*?"

Her mother looked up. "Don't you see that this is a reflection on all of us?"

"*I* didn't make the announcement," Emily protested.

"It doesn't matter how it happened," her mother interrupted. "What matters is that it's out there." She stood up and regarded the couch, then picked up a decorative pillow and smacked it with her fist to fluff it up. She set it back down, picked up another, and started all over again. *Thwack.* She was punching them harder than she needed to.

"It was so shocking to see that picture of you, Emily," Mrs. Fields said. "*Horribly* shocking. And to hear that it's something you've done *more than once*, well . . ."

"I'm sorry," Emily whimpered. "But maybe it's not—"

"Have you even thought about how hard this is for the rest of us?" Mrs. Fields interrupted. "We're all . . . well, Carolyn came home crying. And your brother and sister both called me, offering to fly home."

She picked up another pillow. *Thwack, thwack.* A few feathers spewed out and floated through the air before settling on the carpet. Emily wondered what this would look like to someone passing by the window. Perhaps they'd see the feathers flying and think that something silly and happy was happening, instead of what actually was.

Emily's tongue felt leaden in her mouth. A gnawing hole at the pit of her stomach remained. "I'm sorry," she whispered.

Her mother's eyes flashed. She nodded to Emily's father. "Go get it." Her father disappeared into the living room, and Emily listened to him rooting through the drawers of their old antique bureau. Seconds later, he returned with a printout from Expedia. "This is for you," Mr. Fields said.

It was an itinerary, flying from Philadelphia to Des Moines, Iowa. With her name on it. "I don't understand."

Mr. Fields cleared his throat. "Just to make things perfectly clear, either you do Tree Tops—*successfully*—or you will go live with your aunt Helene."

Emily blinked. "Aunt Helene . . . who lives on a farm?"

"Can you think of another Aunt Helene?" he asked.

Emily felt dizzy. She looked to her mom. "You're going to send me *away*?"

"Let's hope it doesn't come to that," Mrs. Fields answered.

Tears dotted Emily's eyes. For a while, she couldn't speak. It felt as if a block of cement were sitting on her chest. "Please don't send me away," she whispered. "I'll . . . I'll do Tree Tops. Okay?"

She lowered her gaze. This felt like when she and Ali used to arm wrestle—they were matched for strength and could do it for hours, but eventually, Emily would surrender, letting her arm go limp. Maybe she was giving up too easily, but she couldn't fight this.

A small, relieved smile crept over her mother's face. She put the itinerary in her cardigan pocket. "Now, that wasn't so hard, was it?"

Before she could respond, Emily's parents left the room.

14

SPENCER'S BIG CLOSE-UP

Wednesday morning, Spencer stared at herself in her mahogany Chippendale vanity mirror. The vanity and dressing table had been in the Hastings family for two hundred years, and the watermark stain on the top had allegedly been made by Ernest Hemingway—he'd set his sweaty glass of whisky on it during one of Spencer's great-great-grandmother's cotillions.

Spencer picked up her round boar-bristle brush and began raking it through her hair until her scalp hurt. Jordana, the reporter from the *Philadelphia Sentinel*, would be showing up soon for her big interview and photo shoot. A stylist was bringing wardrobe options, and Spencer's hairdresser, Uri, was due any minute to give her a blowout. She just finished her own makeup, going for a subtle, refined, fresh-faced look, which hopefully made her look smart, put-together—and absolutely *not* a plagiarist.

Spencer gulped and glanced at a photo she kept wedged

in the corner of the mirror. It was of her old friends on
Ali's uncle's yacht in Newport, Rhode Island. They were
all smashed together, wearing matching J. Crew bikinis
and wide-brimmed straw hats, grinning like they were god-
desses of the sea.

This will go fine, Spencer told the mirror, taking a deep
breath. The article would probably end up being a tiny
item in the Style section, something no one would even
see. Jordana might ask her two or three questions, tops.
A's note from yesterday—*I know what you did*—had only
been meant to scare her. She tried to sweep it to the back
of her mind.

Suddenly, her Sidekick bleeped. Spencer picked it up,
pushed a few buttons to get into her texts inbox, and
squinted at the screen.

Need another warning, Spence? Ali's murderer is right in
front of you. —A

Spencer's phone clattered to the floor. *Ali's murderer?*
She stared at her reflection in the mirror. Then at the
picture of her friends in the corner. Ali was holding the
yacht's wheel, and the others were grinning behind her.

And then, something in the window caught her eye.
Spencer wheeled around, but there was nothing. No
one in her yard except for a lost-looking mallard duck.
Nobody in the DiLaureuntises' or the Cavanaughs' yards,
either. Spencer turned back to the mirror and ran her cool

hands down the length of her face.

"Hey."

Spencer jumped. Melissa stood behind her, leaning against Spencer's four-poster bed. Spencer whirled around, not sure if Melissa's reflection was real. She'd sneaked up on Spencer so . . . stealthily.

"Are you all right?" Melissa asked, fiddling with the ruffled collar of her green silk blouse. "You look like you've seen a ghost."

"I just got the weirdest text," Spencer blurted out.

"Really? What did it say?"

Spencer glanced at her Sidekick on the cream-colored rug, then kicked it farther under the dressing table. "Never mind."

"Well, anyway, your reporter is here." Melissa wandered out of Spencer's room. "Mom wanted me to tell you."

Spencer stood up and walked to her door. She couldn't believe she'd almost told Melissa about A's note. But what had A meant? How could Ali's killer be right in front of her, when she was staring in the mirror?

A vision flashed in front of her eyes. *Come on,* Ali cackled nastily. *You read it in my diary, didn't you?*

I wouldn't read your diary, Spencer replied. *I don't care.*

There were a few spots and flashes, and a white rush of movement. And then, *poof,* gone. Spencer blinked furiously for a few seconds, standing dazed and alone in the middle of the upstairs hallway. It felt like a continuation of the strange, fuzzy memory from the other day. But what was it?

She strode slowly down the stairs, gripping the railing for support. Her parents and Melissa were gathered around the couch in the living room. A plump woman with frizzy black hair and black plastic cat's-eye glasses, a skinny guy with a patchy goatee and a ginormous camera around his neck, and a petite Asian girl who had a pink streak in her hair stood near the front door.

"Spencer Hastings!" the frizzy-haired woman cried when she spied Spencer. "Our finalist!"

She threw her arms around Spencer, and Spencer's nose smushed into the woman's blazer, which smelled like the maraschino cherries Spencer used to get in her Shirley Temples at the country club. Then, she stepped back and held Spencer at arm's length. "I'm Jordana Pratt, style editor of the *Philadelphia Sentinel*," she cried. Jordana gestured to the other two strangers. "And this is Bridget, our stylist, and Matthew, our photographer. It's so nice to meet you!"

"Likewise," Spencer sputtered.

Jordana greeted Spencer's mother and father. She passed over Melissa, not even looking at her, and Melissa cleared her throat. "Um, Jordana, I believe we've met too."

Jordana narrowed her eyes and wrinkled her nose, as if a bad smell had just permeated the air. She stared at Melissa for a few seconds. "We have?"

"You interviewed me when I ran the Philadelphia

Marathon a couple years ago," Melissa reminded her, standing up straighter and pushing her hair behind her ears. "At the Eames Oval, in front of the art museum?"

Jordana still looked lost. "Great, great!" she cried distractedly. "Love the marathon!" She gazed at Spencer again. Spencer noticed she was wearing a Cartier Tank Americaine watch—and not one of the cheap stainless ones, either. "So. I want to know everything about you. What you like to do for fun, your favorite foods, who you think is going to win on *American Idol*, everything. You're probably going to be famous someday, you know! All Golden Orchid winners end up stars."

"Spencer doesn't watch *American Idol*," Mrs. Hastings volunteered. "She's too busy with all her activities and studies."

"She got a 2350 on her PSATs this year," Mr. Hastings added proudly.

"I think that Fantasia girl is going to win," Melissa said. Everyone stopped and looked at her. "On *American Idol*," Melissa qualified.

Jordana frowned. "That was practically the first season." She turned back to Spencer and pursed her glossy red lips. "So. Miss Finalist. We want to emphasize how fantastic and smart and wonderful you are, but we want to keep it fun, too. You were nominated for an economics essay—which is business stuff, right? I was thinking the shoot could be a spoof on *The Apprentice*. The photo could scream, *Spencer Hastings, You're Hired!* You'll be in a sleek black suit, sitting behind a big desk, telling a man he's fired. Or hired. Or that you want him to make you a martini. I don't care."

Spencer blinked. Jordana spoke very fast and gesticulated wildly with her hands.

"The desk in my study might work," Mr. Hastings offered. "It's down the hall."

Jordana looked at Matthew. "Wanna go check it out?" Matthew nodded.

"And I have a black suit she could borrow," Melissa piped up.

Jordana pulled her BlackBerry off her hip-holster and started feverishly typing on the keypad. "That won't be necessary," she murmured. "We've got it covered."

Spencer took a seat on the striped chaise in the living room. Her mother plopped onto the piano bench. Melissa joined them, perching near the antique harp. "This is so exciting," Mrs. Hastings cooed, leaning over to push some hair out of Spencer's eyes.

Spencer had to admit, she loved when people fawned over her. It was such a rare occurrence. "I wonder what she's going to ask me," she mused.

"Oh, probably about your interests, your education," Mrs. Hastings singsonged. "Be sure to tell her about those educational camps I sent you to. And remember how I started teaching you French when you were eight? You were able to go straight to French II in sixth grade because of that."

Spencer giggled into her hand. "There are going to be other stories in Saturday's edition of the *Sentinel,* Mom. Not just mine."

"Maybe she'll ask you about your essay," Melissa said flatly.

Spencer looked up sharply. Melissa was calmly flipping through a *Town & Country,* her expression giving nothing away. Would Jordana ask about the essay?

Bridget waltzed back in with a rolling rack of garment bags. "Start unzipping these and see if there's anything you like," she instructed. "I just have to run out to the car and get the bag of shoes and accessories." She wrinkled her nose. "An assistant would be great right now."

Spencer ran her hands along the vinyl bags. There had to be at least twenty-five. "All these are just for my little photo shoot?"

"Didn't Jordana tell you?" Bridget widened her gray eyes. "The managing editor loved this story, especially since you're local. We're putting you on the front page!"

"Of the Style section?" Melissa seemed incredulous.

"No, of the whole paper!" Bridget cried.

"Oh my God, Spencer!" Mrs. Hastings took Spencer's hand.

"That's right!" Bridget beamed. "Get used to this. And if you win, you'll be on one wild ride. I styled 2001's winner for *Newsweek.* Her schedule was crazy."

Bridget strode back toward the front door, her jasmine

perfume punctuating the air. Spencer tried to breathe yoga fire breaths. She unzipped the first garment bag, running her hands over a dark wool blazer. She checked the tag. Calvin Klein. The next one was Armani.

Her mother and Melissa joined her in unzipping. They were quiet for a few seconds, until Melissa said, "Spence, there's something taped on this bag."

Spencer looked over. A folded piece of lined paper was affixed to a navy garment bag with duct tape. On the front of the note was a single, handwritten initial: *S*.

Spencer's legs stiffened. She pulled the note off slowly, angling her body so that Melissa and her mother couldn't see it, and then opened it up.

"What is it?" Melissa moved away from the rack.

"J-just directions for the stylist." Her words came out garbled and thick.

Mrs. Hastings continued to calmly unzip the garment bags, but Melissa held Spencer's gaze for a beat longer. When Melissa finally looked away, Spencer slowly unfolded the note again.

Dear Ms. Finalist, How'd you like it if I told your secret RIGHT NOW? I can, you know. And if you don't watch it, maybe I will. —A

15

NEVER, *EVER* TRUST SOMETHING
AS OBSOLETE AS A FAX MACHINE

Wednesday afternoon at lunch, Hanna sat at a teak farmhouse table that overlooked the Rosewood Day practice fields and the duck pond. Mount Kale rose up in the distance. It was a perfect afternoon. Tiffany-blue sky, no humidity, the smell of leaves and clean air all around them. The ideal setting for Hanna's perfect birthday present to Mona—now all Mona had to do was show up. Hanna hadn't been able to get a word in while they were fitted for their champagne-colored Zac Posen court dresses at Saks yesterday—not with Naomi and Riley around. She'd tried to call Mona to talk to her about it last night, too, but Mona had said she was in the middle of studying for a big German test. If she failed, the Sweet Seventeen was off.

But whatever. Mona was due any minute, and they'd make up for all the private Hanna-Mona time they'd missed. And yesterday's note from A about Mona not being trustworthy? *Such* a bluff. Mona might still be a little pissed about the Frenniversary misunderstanding, but there was no way she'd bail on their friendship. Anyway, Hanna's birthday surprise would make everything all better. So Mona had better speed it up before she missed the whole thing.

As Hanna waited, she scrolled through her BlackBerry. She had it programmed to keep messages until manually erased, so all her old Alison text conversations were still stored right in her inbox. Most of the time, Hanna didn't like going through them—it was too sad—but today, for some reason she wanted to. She found one from the first day of June, a few days before Ali went missing.

Trying to study for the health final, Ali had written. I have all this nervous energy.

Y? had been Hanna's answer.

Ali: I don't know. Maybe I'm in love. Ha ha.

Hanna: Yr in love? w/ who?

Ali: Kidding. Oh shit, Spencer's at my door. She wants to practice field hockey drills . . . AGAIN.

Tell her no, Hanna had written back. Who do U love?

You don't tell Spencer no, Ali argued. She'll, like, hurt you.

Hanna stared at her BlackBerry's bright screen. At the time, she'd probably laughed. But now Hanna looked at the old texts with a fresh eye. A's note—saying one of Hanna's friends was hiding something—scared her. Could *Spencer* be hiding something?

All of a sudden, Hanna recalled a memory she hadn't thought of in a long time: A few days before Ali went missing, the five of them had gone on a field trip to the People's Light Playhouse to see *Romeo and Juliet*. There weren't many seventh-graders who'd opted to go—the rest of the field-trippers had been high-schoolers. Practically all of the Rosewood Day senior class had been there— Ali's older brother, Jason, Spencer's sister, Melissa, Ian Thomas, Katy Houghton, Ali's field hockey friend, and Preston Kahn, one of the Kahn brothers. After the play was over, Aria and Emily disappeared to the bathroom, Hanna and Ali sat on the stone wall and started eating their lunches, and Spencer sprinted over to talk to Mrs. Delancey, the English teacher, who was sitting near her students.

"She's only over there because she wants to be near the older boys," Ali muttered, glaring at Spencer.

"We could go over too, if you want," Hanna suggested.

Ali said no. "I'm mad at Spencer," she declared.

"Why?" Hanna asked.

Ali sighed. "Long, boring story."

Hanna let it drop—Ali and Spencer often got mad at each other for no reason. She started daydreaming about how the hot actor who played Tybalt had stared right at her all through his death scene. Did Tybalt think Hanna was cute . . . or fat? Or perhaps he wasn't staring at her at all—maybe he was just acting dead with his eyes open. When she looked up again, Ali was crying.

"Ali," Hanna had whispered. She'd never seen Ali cry before. "What's wrong?"

Tears ran silently down Ali's cheeks. She didn't even bother wiping them away. She stared off in the direction of Spencer and Mrs. Delancey. "Forget it."

"Shit! Look at that!" Mason Byers cried out, breaking Hanna out of her old seventh-grade thoughts. Up in the sky, a biplane cut a line through the clouds. It passed over Rosewood Day, swooped around, and then zoomed by again. Hanna jiggled up and down in her seat and swiveled around. Where the hell was Mona?

"Is that an old Curtiss?" James Freed asked.

"I don't think so," Ridley Mayfield answered. "I think it's a Travel Air D4D."

"Oh, right," James said, as if he'd known it all along.

Hanna's heart fluttered excitedly. The plane made a few long, sweeping strokes through the air, puffing out a trail of clouds that formed a perfect letter *G*. "It's writing something!" a girl near the door called out.

The plane moved on to the *E*, then the *T*, and then, after a space, the *R*. Hanna was practically bursting. This was the coolest party court gift *ever*.

Mason squinted at the plane, which was dipping and weaving in the sky. "Get . . . ready . . . to . . ." he read.

Just then, Mona slid into the seat next to her, throwing her charcoal gray quilted Louis Vuitton bag over her chair. "Hey, Han," she said, opening her Fresh Fields bento box and sliding the paper off her wooden chopsticks. "So you'll never believe who Naomi and Riley got to play at my birthday party. It's the best gift ever."

"Forget that," Hanna squealed. "I got you something cooler."

Hanna tried to point out the plane in the sky, but Mona was riled up. "They got Lexi," she rushed on. "*Lexi!* For me! At my party! Can you believe it?"

Hanna let her spoon drop back in the yogurt container. Lexi was a female hip-hop artist from Philadelphia. A major label had signed her and she was going to be a megastar. How had Naomi and Riley managed that? "Whatever," she said quickly, and steered Mona's chin toward the clouds. "Look what *I* did for you."

Mona squinted into the sky. The plane had finished writing the message and was now doing loops over the letters. When Hanna took in the whole message, her eyes widened.

"Get ready to . . ." Mona's mouth fell open. ". . . *fart* with Mona?"

"Get ready to fart with Mona!" Mason cried. Others who saw it were repeating it, too. A freshman boy by the abstract wall mural blew into his hands to make a farting sound.

Mona stared at Hanna. She looked a little green. "What the hell, Hanna?"

"No, that's wrong!" Hanna squeaked. "It was supposed to say, 'Get ready to *party* with Mona!' P-A-R-T-Y! They messed up the letters!"

More people made fart noises. "Gross!" a girl near them screamed. "Why would she *write* that?"

"This is horrible!" Mona cried. She pulled her blazer over her head, just like celebrities did when they were avoiding the paparazzi.

"I'm calling them right now to complain," Hanna exclaimed, whipping out her BlackBerry and shakily scrolling for the skywriting company's number. This wasn't fair. She'd used the clearest, neatest handwriting possible when she faxed Mona's party message to the skywriter. "I'm so sorry, Mon. I don't know how this happened."

Mona's face was shadowed under her blazer. "You're sorry, huh?" she said in a low voice. "I bet you are." She slid her blazer back around her shoulders, lurched up, and strode away as fast as her raffia Celine wedges would carry her.

"Mona!" Hanna jumped up after her. She touched Mona's arm and Mona spun around. "It was a mistake! I'd never do that to you!"

Mona took a step closer. Hanna could smell her French lavender laundry soap. "Ditching the Frenniversary is one thing, but I never thought you'd try to ruin my party," she growled, loud enough for everyone to hear. "But you want to play that way? Fine. Don't come. You're officially uninvited."

Mona stomped through the cafeteria doors, practically pushing two nerdy-looking freshmen aside into the large stone planters. "Mona, wait!" Hanna cried weakly.

"Go to hell," Mona yelled over her shoulder.

Hanna took a few steps backwards, her whole body trembling. When she looked around the courtyard, everyone was staring at her. "Oh, *snap*," Hanna heard Desdemona Lee whisper to her softball-playing friends. *"Mrow,"* a group of younger boys hissed from the moss-covered birdbaths. "Loser," an anonymous voice muttered.

The wafting smell of the cafeteria's overly sauced, mushy-crusted pizza was beginning to give Hanna that old, familiar feeling of being both hideously nauseated and crazily ravenous at the same time. She returned to her purse and rifled absentmindedly through the side pouch to find her emergency package of white cheddar Cheez-Its. She pushed one into her mouth after another, not even tasting them. When she looked up into the sky, the puffy, letter-shaped clouds announcing Mona's party had drifted.

The only letter that remained intact was the last one the plane had written: a crisp, angular letter *A*.

16

SOMEONE'S BEEN KISSING IN THE KILN. . . .

That same Wednesday lunch period, Emily strode quickly through the art studio hallway. "Heeeyyy, Emily," crooned Cody Wallis, Rosewood Day's star tennis player.

"Hi?" Emily looked over her shoulder. She was the only person around—could Cody really be saying hi to *her*?

"Looking good, Emily Fields," murmured John Dexter, the unbelievably hot captain of Rosewood Day's crew team. Emily couldn't even muster a hello—the last time John had spoken to her was in fifth-grade gym class. They'd been playing dodgeball, and John had beaned Emily's chest to tag her out. Later, he'd come up to her and said, snickering, "Sorry I hit your boobie."

She'd never had so many people—especially guys—smile, wave, and say hi to her. This morning, Jared Coffey, a brooding senior who rode a vintage Indian motorcycle to school and was usually too cool to speak to anyone, had insisted on buying her a blueberry muffin out of the vending machine. And as Emily had walked from second to third period this morning, a small convoy of freshman boys followed. One filmed her on his Nokia—it was probably already up on YouTube. She had come to school prepared to be taunted about the photo A had passed around at the meet yesterday, so this was sort of . . . unexpected.

When a hand shot out of the pottery studio, Emily flinched and let out a small shriek. Maya's face materialized at the door. "*Psst*. Em!"

Emily stepped out of the stream of traffic. "Maya. Hey."

Maya batted her eyelashes. "Come with me."

"I can't right now." Emily checked her chunky Nike watch. She was late for her lunch with Becka—Little Miss Tree Tops. "How about after school?"

"Nah, this'll just take a second!" Maya darted inside the empty studio and around a maze of desks toward the walk-in kiln. To Emily's surprise, she pushed the kiln's heavy door open and slid inside. Maya poked her head back out and grinned. "Coming?"

Emily shrugged. Inside the kiln, everything was dark, wooden, and warm—like a sauna. Dozens of students' pots sat on the shelves. The ceramics teacher hadn't fired them yet, so they were still brick red and gooey.

"It's neat in here," Emily mused softly. She'd always liked the earthy, wet smell of raw clay. On one of the shelves was a coil pot she'd made two periods ago. She'd thought she'd done a good job, but seeing it again, she noticed that one side caved in.

Suddenly, Emily felt Maya's hands sliding up her back to her shoulders. Maya spun Emily around, and their noses touched. Maya's breath, as usual, smelled like banana gum. "I think this is the sexiest room in the school, don't you?"

"Maya," Emily warned. They had to stop . . . only, Maya's hands felt so good.

"No one will see," Maya protested. She raked her hands through Emily's dry, chlorine-damaged hair. "And besides, everyone knows about us anyway."

"Aren't you bothered by what happened yesterday?" Emily asked, pulling away. "Don't you feel . . . violated?"

Maya thought for a moment. "Not particularly. And no one really seems to care."

"That's the weird thing," Emily agreed. "I thought everyone was going to be mean today—like, teasing me or whatever. But instead . . . I'm suddenly crazily popular. People didn't even pay this much attention to me after Ali disappeared."

Maya grinned and touched Emily's chin. "See? I told you it wouldn't be so bad. Wasn't it a good idea?"

Emily stepped back. In the kiln's pale light, Maya's face shone a ghoulish green. Yesterday, she'd noticed Maya in the natatorium stands . . . but when she'd looked after discovering the photo, she couldn't find Maya anywhere. Maya had wanted their relationship to be more open. A sick feeling washed over her. "What do you mean, *good idea*?"

Maya shrugged. "I just mean, whoever did this made things much easier for us."

"B-but it's *not* easier," Emily stammered, remembering where she was supposed to be right now. "My parents are livid about that photo. I have to go into a counseling program to prove to them I'm not gay. And if I don't, they're going to send me to Iowa to live with my aunt Helene and uncle Allen. For *good*."

Maya frowned. "Why didn't you tell your parents the truth? That this is who you are, and it's not something you can, like, change. Even in Iowa." She shrugged. "I told my family I was bi last year. They didn't take it *that* well at first, but they got better."

Emily moved her feet back and forth against the kiln's smooth cement floor. "Your parents are different."

"Maybe." Maya stood back. "But listen. Since last year, when I was finally honest with myself and with everybody else? Ever since then, I've felt so great."

Emily's eyes instinctively fell to the snakelike scar on the inside of Maya's forearm. Maya used to cut herself—she said it was the only thing that made her feel okay. Had being honest about who she was changed that?

Emily closed her eyes and thought of her mother's angry face. And getting on a plane to live in Iowa. Never sleeping in her own bed again. Her parents hating her forever. A lump formed in her throat.

"I have to do what they say." Emily focused on a petrified piece of gum someone had stuck on a kiln shelf. "I should go." She opened the kiln door and stepped back into the classroom.

Maya followed her. "Wait!" She caught Emily's arm, and as Emily spun around, Maya's eyes searched her face. "What are you saying? Are you breaking up with me?"

Emily stared across the room. There was a sticker above the pottery teacher's desk that said, I LOVE POTS! Only, someone had crossed out the *s* and drawn a marijuana leaf over the exclamation point. "Rosewood's my home, Maya. I want to stay here. I'm sorry."

She snaked around the vats of glaze and potter's wheels. "Em!" Maya called behind her. But Emily didn't turn around.

She took the exit door that led straight out of the pottery studio to the quad, feeling like she'd just made a huge mistake. The area was empty—everyone was at lunch—but for a second, Emily could have sworn she saw a figure standing on Rosewood Day's bell tower roof. The figure had long blond hair and held binoculars to her face. It almost looked like Ali.

After Emily blinked, all she saw was the tower's

weathered bronze bell. Her eyes must have been playing tricks on her. She'd probably just seen a gnarled, twisted tree.

Or . . . had she?

Emily shuffled down the little footpath that led to Lorence chapel, which looked less like a chapel and more like the gingerbread house Emily had made for the King James Mall Christmas competition in fourth grade. The building's scalloped siding was cinnamon brown, and the elaborate trim, balusters, and gables were a creamy white. Gumdrop-colored flowers lined the window boxes. Inside, a girl was sitting in one of the front pews, facing forward in the otherwise empty chapel.

"Sorry I'm late," Emily huffed, sliding onto the bench. There was a Nativity scene placed on the altar at the front of the room, waiting to be set up. Emily shook her head. It wasn't even November yet.

"It's cool." The girl put out her hand. "Rebecca Johnson. I go by Becka."

"Emily."

Becka wore a long lacy tunic, skinny jeans, and demure pink flats. Delicate, flower-shaped earrings dangled from her ears, and her hair was held back with a lace-trimmed headband. Emily wondered if she'd end up looking as girly as Becka if she completed the Tree Tops program.

A few seconds passed. Becka took out a tube of pink lip gloss and applied a fresh coat. "So, do you want to know anything about Tree Tops?"

Not really, Emily wanted to answer. Maya was probably right—Emily would never be truly happy until she stopped feeling ashamed and denying her feelings. Although . . . she eyed Becka. *She* seemed okay.

Emily opened her Coke. "So, *you* liked girls?" She didn't entirely believe it.

Becka looked surprised. "I–I did . . . but not anymore."

"Well, when you did . . . how did you know for sure?" Emily asked, realizing she was brimming with questions.

Becka took a minuscule bite out of her sandwich. Everything about her was small and doll-like, including her hands. "It felt different, I guess. Better."

"Same here!" Emily practically shouted. "I had boyfriends when I was younger . . . but I always felt *differently* about girls. I even thought my Barbies were cute."

Becka daintily wiped her mouth with a napkin. "Barbie was never my type."

Emily smiled, as another question came to her. "Why do you think we like girls? Because I was reading that it was genetic, but does that mean that if I had a daughter, she would think her Barbies were cute, too?" She thought for a moment, before rambling on. No one was around and it felt good to ask some of the things that had been circling around in her brain. That's what this meeting was supposed to be about, right? "Although . . . my mom seems like the straightest woman on earth," Emily continued, a little manically. "Maybe it skips a generation?"

Emily stopped, realizing that Becka was staring at her with a weirded-out expression on her face. "I don't think so," she said uneasily.

"I'm sorry," Emily admitted. "I'm kind of babbling. I'm just really . . . confused. And nervous." *And aching,* she wanted to add, dwelling for a second on how Maya's face had collapsed when Emily told her it was over.

"It's okay," Becka said quietly.

"Did you have a girlfriend before you went into Tree Tops?" Emily asked, more quietly this time.

Becka chewed on her thumbnail. "Wendy," she said almost inaudibly. "We worked together at the Body Shop at the King James Mall."

"Did you and Wendy . . . fool around?" Emily nibbled on a potato chip.

Becka glanced suspiciously at the manger figurines on the altar, like she thought that Joseph and Mary and the three wise men were listening in. "Maybe," she whispered.

"What did it feel like?"

A tiny vein near Becka's temple pulsed. "It felt *wrong.* Being . . . gay . . . it's not easy to change it, but I think you can. Tree Tops helped me figure out why I was with Wendy. I grew up with three brothers, and my counselor said I was raised in a very boy-centric world."

That was the stupidest thing Emily had ever heard. "I have a brother, but I have two sisters too. I wasn't raised in a boy-centric world. So what's wrong with me?"

"Well, maybe the root of your problem is different." Becka shrugged. "The counselors will help you figure that out. They get you to let go of a lot of feelings and memories. The idea is to replace them with new feelings and memories."

Emily frowned. "They're making you *forget* stuff?"

"Not exactly. It's more like letting go."

As much as Becka tried to sugarcoat it, Tree Tops sounded horrible. Emily didn't want to let go of Maya. Or Ali, for that matter.

Suddenly, Becka reached out and put her hand over Emily's. It was surprising. "I know this doesn't make much sense to you now, but I learned something huge in Tree Tops," Becka said. "Life is hard. If we go with these feelings that are . . . that are *wrong*, our lives are going to be even more of an uphill battle. Things are hard enough, you know? Why make it worse?"

Emily felt her lip quiver. Were all lesbians' lives an uphill battle? What about those two gay women who ran the triathlon shop two towns over? Emily had bought her New Balances from them, and they seemed so happy. And what about Maya? She used to cut herself, but now she was better.

"So is Wendy okay that you're in Tree Tops now?" Emily asked.

Becka stared at the stained-glass window behind the altar. "I think she gets it."

"Do you guys still hang out?"

Becka shrugged. "Not really. But we're still friends, I guess."

Emily ran her tongue over her teeth. "Maybe we could all hang out some time?" It might be good to see two *ex-gays* who were actually friends. Maybe she and Maya could be friends, too.

Becka cocked her head, seeming surprised. "Okay. How about Saturday night?"

"Sounds good to me," Emily answered.

They finished their lunch and Becka said good-bye. Emily started down the sloped green, falling in line with the other Rosewood Day kids heading back to class. Her brain was overloaded with information and emotions. The lesbian triathletes might be happy and Maya might be better, but maybe Becka had a point, too. What would it be like at college, then after college, then getting a job? She would have to explain her sexuality to people over and over again. Some people wouldn't accept her.

Before yesterday, the only people who knew how Emily truly felt were Maya, her ex, Ben, and Alison. Two out of the three hadn't taken it very well.

Maybe they were right.

17

BECAUSE ALL CHEESY RELATIONSHIP MOMENTS HAPPEN IN CEMETERIES

Wednesday after school, Aria watched Sean pedal his Gary Fisher mountain bike farther in front of her, easily climbing West Rosewood's hilly country roads. "Keep up!" he teased.

"Easy for you to say!" Aria answered, pedaling furiously on Ella's old beat-up Peugeot ten-speed from college—she'd brought it with her when she moved into Sean's. "I don't run six miles every morning!"

Sean had surprised Aria after school by announcing he was ditching soccer so they could hang out. Which was a huge deal—in the 24 hours she had lived with him, Aria had learned that Sean was über-soccer boy, the same way her brother was manic about lacrosse. Every morning, Sean ran six miles, did drills, and kicked practice goals into a net set up on the Ackards' lawn until it was time to leave for school.

Aria struggled up the hill and was happy to see that there was a long descent in front of them. It was a gorgeous day, so they'd decided to take a bike ride around West Rosewood. They rode past rambling farmhouses and miles of untouched woods.

At the bottom of the hill, they passed a wrought-iron fence with an ornate entrance gate. Aria hit her brakes. "Hold on. I completely forgot about this place."

She had stopped in front of St. Basil's cemetery, Rosewood's oldest and spookiest, where she used to do gravestone rubbings. It was set on acres and acres of rolling hills and beautifully tended lawns, and some of the headstones dated back to the 1700s. Before Aria found her niche with Ali, she'd gone through a goth phase, embracing everything having to do with death, Tim Burton, Halloween, and Nine Inch Nails. The cemetery's leafy oaks had provided the perfect shade for lounging and acting morose.

Sean stopped beside her. Aria turned to him. "Can we go in for a sec?"

He looked alarmed. "Are you *sure*?"

"I used to love coming here."

"Okay." Sean reluctantly chained his bike to a wrought-iron trash can along with Aria's and started behind her past the first line of headstones. Aria read the names and the dates that she had practically memorized a few years back. EDITH JOHNSTON, 1807–1856. BABY AGNES, 1820–1821. SARAH WHITTIER, with that Milton quote, DEATH IS THE GOLDEN KEY THAT OPENS THE PALACE OF ETERNITY. Over the hill, Aria knew, were the graves of a dog named Puff, a cat named Rover, and a parakeet named Lily.

"I love graves," Aria said as they passed a big one with an angel statue on the top. "They remind me of 'The Tell-Tale Heart.'"

"The *what*?"

Aria raised an eyebrow. "Oh, come on. You've read that short story. Edgar Allan Poe? The dead guy's buried in the floor? The narrator can still hear his heart beating?"

"Nope."

Aria put her hands on her hips, dumbstruck. How could Sean not have read that? "When we get back, I'll find my Poe book so you can."

"Okay," Sean agreed, then changed the subject. "You sleep okay last night?"

"Great." A white lie. Her Paris-hotel-like room was beautiful, but Aria had actually found it difficult to sleep. Sean's house was . . . *too* perfect. The duvet seemed *too* fluffy, the mattress *too* quilted, the room *too* quiet. It smelled too nice and clean as well.

But more than that, she'd been too worried about the movement outside her guest bedroom window, about the possible stalker sighting, *and* about A's note—saying that Ali's killer was closer than she thought. Aria had thrashed around for hours, alone, certain she'd look over and see the stalker—or Ali's killer—at the foot of her bed.

"Your stepmom got all anal on me this morning, though," Aria said, skirting around a Japanese cherry blossom tree. "I forgot to make my bed. She made me go back upstairs and do it." She snorted. "My mom hasn't done that in about a billion years."

When she looked over, Sean wasn't laughing along. "My stepmom works hard to keep the house clean. Rosewood Historic House tours come through it almost every day."

Aria bristled. She wanted to tell him that the Rosewood Historic Society had considered her house for the tour, too—some Frank Lloyd Wright protégé had designed it. Instead, she sighed. "I'm sorry. It's just . . . my mom hasn't even called me since I left a message telling her I was staying with you. I feel so . . . abandoned."

Sean stroked her arm. "I know, I know."

Aria poked her tongue into the spot at the back of her mouth where her lone wisdom tooth had been. "That's the thing," she said softly. "You don't know." Sean's family was perfect. Mr. Ackard had made them Belgian waffles this morning, and Mrs. Ackard had packed everyone's lunches—including Aria's. Even their dog, an Airedale, was well mannered.

"So explain it to me," Sean said.

Aria sighed. "It's not as easy as that."

They passed a gnarled, knotty tree. Suddenly, Aria looked down . . . and stopped short. Right in front of her was a new gravesite. The groundskeeper hadn't dug the hole for the coffin yet, but there was a taped-off, coffin-size space. The marble headstone was up, though. It read, plainly, ALISON LAUREN DILAURENTIS.

A small, gurgling noise escaped from the back of Aria's throat. The authorities were still examining Ali's remains for signs of poison and trauma, so her parents hadn't buried her yet. Aria hadn't known they were planning to bury her *here*.

She looked helplessly at Sean. He went pale. "I thought you knew."

"I had no idea," she whispered back.

The headstone said nothing but Ali's name. No *devoted daughter,* or *wonderful field hockey playe*r, or *most beautiful girl in Rosewood*. There wasn't even the day, month, or year she'd died. That was probably because no one *knew* the exact date.

She shivered. "Do you think I should say something?"

Sean pursed his pink lips. "When I visit my mom's grave, sometimes I do."

"Like what?"

"I fill her in on what's going on." He looked at her sideways and blushed. "I went after Foxy. I told her about you."

Aria blushed too. She stared at the headstone but felt self-conscious. Talking to dead people wasn't her thing. *I can't believe you're dead,* Aria thought, not able to say the words out loud. *I'm standing here, looking at your grave, and it still isn't real. I hate that we don't know what happened. Is the killer still here? Is A telling the truth?*

Yesssss, Aria swore she heard a far-off voice call. It sounded like Ali's voice.

She thought about A's note. Someone had wanted something of Ali's—and had killed her for it. What? Everyone had wanted *something* of Ali's—even her best friends. Hanna had wanted Ali's personality, and seemed to have appropriated it after Ali vanished. Emily had loved Ali more than anyone—they used to call Emily "Killer," as in Ali's personal pit bull. Aria had wanted Ali's ability to flirt, her beauty, her charisma. And Spencer had always been so jealous of her.

Aria stared into the taped-off area that would be Ali's grave and asked the question that had been slowly forming in her mind: *What were you guys really fighting about?*

"This isn't working for me," Aria whispered after a moment. "Let's go."

She gave Ali's future grave a parting glance. As she turned away, Sean's fingers entwined with hers. They walked quietly for a while, but halfway to the gate, Sean stopped. "Bunny rabbit," he said, pointing at a rabbit across the clearing. He kissed Aria's lips.

Aria's mouth curled up into a smile. "I get a kiss just because you saw a rabbit?"

"Yep." Sean nudged her playfully. "It's like the game

where you punch someone when you see a VW Bug. With us, it can be kisses—and rabbits. It's our couple game."

"Couple game?" Aria snickered, thinking he was joking.

But Sean's face was serious. "You know, a game that's only for us. And it's a good thing it's rabbits, because there are *tons* of rabbits in Rosewood."

Aria was afraid to make fun of him, but really—a *couple* game? It reminded her of something Jennifer Thatcher and Jennings Silver might do. Jennifer and Jennings were a couple in her grade who had been going out since *before* Aria had left for Iceland at the end of seventh grade. They were known only as Double-J, or Dub-J, and were called that even individually. Aria could *not* be a Dub-J.

As she watched Sean walk in front of her, heading toward their bikes, the delicate hairs on the back of her neck stood up. It felt like someone was looking at her. But when she turned around, all she saw was a giant black crow standing on top of Ali's headstone.

The crow glared at her, unblinking, and then spread its massive wings and took off toward the trees.

18

A GOOD SMACK UPSIDE THE HEAD
NEVER HURT ANYONE

On Thursday morning, Dr. Evans shut her office door, settled into her leather chair, folded her hands placidly, and smiled at Spencer, who was sitting opposite her. "So. I hear you had a photo shoot and interview yesterday with the *Sentinel*."

"That's right," Spencer answered.

"And how did that go?"

"Fine." Spencer took a sip of her extra-large Starbucks vanilla latte. The interview actually *had* gone fine, even after all of Spencer's worrying—and A's threats. Jordana had barely asked her about the essay, and Matthew had told her the pictures looked exquisite.

"And how did your sister deal with you being in the spotlight?" Dr. Evans asked. When Spencer raised an eyebrow, Dr. Evans shrugged and leaned forward. "Have you ever thought she might be jealous of you?"

Spencer glanced anxiously at Dr. Evans's closed door. Melissa was sitting outside on the waiting room couch, reading *Travel + Leisure*. Yet again, she'd scheduled her session for right after Spencer's.

"Don't worry, she can't hear you," Dr. Evans assured her.

Spencer sighed. "She seemed sort of . . . pissed," she said in a low voice. "Usually, it's all about Melissa. Even when my parents just ask me a question, Melissa immediately tries to steer the conversation back to her." She stared at the undulating silver Tiffany ring on her pointer finger. "I think she hates me."

Dr. Evans tapped her notebook. "You've felt like she hates you for a long time, right? How does that make you feel?"

Spencer shrugged, hugging one of Dr. Evans's forest green chenille pillows to her chest. "Angry, I guess. Sometimes I get so frustrated about the way things are, I just want to . . . hit her. I don't, obviously, but—"

"But it would feel good though, wouldn't it?"

Spencer nodded, staring at Dr. Evans's chrome gooseneck lamp. Once, after Melissa told Spencer she wasn't a very good actress, Spencer had come really close to punching Melissa in the face. Instead, she'd flung one of her mother's Spode Christmas plates across the dining room. It had shattered, leaving a butterfly-shaped crack in the wall.

Dr. Evans flipped a page in her notebook. "How do your

parents deal with your and your sister's . . . animosity?"

Spencer raised one shoulder. "Mostly, they don't. If you asked my mom, she'd probably say that we get along perfectly."

Dr. Evans sat back and thought for a long time. She tapped the drinking-bird toy on her desk, and the plastic bird started taking measured sips of water out of an I HEART ROSEWOOD, PA, coffee mug. "This is just an early theory, but perhaps Melissa is afraid that if your parents recognize something you've done well, they'll love you instead of her."

Spencer cocked her head. "Really?"

"Maybe. You, on the other hand, think your parents don't love you at all. It's all about Melissa. You don't know how to compete with her, so that's where her boyfriends come in. But maybe it's not that you want Melissa's boyfriends exactly, but more that you want to hurt Melissa herself. Sound right?"

Spencer nodded thoughtfully. "Maybe . . ."

"You girls are both in a lot of pain," Dr. Evans said quietly, her face softening. "I don't know what started this behavior—it could have been something long ago, something you might not even remember—but you've fallen into a pattern of dealing with each other this way, and you'll continue the pattern unless you recognize what it's based on and learn how to respect each other's feelings and change. The pattern might be repeating in your other relationships, too—you might choose friends and boyfriends who treat you like Melissa does, because you're comfortable with the dynamic, and you know your role."

"What do you mean?" Spencer asked, hugging her knees. This sounded awfully psychobabblish to her.

"Are your friends sort of . . . the center of everything? They have everything you want, they push you around, you never feel good enough?"

Spencer's mouth went dry. She certainly used to have a friend like that: Ali.

She closed her eyes and saw the strange Ali memory that had been plaguing her all week. The memory was of a fight, Spencer was sure of it. Only, Spencer usually remembered all of her fights with Ali, better than she remembered the good moments of their friendship. Was it a dream?

"What are you thinking?" Dr. Evans asked.

Spencer took a breath. "About Alison."

"Ah." Dr. Evans nodded. "Do you think Alison was like Melissa?"

"I don't know. Maybe."

Dr. Evans plucked a Kleenex out of the box on her desk and blew her nose. "I saw that video of you girls on TV. You and Alison seemed angry at each other. Were you?"

Spencer took a deep breath. "Sort of."

"Can you remember why?"

She thought for a moment and gazed around the

room. There was a plaque on Dr. Evans's desk that she hadn't noticed the last time she'd been here. It said THE ONLY TRUE KNOWLEDGE IN LIFE IS KNOWING YOU KNOW NOTH-ING. —SOCRATES. "Those weeks before Alison went missing, she started acting . . . different. Like she hated us. None of us wanted to admit it, but I think she was planning on dropping us that summer."

"How did that make you feel? Angry?"

"Yeah. Sure." Spencer paused. "Being Ali's friend was great, but we had to make a lot of sacrifices. We went through a lot together, and some of it wasn't good. It was like, 'We go through all this for you, and you repay us by ditching us?'"

"So you felt owed something."

"Maybe," Spencer answered.

"But you feel guilty too, right?" Dr. Evans suggested.

Spencer lowered her shoulders. "Guilty? Why?"

"Because Alison's dead. Because, in some ways, you resented her. Maybe you wanted something bad to happen to her because she was hurting you."

"I don't know," Spencer whispered.

"And then your wish came true. Now you feel like Alison's disappearance is your fault—that if you hadn't felt this way about her, she wouldn't have been murdered."

Spencer's eyes clouded with tears. She couldn't respond.

"It's not your fault," Dr. Evans said forcefully, leaning

forward in the chair. "We don't always love our friends every minute. Alison hurt you. Just because you had a mean thought about her doesn't mean you caused her death."

Spencer sniffed. She stared at the Socrates quote again. *The only true knowledge in life is knowing you know nothing.* "There's a memory that keeps popping into my head," she blurted out. "About Ali. We're fighting. She talks about something I read in her diary—she always thought I was reading her diary, but I never did. But I'm . . . I'm not even sure the memory is real."

Dr. Evans put her pen to her mouth. "People cope with things in different ways. For some people, if they witness or do something disturbing, their brain some-how . . . edits it out. But often the memory starts pushing its way back in."

Spencer's mouth felt scratchy, like steel wool. "Nothing disturbing happened."

"I could try to hypnotize you to draw out the memory."

Spencer's mouth went dry. *"Hypnotize?"*

Dr. Evans was staring at her. "It might help."

Spencer chewed on a piece of hair. She pointed at the Socrates quote. "What does that mean?"

"That?" Dr. Evans's shrugged. "Think about it yourself. Draw your own conclusion." She smiled. "Now, are you ready? Lie down and get comfy."

Spencer slumped on the couch. As Dr. Evans pulled down the bamboo blinds, Spencer cringed. *This was just like what Ali did that night in the barn before she died.*

"Just relax." Dr. Evans turned off her desk lamp. "Feel yourself calming down. Try to let go of everything we talked about today. Okay?"

Spencer wasn't relaxed at all. Her knees locked and her muscles shook. Even her teeth ground together. *Now she's going to walk around and count down from one hundred. She'll touch my forehead, and I'll be in her power.*

When Spencer opened her eyes, she wasn't in Dr. Evans's office anymore. She was outside her barn. It was night. Alison was staring at her, shaking her head just like she had in the other flashes of memory Spencer had recalled during the week. Spencer suddenly knew it was the night Ali went missing. She tried to claw her way out of the memory, but her limbs felt heavy and useless.

"You try to steal everything away from me," Ali was saying with a tone and inflection that were now eerily familiar. "But you can't have this."

"Can't have what?" The wind was cold. Spencer shivered.

"Come on," Ali taunted, putting her hands on her hips. "You read about it in my diary, didn't you?"

"I wouldn't read your diary," Spencer spat. "I don't care."

"You care way too much," Ali said. She leaned forward. Her breath was minty.

"You're delusional," Spencer sputtered.

"No, I'm not," Ali snarled. "*You* are."

Rage suddenly filled Spencer. She leaned forward and shoved Ali's shoulder.

Ali looked surprised. "Friends don't shove friends."

"Well, maybe we're not friends," Spencer answered.

"Guess not," Ali said. She took a few steps away but turned back. Then she said something else. Spencer saw Ali's mouth move, then felt her own mouth move, but she couldn't hear their words. All she knew was that whatever Ali said made her angry. From somewhere far away was a sharp, splintering *crack*. Spencer's eyes snapped open.

"Spencer," Dr. Evans's voice called. "Hey. Spencer."

The first thing she saw was Dr. Evans's plaque across the room. *The only true knowledge is knowing you know nothing.* Then, Dr. Evans's face swam into view. She had an uncertain, worried look on her face. "Are you okay?" Dr. Evans asked.

Spencer blinked a few times. "I don't know." She sat up and ran the palm of her hand over her sweaty forehead. This felt like waking up from the anesthesia the time she'd had her appendix out. Everything seemed blurry and edgeless.

"Tell me what you see in the room," Dr. Evans said. "Describe everything."

Spencer looked around. "The brown leather couch, the white fluffy rug, the . . ."

What had Ali said? Why couldn't Spencer hear her? Had that really happened?

"A wire mesh trash can," she stammered. "An

Anjou pear candle . . ."

"Okay." Dr. Evans put her hand on Spencer's shoulder. "Sit here. Breathe."

Dr. Evans's window was now open, and Spencer could smell the freshly tarred asphalt on the parking lot. Two morning doves cooed to each other. When she finally got up and told Dr. Evans she'd see her next week, she was feeling clearer. She skidded across the waiting room without acknowledging Melissa. She wanted out of here.

In the parking lot, Spencer slid into her car and sat in silence. She listed all the things she saw here, too. Her tweed bag. The farmer's market placard across the street that read, FRESH OMATOES. The T had fallen to the ground. The blue Chevy truck parked crookedly in the farmer's market lot. The cheerful red birdhouse hanging from a nearby oak. The sign on the office building door that said only service animals were permitted inside. Melissa's profile in Dr. Evans's office window.

The corners of her sister's mouth were spread into a jagged smile, and she was talking animatedly with her hands. When Spencer looked back at the farmer's market, she noticed the Chevy's front tire was flat. There was something slinking behind the truck. A cat, maybe.

Spencer sat up straighter. It wasn't a cat—it was a *person*. Staring at her.

The person's eyes didn't blink. And then, suddenly, whoever it was turned his or her head, crouched into the shadows, and disappeared.

19

IT'S BETTER THAN A
SIGN SAYING, "KICK ME"

Thursday afternoon, Hanna followed her chemistry class across the commons to the flagpole. There had been a fire drill, and now her chem teacher, Mr. Percival, was counting to make sure none of the students had run off. It was another freakishly hot October day, and as the sun beat down on the top of Hanna's head, she heard two sophomore girls whispering.

"Did you *hear* that she's a klepto?" hissed Noelle Frazier, a tall girl with cascading blond ringlets.

"I know," replied Anna Walton, a tiny brunette with enormous boobs. "She, like, organized this huge Tiffany heist. And then she went and wrecked Mr. Ackard's car."

Hanna stiffened. Normally, she wouldn't have been bothered by a couple of lame sophomore girls, but she was feeling sort of vulnerable. She pretended to be really interested in a bunch of tiny pine trees the gardeners had just planted.

"I heard she's at the police station like every day," Noelle said.

"And you know she's not invited to Mona's anymore, right?" Anna whispered. "They had this huge fight because Hanna humiliated her with that skywriting thing."

"Mona's wanted to drop her for a couple months now," Noelle said knowingly. "Hanna's become this huge loser."

That was too much. Hanna whirled around. "Where did you hear that?"

Anna and Noelle exchanged a smirk. Then they sauntered down the hill without answering.

Hanna shut her eyes and leaned against the metal flagpole, trying to ignore the fact that everyone in her chem class was now staring at her. It had been twenty-four hours since the disastrous skywriting debacle, and things had gone from bad to worse. Hanna had left at least ten apologetic messages on Mona's cell last night . . . but Mona hadn't called back. And today, she'd been hearing strange, unsavory things about herself . . . from everyone.

She thought of A's note. *And Mona? She's not your friend, either. So watch your back.*

Hanna scanned the crowd of kids on the commons. Next to the doors, two girls in cheerleading uniforms were pantomiming a cheer. Near the gum tree, a couple of boys were "blazer fighting"—whapping each other with their Rosewood Day blazers. Aria's brother, Mike, walked by playing his PSP. Finally, she spied Mona's white-blond hair. She was heading back into the main building via one of the side doors with a bored, haughty look on her face. Hanna straightened her blazer, clenched and unclenched her fists, and made a beeline for her best friend.

When she reached Mona, she tapped her on her bony shoulder. Mona looked over. "Oh. It's you," she said in a monotone, the way she normally greeted losers not cool enough to be in her presence.

"Are you saying stuff about me?" Hanna demanded, putting her hands on her hips and keeping pace with Mona, who was striding quickly through the side door and down the art studio hallway.

Mona hitched her tangerine Dooney & Bourke tote higher on her shoulder. "Nothing that's not true."

Hanna's mouth fell open. She felt like Wile E. Coyote in one of those old Looney Toons cartoons she used to watch—he would be running and running and running and suddenly run off a cliff. Wile E. would pause, not realizing it for a second, and then rapidly plummet. "So you think I'm a loser?" she squeaked.

Mona raised one eyebrow. "Like I said, nothing that's not true."

She left Hanna standing in the middle of the hall,

students swarming around her. Mona walked to the end
of the corridor and stopped at a clump of girls. At first
they all looked the same—expensive handbags, shiny hair,
skinny fake-tanned legs—but then Hanna's eyes unblurred.
Mona was standing with Naomi and Riley, and they were
all whispering.

Hanna was certain she was going to cry. She fumbled
through the bathroom door and closed herself into a stall
next to Old Faithful, an infamous toilet that randomly
spurted out plumes of water, drenching you if you were
stupid enough to use it. The boys' room had a spewing toilet, too. Through the years, plumbers had tried to fix them
both, but since they couldn't figure out the cause, the Old
Faithfuls had become a legendary part of Rosewood Day
lore. Everyone knew better than to use them.

Except . . . Mona had used Old Faithful just a few
weeks after she and Hanna became friends, back when
Mona was still clueless. She'd frantically texted Hanna
in health class, and Hanna had rushed to the bathroom
to slip Mona the extra uniform skirt and blouse she'd
had in her locker. Hanna remembered balling up Mona's
soaked skirt in a Fresh Fields plastic bag and sliding out
of the stall so Mona could furtively change—Mona had
always been funny about changing in front of other
people.

How could Mona not *remember* that?

As if on cue, Old Faithful erupted. Hanna shrieked
and pressed herself against the opposite stall wall as a

column of blue toilet water shot into the air. A few heavy droplets hit the back of Hanna's blazer, and she curled up against the stall wall and finally started to sob. She hated that Mona no longer needed her. And that Ali had been murdered. And that her dad still hadn't called. Why was this *happening*? What had she done to deserve this?

As Old Faithful quieted down to a gurgle, the main door swung open. Hanna made tiny gasping noises, trying to keep quiet. Whoever it was walked to the sink, and Hanna peered under the door. She saw a pair of clunky, black, boyish loafers.

"Hello?" a boy's voice said. "Is . . . is someone in there?"

Hanna put her hand to her mouth. What was a *guy* doing in this bathroom?

Unless . . . *No*. She hadn't.

"Hanna?" The shoes stood in front of her stall. Hanna recognized the voice, too.

She peeked out the crack in the door. It was Lucas, the boy from Rive Gauche. She could see the edge of his nose, a long piece of white blond hair. There was a big GO ROSEWOOD SOCCER! pin on his lapel. "How did you know it was me?"

"I saw you come in here," he answered. "You know this is the boys' room, right?"

Hanna answered with an embarrassed sniff. She took off her wet blazer, shuffled out of the stall, walked to the sink, and forcefully pumped the soap dispenser. The soap had that fake almond smell Hanna hated.

Lucas's eyes cut to the Old Faithful stall. "Did that thing erupt?"

"Yes." And then Hanna couldn't control her emotions anymore. She hunched over the sink, her tears dripping into the basin.

Lucas stood there a moment, then put his hand on the middle of her back. Hanna felt it shake a little. "It's only Old Faithful. It erupts, like, every hour. You know that."

"That's not it." Hanna grabbed a scratchy paper towel and blew her nose. "My best friend hates me. And she's making everyone else hate me, too."

"What? Of course she doesn't. Don't be crazy."

"Yes, she does!" Hanna's high-pitched voice bounced off the bathroom's tiled walls. "Mona's hanging out with these girls now who we used to hate, and she's gossiping about me, all because I missed the Frenniversary and the skywriter wrote, 'Fart with Mona,' instead of, 'Party with Mona,' and she disinvited me to her birthday party, and I'm supposed to be her best friend!"

She said it all in a long sentence without breathing, despite where she was and who she was talking to. When she finished, she stared at Lucas, suddenly irritated that he was there and had heard it all.

Lucas was so tall he practically had to stoop to not hit his head on the ceiling. "I could start spreading rumors about her. Like maybe she's got a disease where she can't help but secretly eat her snot when no one's looking?"

Hanna's heart thawed. That was gross . . . but also funny . . . and sweet. "That's okay."

"Well the offer stands." Lucas had an earnest look on his face. In the hideous green bathroom light, he was actually cute. "But hey! I know something we can do to cheer you up."

Hanna looked at him incredulously. What, did Lucas think they were friends now, because he'd seen her in the bathroom? Still, she was curious. "What?"

"Can't tell you. It's top secret. I'll come get you tomorrow morning."

Hanna shot him a warning look. "Like, *a date*?"

Lucas raised his hands in surrender. "Absolutely not. Just as . . . friends."

Hanna swallowed. She needed a friend right now. *Bad.* "All right," she said quietly, feeling too exhausted to argue. Then, with a sigh, she pushed out of the boys' Old Faithful bathroom and headed for her next class. Strangely, she felt a teensy bit better.

But as she turned the corner to the foreign languages wing, Hanna reached around to put her blazer back on and felt something sticking to the back. She pulled off a wrinkled piece of paper. *Feel sorry for me,* it said, in spiky pink handwriting.

Hanna looked around at the passing students, but no one was paying attention. How long had she been walking around with the note on her? Who could have done this? It could have been anyone. She'd been in that crowd during the fire drill. Everyone had been there.

Hanna looked down at the paper again and turned it over in her hands. On the other side was a typewritten note. Hanna got that familiar sinking feeling in her stomach.

Hanna: Remember when you saw Mona leaving the Bill Beach plastic surgery clinic? Hello, lipo!! But shh! You didn't hear it from me. —A

20

LIFE IMITATES ART

Thursday afternoon at lunch, Aria turned the corner to Rosewood Day's administrative wing. All the teachers had offices here and often tutored or advised students during their lunch periods.

Aria stopped at Ezra's closed office door. It had changed a lot since the beginning of the year. He'd installed a white board, and it was chock-full of blue-inked notes from students. *Mr. Fitz—Want to talk about my Fitzgerald report. I'll stop by after school. —Kelly.* There was a *Hamlet* quote at the bottom: *O villain, villain, smiling, damned villain!* Below the marker board was a cutout of a *New Yorker* cartoon of a dog on a therapist's couch. And on the doorknob was a DO NOT DISTURB sign from a Day's Inn; Ezra had turned it to the DISTURB side: MAID, PLEASE CLEAN UP THIS ROOM.

Aria tentatively knocked. "Come in," she heard him say from the other side. She'd expected Ezra to be with another student—from snippets she heard in class, she'd thought his lunchtime office hours were always busy—but here he was alone, with a Happy Meal box on his desk. The room smelled like McNuggets.

"Aria!" Ezra exclaimed, raising an eyebrow. "This is a surprise. Sit down."

She plopped down on Ezra's scratchy tweed couch—the same kind that was in the Rosewood Day headmaster's office. She pointed at his desk. "Happy Meal?"

He smiled sheepishly. "I like the toys." He held up a car from some kids' movie. "McNugget?" He proffered the box. "I got barbecue."

She waved him away. "I don't eat meat."

"That's right." He ate a fry, his eyes locked with hers. "I forgot."

Aria felt a swoosh of something—a mix of intimacy and discomfort. Ezra looked away, probably feeling it too. She looked around on his desk. It was littered with stacks of paper, a mini zen rock garden, and about a thousand books.

"So . . ." Ezra wiped his mouth with a napkin, not noticing Aria's expression. "What can I do for you?"

Aria leaned her elbow on the couch's arm. "Well, I'm wondering if I can have an extension on the *Scarlet Letter* essay that's due tomorrow."

He set down his soda. "Really? I'm surprised. You're never late with anything."

"I know," she mumbled sheepishly. But the Ackards'

house was not conducive to studying. One, it was too quiet—Aria was used to studying while simultaneously listening to music, the TV, and Mike yammering on the phone in the next room. Two, it was hard to concentrate when she felt like someone was . . . watching her. "But it's not a big deal," she went on. "All I need is this weekend."

Ezra scratched his head. "Well . . . I haven't set a policy on extensions yet. But all right. Just this once. Next time, I'm going to have to mark you down a grade."

She pushed her hair behind her ears. "I'm not going to make a habit of it."

"Good. So, what, are you not liking the book? Or haven't you started it?"

"I finished it today. But I hated it. I hated Hester Prynne."

"Why?"

Aria fiddled with the buckle on her Urban Outfitters ivory suede flats. "She assumes her husband's lost at sea, and so she goes and has an affair," she muttered.

Ezra leaned forward on his elbow, looking amused. "But her husband isn't a very good man, either. That's what makes it complicated."

Aria stared at the books that were crammed into Ezra's cramped, wooden bookshelves. *War and Peace. Gravity's Rainbow.* An extensive collection of e. e. cummings and Rilke poetry, and not one but *two* copies of *No Exit.* There was the Edgar Allan Poe collection Sean hadn't read. All of the books looked creased and worn from reading and rereading. "But I couldn't see past what Hester did," Aria said quietly. "She *cheated.*"

"But we're supposed to feel for her struggle, and how society has branded her, and how she strives to forge her own identity and not allow anyone to create one for her."

"I hated her, okay?" Aria exploded. "And I'll never forgive her!"

She covered her face with her hands. Tears spilled down her cheeks. When she shut her eyes, she pictured Byron and Meredith as the book's illicit lovers, Ella as Hester's vengeful, wronged husband. But if life really imitated art, Byron and Meredith should be suffering . . . *not* Aria. She'd tried to call her house last night, but as soon as Ella picked up and heard Aria's voice on the other end, she hung up. When Aria waved at Mike across the gym, Mike had quickly spun on his heel and marched back into the locker room. No one was on her side.

"Whoa," Ezra said quietly, after Aria let out a stifled sob. "It's okay. So you didn't like the book. It's fine."

"I'm sorry. I'm just . . ." She felt hot tears on her palms. Ezra's room had grown so quiet. There was only the whirring of the computer's hard drive. The buzz of the fluorescent lamp. The happy cries from the lower school playground—all the little kids were out for recess.

"Is there something you want to talk about?" Ezra asked.

Aria wiped her eyes with the back of her blazer sleeve. She picked at a loose button on one of the couch's seat cushions. "My father had an affair with his student three years ago," she blurted out. "He's a professor at Hollis. I knew about it the whole time, but he asked me not to tell my mom. Well, now he's back with the student . . . and my mom found out. She's furious I knew for so long . . . and now my dad's gone."

"Jesus," Ezra whispered. "This just happened?"

"A few weeks ago, yeah."

"God." Ezra stared up at the beamed ceiling for a while. "That doesn't sound very fair of your dad. *Or* your mom."

Aria shrugged. Her chin started to tremble again. "I shouldn't have kept it a secret from my mom. But what was I supposed to do?"

"It's not your fault," Ezra told her.

He got out of his chair, walked around to the front of the desk, pushed a few papers aside, and sat on the edge. "Okay. So, I've never told anyone this, but when I was in high school, I saw my mom kissing her doctor. She had cancer at the time, and since my dad was traveling, she asked me to take her to her chemotherapy treatments. Once, while I was waiting, I had to use the bathroom, and as I was walking back through the hall, I saw this exam room door open. I don't know why I looked in, but when I did . . . there they were. Kissing."

Aria gasped. "What did you do?"

"I pretended like I didn't see it. My mom had no idea that I had. She came out twenty minutes later, all straightened up and proper and in a hurry. I really wanted to bring it up, but at the same time, I couldn't." He shook his head. "Dr. Poole. I never looked at him in the same way again."

"Didn't you say your parents got divorced?" Aria asked, remembering a conversation they'd had at Ezra's house. "Did your mom go off with Dr. Poole?"

"Nah." Ezra reached over and grabbed a McNugget out of the box. "They got divorced a couple years later. Dr. Poole and the cancer were long gone."

"God," was all Aria could think to say.

"It sucks." Ezra fiddled with one of the rocks in the mini zen rock garden that sat at the edge of his desk. "I idolized my parents' marriage. It didn't seem to me like they were having problems. My whole relationship ideal was shattered."

"Mine too," Aria said glumly, running her foot against a stack of paperbacks on the floor. "My parents seemed really happy together."

"It has nothing to do with you," Ezra told her. "That's a big thing I learned. It's their thing. Unfortunately, you have to deal with it, and I think it makes you stronger."

Aria groaned and clunked her head against the couch's stiff back. "I hate when people say things like that to me. That things will make me a better person, even if the things themselves suck."

Ezra chuckled. "Actually, I do too."

Aria shut her eyes, finding this moment bittersweet.

She had been waiting for someone to talk to about all this—someone who really, truly understood. She wanted to kiss Ezra for having as messed-up a family as she did.

Or maybe, she wanted to kiss Ezra . . . because he was Ezra.

Ezra's eyes met hers. Aria could see her reflection in his inky pupils. With his hand, Ezra pushed the little Happy Meal car so that it rolled across his desk, over the edge, and onto her lap. A smile whispered across his face.

"Do you have a girlfriend in New York?" Aria blurted out.

Ezra's forehead furrowed. "A girlfriend . . ." He blinked a few times. "I *did*. But we broke up this summer."

"Oh."

"Where did *that* come from?" Ezra asked.

"Some kids were talking about it, I guess. And I . . . I wondered what she was like."

A devilish look danced in Ezra's eyes, then escaped. He opened his mouth to say something but changed his mind. "What?" Aria asked him.

"I shouldn't."

"What?"

"It's just . . ." He glanced at her askance. "She was nothing compared to you."

A hot feeling swished through Aria. Slowly, without taking his eyes off her, Ezra slid off the desk to stand. Aria inched toward the edge of the couch. The moment stretched on forever. And then, Ezra lunged forward, grabbed Aria at her shoulders, and pressed her to him. Her lips crashed onto his. She held the sides of his face, and he ran his hands up the length of her back. They broke away and stared at each other, then dove back in again. Ezra smelled delicious, like a mix of Pantene and mint and chai tea and something that was just . . . Ezra. Aria had never felt this way from kissing. Not with Sean, not with anyone.

Sean. His image swam into her head. Sean letting Aria lean into him while they watched the BBC version of *The Office* last night. Sean kissing her before bio class, comforting her because they were starting dissections today. Sean holding her hand at dinner with his family. Sean was her *boyfriend.*

Aria pushed Ezra away and jumped up. "I have to go." She felt sweaty, as if someone had jacked up the thermostat about fifty degrees. She quickly gathered up her things, heart thumping and cheeks blazing.

"Thanks for the extension," she blurted out, pushing clumsily through the door.

Out in the hall, she drew in a few deep breaths. Down the corridor, a figure slipped around the corner. Aria tensed. *Someone had seen.*

She noticed something on Ezra's door and widened her eyes. Someone had erased all the old white-board messages, replacing them with a new one in an unfamiliar hot pink marker.

Careful, careful! I'm always watching! —A

And then, in smaller letters, down at the bottom:

Here's a second hint: You all knew every inch of her back-yard. But for one of you, it was so, so easy.

Aria pulled her blazer sleeve down and quickly wiped the letters away. When she got to the signature, she wiped extra hard, scrubbing and scrubbing until there was no trace of *A* left.

21

WHAT DOES
H-O-L-Y C-R-A-P SPELL?

Thursday evening, Spencer settled into the red plushy seats at the Rosewood Country Club restaurant and looked out the bay window. On the golf course, a couple of older guys in V-neck sweaters and khakis were trying to get in a few more holes before the sun went down. Out on the deck, people were taking advantage of the last few warm days of the year, drinking gin and tonics and eating rock shrimp and bruschetta squares. Mr. and Mrs. Hastings stirred their Bombay Sapphire martinis, then looked at each other.

"I propose a toast." Mrs. Hastings pushed her blond bobbed hair behind her ears, her three-carat diamond ring glinting against the setting sun streaming through the window. Spencer's parents always toasted before they took a drink of anything—even water.

Mrs. Hastings raised her glass. "To Spencer making

the Golden Orchid finals."

Mr. Hastings clinked. "*And* to being on the front page of this Sunday's *Sentinel*."

Spencer raised her glass and clinked it with them, but the effort was halfhearted. She didn't want to be here. She wanted to be at home, protected and safe. She couldn't stop thinking about her strange session with Dr. Evans this morning. The vision she'd seen—the forgotten fight with Ali the night she disappeared—was haunting. Why hadn't she remembered it before? Was there more to it? What if she'd *seen* Ali's killer?

"Congrats, Spencer," her mother interrupted her thoughts. "I hope you win."

"Thanks," Spencer mumbled. She worked to fold her green napkin back into an accordion, then went around the table and folded all the others, too.

"Nervous about something?" Her mother nudged her chin at the napkins.

Spencer immediately stopped. "No," she said quickly. Whenever she shut her eyes, she was right back in the Ali memory again. It was so clear now. She could smell the honeysuckle that grew in the woods that paralleled the barn, feel the early summer breeze, see the lightning bugs spatter-painting the dark sky. But it couldn't be real.

When Spencer looked up, her parents were gazing at her peculiarly. They'd probably asked her a question she'd completely missed. For the first time ever, she wished Melissa were here monopolizing the conversation.

"Are you nervous because of the doctor?" her mother whispered.

Spencer couldn't hide her smirk—she loved that her mom called Dr. Evans "the doctor" instead of "the therapist." "No. I'm fine."

"Do you think you've gotten a lot . . ." Her father seemed to search for his words, fiddling with his tie pin. ". . . accomplished, with the doctor?"

Spencer rocked her fork back and forth. *Define accomplished,* she wanted to say.

Before she could answer, the waiter appeared. It was the same waiter they'd had for years, the short little baldish guy who had a Winnie-the-Pooh voice. "Hello, Mr. and Mrs. Hastings." Pooh shook her father's hand. "And Spencer. You're looking lovely."

"Thanks," Spencer mumbled, although she was pretty sure she wasn't. She hadn't washed her hair after field hockey, and the last time she'd looked in the mirror, her eyes had a wild, scared look to them. She kept twitching, too, and looking around the restaurant to see if someone was watching her.

"How is everyone tonight?" Pooh asked. He fluffed up the napkins Spencer had just refolded and spread them on everyone's laps. "Here for a special occasion?"

"Actually, yes," Mrs. Hastings piped up. "Spencer's a finalist in the Golden Orchid competition. It's a major academic prize."

"*Mom,*" Spencer hissed. She hated how her mother

broadcast family accomplishments. Especially since Spencer had cheated.

"That's wonderful!" Pooh bellowed. "It's nice to have some *good* news, for once." He leaned in closer. "Quite a few of our guests think they've seen that stalker everyone's been talking about. Some even say they saw someone near the club last night."

"Hasn't this town been through enough?" Mr. Hastings mused.

Mrs. Hastings worriedly glanced at her husband. "You know, I swore I saw someone staring at me when I met Spencer at the doctor's on Monday."

Spencer jerked her head up, her heart racing. "Did you get a look at him?"

Mrs. Hastings shrugged. "Not really."

"Some people are saying it's a man. Others, a woman," Pooh said.

Everyone *tsk*ed in distress.

Pooh took their orders. Spencer mumbled that she wanted the ahi tuna—the same thing she'd been getting ever since she stopped ordering off the kids' menu. As the waiter trundled away, Spencer looked blearily around the dining room. It was done up in a ramshackle-Nantucket-boat theme, with dark wicker chairs and lots of life buoys and bronze figureheads. The far wall still had the ocean mural, complete with a hideous giant squid, a killer whale, and a merman that had flowing blond hair and a broken, Owen Wilson–style nose. When Spencer, Ali, and the others used to come here to eat dinner alone—a huge deal, back in sixth and seventh grades—they loved sitting next to the merman. Once, when Mona Vanderwaal and Chassey Bledsoe came in here by themselves, Ali demanded that Mona and Chassey both give the merman a big French kiss. Tears of shame had run down their cheeks as both girls stuck their tongues to the painted merman's lips.

Ali was so mean, Spencer thought. Her dream floated back. *You can't have this,* Ali had said. Why did Spencer get so angry? Spencer thought Ali was going to tell Melissa about Ian that night. Was that why? And what did Dr. Evans mean when she said that some people edit out things that happen to them? Had Spencer ever done that before?

"Mom?" Suddenly Spencer was curious. "Do you know if I ever, like, randomly forgot a whole bunch of stuff? Like . . . experienced temporary amnesia?"

Her mother held her drink in midair. "W-why are you asking?"

The back of Spencer's neck felt clammy. Her mother had the same disturbed, *I don't want to deal with this* look she'd had the time her brother, Spencer's uncle Daniel, got too drunk at one of their parties and prattled off a few deeply protected family secrets. That was how Spencer found out her grandmother had a morphine addiction, and that her aunt Penelope had given away a child for adoption when she was seventeen. "Wait, I *have?*"

Her mom felt the plate's scalloped edge. "You were seven. You had the flu."

The cords in her mother's neck stood out, which meant she was holding her breath. And that meant she wasn't telling Spencer everything. *"Mom."*

Her mother ran her hands around the martini glass edge. "It's not important."

"Oh, tell her, Veronica," her father said gruffly. "She can handle it."

Mrs. Hastings took a deep breath. "Well, Melissa, you, and I went to the Franklin Institute—you both loved that walk-through heart exhibit. Remember?"

"Sure," Spencer said. The Franklin Institute heart exhibit spanned five thousand square feet, had veins the size of Spencer's forearm, and throbbed so loudly that when you were inside its ventricles, the beating was the only sound you could hear.

"We were walking back to our car," her mother went on, her eyes on her lap. "On our way, this man stopped us." She paused, and took Spencer's father's hand. They both looked so solemn. "He . . . he had a gun in his jacket. He wanted my wallet."

Spencer widened her eyes. *"What?"*

"He made us get down on our stomachs on the side-walk." Mrs. Hastings's mouth wobbled. "I didn't care that I gave him my wallet, but I was so scared for you girls. You kept whimpering and crying. You kept asking me if we were going to die."

Spencer twisted the end of the napkin in her lap. She didn't remember this.

"He told me to count to one hundred before we could get up again," her mother said. "After the coast was clear, we ran to our car, and I drove us home. I drove nearly thirty miles over the speed limit, I remember. It's a wonder I didn't get stopped."

She paused and sipped her drink. Someone dropped a bunch of plates in the kitchen, and most of the diners craned their necks in the direction of the shattering china, but Mrs. Hastings acted as if she hadn't even heard it. "When we got home, you had a horrible fever," she went on. "It came on suddenly. We took you to the ER. We were afraid you had meningitis—there had been a case of it a few towns over. We had to stay close to home while we waited for the test results, in case we had to rush you back to the hospital. We had to miss Melissa's national spelling bee. Remember when she was preparing for that?"

Spencer remembered. Sometimes, she and Melissa would play Bee—Melissa as the contestant, Spencer as the judge, lobbing Melissa words to spell from a long list. That was back when Melissa and Spencer used to like each other. But the way Spencer remembered it, Melissa had opted out of the competition because she had a field hockey game that same day. "Melissa went to the bee after all?" she sounded out.

"She did, but she went with Yolanda's family.

Remember her friend Yolanda? She and Melissa were in all those knowledge bowls together."

Spencer crinkled her brow. "Yolanda Hensler?"

"That's right."

"Melissa was never Yolanda's—" Spencer stopped herself. She was about to say that Melissa was never Yolanda Hensler's friend. Yolanda was the type of girl who was sweetie-pie around adults but a bossy terror in private. Spencer knew that Yolanda had once forced Melissa to go through every knowledge bowl sample question without stopping, even though Melissa told her a zillion times that she had to pee. Melissa had ended up peeing in her pants, and it seeped all over Yolanda's Lilly Pulitzer comforter.

"Anyway, a week later, your fever broke," her mother said. "But when you woke up, you'd forgotten the whole thing ever happened. You remembered going to the Franklin Institute, and you remembered walking through the heart, but then I asked if you remembered the mean man in the city. And you said, 'What mean man?' You couldn't remember the ER, having tests run, being sick, anything. You just . . . erased it. We watched you the rest of that summer, too. We were afraid you might get sick again. Melissa and I had to miss our mother-daughter kayak camp in Colorado and that big piano recital in New York City, but I think she understood."

Spencer's heart was racing. "Why hasn't anyone ever told me this?"

Her mother looked at her dad. "The whole thing was so strange. I thought it might upset you, knowing you'd missed a whole week. You were such a worrier after that."

Spencer gripped the edge of the table. *I might have missed more than a week of my life,* she wanted to say to her parents. *What if it wasn't my only blackout?*

She shut her eyes. All she could hear was that *crack* from her memory. What if she had blacked out before Ali disappeared? What had she missed that night?

By the time Pooh set down their steaming plates, Spencer was shaking. Her mother cocked her head. "Spencer? What's wrong?" She swiveled her head to Spencer's father. "I knew we shouldn't have told her."

"Spencer?" Mr. Hastings waved his hands in front of Spencer's face. "You okay?"

Spencer's lips felt numb, as if they'd been injected with novocaine. "I'm afraid."

"Afraid?" her father repeated, leaning forward. "Of what?"

Spencer blinked. She felt like she was having the recurring dream where she knew what she wanted to say in her head, but instead of words coming out of her mouth, out came a shell. Or a worm. Or a plume of purple, chalky smoke. Then she clamped her mouth closed. She'd suddenly realized the answer she was looking for—what she feared.

Herself.

22

THERE'S NO PLACE LIKE ROSEWOOD—FROM 3,000 FEET UP

Friday morning, Hanna stepped out of Lucas's maroon Volkswagen Jetta. They were in the parking lot of Ridley Creek State Park, and the sun was barely up.

"This is my big surprise that's supposed to make me feel all better?" She looked around. Ridley Creek Park was full of undulating gardens and hiking trails. She watched as a bunch of girls in running shorts and long-sleeved T-shirts passed. Then a bunch of guys on bikes in colorful spandex shorts rode by. It made Hanna feel lazy and fat. Here it was, not even 6 A.M., and these people were virtuously burning off calories. They probably hadn't binged on a whole box of cheddar-flavored goldfish crackers last night, either.

"I can't tell you," Lucas answered. "Otherwise, it wouldn't be a surprise."

Hanna groaned. The air smelled like burning leaves,

which Hanna always found spooky. As she crunched through the parking lot gravel, she thought she heard snickering. She whipped back around, alert.

"Something wrong?" Lucas said, stopping a few paces away.

Hanna pointed at the trees. "Do you see someone?"

Lucas shaded his eyes with his hand. "You worried about that stalker?"

"Something like that."

Anxiety gnawed at her belly. When they'd driven here in semi-darkness, Hanna felt like a car had been following them. A? Hanna couldn't stop thinking about the bizarre text from yesterday about Mona going to Bill Beach for plastic surgery. In some ways, it made sense—Mona never wore anything that revealed too much skin, even though she was way thinner than Hanna was. But plastic surgery—anything but a boob job, anyway—was kind of . . . embarrassing. It meant genetics were against you, and you couldn't exercise your way down to your ideal body. If Hanna spread that rumor about Mona, her popularity quotient might sink a few notches. Hanna would have done it to another girl without batting an eye . . . but to Mona? Hurting her felt different.

"I think we're okay," Lucas said, walking toward the pebbly path. "They say the stalker only spies on people in their houses."

Hanna rubbed her eyes nervously. For once, she didn't need to worry about smudging her mascara. She'd put on next to no makeup this morning. And she was wearing Juicy velour pants and a gray hoodie she often wore to run laps around the track. This was all to show they were *not* on some queer early morning date.

When Lucas showed up at the door, Hanna was relieved to find that he was wearing ratty jeans, a scruffy tee, and a similar gray hoodie. Then he'd flopped into a leaf pile on their way to the car and squirmed around like Hanna's miniature Doberman, Dot. It was actually kind of cute. Which was totally different from thinking that Lucas was cute, obviously.

They entered a clearing and Lucas turned around. "Ready for your surprise?"

"This better be good." Hanna rolled her eyes. "I could still be in bed."

Lucas led her through the trees. In the clearing was a rainbow-striped hot air balloon. It was limp and lying on its side, with the basket part tipped over. A couple of guys stood around it as fans blew air up into the balloon, making it ripple.

"Ta-daaa!" Lucas cried.

"Okaaay." Hanna shaded her eyes with her hand. "I'm going to watch them blow up a balloon?" She *knew* this wasn't a good idea. Lucas was so lame.

"Not quite." Lucas leaned back on his heels. "You're going *up* in it."

"What?" Hanna shrieked. "By *myself*?"

Lucas knocked her upside the head. "I'm going with

you, duh." He started walking toward the balloon. "I have a license to fly hot air balloons. I'm learning to fly a Cessna, too. But my biggest accomplishment is this." He held up a stainless steel carafe. "I made smoothies for us this morning. It was the first time I'd used the blender—the first time I've used a kitchen appliance at all, actually. Aren't you proud of me?"

Hanna smirked. Sean had always cooked for her, which always made Hanna feel more inadequate than pampered. She liked that Lucas was boyishly clueless.

"I am proud." Hanna smiled. "And sure, I'll go up in that deathtrap with you."

After the balloon got fat and taut, Hanna and Lucas climbed in the basket and Lucas shot a long plume of fire up into the envelope. In seconds, they started to rise. Hanna was surprised her stomach didn't lurch as it sometimes did on an elevator, and when she looked down, she was amazed to see that the two guys who had helped inflate the balloon were tiny specks on the grass. She saw Lucas's red Jetta in the parking lot . . . then the fishing creek, then the winding running path, then Route 352.

"There's the Hollis spire!" Hanna cried excitedly, pointing at it off in the distance.

"Cool, huh?" Lucas smiled.

"It *is*," Hanna admitted. It was so nice and quiet up here. There were no traffic sounds, no annoying birds, just the sound of wind. Best of all, A wasn't up here. Hanna felt so free. Part of her wanted to fly away in a balloon for good, like the Wizard of Oz.

They flew over the Old Hollis neighborhood, with its Victorian houses and messy front lawns. Then the King James Mall, its parking lot nearly empty. Hanna smiled when they passed the Quaker boarding school. It had an avant-garde obelisk on the front lawn that was nicknamed William Penn's Penis.

They floated over Alison DiLaurentis's old house. From up here, it seemed so untroubled. Next to that was Spencer's house, with its windmill, stables, barn, and rock-lined pool. A few houses down was Mona's, a beautiful redbrick bordered by a grove of cherry trees with a garage off to the side of the yard. Once, right after their makeovers, they'd painted $HM + MV = BBBBBFF$ in reflective paint on the roof. They never knew what it actually looked like from above. She reached for her BlackBerry to text Mona the news.

Then she remembered. They weren't friends anymore. She sucked in a breath.

"You all right?" Lucas asked.

She looked away. "Yeah. Fine."

Lucas's eyebrows made a V. "I'm in the Supernatural Club at school. We practice mind reading. I can ESP it out of you." He shut his eyes and put his hands to his temples. "You're upset because of . . . how Mona's having a birthday party without you."

Hanna suppressed a snort. Like that was hard to figure

out. Lucas had been in the bathroom right after it happened. She unscrewed the top to the smoothie carafe. "Why are you in, like, every Rosewood Day club imaginable?" He was like a dorkier version of Spencer in that way.

Lucas opened his eyes. They were such a clear, light blue—like the cornflower crayon from the 64-Crayola box. "I like being busy all the time. If I'm not doing anything, I start thinking."

"About what?"

Lucas's Adam's apple bobbed as he swallowed. "My older brother tried to kill himself a year ago."

Hanna widened her eyes.

"He has bipolar disorder. He stopped taking his medication and . . . something went wrong in his head. He took a whole bunch of aspirin, and I found him passed out in our living room. He's at a psychiatric hospital now. They have him on all these medications and . . . he's not really the same person anymore, so . . ."

"Did he go to Rosewood Day?" Hanna asked.

"Yeah, but he's six years older than us. You probably wouldn't remember him."

"God. I'm so sorry," Hanna whispered. "That sucks."

Lucas shrugged. "A lot of people would probably just sit in their room and get stoned, but keeping busy works better for me."

Hanna crossed her arms over her chest. "My way of

staying sane is to eat a ton of cheese-based snacks and then throw them up."

She covered her mouth. She couldn't believe she just said that.

Lucas raised an eyebrow. "Cheese-based snacks, huh? Like Cheez-Its? Doritos?"

"Uh-huh." Hanna stared at the balloon basket's wooden bottom.

Lucas's fingers fidgeted. His hands were strong and well proportioned and looked like they could give really great back rubs. All of a sudden, Hanna wanted to touch them. "My cousin had that . . . problem . . . too," Lucas said softly. "She got over it."

"How?"

"She got happy. She moved away."

Hanna stared over the basket. They were flying over Cheswold, Rosewood's wealthiest housing development. Hanna had always wanted to live in a Cheswold house, and up here, the estates looked even more amazing than they did at street level. But they also looked stiff and formal and not quite real—more like an *idea* of a house instead of something you'd actually want to live in.

"I used to be happy," Hanna sighed. "I hadn't done . . . the cheese thing . . . in years. But my life's been awful lately. I *am* upset about Mona. But there's more. It's everything. Ever since I got that first note, things have gone from bad to worse."

"Rewind." Lucas leaned back. "Note?"

Hanna paused. She hadn't meant to mention A. "Just these notes I've been getting. Someone's teasing me with all this personal stuff." She peeked at Lucas, hoping he wasn't interested—most boys wouldn't be. Unfortunately, he looked worried.

"That sounds mean." Lucas furrowed his brow. "Who's sending them?"

"Don't know. At first, I thought it was Alison DiLaurentis." She paused, pushing the hair out of her eyes. "I know that's moronic, but the first notes talked about this thing that only she knew."

Lucas made a disgusted face. "Alison's body was found, what, a month ago? Someone's impersonating her? That's . . . that's freaky."

Hanna waved her arms. "No, I started getting the notes before Ali's body was found, so no one knew she was dead yet. . . ." Her head started to hurt. "It's confusing and . . . don't worry about it. Forget I said anything."

Lucas looked at her uneasily. "Maybe you should call the cops."

Hanna sniffed. "Whoever it is isn't breaking any laws."

"You don't know who you're dealing with, though," Lucas said.

"It's probably some dumb kid."

Lucas paused. "Don't the cops say that if you're being harassed, like getting prank calls, it's most likely from someone you know? I saw that on a crime show once."

A chill went through Hanna. She thought of A's note—*One of your old friends is hiding something from you. Something big.* She thought again about Spencer. Once, not long after Ali vanished, Spencer's dad had taken the four of them to Wildwater Kingdom, a water park not too far from their house. As Hanna and Spencer were climbing the steps to the Devil's Drop, Hanna had asked her if she and Ali were mad at each other about something.

Spencer's face had turned the exact shade of her merlot-colored Tommy Hilfiger string bikini. "Why are you asking that?"

Hanna frowned, holding her foamy raft to her chest. "I was just curious."

Spencer stepped closer. The air became very still, and all splashing and squealing sounds seemed to evaporate. "I wasn't mad at Ali. She was mad at me. I have no clue why, okay?" Then she did a 180 and started marching back down the wooden staircase, practically knocking over other kids as she went.

Hanna curled her toes. She hadn't thought of that day in a while.

Lucas cleared his throat. "What are the notes about? The cheese thing?"

Hanna stared at the skylights on top of the Rosewood Abbey, the site of Ali's memorial. *Screw it,* she thought. She'd told Lucas about A—why not everything else? It was like that trust exercise she'd done on her sixth-grade camping trip: a girl in her bunk named Viviana Rogers had stood behind her and Hanna had to fall into her arms, having faith that she would catch Hanna instead of letting her clunk to the grass.

"Yeah, the cheese," she said quietly. "And . . . well, you may have heard some of the other things. Plenty of stuff is going around about me. Like my father. He moved out a couple years ago and now lives with his beautiful step-daughter. She wears a size *two*."

"What size do you wear?" Lucas asked, confused.

She took a deep breath, ignoring that question. "And I got caught stealing, too—some jewelry from Tiffany, and Sean Ackard's father's car."

She looked up, surprised to see that Lucas hadn't jumped over the side of the balloon in disgust. "In seventh grade, I was a fat, ugly spaz. Even though I was friends with Alison, I still felt . . . like a nothing. Mona and I worked hard to change, and I thought we'd both become . . . *Alison*. It worked for a while, but not anymore."

Hearing her problems out loud, she sounded like such a loser. But it also felt like the time she'd gone with Mona to a spa in the country and had a colonic. The process was gross, but afterward she felt so free.

"I'm glad you're not Alison," Lucas said quietly.

Hanna rolled her eyes. "Everyone loved Alison."

"I didn't." Lucas avoided Hanna's startled look. "I know that's terrible to say, and I feel horrible about what happened to her. But she wasn't very nice to me." He blew a plume of fire into the balloon. "In seventh grade, Ali started a rumor that I was a hermaphrodite."

Hanna looked up sharply. "Ali didn't start that rumor."

"She did. Actually, I started it for her. She asked if I was a hermaphrodite at a soccer game. I said I didn't know—I had no idea what a hermaphrodite *was*. She laughed and told everyone. Later, when I looked it up, it was too late—it was everywhere."

Hanna stared at him in disbelief. "Ali wouldn't do that."

But . . . Ali *would* do that. It was Ali who had gotten everyone to call Jenna Cavanaugh Snow. She'd spread the rumor that Toby had fish gills. Everyone had taken everything Ali said as gospel.

Hanna peered over the edge of the basket. That rumor about Lucas being a hermaphrodite had started after they found out he was going to send Hanna a heart-shaped box on Candy Day. Ali had even gone with Hanna to buy new glitter-pocketed Sevens to mark the occasion. She'd said she loved them, but she was probably lying about that, too.

"And you shouldn't say you're ugly, Hanna," Lucas said. "You're so, *so* pretty."

Hanna stuck her chin into the collar of her shirt, feeling surprisingly shy.

"You are. I can't stop looking at you." Lucas grimaced. "Yikes. I probably *way* overstepped the friends thing, huh?"

"It's okay." Heat spread over her skin. It made her feel so good to hear she was pretty. When had someone last told her that? Lucas was as different from perfect Sean as a boy could get. Lucas was tall and lanky, and not in the slightest bit cool, with his Rive Gauche job and ESP club and the sticker on the back of his car that said, SCISSOR SISTERS, which could be a band or a salon or a cult. But there was something else there, too—you just had to dig down to get to it, like how Hanna and her dad had once plundered the New Jersey beaches with their metal detector. They'd searched for hours and had found not one but two diamond earrings hiding under the sand.

"So listen," Lucas said. "I'm not invited to Mona's party, either. Do you want to get together on Saturday and have an anti-party? I have a negative-edge pool. It's heated. Or, you know, if that's not your thing, we could . . . I don't know. Play poker."

"Poker?" Hanna glanced at him askance. "*Not* strip."

"What do you take me for?" Lucas put his hand to his chest. "I'm talking Texas Hold 'Em. You'd better watch it, though. I'm good."

"All right. Sure. I'll come over and play poker." She leaned back in the balloon, realizing she was looking forward to it. She gave Lucas a coy smile. "Don't change the subject, though. Now that I've made an ass out of myself, you've got to fess up about some embarrassing stuff, too. What else are you avoiding by joining all your activities?"

Lucas leaned back. "Let's see. There's the fact that I'm a hermaphrodite."

His face was dead serious. Hanna widened her eyes, caught off guard. But then Lucas grinned and started laughing, so Hanna laughed, too.

23

THE ROSEBUSHES HAVE EYES

Friday at lunch, Emily sat in the Rosewood Day green-house, where tall, leafy plants and a few species of butterflies flourished in the humidity. Even though it was hot and smelled like dirt, a lot of people were eating lunch in here. Maybe it was to escape the drizzly weather—or maybe they just wanted to be near Rosewood Day's new It Girl, Emily Fields.

"So are you going to Mona's party?" Aria's brother, Mike, gazed expectantly at Emily. He and a few other boys on the lacrosse team had plopped down on a bench across from her and were hanging on her every word.

"I don't know," Emily replied, finishing the last of her potato chips. It was doubtful her mom would let her go to Mona's, and Emily wasn't sure if she wanted to.

"You should come hang out in my hot tub after-ward." Noel Kahn scribbled his number on a piece of lined notebook paper. He tore it off and handed it to her. "That's when the *real* party's going to start."

"Bring your girlfriend, too," Mike suggested, a hungry look in his eye. "And feel free to make out around us. We're very open-minded."

"I could even get my photo booth back out for you," Noel offered, giving Emily a wink. "Whatever turns you on."

Emily rolled her eyes. As the boys sauntered off, she leaned over her thighs and let out a frazzled breath. It was too bad she wasn't the exploitative type—she could probably make a lot of money off these sexed-up, girl-on-girl-loving Rosewood boys.

Suddenly, she felt someone's small hand curl around her wrist. "You dating a lax boy?" Maya whispered in her ear. "I saw him slip you his number."

Emily looked up. Her heart swooped. It felt like she hadn't seen Maya in weeks, and she couldn't stop thinking about her. Maya's face swam before her whenever she shut her eyes. She thought about the feel of her lips during their make-out sessions on the rock by the creek.

Not that those make-out sessions could ever happen again.

Emily pulled her hand away. "Maya. We can't."

Maya stuck out her bottom lip. She looked around. Kids were sitting on the fountains or on the wooden benches next to the flower beds or near the butterfly sanctuary, calmly talking and eating their lunches. "It's not like anyone's watching."

Emily shivered. It *felt* like someone was. This whole lunch, she'd had the most eerie feeling that there was someone right behind her, spying. The greenhouse plants were so tall and thick, they provided easy coverage for people to hide behind.

Maya unclipped her pink Swiss Army knife from her backpack and snipped off a rose from the lush bushes behind them. "Here," she said, handing it to Emily.

"Maya!" Emily dropped the rose on her lap. "You can't pick flowers in here!"

"I don't care," Maya insisted. "I want you to have it."

"Maya." Emily forcefully slapped her palms on her thighs. "You should go."

Maya scowled at her. "You're seriously doing the Tree Tops thing?" When Emily nodded, Maya groaned. "I thought you were stronger than that. And it seems so creepy."

Emily crumpled up her lunch bag. Hadn't she already gone through this? "If I don't do Tree Tops, I have to go to Iowa. And I can't—my aunt and uncle are crazy."

She closed her eyes and thought of her aunt, her uncle, and her three Iowa cousins. She hadn't seen them in years, and all she could picture were five disapproving frowns. "The last time I visited, my aunt Helene told me that I should eat Cheerios *and only Cheerios* for breakfast because they suppressed sexual urges. My two male cousins went on extra-long runs through the corn-fields every morning to drain their sexual energy. And my cousin Abby—she's my age—wanted to be a nun. She probably *is* one now. She carried around a notebook that she called Abby's Little Book of Evil—and she wrote down everything she thought was a sin. She recorded *thirty* sin-ful things about me. She even thought going *barefoot* was evil!"

Maya chuckled. "If you have really ganked-up feet, it is."

"It's not funny!" Emily cried. "And this isn't about me being strong or thinking Tree Tops is right or lying to myself. I *can't* move there."

Emily bit her lip, feeling the hot rush she always got before she was about to cry. In the past two days, if her family passed her in the halls or the kitchen, they wouldn't even look in her direction. They said nothing to her at meals. She felt weird about joining them on the couch to watch TV. And Emily's sister Carolyn seemed to have no idea how to deal with her. Since the swim meet, Carolyn had stayed away from their shared bedroom. Usually, the sisters did their homework at their desks, murmuring to each other about math problems, history essays, or random gossip they'd heard at school. Last night, Carolyn came upstairs when Emily was already in bed. She changed in the dark and climbed into her own bed without saying a word.

"My family won't love me if I'm gay," Emily explained,

looking into Maya's round brown eyes. "Imagine if your family woke up and decided they hated you."

"I just want to be with you," Maya mumbled, twirling the rose between her hands.

"Well, me too," Emily answered. "But we can't."

"Let's hang out in secret," Maya suggested. "I'm going to Mona Vanderwaal's party tomorrow. Meet me there. We'll ditch and find somewhere to be alone."

Emily chewed on her thumbnail. She wished she could . . . but Becka's words haunted her. *Life is hard already. Why make it harder?* Yesterday, during her free period, Emily had logged into Google and typed, *Are lesbians' lives hard?* Even as she typed that word—*lesbian*—her right hand pecking the *L* key and her left the *E*, *S*, and *B*, it seemed strange to think that it applied to her. She didn't like it, as a word—it made her think of rice pudding, which she despised. Every link in the list was to a blocked porn site. Then again, Emily had put the words *lesbian* and *hard* in the same search field.

Emily felt someone's eyes on her. She glanced around through the whirling vines and bushes and saw Carolyn and a few other swim team girls sitting by the bougain-villea. Her sister glared right at them, a disgusted look on her face.

Emily leapt up from the bench. "Maya, go. Carolyn sees us."

She took a few steps away, pretending to be fascinated by a planter of marigolds, but Maya didn't move. "Hurry!"

Emily hissed. "Get out of here!"

She felt Maya's eyes on her. "I'm going to Mona's party tomorrow," she said in a low voice. "Are you going to be there or not?"

Emily shook her head, not meeting Maya's eye. "I'm sorry. I need to change."

Maya violently yanked up her green-and-white canvas tote. "You can't change who you are. I've told you that a thousand times."

"But maybe I can," Emily answered. "And maybe I want to."

Maya dropped Emily's rose on the bench and stomped away. Emily watched her weave through the rows of planters past the foggy windows for the exit and wanted to cry. Her life was a horrible mess. Her old, simple life—the one she'd had before this school year started—seemed like it belonged to a different girl entirely.

Suddenly, she felt someone's fingernails trace the back of her neck. A chill ran up her back, and she whirled around. It was only a tendril from another rosebush, its thorns fat and sharp, the roses plump. Then, Emily noticed something on one of the windows a few feet away. Her mouth fell open. There was writing in the condensation. *I see you.* Two wide-open, heavily lashed eyes were drawn next to the words. It was signed *A*.

Emily rushed to the writing to wipe it away with her sleeve. Had it been here all along? Why hadn't she seen it? Then, something else struck her. Because of the greenhouse's humidity, water only condensed on its inside walls, so whoever had written this had to be . . . inside.

Emily turned around, looking for some kind of telltale sign, but the only people glancing in her direction were Maya, Carolyn, and the lacrosse boys. Everyone else was milling around the greenhouse door, waiting for lunch period to end, and Emily couldn't help but wonder if A was among them.

24

AND IN ANOTHER
GARDEN ACROSS TOWN . . .

Friday afternoon, Spencer leaned over her mother's flower bed, pulling out the thick, stubborn weeds. Her mother usually did the gardening herself, but Spencer was doing it in an attempt to be nice—and to absolve herself of something, although she wasn't sure what.

The multicolored balloons her mother had bought a few days ago to celebrate the Golden Orchid were still tied to the patio rail. *Congratulations, Spencer!* they all said. Next to the words were pictures of blue ribbons and trophies. Spencer glanced into the balloons' shiny Mylar fabric; her warped reflection stared back. It was like looking into a funhouse mirror—her face looked long instead of round, her eyes were small instead of large, and her button nose looked wide and enormous. Maybe it was this balloon girl, not Spencer, who'd cheated to become a Golden Orchid finalist. And maybe Balloon Girl had been the one who'd fought with Ali the night she disappeared, too.

The sprinkler system came on next door at the DiLaurentises' old house. Spencer stared up at Ali's old window. It was the last one at the back, directly across from Spencer's. She and Ali had felt so lucky their rooms faced each other. They had window signals when it was past phone curfew—one blink of the flashlight meant, *I can't sleep, can you?* Two blinks meant, *Good night.* Three meant, *We need to sneak out and talk in person.*

The memory from Dr. Evans's office floated into her head again. Spencer tried to push it down, but it bobbed right back up. *You care way too much,* Ali had said. And that far-off *crack.* Where had it come from?

"Spencer!" a voice whispered. She whirled around, heart pounding. She faced the woods that bordered the back of her house. Ian Thomas stood between two dogwoods.

"What are you doing here?" she hissed, glancing toward the edge of the yard. Melissa's barn was just a few hundred yards away.

"Watching my favorite girl." Ian's eyes grazed down her body.

"There's a stalker running around," Spencer warned him sternly, trying to suppress the hot, excited feeling in her stomach she always got when Ian looked at her. "You should be careful."

Ian scoffed. "Who's to say I'm not part of the

neighborhood watch? Maybe I'm protecting you *from* the stalker?" He pushed his palm flat up against the tree.

"Are you?" Spencer asked.

Ian shook his head. "Nah. I actually cut through here from my house. I was coming to see Melissa." He paused, shoving his hands into his jeans pockets. "What do you think of me and Melissa being back together?"

Spencer shrugged. "It's none of my business."

"It isn't?" Ian held her gaze, not even blinking. Spencer looked away, her cheeks hot. Ian wasn't making a reference to their kiss. He *couldn't* be.

She revisited that moment again. Ian's mouth had hit hers so roughly that their teeth had smacked together. Afterward, her lips had felt achy and sore. When Spencer told Ali the exciting news, Ali had cackled. "What, do you think Ian's going to go out with you?" she taunted. "Doubtful."

She eyed Ian now, calm and casual and oblivious that he'd been the cause of all that strife. She sort of wished she hadn't kissed him. It seemed like it had started a domino effect—it had led to the fight in the barn, which had led to Ali leaving, which had led to . . . what?

"So Melissa told me you're in therapy, huh?" Ian asked. "Pretty crazy."

Spencer stiffened. It seemed odd, Melissa talking about therapy to Ian. The sessions were supposed to be private. "It isn't that crazy."

"Really? Melissa said she heard you screaming."

Spencer blinked. "Screaming?" Ian nodded. "W-what was I saying?"

"She didn't say you were saying anything. Just that you were screaming."

Spencer's skin prickled. The DiLaurentises' sprinkler system sounded like a billion little guillotines, chopping off grass-blade heads. "I have to go." She walked crookedly toward the house. "I think I need some water."

"One more sec." Ian stepped toward her. "Have you *seen* what's in your woods?"

Spencer stiffened. Ian had such a strange look on his face that Spencer wondered if maybe it was something of Ali's. One of her bones. A clue. Something to make sense of Spencer's memory.

Then Ian thrust out his open fist. Inside were six plump, pulpy blackberries. "You have the most amazing blackberry bushes back here. Want one?"

The berries had stained Ian's palm a dark, bloody purple. Spencer could see his love line and life line and all the strange etchings near his fingers.

She shook her head. "I wouldn't eat anything from those woods," she said.

After all, Ali had been killed there.

25

SPECIAL DELIVERY FOR HANNA MARIN

Friday evening, a pimply, over-gelled T-Mobile sales-person inspected Hanna's BlackBerry screen. "Your phone looks okay to me," he said. "And your battery is functioning."

"Well, you must not be looking hard enough," Hanna replied gruffly, leaning up against the store's glass counter. "What about the service? Is T-Mobile down?"

"No." The sales boy pointed to the bars in the Black-Berry's window. "See? Five bars. Looks great."

Hanna breathed forcefully through her nose. *Something* was going on with her BlackBerry. Her phone hadn't rung *once* all night. Mona might have ditched her, but Hanna refused to believe that everyone else would follow so quickly. And she thought A might text again, filling Hanna in with more information about Mona and her possible lipo, or explaining what it meant when A said that one of her friends had a big secret that had yet to be revealed.

"Do you just want to buy a new BlackBerry?" the sales guy asked.

"Yes," Hanna said sharply, conjuring up a voice that sounded surprisingly like her mother's. "One that works this time, please."

The sales guy looked tired. "I'm not going to be able to transfer over your information from this one, though. We don't do that at this location."

"It's fine," Hanna snapped. "I have a hard copy of everything at home."

The sales guy retrieved a new phone from the back, pulled it out of its Styrofoam bed, and started hitting some buttons. Hanna leaned on the counter and watched the shoppers stream through the King James Mall concourse, trying not to think about what she and Mona usually did on Friday nights. First, they'd buy a Happy Friday outfit to reward themselves for making it through another week; next, they'd hit a sushi place for the salmon platter; and then—Hanna's favorite part—they'd go home and gossip on Hanna's queen-size bed, laughing and making fun of the "Ouch! of the Day" column in *CosmoGirl!*. Hanna had to admit that it was hard to talk to Mona about certain things—she'd sidestepped any emotional conversations about Sean because Mona thought he was gay, and they were never able to talk about Ali's disappearance because Hanna didn't want to dredge up bad memories about her old friends. In fact, the more she thought about it, she wondered what she and Mona *did* talk about. Boys? Clothes? Shoes? People they hated?

"It'll be a minute," the sales guy said, frowning and looking at something on his computer monitor. "For some reason, our network isn't responding."

Ha! Hanna thought. There *was* something wrong with the network.

Someone laughed as they entered T-Mobile, and Hanna looked up. She had no time to duck when she saw Mona walking in with Eric Kahn.

Mona's light blond hair stood out against her charcoal gray turtleneck sweater dress, black tights, and tall black boots. Hanna wished she could hide, but she didn't know where—the T-Mobile register counter was an island in the middle of the store. This stupid place didn't even have any aisles to sneak down or shelves to hide under, just four walls of cell phones and mobile devices.

Before she could do anything, Eric saw her. His eyes flashed with recognition, and he gave Hanna a nod. Hanna's limbs froze. Now she knew how a deer felt when it was face-to-face with an oncoming tractor-trailer.

Mona followed Eric's gaze. "Oh," she said flatly when her eyes met Hanna's.

Eric, who must have sensed girl trouble, shrugged and wandered to the back of the store. Hanna took a few steps toward Mona. "Hi."

Mona stared at a wall of phone headsets and car adapters. "Hey."

A long beat passed. Mona scratched the side of her nose. She had painted her nails with Chanel's limited edition La Vernis black lacquer–Hanna remembered the time they'd stolen two bottles from Sephora. The memory nearly brought tears to Hanna's eyes. Without Mona, Hanna felt like a great outfit without matching accessories, a screwdriver that was all orange juice and no vodka, an iPod without headphones. She just felt *wrong*. Hanna thought about the time in the summer after eighth grade when she'd tagged along with her mom on a work trip. Hanna's cell didn't get service there, and when she came back, there had been twenty voice mails from Mona. "It felt weird not talking to you every day, so I decided to tell you everything in messages instead," Mona had said.

Hanna let out a long, shaky breath. T-Mobile smelled overwhelmingly like carpet cleaner and sweat–she hoped it wasn't her own. "I saw that message we painted on top of your garage the other day," she blurted out. "You know, *HM + MV = BBBBBFF*? You can see it from the sky. Clear as day."

Mona seemed startled. Her expression softened. "You can?"

"Uh-huh." Hanna stared at one of T-Mobile's promo posters across the room. It was a cheesy photo of two girls giggling over something, holding their cell phones in their laps. One was auburn-haired, the other blond—like Hanna and Mona.

"This is so messed up," Hanna said quietly. "I don't even know how this started. I'm sorry I missed the Frenniversary, Mon. I didn't want to be hanging out with my old friends. I'm not getting close with them or anything."

Mona tucked her chin into her chest. "No?" Hanna could barely hear her over the mall's kiddie train, which was rumbling by right outside the T-Mobile store. There was only one pudgy, miserable-looking boy on the ride.

"Not at all," Hanna answered, after the kiddie train passed. "We're just . . . weird stuff is happening to us. I can't explain all of it right now, but if you're patient with me, I'll be able to tell you soon." She sighed. "And you know I didn't do that skywriting thing on purpose. I wouldn't do that to you."

Hanna let out a small, squeaky hiccup. She always got the hiccups before she was about to start bawling, and Mona knew it. Mona's mouth twitched, and for a second, Hanna's heart leapt. Maybe things would be okay.

Then, it was like the cool-girl software inside Mona's head re-booted. Her face snapped back to being glossy and confident. She stood up straighter and smiled icily. Hanna knew exactly what Mona was doing—she and Hanna agreed never, *ever* to cry in public. They even had a rule about it: if they even thought they were going to cry, they had to squeeze their butt cheeks together, remind themselves that they were beautiful, and smile. A few days ago, Hanna would've done the same thing, but now, she couldn't see the point. "I miss you, Mona," Hanna said. "I want things to go back to the way they were."

"Maybe," Mona answered primly. "We'll have to see."

Hanna tried to force a smile. *Maybe?* What did *maybe* mean?

When she pulled into her driveway, Hanna noticed Wilden's police cruiser next to her mother's Lexus. Inside, she found her mother and Darren Wilden snuggled up on the couch watching the news. There was a bottle of wine and two glasses on the coffee table. By the looks of Wilden's T-shirt and jeans, Hanna guessed Supercop was off duty tonight.

The news was showing the leaked video of the five of them again. Hanna leaned against the doorjamb between the living room and the kitchen and watched as Spencer threw herself at her sister's boyfriend, Ian, and Ali sat at the corner of the couch, looking bored. When the clip ended, Jessica DiLaurentis, Alison's mother, appeared on the screen. "The video is hard to watch," Mrs. DiLaurentis said. "All of this has made us go through our suffering all over again. But we want to thank everyone in Rosewood—you've all been so wonderful. The time we've spent back here for Alison's investigation has made my husband and me realize how much we've missed it."

For a brief second, the camera panned on the

people behind Mrs. DiLaurentis. One of them was Offi-cer Wilden, all gussied up in his cop uniform. "There you are!" Hanna's mother cried, squeezing Wilden's shoulder. "You look *great* on camera."

Hanna wanted to vomit. Her mom hadn't even gotten that excited last year when Hanna had been named Snow-flake Queen and had ridden on a float in the Philadelphia Mummers parade.

Wilden swiveled around, sensing Hanna's presence in the doorway. "Oh. Hi, Hanna." He moved slightly away from Ms. Marin, as if Hanna had just caught him doing something wrong.

Hanna grunted a hello, then turned and opened a kitchen cupboard and pulled down a box of peanut but-ter Ritz Bits.

"Han, a package came for you," her mother called, turning down the TV volume.

"Package?" Hanna repeated, her mouth full of crackers.

"Yep. It was on the doorstep when we got here. I put it in your room."

Hanna carried the box of Ritz Bits upstairs with her. There was indeed a large box propped up against her bureau, right next to her miniature pinscher Dot's Gucci dog bed. Dot stretched off the bed, his tiny nubby tail wagging. Hanna's fingers trembled as she used her nail scissors to slice open the packing tape. As she ripped open the box, a few sheets of tissue paper cascaded through the room. And then . . . a champagne-colored Zac Posen slip dress sat at the bottom.

Hanna gasped. Mona's court dress. All tailored and pressed and ready to wear. She rooted around the bottom of the box for a note of explanation but couldn't find one. Whatever. This could only mean one thing—she was forgiven.

The corners of Hanna's lips slowly spread into a grin. She leapt onto her bed and started jumping, making her bedsprings squeak. Dot circled around her, yapping crazily. *"Yessss,"* Hanna cried, relieved. She'd known Mona would come to her senses. She would be crazy to stay mad at Hanna for long.

She sat back down on the bed and picked up her new BlackBerry. This was short notice—she probably wouldn't be able to rebook the hair and makeup appointments she'd cancelled when she thought she wasn't going to the party. Then she remembered something else: Lucas. *I'm not invited to Mona's party, either,* he'd said.

Hanna paused, drumming her hands on the Black-Berry's screen. She obviously couldn't bring him to Mona's party. Not as her *date*. Not as anything. Lucas was cute, sure, but he was definitely not party-worthy.

She sat up straighter and flipped through her red leather Coach organizer for Lucas's e-mail address. She would write him a short, snippy e-mail so he'd know exactly where he stood with her: nowhere. He'd be crushed, but really, Hanna couldn't please everyone now, could she?

26

SPENCER GETS IN HOT WATER . . .
LITERALLY AND FIGURATIVELY

Friday evening, Spencer was soaking in the family hot tub. It was one of her favorite things to do, especially at night, when all of the stars glittered in the dark sky. Tonight the only sounds around her were the burbling of the hot tub's jets and the slobbery crunching sounds of Beatrice, one of the family's labradoodles, chewing on a rawhide bone.

Then suddenly, she heard a twig snap. Then another. Then . . . someone breathing. Spencer turned as her sister, clad in a Nova-check plaid Burberry bikini, climbed down the stairs and settled into the tub, too.

For a while, neither of them said anything. Spencer hid under a beard of bubbles, and Melissa was looking at the umbrella table next to the pool. Suddenly, Melissa inspected her sister. "So I'm a little annoyed at Dr. Evans."

"Why?"

Melissa swished her hands around in the water. "Sometimes she says all this stuff about me like she's known me for years. Does she do that to you?"

Spencer shrugged. Hadn't Melissa warned her Dr. Evans would do that?

Melissa pressed the flat of her hand against her forehead. "She told me that I choose untrustworthy men to date. That I actually go after guys I know will never commit or turn into anything long-term because I'm afraid of getting close to anyone."

Melissa reached over and drank from her big bottle of Evian, which was sitting next to the tub. Above her head, Spencer saw the silhouette of a large bird—or perhaps a bat—flap past the moon. "I was angry about it at first, but now . . . I don't know." Melissa sighed. "Maybe she's right. I've started to think about all my relationships. Some of the guys I've gone out with *have* seemed really untrustworthy, right from the start."

Her eyes needled into Spencer, and Spencer blushed.

"Wren's an obvious one," Melissa went on, as if reading Spencer's thoughts. Spencer looked away, staring at the waterfall installation that was on the other side of the pool. "She's got me wondering about Ian, too. I think he was cheating on me when we were in high school."

Spencer tensed. "Really?"

"Uh-huh." Melissa inspected her perfectly manicured pale peach nails. Her eyes were dark. "I'm almost *certain*. And I think I know who it was."

Spencer bit a hangnail on her thumb. What if Melissa had overheard Spencer and Ian in the yard earlier? Ian had alluded to their kiss. Or, worse: what if Ali *had* told Melissa what Spencer had done, years ago?

Not long before Ali vanished, Spencer's dad had taken the five of them to play paintball. Melissa had come along, too. "I'm going to tell Melissa what you did," Ali sing-songed to Spencer as they put on their jumpsuits in the changing room.

"You wouldn't," Spencer hissed back.

"Oh no?" Ali teased. "Watch me."

Spencer had followed Ali and the others to the field. They all crouched behind a large bale of hay, waiting for the game to start. Then Ali leaned over and tapped Melissa on the shoulder. "Hey, Melissa. I have something to tell you."

Spencer nudged her. "Stop it."

The whistle blew. Everyone shot forward and started pelting the other team. Everyone, that was, except for Ali and Spencer. Spencer took Ali's arm and dragged her behind a nearby hay bale. She was so angry her muscles were quivering.

"Why are you doing this?" Spencer demanded.

Ali snickered, leaning against the hay. *"Why are you doing this?"* she imitated in a high falsetto. "Because it's wrong. Melissa deserves to know."

Anger gathered in Spencer's body like clouds before a huge thunderstorm. Didn't friends keep each other's

secrets? They'd kept the Jenna secret for Ali, after all—
Ali was the one who'd lit that firework, *Ali* was the one
who had blinded Jenna—and they'd all vowed not to tell.
Didn't Ali remember that?

Spencer didn't mean to pull the trigger of the paintball
gun . . . it just happened. Blue paint splattered all over
Ali's jumpsuit, and Ali let out a startled cry. Then she
glared at Spencer and stormed away. What if she'd gone
and told Melissa then, and Melissa had been waiting all
this time for the right moment to drop it on Spencer?
Maybe this was it.

"Any guesses who it was?" Melissa goaded, breaking
Spencer out of the memory.

Spencer sank down farther into the hot tub's bubbles,
her eyes stinging with chlorine. A kiss hardly qualified as
cheating, and it had been so long ago. "Nope. No clue."

Melissa sighed. "Maybe Dr. Evans is full of it. What
does she know, really?"

Spencer studied her sister carefully. She thought about
what Dr. Evans had said about Melissa—that her sister
needed validation. That she was jealous of Spencer. It was
such a weird possibility to consider. And could Melissa's
issues have something to do with the time they'd been
mugged, Spencer had gotten sick, and Melissa had had to
go to her Bee with Yolanda? How many other things had
her sister missed out on that summer because her parents
were too busy hovering over Spencer? How many times
had she been shoved to the side?

I liked when we were friends, said a voice inside Spencer's head. *I liked quizzing you with your spelling words. I hate the way things are now. I've hated it for a long time.*

"Does it really matter if Ian cheated on you in high school?" Spencer said quietly. "I mean, it was so long ago."

Melissa stared up at the dark, clear sky. All the stars had come out. "Of course it matters. It was *wrong.* And if I ever find out it's true, Ian is going to regret it for the rest of his life."

Spencer flinched. She'd never heard Melissa sound so vengeful. "And what will you do to the girl?"

Melissa turned very slowly and gave Spencer a poisonous smile. At that very moment, the backyard's timed lights snapped on. Melissa's eyes glowed. "Who says I haven't done something to her already?"

27

OLD HABITS DIE HARD

Late Saturday afternoon, Aria slumped down behind a maple in the McCreadys' yard, which was across the street from her own house. She watched as three cookie-selling Girl Scouts strode to her family's front door. *Ella's not home, but put her down for a couple boxes of Thin Mints,* she wanted to tell the girls. *They're her favorite.*

The girls waited. When no one answered, they went to the next house.

Aria knew it was weird to have biked here from Sean's, stalking her own house as if it were a velvet-rope celebrity club and she were a paparazzo, but she missed her family so badly. The Ackards were like the bizarro-Montgomerys. Mr. and Mrs. Ackard had joined the Rosewood Stalker Community Watch Board. They'd established a twenty-four-hour tip hotline, and in a few days, it would be Mr. and Mrs. Ackard's turn to make the nightly rounds. And every time any of them looked at her, Aria felt like they could tell what she'd done with Ezra in his office. It was as though she had a big scarlet *A* on her shirt now, too.

Aria needed to clear her head and purge herself of Ezra. Only, she couldn't stop thinking about him. This whole bike ride had been one Ezra reminder after another. She'd passed a chubby man eating Chicken McNuggets and had gotten weak-kneed from the smell. She'd seen a girl with black plastic glasses just like Ezra's and felt chills. Even a cat on a garden wall had reminded her of Ezra, for no good reason at all. But what was she thinking? How could something be so wrong . . . yet so right at the same time?

As she passed a stone house with its own water-wheel, a Channel 7 news van whizzed by. It disappeared over the hill, the wind slid through the trees, and the sky suddenly darkened. All at once, Aria felt as if a hundred spiders were crawling over her. Someone was watching.

A?

When her Treo let out a whirly little ring, she nearly fell off her bike. She hit the brakes, pulled onto the sidewalk, and reached for it in her pocket. It was Sean.

"Where are you?" he asked.

"Um . . . I went out for a bike ride," she answered, chewing on the cuff of her beat-up red hoodie.

"Well, come home soon," Sean said. "Otherwise we'll be late to Mona's."

Aria sighed. She'd completely forgotten about Mona

Vanderwaal's party.

He sighed back at her, too. "Do you not want to go?"

Aria squeezed the bike's brakes and stared at the beautiful Gothic Revival house in front of her. The owners had decided to paint it royal purple. Aria's parents were the only people in the neighborhood who hadn't signed a petition demanding the artist-owners paint it a more conservative color, but the petition hadn't held up in court. "I'm not really friends with Mona," Aria mumbled. "Or anyone else going to that party."

"What are you talking about?" Sean sounded baffled. "They're my friends, so they're your friends. We're going to have a great time. And, I mean, other than our bike ride, I feel like I haven't seen you, really, since you moved in with me. Which is weird, if you think about it."

Suddenly, Aria's call waiting beeped. She brought her phone away from her ear and looked at the screen. *Ezra.* She clapped her hand over her mouth.

"Sean, can I put you on hold for a sec?" She tried to contain the exhilaration in her voice.

"Why?" Sean asked.

"Just . . . hang on." Aria clicked over. She cleared her throat and smoothed down her hair, as if Ezra were watching her on a video screen. "Hello?" She tried to sound cool yet seductive.

"Aria?" She swooned at Ezra's sleepy, gravelly voice.

"Ezra." Aria feigned surprise. "Hi."

A few seconds of silence passed. Aria spun her bike's

pedals with her foot and watched a squirrel run across the purple house's lawn. "I can't stop thinking about you," Ezra finally admitted. "Can you meet me?"

Aria squeezed her eyes shut. She knew she shouldn't go. But she so wanted to. She swallowed hard. "Hang on."

She clicked back over to Sean. "Um, Sean?"

"Who was it?" he asked.

"It was . . . my mom," Aria fumbled.

"Really? That's great, right?"

Aria bit down hard on the inside of her cheek. She focused intently on the intricately carved pumpkins on the purple house's steps. "I have to go do something," she blurted out. "I'll call you later."

"Wait," Sean cried. "What about Mona's?"

But Aria's finger was already switching back to Ezra. "I'm back," she said breathlessly, feeling as if she'd just competed in some sort of boy triathlon. "And I'll be right over."

When Ezra opened the door to his apartment, which was in an old Victorian house in Old Hollis, he was holding a Glenlivet bottle in his right hand. "Want some Scotch?" he asked.

"Sure," Aria answered. She walked into the middle of Ezra's living room and sighed happily. She'd thought about this apartment a lot since she'd been here last. The billions of books on the shelves, the blue melted candle wax spilling over the mantel in Smurf-like lumps, and the big, useless bathtub in the middle of the room . . . it all made Aria feel so comfortable. She felt like she'd just come home.

They plopped down on Ezra's springy, mustard-yellow love seat. "Thanks for coming over," Ezra said softly. He was wearing a pale blue T-shirt with a little rip in the shoulder. Aria wanted to stick her finger through the hole.

"You're welcome," Aria said, sliding out of her checkerboard Vans slip-ons. "Should we toast?"

Ezra thought for a moment, a lock of dark hair falling over his eyes. "To coming from messed-up homes," he decided, and touched his glass to hers.

"Cheers." Aria tipped the Scotch back. It tasted like glass cleaner and smelled like kerosene, but she didn't care. She drained the Scotch fast, feeling it burn down her esophagus.

"Another?" he asked, bringing the Glenlivet bottle with him as he sat back down.

"Sure," Aria answered. Ezra got up to get more ice cubes and glanced at the tiny muted TV in the corner. There was an iPod commercial on. It was funny to watch someone dance so enthusiastically with no sound.

Ezra returned and poured Aria another drink. With every sip of the Scotch, Aria's tough exterior melted away. They talked for a while about Ezra's parents—his mom lived in New York City now, his dad in Wayne, a town not too far away. Aria began to talk about her family again. "You know what my favorite memory of my parents is?" she said, hoping she wasn't slurring. The bitter Scotch was doing a number on her motor skills. "My thirteenth birthday at Ikea."

Ezra raised an eyebrow. "You're kidding. Ikea's a nightmare."

"It sounds weird, right? But my parents knew someone who was really high up who ran the Ikea store near here, and we rented it out after-hours. It was so much fun—Byron and Ella went there early and planned this whole big scavenger hunt all around the Ikea bedrooms and kitchens and offices. They were so giddy about it. We all had Swedish furniture names for the party—Byron's was Ektorp, I think, and Ella's was Klippan. They seemed so . . . together."

Tears dotted Aria's eyes. Her birthday was in April; Aria had found Bryon with Meredith in May, and then Ali had vanished in June. It seemed like that party had been the last perfect, uncomplicated night of her life. Everyone had been so happy, even Ali—especially Ali. At one point in a cavern of Ikea shower curtains, Ali had grabbed Aria's hands and whispered, "I'm so happy, Aria! I'm *so* happy!"

"Why?" Aria had asked.

Ali grinned and wiggled. "I'll tell you soon. It's a surprise."

But she'd never had the chance.

Aria traced her finger around the top of the Scotch glass. The news had just come on the TV. They were talking about Ali—again. *Murder investigation,* the banner at the bottom of the screen said. Ali's seventh-grade school picture was in the left-hand corner: Ali flashing her brilliant smile, the diamond hoops glinting in her ears, her blond hair wavy and lustrous, her Rosewood Day blazer perfectly fitted and lint-free. It was so odd that Ali would be a seventh grader forever.

"So," Ezra said. "Have you spoken to your dad?"

Aria turned away from the TV. "Not really. He wanted to talk to me, although he probably doesn't now. Not after the Scarlet *A* thing."

Ezra frowned. "Scarlet *A* thing?"

Aria picked at a loose thread in her favorite APC jeans from Paris. This was *not* something she could explain to someone who had a degree in English literature. But Ezra was learning forward, his beautiful lips parted in expectation. So she took another sip of Scotch and told him all about Meredith, Hollis, and the dripping red *A.*

To her horror, Ezra burst out laughing. "You're *kidding* me. You really did that?"

"Yes," Aria snapped. "I shouldn't have told you."

"No, no, it's great. I love it." Ezra impetuously grabbed Aria's hands. His palms were warm and big and slightly sweaty. He met her eyes . . . then kissed her. First lightly, then Aria leaned in and kissed him harder. They stopped for a moment, and Aria slumped back on the couch.

"You okay?" Ezra asked softly.

Aria had no idea if she was okay. She'd never felt so

much in her life. She couldn't quite figure out what to do with her mouth. "I don't—"

"I know we shouldn't be doing this," Ezra interrupted. "You're my student. I'm your teacher. But . . ." He sighed, pushing back a lock of hair. "But . . . I wish that maybe . . . somehow . . . this could work."

How badly had she wanted Ezra to say these things weeks ago? Aria felt perfect with him—more alive, more *herself*. But then Sean's face appeared in Aria's mind. She saw him leaning over to kiss her the other day in the cemetery when he saw a rabbit. And she saw A's note: *Careful, careful! I'm always watching.*

She glanced at the television again. The familiar video clip came on for the billionth time. Aria could read Spencer's lips: *Want to read her texts?* The girls crowded around the phone. Ali swam into the picture. For a moment, Ali looked squarely into the camera, her eyes round and blue. It seemed like she was staring out of the TV screen into Ezra's living room . . . straight at Aria.

Ezra turned his head and noticed what was on. "Shit," he said. "I'm sorry." He rooted around in the pile of magazines and Thai takeout menus on his coffee table and finally found the remote. He switched one channel up, which was QVC. Joan Rivers was selling a giant dragonfly-shaped brooch.

Ezra pointed at the screen. "I'll buy that for you, if you want."

Aria giggled. "No thanks." She put her hand on Ezra's

and took a deep breath. "So, what you said . . . about making this work. I . . . I think I want it to work with you, too."

He brightened and Aria could see her reflection in his glasses. The old grandfather clock near Ezra's dining room table chimed out the hour. "R-really?" he murmured.

"Yes. But . . . but I also want to do it right." She swallowed hard. "I have a boyfriend right now. So . . . I have to take care of that, you know?"

"Sure," Ezra said. "I understand."

They stared at each other for at least a minute more. Aria could have reached over, torn his glasses off, and kissed him a billion times. "I think I should go now," she said wistfully.

"Okay," Ezra answered, his eyes not leaving hers. But when she slid off the couch and tried to put on her shoes, he pulled at the edge of her T-shirt. Even though she'd wanted to leave, she just . . . couldn't.

"Come here," Ezra whispered, and Aria fell back into him. Ezra reached out his arms and caught her.

28

SOME OF HER LETTERS
ALSO SPELL *JAIL*

A little before eight on Saturday night, Spencer was lying on her bed, watching her palm-leaf ceiling fan go around and around. The fan cost more than a decent-running car, but Spencer had begged her mom to buy it because it looked identical to the fan in her private cabana the time her family stayed at the Caves in Jamaica. Now, however, it looked so . . . Spencer at thirteen.

She got out of bed and slid her feet into her black Chanel sling-backs. She knew she should muster up some enthusiasm for Mona's party. She would have last year—then again, everything had been different last year. All day, she'd been having strange visions—fighting with Ali outside the barn, Ali's mouth moving but Spencer not hearing the words, Spencer taking a step toward her, a *crack*. It was as if the memory, pent up for all these years, wanted to be the star.

She swiped more toasted almond-colored gloss on her lips, straightened her kimono-sleeve black dress, and clomped downstairs. When she reached the kitchen, she was surprised to see that her mother, father, and Melissa were sitting at the table around an empty Scrabble board. The two dogs snuggled at their feet. Her father wasn't wearing his standard uniform of either a suit or cycling clothes, but a soft white T-shirt and jeans. Her mom was in yoga pants. The room smelled like steamed milk from the Miele espresso maker.

"Hey." Spencer couldn't remember the last time she'd seen her parents home on a Saturday night. They were all about being seen—whether it was at a restaurant opening or at the symphony or at one of the dinner parties the partners at her father's firm were always having.

"Spencer! There you are!" Mrs. Hastings cried. "Guess what we just got?" With a flourish, she presented a printout she had been holding behind her back. It had the *Philadelphia Sentinel*'s gothic-script logo on the top. Underneath was the headline, *Move Over, Trump! Spencer Hastings Is Coming!* Spencer stared at the photo of herself sitting at her father's desk. The battleship gray Calvin Klein suit with the raspberry silk camisole underneath had been a good choice.

"Jordana just e-mailed us the link," her mother chirped. "Sunday's front page won't be ready until tomorrow morning, of course, but your story is already up online!"

"Wow," Spencer said shakily, too unfocused to actually read the story. So this was really happening. How far was this going to go? What if she actually *won*?

"We're going to open a bottle of champagne to celebrate," Mr. Hastings said. "You can even have some, Spence. Special occasion and all."

"And maybe you want to play Scrabble?" Mrs. Hastings asked.

"Mom, she's all dressed up for a party," Melissa urged. "She doesn't want to sit here and drink champagne and play Scrabble."

"Nonsense," Mrs. Hastings said. "It's not even eight yet. Parties don't start this early, do they?"

Spencer felt trapped. They were all staring at her. "I . . . I guess not," she said.

She dragged a chair back, sat down, and kicked off her shoes. Her father got a bottle of Moët out of the fridge, popped the cork, and took out four Riedel glasses from the cabinet. He poured a whole glass for himself, Spencer's mother, and Melissa, and a half glass for Spencer. Melissa put a Scrabble rack in front of her.

Spencer plunged her hand into the velvet bag and selected letters. Her father selected his letters next. Spencer was amazed he knew how to do it—she'd never seen him play a game, not even on vacation. "When do you hear what the judges' final decision is?" he asked, taking a sip of his champagne.

Spencer shrugged. "I don't know." She glanced at

Melissa, who gave her a brief, indecipherable smile. Spencer hadn't talked to Melissa since their hot-tub session last night, and she felt a little strange around her sister. Apprehensive, almost.

"I had a chance to read it yesterday," Mr. Hastings continued, folding his hands. "I love how you updated the concept for modern times."

"So who goes first?" Spencer asked shrilly. There was no way they were talking about the *content* of the essay. Not around Melissa.

"Didn't 1996's Golden Orchid winner win a Pulitzer last year?" Mrs. Hastings asked.

"No, it was a National Book Award," Melissa said.

Please stop talking about the Golden Orchid, Spencer thought. Then, she realized: for once, they were talking about *her*—not Melissa.

Spencer looked at her tiles. She had *I, A, S, J, L, R,* and *H.* She rearranged the letters and almost choked on her tongue. LIAR SJH. SJH, as in Spencer Jill Hastings.

Outside, the sky was raven-colored. A dog howled. Spencer grabbed her champagne flute and drained its contents in three seconds flat. "Someone's not driving for at least an hour," her father mock-scolded.

Spencer tried to laugh, sitting on her hands so her dad wouldn't see that they were shaking.

Mrs. Hastings spelled WORM with her tiles. "Your turn, Spence," she said.

As Spencer picked up her *L* tile, Melissa's slim

Motorola lit up. A fake cello vibrated out of the cell's speaker, playing the theme to *Jaws. Duh-DUH. Duh-DUH.* Spencer could see the screen from here: new text message.

Melissa flipped the screen open, angling it away from Spencer's view. She frowned. "Huh?" she said aloud.

"What is it?" Mrs. Hastings asked, raising her eyes from her tiles.

Melissa scratched her head. *"The great Scottish economist Adam Smith's invisible-hand concept can be summed up very easily, whether it's describing the markets of the nineteenth century or those of the twenty-first: you might think people are doing things to help you, but in reality, everyone is only out for himself.* Weird! Why would someone send me part of an essay I wrote when I was in *high school?"*

Spencer opened her mouth to speak, but only a dry exhalation came out.

Mr. Hastings put down his glass. "That's Spencer's Golden Orchid essay."

Melissa examined the screen. "No, it's not, it's my . . ." She looked at Spencer. *"No."*

Spencer shrank down in her chair. "Melissa, it was a mistake."

Melissa's mouth was open so wide, Spencer saw the silver fillings in her molars. "You bitch!"

"Things got out of hand!" Spencer cried. "The situation slipped away from me!"

Mr. Hastings frowned, confused. "What's going on?"

Melissa's face contorted, the corners of her eyes turning down and her lips curling up sinisterly. "First you steal my boyfriend. And then my *paper*? Who do you think you are?"

"I said I was sorry!" Spencer cried at the same time.

"Wait. It's . . . Melissa's paper?" Mrs. Hastings said, growing pale.

"There must be some mistake," Mr. Hastings insisted.

Melissa put her hands on her hips. "Should I tell them? Or would you like to?"

Spencer jumped up. "Tell on me like you always do." She ran down the hall toward the stairs. "You've gotten so good at it by now."

Melissa followed. "They need to know what a liar you are."

"They need to know what a bitch *you* are," Spencer shot back.

Melissa's lips spread into a smile. "You're so lame, Spencer. Everyone thinks so. Including Mom and Dad."

Spencer scrambled up the stairs backwards. "They do not!"

"Yes, they do!" Melissa taunted. "And it's the truth, isn't it? You're a boyfriend-stealing, plagiarizing, pathetic little bitch!"

"I'm so sick of you!" Spencer screamed. "Why don't you just *die*?"

"Girls!" Mr. Hastings cried.

But it was as if the sisters were in a force-field bubble

all their own. Melissa didn't break her stare from Spencer. And Spencer started shaking. It was true. She *was* pathetic. She *was* worthless.

"Rot in hell!" Spencer screamed. She took two stairs at a time.

Melissa was right behind her. "That's right, little baby who means nothing, run away!"

"Shut *up!*"

"Little baby who steals my boyfriends! Who isn't even smart enough to write her own papers! What were you going to say on TV if you won, Spencer? *Yes, I wrote every word of it myself. I'm such a smart, smart girl!* What, did you cheat on the PSATs, too?"

It felt like fingernails scraping against Spencer's heart. "Stop it!" she rasped, nearly tripping over an empty J. Crew box her mother had left on the steps.

Melissa grabbed Spencer's arm and swung her around. She put her face right up to Spencer's. Her breath smelled like espresso. "Little baby wants everything of mine, but you know what? You can't have what I have. You never will."

All the anger that Spencer had held in for years broke free and flooded her body, making her feel hot, then wet, then shaky. Her insides were so bathed in fury they were starting to prune. She braced herself against the railing, grabbed Melissa by the shoulders and started to shake her as if she were a Magic Eight Ball. Then she shoved her. "I said, *stop* it!"

Melissa stumbled, grabbing the railing for support. A frightened look danced over her face.

A crack started to form in Spencer's brain. But instead of Melissa she saw Ali. They both wore the same smug, *I'm everything and you're nothing* expression. *You try to steal everything away from me. But you can't have this.* Spencer smelled the dewy humidity and saw the lightning bugs and felt Ali's breath close to her face. And then, a strange force invaded Spencer's body. She let out an agonized grunt from somewhere deep inside her and shot forward. She saw herself reaching out and pushing Ali—or was it Melissa?—with all her strength. Both Melissa and Ali fell backward. Their heads both made skull-shattering cracks as they fell against something. Spencer's vision cleared and she saw Melissa tumbling down, down, down the stairs, falling into a heap at the bottom.

"Melissa!" Mrs. Hastings cried.

And then, everything went black.

29

THERE'S A FULL MOON AT THE HOLLIS PLANETARIUM

Hanna staggered to the planetarium gates a little after nine. It was the weirdest thing, but it was kind of hard to walk in the court dress. Or sit down. Or, well, breathe.

Okay, so the whole thing was too damn tight. It had taken Hanna forever to wriggle into the thing and then even longer to zip up the back. She had even considered borrowing her mom's Spanx girdle, but that would have meant taking the dress off and going through the zipper torture again. The process had taken so long, in fact, she'd hardly had time to do anything else before coming here, like touch up her makeup, tally the calories she'd eaten today, or import her old phone numbers into her new BlackBerry.

Now the dress fabric seemed to have shrunk even more. It cut into her skin and clung so tightly to her hips that she had no idea how she would pull it up to pee. Every time she moved, she could hear tiny threads tearing. There were certain spots, too, like around the belly, the side of her boobs, and across her butt, that . . . bulged.

She *had* eaten a lot of Cheez-Its over the past few days . . . and she'd tried really hard not to throw any of them up. Could she have gained weight that fast? What if something was suddenly wrong with her metabolism? What if she had turned into one of those girls who gained weight by simply *looking* at food?

But she had to wear this dress. Maybe the fabric would loosen the more she wore it, like leather. The party would probably be dark, too, so no one would notice. Hanna tottered up the planetarium's steps, feeling a bit like a stiff, champagne-colored penguin.

She heard the pumping bass from inside the building and steeled herself. She hadn't felt this nervous about a party since Ali's seventh-grade Halloween bash, when she'd still felt like she was teetering on the edge of dork-dom. Not long after Hanna had arrived, Mona and her geeky friends Chassey Bledsoe and Phi Templeton had shown up as three Hobbits from *The Lord of the Rings*. Ali had taken one look at them and turned them away. "You look like you're covered in fleas," she'd said, laughing in their faces.

The day after Ali's party, when Hanna had gone with her mom to the grocery store, she'd seen Mona and her dad in the checkout line. There, on the lapel of Mona's denim jacket, was the crystal-studded jack-o'-lantern pin that had been in Ali's party gift bag. Mona was wearing it proudly, as if she belonged.

Hanna felt a twinge of guilt about ditching Lucas—he hadn't e-mailed her back after she cancelled on him—but what choice did she have? Mona had all but forgiven her in T-Mobile and then sent her the dress. Best friends always came first, especially best friends like Mona.

She carefully pushed through the large metal front door. Immediately, the music washed over her like a wave. She saw bluish ice sculptures in the main hall, and farther back, a giant trapeze. Glittering planets hung from the ceiling, and an enormous video screen loomed over the stage. A larger-than-life Noel Kahn gazed through a telescope on the Jumbotron.

"Oh my God," Hanna heard behind her. She turned around. Naomi and Riley stood by the bar. They wore matching emerald sheaths and carried tiny satin clutches. Riley smirked behind her hand, giving Hanna the once-over. Naomi let out a loud guffaw. Hanna would have nervously pulled in her stomach if the dress hadn't already unnaturally been doing it for her.

"Nice *dress*, Hanna," Riley said smoothly. With her blazing red hair and shiny bright green dress, she looked like an inverted carrot.

"Yeah, it looks really good on you," Naomi simpered.

Hanna stood up straighter and strode away. She skirted around a black-suited waitress carrying a tray of mini crab cakes and tried not to look at them, worried she really might gain a pound. Then she watched as the image on the Jumbotron changed. Nicole Hudson and Kelly Hamilton, Riley and Naomi's bitchy underlings, appeared on the screen. They also wore slinky green sheaths and carried the same delicate satin bags. "Happy birthday, Mona, from your party court posse!" they cried, blowing kisses.

Hanna frowned. *Party court?* No. The court dress wasn't green—it was champagne. Right?

Suddenly, a crowd of dancing kids parted. A beautiful blond girl strode right up to Hanna. It was *Mona*. She wore the exact same champagne-colored Zac Posen gown as Hanna—the one they'd both been fitted for at Saks. Except hers didn't pull across the stomach or the ass. The zipper didn't look puckered and strained, and there were no bulges. Instead, it accentuated Mona's thin waist and showed off her long, lithe legs.

Mona's eyes boggled. "What are *you* doing here?" She looked Hanna up and down, her mouth wobbling into a smile. "And where the *hell* did you get that dress?"

"You sent it to me," Hanna answered.

Mona stared at her like she was crazy. She pointed at Riley. "*That's* the court dress. I changed it. I wanted to be the only one wearing champagne—not all of us." She looked Hanna up and down. "And certainly not any whales."

Everyone tittered, even the waitresses and the bartender.

Hanna stepped back, confused. The room was quieter for a moment—the DJ was between songs. Mona wrinkled her nose and Hanna suddenly felt like a drawstring had pulled her throat closed. It all made horrible, sickening sense.

Of course Mona hadn't sent the dress. *A had.*

"Please leave." Mona crossed her arms over her chest and stared pointedly at Hanna's various bulges. "I disinvited you, remember?"

Hanna walked toward Mona, wanting to explain, but she stepped down unsteadily on her gold Jimmy Choo heel. She felt her ankle twist, her legs go out from under her, and her knees hit the ground. Worse, Hanna heard a loud, undeniable *riiiiiiip.* Suddenly, her butt felt a lot less constricted. As she twisted around to assess the damage, her side seam gave way, too. The whole side of the dress burst open from Hanna's ribs to her hip, exposing the thin, lacy straps of her Eberjey bra and thong.

"Oh my God!" Riley cried. Everyone howled with laughter. Hanna tried to cover herself up, but she didn't know where to start. Mona just stood there and let it happen, beautiful and queenlike in her perfect-fitting gown. It was hard for Hanna to imagine that only days ago, they'd loved each other as only best friends could.

Mona placed her hands on her hips and looked over at the others. "Come on, girls," she sniffed. "This train wreck isn't worth our time."

Hanna's eyes filled with tears. Kids started to trample

away, and someone tripped over Hanna, spilling warm beer on her legs. *This train wreck isn't worth our time.* Hanna heard the words echo in her head. Then she thought of something.

Remember when you saw Mona leaving the Bill Beach plastic surgery clinic? Hello, lipo!!

Hanna propped herself up against the cool marble floor. "Hey, Mona."

Mona turned and stared at her.

Hanna took a deep breath. "You look a lot skinnier since I saw you leaving Bill Beach. For *lipo*."

Mona cocked her head. But she didn't look horrified or embarrassed—just confused. She let out a snort and rolled her eyes. "Whatever, Hanna. You're so pathetic."

Mona tossed her hair over her shoulder and wove toward the stage. A wall of kids quickly separated them. Hanna sat up, covering the tear on her side with one hand and the tear on her ass with the other. And then, she saw it: her face, magnified a billion times on the Jumbotron screen. There was a long, panning shot of her dress. The fat under her arms bulged. The lines of her thong showed through the tight fabric. The Hanna on the screen took a step toward Mona and toppled over. The camera captured her dress splitting apart.

Hanna screamed and covered her eyes. Everyone's laughter felt like needles tattooing her skin. Then she felt a hand on her back. "Hanna."

Hanna peeped through her hands. *"Lucas?"*

He was wearing dark trousers, an Atlantic Records T-shirt, and a pinstriped jacket. His longish blond hair looked thick and wild. The look on his face said he'd seen everything.

He took off his jacket and handed it to her. "Here. Put this on. Let's get you out of here."

Mona was climbing onstage. The crowd quivered with anticipation. On any normal party night, Hanna would have been front and center, ready to grind to the music. But instead, she grabbed Lucas's arm.

30

CHANGE IS GOOD . . .
EXCEPT WHEN IT'S NOT

On Saturday evening, Emily laced up her rental ice skates until she could barely feel the circulation in her feet. "I can't believe we have to wear three pairs of socks," she complained to Becka, who was next to her on the bench, lacing up the pair of white skates she'd brought from home.

"I know," Becka agreed, adjusting her lace headband. "But it keeps your feet from getting cold."

Emily tied her skate laces in a bow. It had to be about fifty degrees in the rink, but she was only in a Rosewood Swimming short-sleeve T-shirt. She felt so numb, cold didn't affect her. On the way here, Emily told Becka that her first Tree Tops session was Monday. Becka seemed startled, then happy. Emily didn't say much else the rest of the ride over. All she was thinking about was how she'd rather be with Maya.

Maya. Whenever Emily shut her eyes, she saw Maya's angry face in the greenhouse. Emily's cell phone had been quiet all day. Part of her wanted Maya to call, to try to get Emily back. And then of course, part of her didn't. She tried to look at the positives—now that her parents saw that she was really making a commitment to Tree Tops, they had been kinder to her. At Saturday swim practice, Coach Lauren had told her that the U of A swim coach still wanted to meet with her. All the swim team boys were still hitting on her and inviting Emily to hot-tub parties, but it was better than them making fun of her. And as they were driving home from practice, Carolyn had said, "I like this CD," when Emily slid some old No Doubt into the player. It was a start.

Emily stared at the ice rink. After The Jenna Thing, she and Ali used to come here practically every weekend, and nothing about the place had changed since then. There were still the same blue benches that everyone sat on to lace up their boots, the machine that dispensed hot chocolate that tasted like aspirin, the giant plastic polar bear that greeted everyone at the main entrance. The whole thing was so eerily nostalgic, Emily almost expected to see Ali out on the ice practicing her backward crossovers. The rink was practically empty tonight, though—there were clusters of kids, but no one Emily's age. Most likely, they were all at Mona's party—in a parallel world, Emily would have been there too.

"Becka?"

Emily and Becka looked up. A tall girl with short dark curly hair, a button nose, and hazel eyes stared at them. She had on a pink A-line dress, white cable-knit tights, a delicate pearl bracelet, and hot pink lip gloss. A pair of white ice skates with rainbow laces dangled from her wrists.

"Wendy!" Becka cried, standing up. She went to hug Wendy but then seemed to correct herself and stood back. "You're . . . you're here!"

Wendy had a big smile on her face. "Wow, Becks. You look . . . great."

Becka smiled sheepishly. "So do you." She inspected Wendy almost in disbelief, as if Wendy had been resurrected from the dead. "You cut your hair."

Wendy touched it self-consciously. "Is it too short?"

"No!" Becka said quickly. "It's really cute."

Both of them kept smiling and giggling. Emily coughed, and Becka looked over. "Oh! This is Emily. My new Tree Tops friend."

Emily shook Wendy's hand. Wendy's short fingernails were painted seashell pink, and there was a Pokémon appliqué on her thumb.

Wendy sat down and started lacing up her skates. "Do you guys skate a lot?" Emily asked. "You both have your own skates."

"We used to," Wendy said, glancing at Becka. "We took lessons together. Well . . . sort of."

Becka giggled and Emily glanced at her, confused. "What?"

"Nothing," Becka answered. "Just . . . remember the skate rental room, Wendy?"

"Oh my God." Wendy clapped a hand over her mouth. "The look on that guy's face!"

Oh-*kaaay*. Emily coughed again, and Becka immediately stopped laughing, as if she realized where she was—or, perhaps, *who* she was.

When Wendy finished lacing up, they all stepped onto the rink. Wendy and Becka immediately twirled around and began skating backward. Emily, who only knew how to skate forward in a somewhat jerky fashion, felt bumbling and oafish next to them.

No one said anything for a while. Emily listened to the slicing noises their skates made in the ice. "So, are you still seeing Jeremy?" Wendy asked Becka.

Becka chewed on the end of her wool mitten. "Not really."

"Who's Jeremy?" Emily asked, skirting around a blond girl in a Brownie uniform.

"A guy I met at Tree Tops," Becka answered. She glanced at Wendy uncomfortably. "We went out for a month or two. It didn't really work out."

Wendy shrugged and pushed a lock of hair behind her ear. "Yeah, I was going out with a girl from history class, but it didn't go anywhere either. And I have a blind date next week, but I'm not sure if I'll go. Apparently she's into hip-hop." She wrinkled her nose.

Emily suddenly realized that Wendy had said *she*.

Before she could ask, Becka cleared her throat. Her jaw was tense. "I might go on a blind date, too," she said, louder than usual. "With another boy from Tree Tops."

"Well, good luck with that," Wendy said stiffly, spinning to skate forward again. Only, she didn't take her eyes off Becka, and Becka didn't take her eyes off Wendy. Becka skated up next to Wendy, it seemed like she purposefully bumped hands.

The lights dimmed. A disco ball descended from the ceiling and colored lights swirled around the rink. Everyone except for a few couples tottered off the ice. "Couples skate," said an Isaac Hayes imposter over the loudspeaker. "Grab the one you love."

The three of them collapsed on a nearby bench as Unchained Melody belted out of the speakers. Ali had once remarked that she was tired of sitting out of couples skate. "Why don't we just skate together, Em?" she suggested, offering Emily her hand. Emily would never forget what it felt like to wrap her arms around Ali. To smell the sweet, Granny Smith apple scent of Ali's neck. To squeeze Ali's hands when Ali lost her balance, to accidentally brush her arm against Ali's bare skin.

Emily wondered if she'd remember that event differently next week. Would Tree Tops wipe those feelings from her mind, the way the Zamboni machine smoothed away all the nicks and skate-marks from the ice?

"I'll be back," Emily murmured, stumbling clumsily on the blades of her skates to the bathroom. Inside, she ran her hands under scalding hot water and stared at herself in the streaky mirror. *Doing Tree Tops was the right decision,* she told her reflection. It was the *only* decision. After Tree Tops, she would probably date boys just like Becka did. Right?

When she walked back to the rink, she noticed that Becka and Wendy had left the bench. Emily plopped down, figuring they'd gone to get a snack, and stared at the darkened rink. She saw couples with their hands intertwined. Others were attempting to kiss while skating. One couple hadn't even made it to the ice—they were going at it by one of the entrances. The girl plunged her hands into the guy's curly dark hair.

The slow song abruptly ended and the fluorescent lights snapped back on. Emily's eyes widened at the couple by the door. The girl wore a familiar lace headband. Both were wearing white ice skates. The guy's had rainbow laces. And . . . he was in a pink A-line dress.

Becka and Wendy saw Emily at the same time. Becka's mouth went round, and Wendy looked away. Emily could feel herself shaking.

Becka walked over and stood next to Emily. She exhaled a puff of frosty air. "I guess I should explain, huh?"

The ice smelled cold, like snow. Someone had left a single, child-size red mitten on the next bench over. On the rink, a child swooped by and cried, "I'm an airplane!" Emily stared at Becka. Her chest felt tight.

"I thought Tree Tops worked," Emily said quietly.

Becka ran her hands through her long hair. "I thought it did, too. But after seeing Wendy . . . well, I guess you got the picture." She pulled her Fair Isle sweater's cuffs down over her hands. "Maybe you can't really change."

A hot feeling spread in Emily's stomach. Thinking that Tree Tops could change something so fundamental about her had scared her. It seemed so against the principles of . . . of being human, maybe. But it couldn't. Maya and Becka were right—you *couldn't* change who you were.

Maya. Emily clapped her hand over her mouth. She needed to talk to Maya, right now. "Um, Becka," she said quietly. "Can I ask you a favor?"

Becka's eyes softened. "Sure."

Emily skated for the exit. "I need you to drive me to a party. Right now. There's someone I have to see."

31

THEY FOUGHT THE LAW
AND THE LAW WON

Aria squinted into the lens of her Sony Handycam as Spencer adjusted the rhinestone crown perched atop her head. "Hey, guys," Spencer whispered, sauntering over to an LG flip phone that was lying right side up on the Hastingses' leather couch. "Want to read her texts?"

"I do," Hanna whispered.

Emily stood up from her perch on the leather couch's arm. "I don't know. . . ."

"C'mon. Don't you want to know who texted her?" Spencer demanded. Spencer, Hanna, and Emily gathered around Ali's cell phone. Aria took the camera off the tripod and moved closer, too. She wanted to get all of this on film. All of Ali's secrets. She zoomed in to get a good shot of the cell phone's screen when suddenly she heard a voice from the hall.

"Were you looking at my phone?" Ali shrieked, marching into the room.

"Of course not!" Hanna cried. Ali eyed her cell on the couch, but then turned her attention to Melissa and Ian, who had just come into the kitchen.

"Hey, girls," Ian said, stepping into the family room. He glanced at Spencer. "Cute crown."

Aria retreated back to her tripod. Spencer, Ian, and Ali gathered on the couch, and Spencer began playing talk-show host. Suddenly, a second Ali walked right up to the camera. Her skin looked gray. Her irises were black and her neon-red lipstick was applied clownishly, in wriggly lines around her mouth.

"Aria," Ali's doppelganger commanded, staring straight into the lens. "*Look*. The answer is right in front of you."

Aria furrowed her brow. The rest of the scene was rolling forward as usual—Spencer was asking Ian about base-jumping. Melissa was growing more pissed off as she put away their takeout bags. The other Ali—the normal-looking one on the couch—seemed bored. "What do you mean?" Aria whispered to the Ali in front of the lens.

"It's right in front of you," Ali urged. "Look!"

"Okay, okay," Aria said hastily. She searched the room again. Spencer was leaning into Ian, hanging on his every word. Hanna and Emily were perched against the credenza, seeming relaxed and chill. What was Aria supposed to be looking for?

"I don't understand," she whimpered.

"But it's there!" Ali screamed. "It's. Right. There!"

"I don't know what to do!" Aria argued helplessly.

"Just *look*!"

Aria sprang up in bed. The room was dark. Sweat poured down her face. Her throat hurt. When she looked over, she saw Ezra lying on his side next to her, and jumped.

"It's okay," Ezra said quickly, wrapping his arms around her. "It was just a dream. You're safe."

Aria blinked and looked around. She wasn't in the Hastingses' living room but under the covers of Ezra's futon. The bedroom, which was right off the living room, smelled like mothballs and old-lady perfume, the way all Old Hollis houses smelled. A light, peaceful breeze rippled the blinds, and a William Shakespeare bobblehead nodded on the bureau. Ezra's arms were around her shoulders. His bare feet rubbed her ankles.

"Bad dream?" Ezra asked. "You were screaming."

Aria paused. Was her dream trying to tell her something? "I'm cool," she decided. "It was just one of those weird nightmares."

"You scared me," Ezra said, squeezing her tight.

Aria waited until her breathing returned to normal, listening to the wooden, fish-shaped wind chimes knocking together right outside Ezra's window. Then she noticed that Ezra's glasses were askew. "Did you fall asleep in your glasses?"

Ezra put his hand to the bridge of his nose. "I guess," he said sheepishly. "I fall asleep in them a lot."

Aria leaned forward and kissed him. "You're such a weirdo."

"Not as weird as you, screamer," Ezra teased, pulling her on top of him. "I'm going to get you." He started to tickle her waist.

"No!" Aria shrieked, trying to wriggle away from him. "Stop!"

"Uh-uh!" Ezra bellowed. But his tickling hastily turned into caressing and kissing. Aria shut her eyes and let his hands flutter over her. Then, Ezra flopped back on the pillow. "I wish we could just go away and live somewhere else."

"I know Iceland really well," Aria suggested. "Or what about Costa Rica? We could have a monkey. Or maybe Capri. We could hang out in the Blue Grotto."

"I always wanted to go to Capri," Ezra said softly. "We could live on the beach and write poems."

"As long as our pet monkeys can write poems with us," Aria bargained.

"Of course," Ezra said, kissing her nose. "We can have as many monkeys as you want." He got a far-off look on his face, as if he were actually considering it. Aria felt her insides swell. She'd never felt so happy. This felt . . . right. They would make it work. She would figure out the rest of her life—Sean, A, her parents—tomorrow.

Aria snuggled into Ezra. She started dozing off again,

thinking about dancing monkeys and sandy beaches when suddenly, there was pounding at the front door. Before Aria and Ezra could react, the door split open and two policemen burst inside. Aria screamed. Ezra sat up and straightened his boxers, which had pictures of fried eggs, sausages, and pancakes all over them. The words *Tasty Breakfast!* were scrolled around the waistband. Aria hid under the covers—she was wearing an oversized Hollis University T-shirt of Ezra's that barely covered her thighs.

The cops stomped through Ezra's living room and into his bedroom. They shined their flashlights first over Ezra, then on Aria. She wrapped the sheets around her tighter, scanning the floor for her clothes and undies. They were gone.

"Are you Ezra Fitz?" demanded the cop, a burly, Popeye-armed man with slick black hair.

"Uh . . . yeah," Ezra stammered.

"And you teach at Rosewood Day School?" Popeye asked. "Is this the girl? Your *student?*"

"What the hell is going on?" Ezra shrieked.

"You're under arrest." Popeye unhooked silver handcuffs from his belt. The other cop, who was shorter and fatter and had shiny skin that Aria could only describe as ham-colored, yanked Ezra out of bed. The threadbare, grayish sheets went with him, exposing Aria's bare legs. She screamed and dropped to the other side of the bed to hide. She found a pair of plaid pajama pants balled up behind the radiator. She stuffed her legs into them as fast as she could.

"You have the right to remain silent," Ham-face began. "Anything you say can and will be used against you in a court of law."

"Wait!" Ezra screamed.

But the cops didn't listen. Ham-face spun Ezra around and snapped the cuffs on his wrists. He glanced disgustedly at Ezra's futon. Ezra's jeans and T-shirt were snarled up near the headboard. Aria suddenly noticed that the lacy black bra she'd had custom-fitted in Belgium was snagged on one of the bedposts. She quickly ripped it down.

They shoved Ezra through the living room and out his own door, which hung precariously on one hinge. Aria ran after them, not even bothering to put on her check-erboard Vans, which waited in the second ballet position on the floor near the television. "You can't do this!" she shouted.

"We'll deal with you next, little girl," Popeye growled.

She hesitated in the dingy, dimly lit front hall. The cops restrained Ezra like he was a skinny, breakfast-boxer-clad mental patient. Ham-face kept stepping on his knobby bare feet. It made Aria love him even more.

As they bumbled out the door and onto the front porch, Aria realized someone else was in the hall with her. Her mouth fell open.

"Sean," Aria sputtered. "What . . . what are you doing here?"

Sean was crumpled up against the gray mailbox unit, staring at Aria with dread and disappointment. "What are you doing here?" he demanded, staring pointedly at Ezra's oversize pajama pants, which were threatening to fall down to her ankles. She quickly yanked them back up.

"I was going to explain," Aria mumbled.

"Oh yeah?" Sean challenged, putting his hands on his hips. He looked sharper tonight, meaner. Not the soft Sean she knew. "How long have you been with him?"

Aria silently stared at an Acme market coupon circular that had fallen on the floor.

"I've packed up all your stuff," Sean went on, not even waiting for her answer. "It's on the porch. There's no way you're coming back to my house."

"But . . . Sean . . ." Aria said weakly. "Where will I go?"

"That's not my problem," he snapped, storming out the front door.

Aria felt woozy. Through the open door, she could see the cops guiding Ezra down his front walk and pushing him into a Rosewood Police cruiser. After they slammed the back door, Ezra glanced toward his house again. He looked at Aria, then Sean, then back again. There was a betrayed look on his face.

A light switched on in Aria's head. She followed Sean to the porch and grabbed his arm. "*You* called the police, didn't you?"

Sean crossed his arms over his chest and looked away. She felt dizzy and sick, and clutched the porch's rusty blue-gray glider for balance.

"Well once I got this . . ." Sean whipped out his cell phone and brought it close to Aria's face. On the screen was a picture of Aria and Ezra kissing in Ezra's office. Sean hit the side arrow. There was another photo of them kissing, just from a different angle. "I figured I should let the authorities know a teacher was with a student." His lips curled around the word *student,* as if it was disgusting to him. "And on school property," he added.

"I didn't mean to hurt you," Aria whispered. And then, she noticed the text message that accompanied the last photo. Her heart sank a few thousand feet deeper.

Dear Sean, I think someone's girlfriend has a LOT of explaining to do. —A

32

NOT-SO-SECRET LOVERS

"And they were all over each other!" Emily took a huge sip of the sangria Maya had gotten for them from the planetarium bar. "All this time, I was afraid they could, like, change you, but it turns out that it's fake! My sponsor's back with her girlfriend and everything!"

Maya gave Emily a crazy look, poking her in the ribs. "You seriously thought they could change you?"

Emily leaned back. "I guess that *is* stupid, isn't it?"

"*Yes.*" Maya smiled. "But I'm glad it doesn't work too."

About an hour ago, Becka and Wendy had dropped Emily off at Mona's party and she had torn through the rooms, searching for Maya, terrified that she had left—or worse, that she was with someone else. She'd found Maya by herself near the DJ booth, wearing a black-and-white striped dress and patent-leather Mary Janes. Her hair was up in white butterfly clips.

They had escaped outside to a little patch of grass in

the planetarium's garden. They could see the party still raging through the two-story, frosted-glass windows, but they couldn't hear it. Shady trees, telescopes, and bushes pruned into the shapes of planets filled the garden. A few of the partygoers had spilled out and were sitting on the other side of the patio, smoking and laughing, and there was a couple making out by the giant, Saturn-shaped topiary, but Emily and Maya were pretty much sequestered. They hadn't kissed or anything, but were merely staring up at the sky. It had to be almost midnight, which was normally Emily's curfew, but she'd called her mom to say that she would be staying the night at Becka's. Becka had agreed to corroborate the story, if need be.

"Look," Emily said, pointing at the stars. "That section of stars up there, don't they look like they could form an *E* if you drew lines between them?"

"Where?" Maya squinted.

Emily positioned Maya's chin correctly. "There are stars next to them that form an *M*." She smiled in the darkness. "*E* and *M*. Emily and Maya. It's, like, a sign."

"You and your signs," Maya sighed. They were comfortably quiet for a second.

"I was furious at you," Maya said softly. "Breaking up with me in the kiln like that. Refusing to even look at me in the greenhouse."

Emily squeezed her hand and stared at the constellations. A tiny jet streaked past, a thousand feet up. "I'm sorry," she said. "I know I haven't exactly been fair."

Now Maya eyed Emily carefully. Glittery bronzer illuminated her forehead, cheeks, and nose. She looked more beautiful than Emily had ever seen her. "Can I hold your hand?" she whispered.

Emily gazed at her own rough, square hand. It had held pencils and paintbrushes and pieces of chalk. Gripped the starting blocks before a swimming race. Clutched a balloon on the swim team's homecoming float last year. It had held her boyfriend Ben's hand . . . and it had even held Maya's, but it seemed like this time it was more official. It was real.

She knew there were people around. But Maya was right—everyone already knew. The hard part was over, and she'd survived. She'd been miserable with Ben, and she hadn't been kidding anybody with Toby. Maybe she should be out there with this. As soon as Becka had said it, Emily knew she was right: she *couldn't* change who she was. The idea was terrifying but thrilling.

Emily touched Maya's hand. First lightly, then harder. "I love you, Em," Maya said, squeezing back. "I love you so much."

"I love you, too," Emily repeated, almost automatically. And she realized—she did. More than anyone else, more than Ali, even. Emily had kissed Ali, and for a split second, Ali had kissed her back. But then Ali had pulled back, disgusted. She'd quickly started talking about some boy she was really into, a boy whose name she wouldn't tell Emily because Emily might "really freak." Now Emily wondered if there even *had* been a boy, or if Ali had said it to undo the tiny moment when she had kissed Emily for real. To say, *I'm not a lesbo. No frickin' way.*

All this time, Emily had fantasized about what things would have been like if Ali hadn't disappeared, and if that summer and their friendship had proceeded as planned. Now she knew: it wouldn't have gone on. If Ali hadn't disappeared, she would have drifted farther and farther away from Emily. But maybe Emily would still have found her way to Maya.

"You okay?" Maya asked, noting Emily's silence.

"Yeah." They sat quietly for a few minutes, holding hands. Then Maya lifted her head, frowning at something inside the planetarium. Emily followed her eyes to a shadowy figure, staring straight at them. The figure knocked on the glass, making Emily jump.

"Who is that?" Emily murmured.

"Whoever it is," Maya said, squinting, "they're coming outside."

Every hair on Emily's body stood up. *A?* She scooted backward. Then she heard an all-too-familiar voice. "Emily Catherine Fields! Get over here!"

Maya's mouth dropped open. "Oh my God."

Emily's mother stepped under the courtyard spotlights. Her hair was uncombed, she wore no makeup, she had on a ratty T-shirt, and her sneaker lace was untied. She looked ridiculous among the throng of done-up partygoers. A few kids gaped at her.

Emily clumsily struggled off the grass. "W-what are you doing here?"

Mrs. Fields grabbed Emily's arm. "I *cannot* believe you. I get a call fifteen minutes ago saying you're with *her*. And I don't believe them! Silly me! I don't believe them! I say they're lying!"

"Mom, I can explain!"

Mrs. Fields paused and sniffed the air around Emily's face. Her eyes widened. "You've been drinking!" she screamed, enraged. "What has *happened* to you, Emily?" She glanced down at Maya, who was sitting very still on the grass, as if Mrs. Fields had put her in suspended animation. "You're *not* my daughter anymore."

"Mom!" Emily screamed. It felt like her mother had thrust a curling iron into her eye. That statement sounded so . . . legal and binding. So final.

Mrs. Fields dragged her to the little gate that led from the courtyard to a back alley that led to the street. "I'm calling Helene when we get home."

"No!" Emily broke free, then faced her mother halfway hunched over, the way a sumo wrestler squares off when he's about to fight. "How can you say I'm not your daughter?" she screeched. "How can you send me away?"

Mrs. Fields reached for Emily's arm again, but Emily's sneakers caught on an uneven divot in the grass. She fell backward, hitting the ground on her tailbone, experiencing a white, blinding flash of pain.

When she opened her eyes, her mother was above her. "Get up. Let's go."

"No!" Emily bellowed. She tried to get up, but her mother's nails pierced her arm. Emily struggled but knew it was hopeless. She glanced once more at Maya, who still hadn't moved. Maya's eyes were huge and watery, and she looked tiny and alone. *I might never see her again*, Emily thought. *This might be it.*

"What's so wrong with it?" she screamed at her mother. "What's so wrong with being different? How can you *hate* me for that?"

Her mother's nostrils flared. She balled up her fists and opened her mouth, ready to scream something back. And then, suddenly, she seemed to deflate. She turned away and made a small noise at the back of her throat. All at once, she looked so spent. And scared. And ashamed. Without any makeup on and in her pajamas, she seemed vulnerable. There was a redness around her eyes, as if she had been crying for a long time. "Please. Let's just go."

Emily didn't know what else to do but get up. She followed her mother down the dark, deserted alley and into a parking lot, where Emily saw their familiar Volvo. The parking lot attendant met her mother's eyes and gave Emily a judging sneer, as if Mrs. Fields had explained why she was parking here and retrieving Emily from the party.

Emily threw herself in the front seat. Her eyes landed

on the Dial-a-Horoscope laminated wheel that was in the car's seat pocket. The wheel foretold every sign's horoscopes for all the twelve months of this year, so Emily pulled it out, spun the wheel to Taurus, her sign, and looked at October's predictions. *Your love relationships will become more fulfilling and satisfying. Your relationships may have caused difficulties with others in the past, but all will be smooth sailing from now on.*

Ha, Emily thought. She hurled the horoscope card out the window. She didn't believe in horoscopes anymore. Or tarot cards. Or signs or signals or anything else that said things happened for a reason. What was the reason *this* was happening?

A chill went through her. *I get a call fifteen minutes ago saying you're with her.*

She dug through her bag, her heart pounding. Her phone had one new message. It had been in her inbox for nearly two hours.

Em, I see you! And if you don't stop it, I'm calling you-know-who. —A

Emily put her hands over her eyes. Why didn't A just kill her instead?

33

SOMEONE SLIPS UP. BIG TIME.

First, Lucas gave Hanna a shrunken Rosewood Day sweatshirt and a pair of red gym shorts from his car. "An Eagle Scout is always prepared for anything," he proclaimed.

Second, he led Hanna to the Hollis College Reading Room so she could change. It was a few streets over from the planetarium. The reading room was simply that—a big room in a nineteenth-century house completely devoted to chilling out and reading. It smelled like pipe smoke and old leather bookbindings and was filled with all sorts of books, maps, globes, encyclopedias, magazines, newspapers, chessboards, leather couches, and cozy love seats for two. Technically, it was only open to college students and faculty, but it was easy enough to jimmy your way in the side door.

Hanna went into the tiny bathroom, removed her ripped dress, and threw it into the little chrome trash can, stuffing it in so it would fit. She slumped out of the bathroom, threw herself on the couch next to Lucas, and just . . . lost it. Sobs that had been pent up inside of her for weeks—maybe even years—exploded out of her. "No one will like me anymore," she said chokingly, between sobs. "And I've lost Mona forever."

Lucas rubbed her hair. "It's all right. She doesn't deserve you anyway."

Hanna cried until her eyes swelled and her throat stung. Finally, she pressed her head into Lucas's chest, which was more solid than it looked. They lay there in silence for a while. Lucas ran his fingers through her hair.

"What made you come to her party?" she asked after a while. "I thought you weren't invited."

"I was invited." Lucas lowered his eyes. "But . . . I wasn't going to go. I didn't want you to feel bad, and I wanted to spend the night with you."

Little sparkles of giddiness snapped through her stomach. "I'm so sorry," she said quietly. "Bagging our poker game at the last minute like that, for Mona's stupid party."

"It's okay," Lucas said. "It doesn't matter."

Hanna stared at Lucas. He had such soft blue eyes and adorably pink cheeks. It *did* matter to her, a lot. She was so consumed with doing the perfect thing all the time—wearing the perfect outfit, picking out the perfect ringtone, keeping her body in perfect shape, having the perfect best friend and the perfect boyfriend—but what was all that perfection for? Maybe Lucas was perfect, just in a different way. He *cared* about her.

Hanna didn't quite know how it had happened, but they'd settled in on one of the cracked-leather love seats, and she was on Lucas's lap. Strangely, she didn't feel self-conscious that she was breaking Lucas's legs. Last summer, to prepare for her trip with Sean's family to Cape Cod, Hanna had eaten nothing but grapefruit and cayenne pepper, and she hadn't let Sean touch her when she was wearing her bathing suit, afraid he'd find her Jell-O-ish. With Lucas, she didn't worry.

Her face moved closer to Lucas's. His face moved closer to hers. She felt his lips touch her chin, then the side of her mouth, then her mouth itself. Her heart pounded. His lips whispered across hers. He pulled her toward him. Hanna's heart was beating so fast and excitedly, she was afraid it would burst. Lucas cradled Hanna's head in his hands and kissed her ears. Hanna giggled.

"What?" Lucas said, pulling away.

"Nothing," Hanna answered, grinning. "I don't know. This is fun."

It *was* fun—nothing like the serious, important make-out sessions she'd had with Sean, where she felt like a panel of judges was scoring each and every kiss. Lucas was sloppy, wet, and overly joyful, like a boy Labrador. Every so often, he'd grab her and squeeze. At one point, he started tickling her, making Hanna squeal and roll off the couch right onto the floor.

Eventually, they were lying on one of the couches,

Lucas on top of her, his hands drifting up and down her bare stomach. He took off his shirt and pressed his chest against hers. After a while, they stopped and lay there, saying nothing. Hanna's eyes grazed across all the books, chess sets, and busts of famous authors. Then, suddenly, she sat up.

Someone was looking in the window.

"Lucas!" She pointed to a dark shape moving toward the side door.

"Don't panic," Lucas said, easing off the couch and creeping toward the window. The bushes shook. A lock began to turn. Hanna clamped down on Lucas's arm.

A was here.

"Lucas . . ."

"Shhh." Another click. Somewhere, a lock was turning. Someone was coming in. Lucas cocked his head to listen. Now there were footsteps coming from the back hall. Hanna took a step backward. The floor creaked. The footsteps came closer.

"Hello?" Lucas grabbed his shirt and pulled it on backward. "Who's there?"

No one answered. There were more creaks. A shadow slithered across the wall.

Hanna looked around and grabbed the largest thing she could find—a *Farmer's Almanac* from 1972. Suddenly, a light flicked on. Hanna screamed and raised the almanac over her head. Standing before them was an older man with a beard. He wore small, wire-framed glasses and a corduroy jacket and held his hands over his head in surrender.

"I'm with the history department!" the old man sputtered. "I couldn't sleep. I came here to read. . . ." He looked at Hanna strangely. Hanna realized the neck of Lucas's sweatshirt was pulled to the side, exposing her bare shoulder.

Hanna's heart started to slow down. She put the book back on the table. "Sorry," she said. "I thought–"

"We'd better go anyway." Lucas sidestepped the old man and pulled Hanna out the side door. When they were next to the house's iron front gate, he burst into giggles.

"Did you see that guy's face?" he hooted. "He was terrified!"

Hanna tried to laugh along, but she felt too shaken. "We should go," she whispered, her voice trembling. "I want to go home."

Lucas walked Hanna to the valet at Mona's party. She gave the valet the ticket for her Prius, and when he brought it back, she made Lucas look all through it to make sure no one was hiding in the backseat. When she was safely inside with the door locked, Lucas tapped his hand against the window and mouthed that he'd call her tomorrow. Hanna watched him walk away, feeling both excited and horribly distracted.

She started down the planetarium's spiral drive. Every twenty feet or so was a banner advertising the new exhibit. THE BIG BANG, they all said. They showed a picture of the universe exploding.

When Hanna's cell phone beeped, she jumped so

violently, she nearly broke out of the seat belt. She pulled over into the bus lane and whipped her phone out of her bag with trembling fingers. She had a new text.

Oops, guess it wasn't lipo! Don't believe everything you hear! —A

Hanna looked up. The street outside the planetarium was quiet. All the old houses were closed up tight, and there wasn't a single person on the street. A breeze kicked up, making the flag on the porch of an old Victorian house flap and a jack-o'-lantern-shaped leaf bag on its front lawn flutter.

Hanna looked back down at the text. This was odd. A's latest text wasn't from *caller unknown*, as it usually was, but an actual number. And it was a 610 number—Rosewood's area code.

The number seemed familiar, although Hanna never memorized anyone's number—she'd gotten a cell in seventh grade and had since relied on speed dial. There was something about this number, though. . . .

Hanna covered her mouth with her hand. "Oh my God," she whispered. She thought about it another moment. Could it *seriously* be?

Suddenly, she knew exactly who A was.

34

IT'S RIGHT THERE IN FRONT OF YOU

"Another coffee?" A waitress who smelled like grilled cheese and had a very large mole on her chin hovered over Aria, waving a coffee carafe around.

Aria glanced at her nearly empty mug. Her parents would probably say this coffee was loaded with carcinogens, but what did they know? "Sure," she answered.

This was what it had come to. Aria sitting in a booth at the diner near Ezra's house in Old Hollis with all of her worldly goods—her laptop, her bike, her clothes, her books—around her. She had nowhere to go. Not Sean's, not Ezra's, not even her own family's. The diner was the only place open right now, unless you counted the twenty-four-hour Taco Bell, which was a total stoner hangout.

She stared at her Treo, weighing her options. Finally, she dialed her home number. The phone rang six times before the answering machine picked up. "Thanks for calling the Montgomerys," Ella's cheery voice rang out.

"We're not home right now. . . ."

Please. Where on earth would Ella be after midnight on a Saturday? "Mom, pick up," Aria said into the machine after it beeped. "I know you're there." Still nothing. She sighed. "Listen. I need to come home tonight. I broke up with my boyfriend. I have nowhere else to stay. I'm sitting at a diner, homeless."

She paused, waiting for Ella to answer. She didn't. Aria could imagine her standing over the phone, listening. Or maybe she wasn't at all. Maybe she'd heard Aria's voice and walked back up the stairs to bed. "Mom, I'm in danger," she pleaded. "I can't explain how, exactly, but I'm . . . I'm afraid something's going to happen to me."

Beep. The answering machine tape cut her off. Aria let her phone clatter to the Formica tabletop. She could call back, but what would be the point? She could almost hear her mother's voice: *I can't even look at you right now.*

She lifted her head, considering something. Slowly, Aria picked up her Treo again and scrolled through her texts. Byron's text with his number was still there. Taking a deep breath, she dialed. Byron's sleepy voice answered.

"It's Aria," she said quietly.

"Aria?" Byron echoed. He sounded stunned. "It's, like, two in the morning."

"I know." The diner's jukebox switched records. The waitress married two ketchup bottles. The last remaining people besides Aria got up from their booth, waved good-bye to the waitress, and pushed through the front door. The diner's bells jingled.

Byron broke the silence. "Well, it's nice to hear from you."

Aria curled her knees into her chest. She wanted to tell him that he'd messed up everything, making her keep his secret, but she felt too drained to fight. And also . . . part of her really missed Byron. Byron was her dad, the only dad she knew. He had warded off a snake that had slithered into Aria's path during a hiking trip to the Grand Canyon. He'd gone down to talk to Aria's fifth-grade art teacher, Mr. Cunningham, when he gave Aria an F on her self-portrait because she had drawn herself with green scales and a forked tongue. "Your teacher simply doesn't understand postmodern expressionism," Byron had said, grabbing his coat to go do battle. Byron used to pick her up, throw her over his shoulder, carry her to bed, and tuck her in. Aria missed that. She *needed* that. She wanted to tell him she was in danger. And she wanted him to say, "I'll protect you." He would, wouldn't he?

But then she heard someone's voice in the background. "Everything okay, Byron?"

Aria bristled. *Meredith.*

"Be there in a sec," Byron called.

Aria fumed. A *sec*? That was all he planned to devote to this conversation? Byron's voice returned to the phone. "Aria? So . . . what's up?"

"Never mind," Aria said icily. "Go back to bed, or

whatever you were doing."

"Aria—" Byron started.

"Seriously, go," Aria said stiffly. "Forget I called."

She hit END and put her head on the table. She tried to breathe in and out, thinking calm thoughts, like about the ocean, or riding a bicycle, or the mindlessness of knitting a scarf.

A few minutes later, she looked around the diner and realized she was the only person there. The ripped, faded counter stools were all vacant, the booths all cleaned off and empty. Two carafes of coffee sat on warmers behind the counter, and the cash register's screen still glowed WELCOME, but the waitresses and cooks had all vanished. It was like one of those horror movies where somehow, all at once, the main character looks up to find everyone dead.

Ali's killer is closer than you think.

Why didn't A just *tell* her who the killer was? She was sick of playing Scooby-Doo. Aria thought of her dream again, of how that pale, ghostly Ali had stepped in front of the camera. "Look closer!" she'd screamed. "It's right in front of you! It's right there!" But *what* was right there? What had Aria missed?

The waitress with the mole trundled out from behind the counter and eyed Aria. "Want a piece of pie? The apple's edible. On the house."

"Th-that's okay," Aria stuttered.

The waitress leaned an ample hip against one of the

counter's pink stools. She had the kind of curly black hair that always looked wet. "You heard about the stalker?"

"Uh-huh," Aria answered.

"You know what I heard?" the waitress said. "It's a *rich* kid." When Aria didn't respond, she went back to washing an already clean table.

Aria blinked a few times. *Look closer,* Ali had said. She reached into her messenger bag and opened her laptop. It took a while to boot up, and then it took even longer for Aria to find the file folder that held her old videos. It had been so long since she'd searched for them. When she finally unearthed it, she realized that none of the video files were labeled very accurately. They were titled things like "Us Five, #1," or "Ali and Me, #6," and the dates were from when they'd last been viewed, not when they were made. She had no idea how to find the video that had been leaked to the press . . . besides going through all of them.

She clicked randomly on a video titled "Meow!" Aria, Ali, and the others were in Ali's bedroom. They were struggling to dress up Ali's Himalayan cat, Charlotte, in a hand-knit sweater, giggling as they stuffed her legs through the armholes.

She watched another movie called "Fight #5," but it wasn't what she thought it would be—she, Ali, and the others were making chocolate-chip cookies and got in a food fight, flinging cookie dough around Hanna's kitchen. In another, they were playing foosball on the table in

Spencer's basement.

When Aria clicked on a new MPEG that was simply called "DQ," she noticed something.

By the looks of Ali's haircut and all their new warm-weather clothes, the video was from a month or so before Ali had gone missing. Aria had zoomed in on a shot of Hanna downing a monster-size Dairy Queen Blizzard in record time. In the background, she heard Ali start making retching noises. Hanna paused, and her face quickly drained of color. Ali giggled in the background. No one else seemed to notice.

A strange sensation slithered over Aria. She'd heard the rumors that Hanna had a bulimia problem. It seemed like something that A—and Ali—would know.

She clicked on another. They were flipping through the channels at Emily's house. Ali stopped on a newscast of a Gay Pride parade that had taken place in Philly earlier that day. She turned pointedly to Emily and grinned. "That looks fun, doesn't it, Em?" Emily turned red and pulled her sweatshirt hood around her head. None of the others batted an eye.

And another. This one was only sixteen seconds long. The five of them were lounging around Spencer's pool. They all wore massive Gucci sunglasses—or, in Emily and Aria's case, knockoffs. Ali sat up and pushed her glasses down her nose. "Hey, Aria," she said abruptly. "What does your dad do if, like, he gets sexy students in his class?"

The clip ended. Aria remembered that day—it had

been shortly after the time she and Ali had discovered Byron and Meredith kissing in Byron's car, and Ali had begun dropping hints that she was going to tell the others.

Ali really *did* know all their secrets, and she'd been dangling them over their heads. It had all been right in front of them, and they hadn't realized it. Ali had known everything. About all of them. And now, A did, too.

Except . . . what was Spencer's secret?

Aria clicked on another video. Finally, she saw the familiar scene. There was Spencer, sitting on her couch with that crown on her head. "Want to read her texts?" She pointed at Ali's LG phone, which was lying between the couch cushions.

Spencer opened Ali's phone. "It's locked."

"Do you know her password?" Aria heard her own voice ask.

"Try her birthday," Hanna whispered.

"Were you looking at my phone?" Ali screamed.

The phone clattered to the ground. Just then, Spencer's older sister, Melissa, and her boyfriend, Ian, walked past the camera. Both of them smiled into the lens. "Hey, guys," Melissa said. "What's up?"

Spencer batted her eyes. Ali looked bored. The camera zoomed in on her face and panned down to the closed phone.

"Oh, this is the clip I've seen on the news," said a voice behind Aria. The waitress was leaning against the counter, filing her nails with a Tweety Bird nail file.

Aria paused the clip and whirled around. "I'm sorry?"

The waitress blushed. "Oops. When it's dead like this, I turn into my evil eavesdropping twin. I didn't mean to look at your computer. That poor boy, though."

Aria squinted at her. She noticed for the first time that the waitress's name tag said ALISON. Spelled the same way and everything. "What poor boy?" she asked.

Alison pointed at the screen. "No one ever talks about the boyfriend. He must have been so heartbroken."

Aria stared at the screen, baffled. She pointed at Ian's frozen image. "That's not her boyfriend. He's with the girl who's in the kitchen. She's not on-screen."

"No?" Alison shrugged and started wiping the counter again. "The way they're sitting . . . I just assumed."

Aria didn't know what to say. She set the video back to the beginning, confused. She and her friends tried to hack Ali's phone, Ali came back, Melissa and Ian smiled, cinematic shot of closed phone, *finis*.

She restarted the movie one more time, this time at half-speed. Spencer slowly readjusted her crown. Ali's cell phone dragged across the screen. Ali came back, every expression languid and contorted. Instead of scurrying past, Melissa plodded. Suddenly, she noticed something in the corner of the screen: the edge of a small, slender hand. Ali's hand. Then came another hand. It was larger and masculine. She slowed down the frame speed. Every so often, the big hand and the little hand bumped each other. Their pinkies intertwined.

Aria gasped.

The camera swung up. It showed Ian, who was looking at something beyond the camera. Off to the right was Spencer, looking longingly at Ian, not realizing he and Ali were touching. The whole thing happened in a blink. But now that she saw it, it was all so obvious.

Someone wanted something of Ali's. Her killer is closer than you think.

Aria felt sick. They all knew Spencer liked Ian. She talked about him constantly: how her sister didn't deserve him, how he was so funny, how cute he was when he ate dinner at their house. And all of them had wondered if Ali was keeping a big secret—it could have been *this*. Ali must have told Spencer. And Spencer couldn't deal.

Aria put more pieces together. Ali had run out of Spencer's barn . . . and turned up not that far away, in a hole in her own backyard. Spencer knew that the workers were going to fill the hole with concrete the very next day. A's note had said: *You all knew every inch of her backyard. But for one of you, it was so, so easy.*

Aria sat motionless for a few seconds, then picked up her own phone and dialed Emily's number. The phone rang six times before Emily answered. "Hello?" Emily's voice sounded like she'd been crying.

"Did I wake you up?" Aria asked.

"I haven't gone to sleep yet."

Aria frowned. "Are you okay?"

"No," Emily's voice cracked. Aria heard a sniffle. "My parents are sending me away. I'm leaving Rosewood in the morning. Because of A."

Aria leaned back. "*What?* Why?"

"It's not even worth getting into." Emily sounded defeated.

"You have to meet me," Aria said. "Right now."

"Didn't you hear what I said? I'm punished. I'm *beyond* punished."

"You have to." Aria turned into the booth, trying to hide what she was about to say from the diner staff as best she could. "I think I know who killed Ali."

Silence. "No, you don't," Emily said.

"I do. We have to call Hanna."

There was scratching at Emily's end of the phone. After a short pause, her voice came back. "Aria," she whispered, "I'm getting another call. It's *Hanna.*"

A shiver went through Aria. "Put her on three-way."

There was a click, and Aria heard Hanna's voice. "You guys," Hanna was saying. She sounded out of breath and the connection was rumbly, like Hanna was talking through a fan. "You're not going to believe this. A messed up. I mean, I think A messed up. I got this note from this number and I suddenly *knew* whose number it was, and . . ."

In the background, Aria heard a horn honk. "Meet me

at our spot," Hanna said. "The Rosewood Day swings."

"Okay," Aria breathed. "Emily, can you come pick me up at the Hollis Diner?"

"Sure," Emily whispered.

"Good," Hanna said. "Hurry."

35

WORDS WHISPERED FROM THE PAST

Spencer shut her eyes. When she opened them, she was standing outside the barn in her backyard. She looked around. Had she been *transported* here? Had she run out here and not remembered?

Suddenly, the barn door swung open and Ali stormed out. "Fine," Ali said over her shoulder, arms swinging confidently. "See ya." She walked right past Spencer, as if Spencer were a ghost.

It was the night Ali went missing again. Spencer started breathing faster. As much as she didn't want to be here, she knew that she needed to see all of this—to remember as much as she could.

"Fine!" she heard herself scream from inside the barn. As Ali stormed down the path, Spencer, younger and smaller, flew to the porch. "Ali!" the thirteen-year-old Spencer screamed, looking around.

Then, it was like the seventeen-year-old Spencer and

the thirteen-year-old Spencer merged into one. She could suddenly feel all the emotions of her younger self. There was fear: what had she done, telling Ali to leave? There was paranoia: none of them had ever challenged Ali. And Ali was angry with her. What was she going to do?

"Ali!" Spencer screamed. The tiny, pagoda-shaped lanterns on the footpath back to the main house provided only a whisper of light. It seemed like things were moving in the woods. Years ago, Melissa had told Spencer that evil trolls lived in the trees. The trolls hated Spencer and wanted to hack off her hair.

Spencer walked to where the path split: she could either go toward her house, or toward the woods that bounded her property. She wished she'd brought a flashlight. A bat swooped out of the trees. As it flew away, Spencer noticed someone far down the path near the woods, hunched over and looking at her cell phone. Ali.

"What are you doing?" Spencer called out.

Ali narrowed her eyes. "I'm going somewhere way cooler than hanging out with you guys."

Spencer stiffened. "Fine," she said proudly. "Go."

Ali sank onto one hip. The crickets chirped at least twenty times before she spoke again. "You try to steal everything away from me. But you can't have this."

"Can't have what?" Spencer shivered in her tissue-thin T-shirt.

Ali laughed nastily. "*You* know."

Spencer blinked. "No . . . I don't."

"Come on. You read about it in my diary, didn't you?"

"I wouldn't read your stupid diary," Spencer spat. "I don't care."

"Right." Ali took a step toward Spencer. "You care way too *much*."

"You're delusional," Spencer sputtered.

"No, I'm not." Ali was right next to her now. "*You* are."

Anger boiled up inside Spencer, and she shoved Ali on the shoulder. It was forceful enough to make Ali stagger back, losing her footing on the path's rocks, which were slippery with dew. The older Spencer winced. She felt like she was a pawn, being dragged along for the ride. A look of surprise crossed Ali's face, but it quickly turned to mocking. "Friends don't shove friends."

"Well, maybe we're not friends," Spencer said.

"Guess not," Ali said. Her eyes danced. The look on her face indicated she had something really juicy to say. There was a long pause before she spoke, as if she was considering her words very, very carefully. *Hang on,* Spencer urged herself. *REMEMBER.*

"You think kissing Ian was so special," Ali growled. "But you know what he told me? That you didn't even know how."

Spencer searched Ali's face. "Ian . . . wait. Ian told you that? When?"

"When we were on our date."

Spencer stared at her.

Ali rolled her eyes. "You're so lame, acting like you don't know we're together. But of course you do, Spence. That's why you liked him, isn't it? Because *I'm* with him? Because your sister's with him?" She shrugged. "The only reason he kissed you the other night was because I asked him to. He didn't want to, but I begged."

Spencer's eyes boggled. *"Why?"*

Ali shrugged. "I wanted to see if he would do *anything* for me." Her face went into a mock pout. "Oh, Spence. Did you really believe he *liked* you?"

Spencer took a step back. Lightning bugs strobed in the sky. There was a poisonous smile on Ali's face. *Don't do it,* Spencer screamed to herself. *Please! It doesn't matter! Don't!*

But it happened anyway. Spencer reached out and pushed Ali as hard as she could. Ali slid backward, her eyes widening in alarm. She fell straight into the stone wall that surrounded the Hastings property. There was a terrible *crack*. Spencer covered her eyes and turned away. The air smelled metallic, like blood. An owl screeched in the trees.

When she took her hands away from her eyes, she was back in her bedroom again, curled up and screaming.

Spencer sat up and checked the clock. It was 2:30 A.M. Her head throbbed. The lights were all still on, she was lying on top of her covers, and she was still wearing her black party dress and Elsa Peretti silver bean necklace. She hadn't washed her face or brushed her hair one hundred times, her typical before-bed rituals. She ran her hands over her arms and legs. There was a purplish bruise on her thigh. She touched it and it ached.

She clapped a hand over her mouth. That memory. She instantly knew all of it was true. Ali was with *Ian*. And she had forgotten all of it. That was the part of the night that was missing.

She walked to her door, but the handle wouldn't turn. Her heart started to pound. "Hello?" she called tentatively. "Is someone there? I'm locked in."

No one answered.

Spencer felt her pulse start to speed up. Something felt really, really wrong. Part of the night surged back to her. The Scrabble game. LIAR SJH. A sending Melissa the Golden Orchid essay. And . . . and then what? She cupped her hands over the crown of her head, as if trying to jostle the memory free. *And then what?*

All at once, she couldn't control her breathing. She started to hyperventilate, sinking to her knees on the ivory carpet. *Calm down,* she told herself, curling into a ball and trying to breathe easily in and out. But it felt like her lungs were filled with Styrofoam peanuts. She felt like she was drowning. "Help!" she cried weakly.

"Spencer?" Her father's voice emerged from the other side of the door. "What's going on?"

Spencer jumped up and ran to the door. "Daddy? I'm locked in! Let me out!"

"Spencer, you're in there for your own good. You scared us."

"Scared you?" Spencer asked. "H-how?" She stared at her reflection in the mirror on the back of her bedroom door. Yes, it was still her. She hadn't woken up in someone else's life.

"We've taken Melissa to the hospital," her father said.

Spencer suddenly lost equilibrium. *Melissa? Hospital? Why?* She shut her eyes and saw a flash of Melissa falling away from her, down the stairs. Or was that Ali falling? Spencer's hands shook. She couldn't *remember*. "Is Melissa all right?"

"We hope so. Stay there," her father said from outside the door, sounding wary. Perhaps he was afraid of her—perhaps that was why he wasn't coming in.

She sat on her bed, stunned, for a long time. How could she not have remembered this? How could she not remember hurting Melissa? What if she did lots of horrible things and, in the next second, erased them?

Ali's murderer is right in front of you, A had said. Just when Spencer was looking in the mirror. Could it be?

Her cell phone, which was sitting on her desk, began to ring. Spencer stood up slowly and looked at the screen on her Sidekick. *Hanna.*

Spencer opened her phone. She pressed her ear to the receiver.

"Spencer?" Hanna jumped right in. "I know something. You have to meet me."

Spencer's stomach tightened and her mind whirled. *Ali's killer is right in front of you. She* killed Ali. She *didn't* kill Ali. It was like pulling petals off a flower: *he loves me, he loves me not.* Perhaps she could meet Hanna and . . . and what? Confess?

No. It couldn't be true. Ali had turned up in a hole in her backyard . . . not on the path against the stone wall. Spencer couldn't have carried Ali to her backyard. She wasn't strong enough, right? She wanted to tell someone about this. Hanna. And Emily. Aria, too. They would tell her she was crazy, that she *couldn't* have killed Ali.

"Okay," Spencer croaked. "Where?"

"At the Rosewood Day Elementary swings. Our place. Get there as fast as you can."

Spencer looked around. She could hoist up her window and shimmy down the face of her house—it would be practically as easy as climbing the rock wall at her gym.

"All right," she whispered. "I'll be right there."

36

IT WILL ALL BE OVER

Hanna's hands were shaking so badly, she could barely drive. The road to the Rosewood Day Elementary School swings seemed darker and spookier than usual. She swerved, thinking she saw something darting out in front of her car, but when she glanced in her rearview mirror, there was nothing. Barely any cars passed her going the other direction, but all of a sudden, as she was cresting a hill not far from Rosewood Day, a car pulled out behind her. Its headlights felt hot against the back of Hanna's head.

Calm down, she thought. *It's not following you.*

Her brain whirled. She *knew* who A was. But . . . how? How was it possible that A knew so much about Hanna . . . things A couldn't possibly know? Perhaps the text had been a mistake. Perhaps A had gotten hold of someone else's cell phone to throw Hanna off the trail.

Hanna was too shocked to think about it carefully. The only thought that cycled in a continuous loop in her brain was: *This makes no sense. This makes no sense.*

She glanced in her rearview mirror. The car was *still there.* She took a deep breath and eyed her phone, considering calling someone. Officer Wilden? Would he come down here on such short notice? He was a cop—he'd have to. She reached for her phone, when the car behind her flashed its brights. Should she pull over? Should she stop?

Hanna's finger was poised over her cell, ready to dial 911. And then, suddenly, the car veered around Hanna and passed her on the left. It was a nondescript car—maybe a Toyota—and Hanna couldn't see the driver inside. The car moved back into her lane, then sped off into the distance. Within seconds, its taillights vanished.

The Rosewood Day Elementary playground's parking lot was wide and deep, separated by a bunch of little landscaped islands, which were full of nearly bare trees, spiny grass, and piles of crisp leaves that gave off that signature leaf-pile smell. Beyond the lot were the jungle gym and climbing dome. They were illuminated by a single fluorescent light, which made them look like skeletons. Hanna slid into a space at the southeast corner of the lot—it was the closest to the park information booth and a police call box. Just being near something that said *Police* made her feel better. The others weren't here yet, so she watched the entrance for any cars.

It was nearly 3 A.M. Hanna shivered in Lucas's sweatshirt. She felt goose bumps form on her bare legs. She'd read once that at 3 A.M., people were in their deepest stages of REM sleep—it was the closest they would come every day to being dead. Which meant that right now, she couldn't rely on too many of Rosewood's inhabitants to help her. They were all corpses. And it was so quiet, she could hear the car's engine winding down and her slow, please-stay-calm breathing. Hanna opened her car door and stood outside it on the yellow line that marked her parking space. It was like her magic circle. Inside it, she was safe.

They'll be here soon, she told herself. In a few minutes, this would all be over. Not that Hanna had any idea what was going to *happen.* She wasn't sure. She hadn't thought that far ahead.

A light appeared at the school's entrance and Hanna's heart lifted. An SUV's headlights slid across the trees and turned slowly into the parking lot. Hanna squinted. Was that them? "Hello?" she called softly.

The SUV hugged the north end of the parking lot, passing the high school art building and the student lot and the hockey fields. Hanna started waving her arms. It had to be Emily and Aria. But the car's windows were tinted.

"Hello?" she yelled again. She got no answer. Then she

saw another car turn into the lot and drive slowly toward her. Aria's head was hanging out the passenger window. Sweet, refreshing relief flooded Hanna's body. She waved and started toward them. First she walked, then she jogged. Then sprinted.

She was in the middle of the lot when Aria called, "Hanna, look out!" Hanna turned her head to the left and her mouth fell open, at first not understanding. The SUV was headed straight for her.

The tires squealed. She smelled burnt rubber. Hanna froze, not sure what to do. "Wait!" she heard herself say, staring into the SUV's tinted window. The car kept coming, faster and faster. *Move,* she told her limbs, but they seemed hardened and dried out, like cacti.

"Hanna!" Emily cried. "Oh my God!"

It only took a second. Hanna didn't even realize she'd been hit until she was in the air, and she didn't realize she was in the air until she was on the pavement. Something in her cracked. And then pain. She wanted to cry out, but she couldn't. Sound was amplified—the car's engine roared, her friends' screams were like sirens, even her heart pumping blood sounded wet in her ears.

Hanna rolled her neck to the side. Her tiny, champagne-colored clutch had landed a few feet away; its contents had sprung out like candy from a burst piñata. The car had run over everything, too: Her mascara, her car keys, her mini bottle of Chloé perfume. Her new BlackBerry was crushed.

"Hanna!" Aria screamed. It sounded like she was coming closer. But Hanna wasn't able to turn her head to look. And then it all faded away.

37

IT WAS NECESSARY

"Oh my God!" Aria screamed. She and Emily crouched down at Hanna's contorted body and started yelling. "Hanna! Oh my God! *Hanna!*"

"She's not breathing," Emily wailed. "Aria, she's not *breathing!*"

"Do you have your cell?" Aria asked. "Call 911."

Emily reached shakily for her phone, but it slid out of her hands and skidded across the parking lot, coming to a stop by Hanna's exploded evening bag. Emily had begun panicking when she picked Aria up and Aria told her everything—about A's cryptic notes, about her dreams, about Ali and Ian, and about how Spencer must have killed Ali.

At first, Emily had refused to believe it, but then a look of horror and realization washed over her. She explained that not long before Ali went missing, Ali had confessed that she was seeing someone.

"And she must have told Spencer," Aria had answered.

"Maybe that's what they'd been fighting about all those months before the end of school."

"911, what's your emergency?" Aria heard a voice say on Emily's speakerphone.

"A car just hit my friend!" Emily wailed. "I'm in the Rosewood Day School parking lot! We don't know what to do!"

As Emily cried out the details, Aria put her mouth against Hanna's lips and tried to give her mouth-to-mouth like she'd learned in lifeguarding class in Iceland. But she didn't know if she was doing it correctly. "C'mon, Hanna, breathe," she wailed, pinching Hanna's nose.

"Just stay on the line until the ambulance gets there," Aria could hear the 911 dispatcher's voice say through Emily's phone. Emily leaned down and reached out to touch Hanna's faded Rosewood Day sweatshirt. Then she pulled back, as if she was afraid. "Oh my God, please don't die. . . ." She glanced at Aria. "Who could have done this?"

Aria looked around. The swings swayed back and forth in the breeze. The flags on the flagpole fluttered. The woods adjacent to the playground were black and thick. Suddenly, Aria saw a figure standing next to one of the trees. She had dirty blond hair and wore a short black dress. Something in her face looked wild and unhinged. She was staring right at Aria, and Aria took a step back across the pavement. *Spencer.*

"Look!" Aria hissed, pointing to the trees. But just as

Emily raised her head, Spencer disappeared into the shadows.

The buzzing startled her. It took Aria a moment to realize it was her cell phone. Then Emily's Call Waiting lit up. One new text message, Emily's screen said. Aria and Emily exchanged a familiar, uneasy look. Slowly, Aria brought her Treo out of her bag and looked at the screen. Emily leaned over to look, too.

"Oh no," Emily whispered.

The wind abruptly stopped. The trees stood still like statues. Sirens wailed in the distance.

"Please, no," Emily wailed. The text was only four chilling words long.

She knew too much. —A

WHAT HAPPENS NEXT . . .

Oooops! So I made one teensy tiny slip-up. It happens. I've got a busy life, things to do, people to torture. Like four pretty little ex-best friends.

Yeah, yeah. I know you're upset about Hanna. Wah. Get over it. I'm already planning my outfit for her funeral: appropriately somber with a touch of flash. Don't you think little Hannakins would want us to mourn in style? But maybe I'm getting ahead of myself—Hanna *does* have a history of rising from the dead. . . .

Meanwhile, Aria just can't catch a break. Her soulmate's in jail. Sean hates her. She's homeless. What's a girl to do? Looks like it's time for a life makeover—new house, new friends, maybe even a new name. But watch out Aria—even if your new BFF is blind to your real identity, *I've* got 20/20 vision. And you know I can't keep a secret.

I wonder how convict is going to look next to class vp on Spencer's college apps? Seems like Little Miss Golden Orchid is about to trade her kelly-green Lacoste polo for a scratchy orange jumpsuit. Then again, Spence wouldn't have that perfect GPA if she didn't have a few tricks up her sleeve—like, say, finding someone *else* to blame for Ali's murder. But know what? She just might be right.

What about Emily, off to live with her wholesome, Cheerios-eating cousins in Iowa? Hey, maybe it won't be so bad—she'll be a girl-loving needle in a big old sexually repressed haystack, far, far away from my prying eyes. As if! She's gonna go haywire when she realizes she can't hide from me. *Yeee-haw!*

And finally, with Hanna out of commission, it's time for me to take on a new victim. Who, you ask? Well nosy-pants, I'm still deciding. It's not like it'll be hard: *everyone* in this town has something to hide. In fact, there's something even juicier than the identity of moi bubbling beneath Rosewood's glistening surface. Something so shocking, you wouldn't believe me if I told you. So I won't even bother. HA. You know, I kind of love being me. . . .

Buckle up, girlies. *Nothing* is as it seems.

Mwah!

—A

ACKNOWLEDGMENTS

Perfect was the toughest *Pretty Little Liars* book to date, because there were so many pieces that had to fit in exactly the right places to make everything work. So I want to thank all of the careful readers, plotters, chart-makers, word arrangers, and other brilliant people who helped in the process: Josh Bank and Les Morgenstern, who saw *Perfect* through its early stages, spending days with me hashing out how exactly Spencer should go mad. I'm very grateful to have you guys on my side. The wonderful people at HarperCollins, Elise Howard and Farrin Jacobs, who puzzled over many drafts, catching all kinds of things I constantly missed. Alloy's Lanie Davis, who drew brilliant charts, was on-call whenever, wherever, and remained an unflagging fan. And, last but not least, my patient, incredibly competent and wonderfully innovative editors—Sara Shandler at Alloy and Kristin Marang at HarperCollins—whose hard work helped to really snap this book into focus. I appreciate all of you for knowing these characters so well, loving this series as much as I do, and really believing in its success. We truly are Team *Pretty Little Liars,* and I propose we start a bowling team, or perhaps a synchronized swimming team, or perhaps we could all just wear matching Lacoste polo shirts.

Many thanks and much love to Nikki Chaiken for professional advice on early drafts about Spencer and Dr. Evans. Love to my wonderful husband, Joel, for his research on what sort of plane would be used to write messages in the sky and the physics of what happens to cars when they crash into each other, and who continues to read all the drafts of this book—amazing! Love also to my wonderful friends and readers, including my fabulous parents, Shep and Mindy (no swanky bar that serves red wine would be complete without either of you), my sweet and loyal cousin, Colleen (no swanky bar would be complete without you, either), and my good friend Andrew Zaeh, who texted me as soon as he stepped off a plane to tell me that someone was reading *Pretty Little Liars,* 20,000 feet up. And thanks to all who have reached out so far with your thoughts and questions about the series. It's great to hear you're out there. You guys are part of Team *Pretty Little Liars,* too.

And thanks to the zany girl this book is dedicated to— my sister, Ali! Because she's nothing like the Alison in this book, because we can still go on for hours about the magical, fictitious world of pelicans, owls, and square-headed creatures we made up when we were six, because she doesn't get mad when I accidentally wear her $380 Rock and Republics, and because tattoos look very nice on the back of her neck—even though I think she should've gone with a certain man's face and a huge eagle tattooed there instead. Ali is quality with a capital Q, and the best sister anyone could ask for.

UNBELIEVABLE

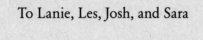
To Lanie, Les, Josh, and Sara

No one can wear a mask for very long

–LUCIUS ANNAEUS SENECA

HOW TO SAVE A LIFE

Ever wish you could go back in time and undo your mistakes? If only you hadn't drawn that clown face on the Bratz doll your best friend got for her eighth birthday, she wouldn't have dropped you for the new girl from Boston. And back in ninth grade, you would never have skipped soccer practice to hit the beach if you'd known Coach would bench you for the rest of the season. If only you hadn't made those bad choices, maybe your ex-BFF would have given you that extra front-row ticket to Marc Jacobs's fashion show. Or maybe you'd be playing goalie for the women's national soccer team by now, with a Nike modeling contract and a beach house in Nice. You could be jet-setting around the Mediterranean instead of sitting in geography class, trying to find it on a map.

In Rosewood, fantasies about reversing fate are as common as girls receiving Tiffany heart pendants for their thirteenth birthdays. And four former best friends would do anything to travel back in time and make things right. But what if they really could go back? Would they be able to keep their fifth best friend alive . . . or is her tragedy part of their destiny?

Sometimes the past holds more questions than answers. And in Rosewood, nothing is *ever* what it seems.

"She's going to be so psyched when I tell her," Spencer Hastings said to her best friends Hanna Marin, Emily Fields, and Aria Montgomery. She straightened her sea-green eyelet T-shirt and pressed Alison DiLaurentis's doorbell.

"Why do *you* get to tell her?" Hanna asked as she hopped from the porch step to the sidewalk and back again. Ever since Alison, their fifth best friend, had told Hanna that only fidgety girls stayed thin, Hanna had been making a lot of extra movements.

"Maybe we should all tell her at the same time," Aria suggested, scratching the temporary dragonfly tattoo she'd pasted on her collarbone.

"That would be fun." Emily pushed her blunt-cut, reddish-blond hair behind her ears. "We could do a choreographed dance and say, 'Ta-da!' at the end."

"No way." Spencer squared her shoulders. "It's my barn—*I* get to tell her." She rang the DiLaurentis's door-bell again.

As they waited, the girls listened to the buzz of the landscapers pruning Spencer's hedges next door and the *thwock-thwock* of the Fairfield twins playing tennis on their backyard court two houses down. The air smelled like lilacs, mown grass, and Neutrogena sunscreen. It was a typical idyllic Rosewood moment—everything about the town was pretty, and that included its sounds, smells, *and* inhabitants. The girls had lived in Rosewood nearly all their lives, and they felt lucky to be part of such a special place.

They loved Rosewood summers best of all. Tomorrow morning, after they completed their last seventh-grade final at Rosewood Day, the school they all attended, they would take part in the school's annual graduation-pin ceremony. One by one Principal Appleton would call each student's name, from kindergarten through eleventh grade, and each student would receive a twenty-four-karat gold pin—the girls' was in the shape of a gardenia, the boys' a horseshoe. After that, they would be released for ten glorious weeks of tanning, cookouts, boating trips, and shopping excursions to Philly and New York. They couldn't *wait*.

But the graduation ceremony wasn't the true rite of passage for Ali, Aria, Spencer, Emily, and Hanna. Summer wouldn't really start for them until tomorrow night, at their end-of-seventh-grade slumber party. And the girls had a surprise for Ali that was going to make this summer's kickoff extra special.

When the DiLaurentis's front door was finally flung open, Mrs. DiLaurentis stood before them, wearing a short pale pink wrap dress that showed off her long, muscular, tanned calves. "Hello, girls," she said coolly.

"Is Ali here?" Spencer asked.

"She's upstairs, I think." Mrs. DiLaurentis stepped out of the way. "Go on up."

Spencer led the group through the hall, her white pleated field hockey skirt swinging, her dirty-blond braid bouncing against the middle of her back. The girls loved Ali's house—it smelled like vanilla and fabric softener, just like Ali. Lush photographs of past DiLaurentis trips to Paris, Lisbon, and Lake Como lined the walls. There were plenty of photos of Ali and her brother, Jason, from grade school on. The girls especially loved Ali's second-grade school picture. Ali's vibrant pink cardigan made her whole face glow. Back then, Ali's family had lived in Connecticut, and Ali's old private school hadn't required her to wear stuffy blue blazers for yearbook pictures like Rosewood Day did. Even as an eight-year-old, Ali was irresistibly cute—she had clear blue eyes, a heart-shaped face, adorable dimples, and a naughty-yet-charming expression, which made it impossible to stay mad at her.

Spencer touched the bottom-right corner of their favorite photo, the one of the five of them camping in the Poconos the previous July. They were all standing next to a giant canoe, drenched in murky lake water, grinning from ear to ear, as happy as five twelve-year-old best friends could be. Aria put her hand on top of Spencer's, Emily put her hand on top of Aria's, and Hanna piled her hand on last. They closed their eyes for a split second, hummed, and broke away. The girls had started the photo-touching habit when the picture first went up, a memento of their first summer of best-friendship. They couldn't believe that Ali, *the* girl of Rosewood Day, had chosen the four of them as her inner circle. It was a little like being joined at the hip with an A-list celebrity.

But admitting that would be . . . well, lame. Especially now.

As they passed the living room, they noticed two graduation robes hanging on the knob of a French door. The white one was Ali's, and the more official-looking navy one was Jason's, who would be going on to Yale in the fall. The girls clasped their hands, excited to put on their own graduation gowns and berets, which Rosewood Day graduates had worn ever since the school had opened in 1897. Just then, they noticed a movement in the living room. Jason was sitting in the leather love seat, staring blankly at CNN.

"Heeyyy, Jason," Spencer called, waving. "Are you *so* psyched for tomorrow?"

Jason glanced at them. He was the hot boy version of Ali, with buttery blond hair and stunning blue eyes. He smirked and went back to the TV without saying a word.

"Oh-kaay," the girls all murmured in unison. Jason had his hilarious side—he was the one who had invented the "not it" game with his friends. The girls had borrowed and reinvented the game for their own uses, which mostly meant making fun of nerdier girls in their presence. But Jason definitely got into funks, too. Ali called them his Elliott Smith moods, after the morose singer-songwriter he liked. Only, Jason certainly didn't have any reason to be upset now—by this time tomorrow, he'd be on a plane to Costa Rica to teach adventure kayaking all summer. Boo-hoo.

"Whatever." Aria shrugged. The four girls turned and bounced up the stairs to Ali's room. As they reached the landing, they noticed that Ali's door was closed. Spencer frowned. Emily cocked her head. Inside the room, Ali let out a giggle.

Hanna gently pushed the door open. Ali had her back to them. Her hair was up in a high ponytail, and she'd tied her striped silk halter top in a perfect bow at her neck. She stared down at the open notebook in her lap, completely entranced.

Spencer cleared her throat, and Ali whirled around, startled. "Guys, hi!" she cried. "What's up?"

"Not much." Hanna pointed at the notebook in Ali's lap. "What's that?"

Ali closed the notebook fast. "Oh. Nothing."

The girls felt a presence behind them. Mrs. DiLaurentis pushed past, waltzing into Ali's bedroom. "We need to talk," she said to Ali, her voice clipped and taut.

"But, Mom . . ." Ali protested.

"Now."

The girls glanced at one another. That was Mrs.

DiLaurentis's you're-in-trouble voice. They didn't hear it often.

Ali's mother faced the girls. "Why don't you girls wait on the deck?"

"It'll just take a second," Ali said quickly, shooting them an apologetic smile. "I'll be right down."

Hanna paused, confused. Spencer squinted, trying to see which notebook Ali was holding. Mrs. DiLaurentis raised an eyebrow. "C'mon, girls. Go."

The four of them swallowed hard and filed back down the stairs. Once on Ali's wraparound porch, they arranged themselves in their usual places around the family's enormous square patio table—Spencer at one end, and Aria, Emily, and Hanna at the sides. Ali would sit at the table's head, next to her father's deck-mounted stone birdbath. For a moment, the four girls watched as a couple of cardinals frolicked in the bath's cold, clear water. When a blue jay tried to join them, the cardinals squawked and quickly sent him away. Birds, it seemed, were just as cliquey as girls.

"That was weird upstairs," Aria whispered.

"Do you think Ali's in trouble?" Hanna whispered. "What if she's grounded and can't come to the sleepover?"

"Why would she be in trouble? She hasn't done anything wrong," whispered Emily, who always stuck up for Ali—the girls called her Killer, as in Ali's personal pit bull.

"Not that *we* know of," Spencer muttered under her breath.

Just then, Mrs. DiLaurentis burst out of the French patio doors and across the lawn. "I want to make sure you have the dimensions right," she screamed to the workers who were perched lazily on an enormous bulldozer at the back of the property. The DiLaurentises were building a twenty-person gazebo for summer parties, and Ali had mentioned that her mom was being very type A about the whole process, even though they were only at the hole-digging stage. Mrs. DiLaurentis marched up to the workers and started chastising them. Her diamond wedding ring glinted in the sun as she waved her arms around frenetically. The girls exchanged glances—it looked like Ali's lecture hadn't taken very long.

"Guys?"

Ali stood at the edge of the porch. She had changed out of her halter into a faded navy blue Abercrombie tee. There was a baffled look on her face. "Uh . . . hi?"

Spencer stood up. "What did she bust you for?"

Ali blinked. Her eyes darted back and forth.

"Were you getting in trouble *without* us?" Aria cried, trying to make it sound like she was teasing. "And why'd you change? That halter you had on was so cute."

Ali still looked flustered . . . and kind of upset. Emily stood up halfway. "Do you want us to . . . go?" Her voice dripped with uncertainty. All the others looked at Ali nervously—was *that* what she wanted?

Ali twisted her blue string bracelet around her wrist three full rotations. She stepped onto the patio and sat down in her rightful seat. "Of course I don't want you to go. My mom was mad at me because I . . . I threw my hockey clothes in with her delicates again." She gave them a sheepish shrug and rolled her eyes.

Emily stuck out her bottom lip. A small beat went by. "She got mad at you for *that*?"

Ali raised her eyebrows. "You know my mom, Em. She's more anal than Spencer." She snickered.

Spencer faux-glared at Ali while Emily ran her thumb along one of the grooves in the teak patio table.

"But don't worry, girls, I'm not grounded or anything." Ali pressed her palms together. "Our sleepover extravaganza can proceed as planned!"

The four of them sighed with relief, and the odd, uneasy mood began to evaporate. Only, each of them had a weird feeling Ali wasn't telling them everything—it certainly wouldn't be the first time. One minute, Ali would be their best friend, and the next, she'd drift away from them, making covert phone calls and sending secret texts. Weren't they supposed to share everything? The other girls had certainly shared enough of themselves—they'd slipped secrets to Ali that no one, absolutely *no one* else, knew. And, of course, there was the big secret that they all shared about Jenna Cavanaugh—the one they'd sworn to take to the grave.

"Speaking of our sleepover extravaganza, I have huge news," Spencer said, breaking them out of their thoughts. "Guess where we're having it?"

"Where?" Ali leaned forward on her elbows, slowly morphing back into her old self.

"Melissa's barn!" Spencer cried. Melissa was Spencer's older sister, and Mr. and Mrs. Hastings had renovated the family's backyard barn and allowed Melissa to use it as her own personal pied-à-terre during her junior and senior years of high school. Spencer would get the same privilege, once she was old enough.

"Sweet!" Ali whooped. "How?"

"She's flying out to Prague tomorrow night after graduation," Spencer answered. "My parents said we could use it, so long as we clean it up before she gets back."

"Nice." Ali leaned back and laced her hands together. Suddenly, her eyes focused on something a bit to the left of the workers. Melissa herself was traipsing through the Hastingses' bordering yard, her posture rigid and proper. Her white graduation gown swung from a hanger in her hand, and she'd slung the school's royal blue valedictorian mantle over her shoulders.

Spencer let out a groan. "She's being so obnoxious about the whole valedictorian thing," she whispered. "She even told me I should feel grateful that Andrew Campbell will probably be valedictorian instead of me when we're all seniors—the honor is 'such a huge responsibility.'" Spencer and her sister hated each other, and Spencer had a new story about Melissa's bitchiness nearly every day.

Ali stood up. "Hey! Melissa!" She started waving.

Melissa stopped and turned around. "Oh. Hey, guys." She smiled cautiously.

"Excited to go to Prague?" Ali singsonged, giving Melissa her brightest smile.

Melissa tilted her head slightly. "Of course."

"Is *Ian* going?" Ian was Melissa's gorgeous boyfriend. Just thinking about him made the girls swoon.

Spencer dug her nails into Ali's arm. *"Ali."* But Ali pulled her arm away.

Melissa shaded her eyes in the harsh sunlight. The royal blue mantle flapped in the wind. "No. He's not."

"Oh!" Ali simpered. "Are you sure that's a good idea—leaving him alone for two weeks? He might get another girlfriend!"

"Alison," Spencer said through her teeth. "Stop it. *Now.*"

"Spencer?" Emily whispered. "What's going on?"

"Nothing," Spencer said quickly. Aria, Emily, and Hanna looked at one another again. This had been happening lately—Ali would say something, one of them would freak, and the rest of them would have no clue what was going on.

But this clearly wasn't nothing. Melissa straightened the mantle around her neck, squared her shoulders, and turned. She looked long and hard at the giant hole at the edge of the DiLaurentises' yard, then walked into the barn, slamming the door behind her so hard that it made the twig-braided wreath on the back of the door thump up and down.

"Something's certainly up *her* butt," Ali said. "I was just kidding, after all." Spencer made a little whimpering noise at the back of her throat, and Ali started giggling. She had a faint smile on her face. It was the same smile Ali gave them whenever she dangled a secret over one of their heads, taunting that she could tell the others if she wanted to.

"Anyway, who cares?" Ali gazed at each of them, her eyes bright. "You know what, girls?" She drummed her fingers excitedly on the table. "I think this is going to be the Summer of Ali. The Summer of *All* of Us. I can just feel it. Can't you?"

A stunned moment passed. It seemed like a humid cloud hung above them, fogging up their thoughts. But slowly, the clouds faded and an idea formed in each of their minds. Maybe Ali was right. This *could* be the best summer of their lives. They could turn their friendship around and make it as strong as it had been last summer. They could forget all the scary, scandalous things that had happened and just start over.

"I can feel it, too," Hanna said loudly.

"Definitely," Aria and Emily said at the same time.

"Sure," Spencer said softly.

They all grabbed hands and squeezed hard.

It rained that night, a hard, pounding rain that made puddles in driveways, watered gardens, and created little mini pools on top of the Hastingses' swimming pool cover.

When the rain stopped in the middle of the night, Aria, Emily, Spencer, and Hanna awakened and sat up in bed at almost the exact same moment. A foreboding feeling had settled over each of them. They didn't know if it was from something they'd just dreamed about, or excitement about the next day. Or maybe it was due to something else entirely . . . something far deeper.

They each looked out their windows onto Rosewood's tranquil, empty streets. The clouds had shifted and all the stars had come out. The pavement shone from the rain. Hanna stared at her driveway—only her mother's car was there now. Her father had moved out. Emily looked at her backyard and the forest beyond it. She'd never braved those woods—she'd heard ghosts lived in them. Aria listened to the sounds emanating from her parents' bedroom, wondering if they'd woken up, too—or perhaps they were fighting again and hadn't fallen asleep yet. Spencer gazed at the DiLaurentises' back porch, then across their yard to the huge hole the workers had dug for the gazebo's foundation. The rain had turned some of the dug-up dirt to mud. Spencer thought about all the things in her life that made her angry. Then she thought about all the things in her life she wanted to have—and all the things she wanted to change.

Spencer reached under her bed, found her red flash-light, and shone it into Ali's window. One flash, two flashes, three flashes. This was her secret code to Ali that she wanted to sneak out and talk in person. She thought she saw Ali's blond head sitting up in bed, too, but Ali didn't flash back.

All four of them fell back onto their pillows, telling themselves that the feeling was nothing and they needed their sleep. In twenty-four short hours, they'd be at the end of their seventh-grade sleepover, the first night of summer. The summer that would change everything.

How right they were.

1

THE ZEN IS MIGHTIER
THAN THE SWORD

Aria Montgomery woke up mid-snore. It was Sunday morning, and she was curled up on a blue vinyl chair in the Rosewood Memorial Hospital waiting room. Everyone—Hanna Marin's parents, Officer Wilden, Hanna's best friend Mona Vanderwaal, and Lucas Beattie, a boy in her class at Rosewood Day who looked like he'd just arrived—was staring at her.

"Did I miss something?" Aria croaked. Her head felt like it was stuffed with marshmallow Peeps. When she checked the Zoloft clock hanging over the waiting room entrance, she saw it was only eight thirty. She'd been out for just fifteen minutes.

Lucas sat down next to her and picked up a copy of *Medical Supplies Today* magazine. According to the cover, the issue featured all the latest colostomy bag models. Who puts a medical supplies magazine in a hospital *waiting room*? "I just got here," he answered. "I heard about the accident on the morning news. Have you seen Hanna yet?"

Aria shook her head. "They still won't let us."

The two of them fell gravely silent. Aria surveyed the others. Ms. Marin wore a rumpled gray cashmere sweater and a pair of great-fitting distressed jeans. She was barking into her little Motorola earpiece, even though the nurses had said they couldn't use cell phones in here. Officer Wilden sat next to her, his Rosewood PD jacket unbuttoned to his mid-chest and showing a frayed white T-shirt beneath it. Hanna's father was slumped in the chair closest to the intensive care unit's two giant double doors, jiggling his left foot. In a pale pink Juicy sweat suit and flip-flops, Mona Vanderwaal looked uncharacteristically disheveled, her face puffy from crying. When Mona looked up and saw Lucas, she gave him an annoyed stare, as if to say, *This is for close friends and family only. What are you doing here?* Aria couldn't blame everyone for feeling testy. She had been here since 3 A.M., after the ambulance came to the Rosewood Day Elementary School parking lot and swept Hanna off to the hospital. Mona and the others had arrived at various points in the morning, when the news had begun to circulate. The last update the doctors had given them was that Hanna had been moved to intensive care. But that was three hours ago.

Aria reviewed the previous night's horrific details. Hanna had called to tell her that she knew the identity of A, the diabolical messenger who had been taunting

Hanna, Aria, Emily, and Spencer for the past month. Hanna hadn't wanted to reveal any details over the phone, so she'd asked Aria and Emily to meet her at the Rosewood Day swings, their old special spot. Emily and Aria had arrived just in time to see a black SUV mow Hanna down and speed away. As the paramedics rushed to the scene, put a cervical collar around Hanna's neck, and carefully lifted her onto a stretcher and into the ambulance, Aria had felt numb. When she pinched herself hard, it didn't hurt.

Hanna was still alive . . . but barely. She had internal injuries, a broken arm, and bruises everywhere. The accident had caused head trauma, and now she was in a coma.

Aria shut her eyes, ready to burst into tears again. The most inconceivable thing about all of this was the text Aria and Emily had received after Hanna's accident. *She knew too much.* It was from A. Which meant . . . A *knew* what Hanna knew. Just like A knew everything else—all their secrets, the fact that it had been Ali, Aria, Spencer, Emily, and Hanna who'd blinded Jenna Cavanaugh, not Jenna's stepbrother, Toby. A probably even knew the truth about who killed Ali.

Lucas tapped Aria on the arm. "You were there when that car hit Hanna, right? Did you get a look at the person who did it?"

Aria didn't know Lucas very well. He was one of those kids who *loved* school activities and clubs, whereas Aria was the type to stay far, far away from all things involving her Rosewood Day peers. She didn't know what connection he had to Hanna, but it seemed sweet that he was here. "It was too dark," she mumbled.

"And you have no idea who it could have been?"

Aria bit down hard on her bottom lip. Wilden and a couple other Rosewood cops had shown up the night before just after the girls received their note from A. When Wilden asked the girls what happened, they all insisted that they hadn't seen the driver's face or the make of the SUV. And they swore over and over that this must have been an accident—they didn't know why anyone would do this on purpose. Maybe it was wrong to withhold this information from the police, but they were all terrified of what A had in store for the rest of them if they told the truth.

A had threatened them about not telling before, and Aria and Emily both had been punished once already for ignoring those threats. A had sent Aria's mother, Ella, a letter telling her that Aria's father was having an affair with one of his university students, and revealed that Aria had kept her dad's secret. Then A had told the entire school that Emily was dating Maya, the girl who had moved into Ali's old house. Aria glanced at Lucas and silently shook her head no.

The door to the ICU swept open, and Dr. Geist strode into the waiting room. With his piercing gray eyes, sloped nose, and shock of white hair, he looked a little like Helmut, the German landlord of the old row house Aria's family had rented in Reykjavík, Iceland. Dr. Geist gave everyone the same judging stare Helmut had given Aria's brother, Mike, when he discovered that Mike had been keeping Diddy, his pet tarantula, in an empty terra-cotta pot Helmut used to grow tulips.

Hanna's parents nervously stood up and walked over to the doctor.

"Your daughter is still unconscious," Dr. Geist said quietly. "Not much has changed. We've set her broken arm and are checking the extent of her internal injuries."

"When can we see her?" Mr. Marin asked.

"Soon," Dr. Geist said. "But she's still in very critical condition."

He turned to go, but Mr. Marin caught his arm. "When will she wake up?"

Dr. Geist fiddled with his clipboard. "She has a lot of swelling in her brain, so it's hard for us to predict the extent of the damage at this point. She might wake up just fine, or there might be complications."

"Complications?" Ms. Marin went pale.

"I've heard that people who are in comas have less of a chance of recovering from them after a certain amount of time," Mr. Marin said nervously. "Is that true?"

Dr. Geist rubbed his hands on his blue scrubs. "That is true, yes, but let's not get ahead of ourselves, okay?"

A murmur went through the room. Mona burst into tears again. Aria wished she could call Emily . . . but Emily was on a plane to Des Moines, Iowa, for reasons she hadn't explained—only that A had done something to send her there. Then there was Spencer. Before Hanna had called with her news, Aria had pieced together something terrifying about Spencer . . . and when Aria had seen her cowering in the woods, twitching like a feral animal just after the SUV hit Hanna, it had only confirmed her worst fears.

Ms. Marin picked up her oversize brown leather tote from the floor, breaking Aria out of her thoughts. "I'm going to go get some coffee," Hanna's mom said softly to her ex-husband. Then, she gave Officer Wilden a kiss on the cheek—before tonight Aria hadn't known there was something going on between them—and disappeared toward the elevator bank.

Officer Wilden slumped back down in his chair. The week before, Wilden had visited Aria, Hanna, and the others, asking them questions about the details surrounding Ali's disappearance and death. In the middle of that interview, A had sent each of them a note saying that if they *dared* tattle about the notes A had been sending them, they'd be sorry. But just because Aria couldn't tell Wilden what A had potentially done to Hanna, that didn't mean she couldn't share the horrible thing she'd realized about Spencer.

Can I talk to you? she mouthed to Wilden across the room. Wilden nodded and stood. They walked out of the waiting room and into a little alcove marked VEND-ING. Inside were six glowing vending machines, offering a range from sodas to full-on meals, unidentifiable sand-wiches, and shepherd's pie, which reminded Aria of the glop her father, Byron, used to make for dinner when her mother, Ella, was working late.

"So listen, if this is about your teacher friend, we let him go." Wilden sat down on the bench next to the microwave and gave Aria a coy little smile. "We couldn't hold him. And just so you know, we've kept it quiet. We won't punish him unless you want to press charges. But I should probably tell your parents."

The blood drained from Aria's face. Of course Wilden knew about what had happened the night before with her and Ezra Fitz, the love of her life *and* her AP English teacher. It was probably the talk of the Rosewood Police Department that a twenty-two-year-old English teacher had been canoodling with a minor—and that it was the minor's *boyfriend* who'd ratted them out. They'd prob-ably gossiped about it at the Hooters that was next to the police station, amid Buffalo wings and cheese fries and girls with big boobs.

"I don't want to press charges," Aria sputtered. "And please, *please* don't tell my parents." The last thing she needed was some sort of big, dysfunctional family dis-cussion.

Aria shifted her weight. "But anyway, that's not why I want to talk to you. I . . . I think I might know who killed Alison."

Wilden raised an eyebrow. "I'm listening."

Aria took a deep breath. "First off, Ali was seeing Ian Thomas."

"Ian Thomas," Wilden repeated, his eyes widening. "Melissa Hastings's boyfriend?"

Aria nodded. "I noticed something in the video that was leaked to the press last week. If you watch it closely, you can see Ian and Ali touching hands." She cleared her throat. "Spencer Hastings had a crush on Ian, too. Ali and Spencer were competitive, and they got into this awful fight the night Ali disappeared. Spencer ran out of the barn after Ali, and she didn't come back for at least ten minutes."

Wilden looked incredulous.

Aria took a deep breath. A had sent Aria various clues about Ali's killer—that it was someone close by, someone who wanted something Ali had, and someone who knew every inch of Ali's backyard. With those clues in place, and once Aria had realized Ian and Ali were together, Spencer was the logical suspect. "After a while, I went outside to look for them," she said. "They weren't anywhere . . . and I just have this horrible feeling that Spencer . . ."

Wilden sat back. "Spencer and Alison weighed about the same, right?"

Aria nodded. "Sure. I guess."

"Could *you* drag someone your size over to a hole and push her in?"

"I–I don't know," Aria stammered. "Maybe? If I was mad enough?"

Wilden shook his head. Aria's eyes filled with tears. She recalled how eerily silent it had been that night. Ali had been just a few hundred yards away from them, and they hadn't heard a sound.

"Spencer also would've had to calm down enough so she didn't seem suspicious when she returned to you guys," Wilden added. "It takes a pretty damn good actor to pull that off–not a seventh-grade girl. I think who-ever did this was obviously nearby, but the whole thing took more time." He raised his eyebrows. "Is this what you Rosewood Day girls do these days? Blame your old friends for murder?"

Aria's mouth dropped open, surprised at Wilden's scolding tone. "It's just–"

"Spencer Hastings is a competitive, high-strung girl, but she doesn't strike me as a killer," Wilden interrupted. Then, he smiled at Aria sadly. "I get it. This must be tough for you–you just want to figure out what happened to your friend. I didn't know that Alison was secretly with Melissa Hastings's boyfriend, though. *That's* interesting."

Wilden gave Aria a terse nod, stood up, and turned back to the hallway. Aria remained by the vending machines, her eyes on the mint-green linoleum floor. She felt overheated and disoriented, as if she'd spent too much time in a sauna. Maybe she should be ashamed of herself, blaming an old best friend. And the holes Wilden had poked in her theory made a lot of sense. Maybe she'd been foolish to trust A's clues at all.

A chill went up Aria's spine. Perhaps A had sent Aria those clues to deliberately throw her off track—and take the heat off the true murderer. And maybe, just maybe, the true murderer was . . . *A*.

Aria was lost in her thoughts when suddenly she felt a hand on her shoulder. She flinched and turned, her heart racing. Standing behind her, wearing a ratty Hollis College sweatshirt and a pair of jeans with a hole through the left front pocket, was Aria's father, Byron. She crossed her arms over her chest, feeling awkward. She hadn't really spoken to her father in a few weeks.

"Jesus, Aria. Are you all right?" Byron blurted out. "I saw you on the news."

"I'm okay," Aria said stiffly. "It was Hanna who was hurt, not me."

As her father pulled her in for a hug, Aria wasn't sure whether to squeeze him tight or let her arms go limp. She'd missed him since he'd moved out of their house a month ago. But Aria was also furious that it had taken a life-threatening accident and a TV appearance to motivate Byron to leave Meredith's side and reach out to his own daughter.

"I called your mother this morning, asking how you were, but she said you weren't living there anymore." Byron's voice quivered with concern. He ran his hand over the top of his head, mussing up his hair even more. "Where *are* you living?"

Aria stared blearily at the brightly printed Heimlich maneuver poster tucked behind the Coke machine. Someone had drawn a pair of boobs on the choking victim's chest, and it looked like the person giving the Heimlich was feeling her up. Aria had been staying at her boyfriend Sean Ackard's house, but Sean had made it clear she wasn't welcome there anymore when he'd ordered a raid on Ezra's apartment and dumped Aria's crap on Ezra's doorstep. Who had tipped Sean off about Aria's affair with Ezra? *Ding ding ding!* A.

She hadn't given a new living situation much thought. "The Olde Hollis Inn?" Aria suggested.

"The Olde Hollis Inn has rats. Why don't you stay with me?"

Aria vigorously shook her head. "You're living with—"

"Meredith," Byron stated firmly. "I want you to get to know her."

"But . . ." Aria protested. Her father, however, was giving her his classic Buddhist monk look. Aria knew the look well—she'd seen it after he'd refused to let Aria go to an arty summer camp in the Berkshires instead of Hollis Happy Hooray day camp for the fourth summer in a row, which meant ten long weeks of making paper-bag puppets and competing in the egg-and-spoon race. Byron had donned the look again when Aria asked if she could finish school at the American Academy in Reykjavík instead of coming back to Rosewood with the rest of the family. The look was often followed by a saying Byron had learned from a monk he'd met during his graduate work in Japan: *The obstacle is the path.* Meaning what wouldn't kill Aria would just make her stronger.

But when she imagined moving in with Meredith, a more appropriate quote came to mind: *There are some remedies worse than the disease.*

2

ABRACADABRA, NOW WE LOVE EACH OTHER AGAIN

Ali sank onto one hip and glared at Spencer Hastings, who stood across from her on the back path that led from the Hastingses' barn to the woods. "You try to steal everything from me," she hissed. "But you can't have this."

Spencer shivered in the cold evening air. "Can't have what?"

"*You* know," Ali said. "You read it in my diary." She pushed her honey-blond hair over her shoulder. "You think you're so special, but you're so lame, acting like you didn't know Ian was with me. Of course you knew, Spence. That's why you liked him in the first place, isn't it? Because *I'm* with him? Because your sister's with him?"

Spencer's eyes boggled. The night air turned sharp, almost acrid-smelling. Ali stuck out her bottom lip. "Oh, Spence. Did you really believe he *liked* you?"

Suddenly, Spencer felt a burst of anger, and her arms

shot out in front of her, pushing Ali in the chest. Ali teetered backward, stumbling against the slippery rocks. Only, it wasn't Ali anymore—it was Hanna Marin. Hanna's body flew up in the air, and she hit the ground with a sharp crack. Instead of all her makeup and BlackBerry bursting out of her purse as from a smashed-open piñata, Hanna's internal organs spewed out of her body, raining down on the concrete like hail.

Spencer shot up, her blond hair damp with sweat. It was Sunday morning, and she was lying in her bed, still in the black satin dress and uncomfortable thong underwear she'd meant to wear to Mona Vanderwaal's birthday party the night before. Soft gold light slanted across her desk, and starlings chirped innocently in the giant oak next to her window. She'd been awake nearly all night, waiting for her phone to ring with news about Hanna. But no one had called. Spencer had no idea if the silence was good . . . or terrible.

Hanna. She'd called Spencer late last night, just after Spencer had recalled her long-suppressed memory of shoving Ali in the woods the night Ali disappeared. Hanna had told Spencer she'd found out something important, and that they had to meet at the Rosewood Day swings. Spencer had pulled up to the parking lot just as Hanna's body flew into the air. She'd maneuvered her car to the side of the road, then run out on foot into the trees, shocked by what she saw. "Call an ambulance!" Aria was shrieking. Emily was sobbing with fear. Hanna remained immobile. Spencer had never witnessed anything so terrifying in her entire life.

Seconds later, Spencer's Sidekick had pinged with a text from A. Still shrouded in the woods, Spencer saw Emily and Aria pull out their phones as well, and her stomach flipped as she realized they must have all received the same creepy message: *She knew too much.* Had A figured out whatever it was that Hanna had discovered—something that A must have been trying to hide—and hit Hanna to shut her up? That had to be it, but it was hard for Spencer to truly believe it had actually happened. It was just so diabolical.

But maybe *Spencer* was just as diabolical. Just hours before Hanna's accident, she'd shoved her sister, Melissa, down the stairs. And she'd finally remembered what had happened the night Ali went missing, recovered those lost ten minutes she'd suppressed for so long. She'd pushed Ali to the ground—maybe even hard enough to kill her. Spencer didn't know what had happened next, but it seemed like A did. A had sent Spencer a text only a couple days ago, hinting that Ali's murderer was right in front of her. Spencer had received the text just as she was looking in the mirror . . . at *herself.*

Spencer hadn't run into the parking lot to join her friends. Instead, she'd sped home, in desperate need to think all this through. *Could* she have killed Ali? Did she have it in her? But after an entire sleepless night, she just couldn't compare what she had done to Melissa and Ali to what A had done to Hanna. Yes, Spencer lost her temper, yes, Spencer could be pushed to the limit, but deep down, she just didn't think she could kill.

Why, then, was A so convinced Spencer was the culprit? Was it possible A was wrong . . . or lying? But A knew about Spencer's seventh-grade kiss with Ian Thomas, her illicit affair with Wren, Melissa's college boyfriend, and that the five of them had blinded Jenna Cavanaugh—all things that were true. A had so much ammo on them, it was hardly necessary to start making stuff up.

Suddenly, as Spencer wiped the sweat off her face, something hit her, sending her heart sinking to her feet. She could think of a very good reason why A might have lied and suggested that Spencer killed Ali. Perhaps A had secrets, too. Perhaps A needed a scapegoat.

"Spencer?" Her mother's voice floated up. "Can you come downstairs?"

Spencer jumped and peeked at her reflection in her vanity mirror. Her eyes looked puffy and bloodshot, her lips were chapped, and her hair had leaves stuck in it from hiding in the woods last night. She couldn't handle a family meeting right now.

The first floor smelled of fresh-brewed Nicaraguan Segovia coffee, Fresh Fields Danishes, and the fresh-cut calla lilies their housekeeper, Candace, bought every morning. Spencer's father stood at the granite-topped island, decked out in his black spandex bike pants and U.S. Postal Service bike jersey. Perhaps that was a good sign—they couldn't be too angry if her dad had gone for his regular 5 A.M. bike ride.

On the kitchen table was a copy of the Sunday *Philadelphia Sentinel*. At first Spencer thought it was there because it had news of Hanna's accident. But then she saw her own face staring back at her from the paper's front page. She wore a sleek black suit and was giving the camera a confident smirk. *Move Over, Trumps!* the headline said. *Golden Orchid Essay Contest Nominee Spencer Hastings Is Coming!*

Spencer's stomach heaved. She'd forgotten. The paper was on everyone's doorsteps right now.

A figure emerged from the pantry. Spencer stepped back in fear. There was Melissa, glaring at her, clutching a box of Raisin Bran so tightly Spencer thought she might crush it. There was a tiny scratch on her sister's left cheek, a Band-Aid over her right eyebrow, a yellow hospital bracelet still around her left wrist, and a pink cast on her right wrist, clearly a souvenir of yesterday's fight with Spencer.

Spencer lowered her eyes, feeling a whole mess of guilty feelings. Yesterday, A had sent Melissa the first few sentences of her old AP economics paper, the very one Spencer had pilfered from Melissa's computer hard drive and disguised as her own AP economics homework. The same essay Spencer's econ teacher, Mr. McAdam, had nominated for a Golden Orchid essay award, the most prestigious high school–level award in the country.

Melissa had figured out what Spencer had done, and although Spencer had begged for forgiveness, Melissa had said horrible things to her—things way worse than Spencer thought she deserved. The fight had ended when Spencer, enraged by Melissa's words, had accidentally shoved her sister down the stairs.

"So, girls." Mrs. Hastings set her coffee cup on the table and gestured for Melissa to sit. "Your father and I have made some big decisions."

Spencer braced for what was coming. They were going to turn Spencer in for plagiarizing. She wouldn't get into college. She'd have to go to trade school. She'd end up working as a telemarketer at QVC, taking orders for ab rollers and fake diamonds, and Melissa would get off scot-free, just like she always did. Somehow, her sister always found a way to come out on top.

"First off, we don't want you girls to see Dr. Evans anymore." Mrs. Hastings laced her fingers together. "She's done more harm than good. Understood?"

Melissa nodded silently, but Spencer scrunched up her nose in confusion. Dr. Evans, Spencer and Melissa's shrink, was one of the few people who didn't try to kiss Melissa's ass. Spencer began to protest but noticed the warning looks on both her parents' faces. "Okay," she mumbled, feeling a bit hopeless.

"Second of all." Mr. Hastings tapped the *Sentinel*, squashing his thumb over Spencer's face. "Plagiarizing Melissa's paper was very wrong, Spencer."

"I know," Spencer said quickly, terrified to look anywhere in Melissa's direction.

"But after some careful thought, we've decided that we don't want to go public with it. This family's been through too much already. So, Spencer, you'll continue to compete for the Golden Orchid. We will tell no one about this."

"What?" Melissa slammed her coffee cup down on the table.

"That's what we've decided," Mrs. Hastings said tightly, dabbing the corner of her mouth with a napkin. "And we also expect Spencer to win."

"To win?" Spencer repeated, shocked.

"You're *rewarding* her?" Melissa shrieked.

"Enough." Mr. Hastings used the tone of voice he typically reserved for underlings at his law practice when they dared call him at home.

"Third thing," Mrs. Hastings said. "You girls are going to bond."

Her mother pulled two snapshots out of her cardigan pocket. The first was of Spencer and Melissa at four and nine years old, respectively, lying on a hammock at their grandmother's beach house in Stone Harbor, New Jersey. The second photo was of them in the same beach house's playroom, a few years later. Melissa wore a magician's hat and cape, and Spencer had on her Tommy Hilfiger stars-and-stripes ruffled bikini. On her feet were the black motorcycle boots she'd worn until they'd gotten so small that they cut off all the circulation to her toes. The sisters were performing a magic show for their parents; Melissa was the magician, and Spencer was her lovely assistant.

"I found these this morning." Mrs. Hastings passed the photos to Melissa, who glanced at them quickly and passed them back. "Remember how you girls used to be such good friends? You were always babbling in the backseat of the car. You never wanted to go anywhere without each other."

"That was ten years ago, Mom," Melissa said wearily.

Mrs. Hastings stared at the photo of Spencer and Melissa on the hammock. "You used to love Nana's beach house. You used to be *friends* at Nana's beach house. So we've decided to take a trip to Stone Harbor today. Nana isn't there, but we have keys. So pack up your things."

Spencer's parents were nodding feverishly, their faces hopeful.

"That's just stupid," Spencer and Melissa said together. Spencer glanced at her sister, astounded they'd thought the same thing.

Mrs. Hastings left the photo on the counter and carried her mug to the sink. "We're doing it, and that's final."

Melissa rose from the table, holding her wrist at an awkward angle. She glanced at Spencer, and for a moment, her eyes softened. Spencer gave her a tiny smile. Perhaps they'd connected just then, finding common ground in hating their parents' naive plan. Perhaps Melissa could forgive Spencer for shoving her down the stairs and stealing her paper. If she did, Spencer would forgive Melissa for saying their parents didn't love her.

Spencer looked down at the photo and thought of the magic shows she and Melissa used to perform. After their friendship had splintered, Spencer had thought that if she muttered some of her and Melissa's old magic words, they'd be best friends again. If only it were that easy.

When she looked up again, Melissa's expression had shifted. She narrowed her eyes and turned away. "Bitch," she said over her shoulder as she sashayed down the hall.

Spencer curled her hands into fists, all of her anger gushing back in. It would take a whole lot more than magic for them to get along. It would take a miracle.

3

EMILY'S OWN AMERICAN GOTHIC

Late Sunday afternoon, Emily Fields followed an old lady with a walker onto the moving sidewalk of the Des Moines International Airport, dragging her ratty blue swim duffel behind her. The bag was stuffed with all her worldly goods—her clothes, shoes, her two favorite stuffed walruses, her journal, her iPod, and various carefully folded notes from Alison DiLaurentis that she couldn't bear to part with. When the plane was over Chicago, she realized she'd forgotten underwear. But then, that was what she got for packing frantically this morning. She'd only gotten three hours of sleep, shell-shocked from seeing Hanna's body fly up into the air when that SUV hit her.

Emily arrived in the main terminal and ducked into the first bathroom she could find, squeezing around a very large woman in too-tight jeans. She stared at her bleary-eyed reflection in the mirror over the sink. Her parents had really done it. They'd really sent her here, to Addams, Iowa, to live with her aunt Helene and her uncle Allen. It was all because A had outed Emily to the entire school, and all because Emily's mother had caught her hugging Maya St. Germain, the girl she loved, at Mona Vanderwaal's party last night. Emily had known the deal—she'd promised to do the "gay-away" Tree Tops program to rid herself of her feelings for Maya or it was good-bye, Rosewood. But when she discovered that even her Tree Tops counselor, Becka, couldn't resist her true urges, all bets were off.

The Des Moines airport was small, boasting only a couple of restaurants, a bookshop, and a store that sold colorful Vera Bradley bags. When Emily reached the baggage claim area, she looked around uncertainly. All she remembered about her aunt and uncle was their super-strictness. They avoided anything that might trigger sexual impulses—even certain *foods*. As she scanned the crowd, Emily half-expected to see the stern, long-faced farmer and his plain, bitter wife from the *American Gothic* painting standing near the baggage carousel.

"Emily."

She whirled around. Helene and Allen Weaver were leaning against a Smarte Carte machine, their hands clasped at their waists. Allen's tucked-in mustard-yellow golf shirt prominently displayed his massive gut. Helene's short gray hair looked shellacked. Neither was smiling.

"Did you check any luggage?" Allen asked gruffly.

"Uh, no," Emily said politely, wondering if she should go in for a hug. Weren't aunts and uncles usually happy to see their nieces? Allen and Helene just looked annoyed.

"Well, then, let's go," Helene said. "It's about two hours to Addams."

Their car was an old, wood-paneled station wagon. The inside smelled like fake pine-tree air freshener, a smell that always made Emily think of long, cross-country drives with her grumpy grandparents. Allen drove at least fifteen miles under the speed limit—even a frail old woman squinting over her steering wheel passed them. Neither her aunt nor her uncle said a word the whole drive—not to Emily, and not to each other. It was so quiet, Emily could hear the sound of her heart breaking into seven million tiny pieces.

"Iowa sure is pretty," Emily commented loudly, gesturing to the endless flat land all around her. She'd never seen a place so desolate—there weren't even any rest stops. Allen made a small grunt. Helene pursed her lips even tighter. If she'd pursed any harder, she'd have swallowed her lips altogether.

Emily's cell phone, cool and smooth in her jacket pocket, felt like one of the last bridges to civilization. She brought it out and stared at the screen. No new messages, not even from Maya. She'd sent Aria a text before she left, asking how Hanna was doing, but Aria hadn't responded.

The newest text in her inbox was the one A had sent last night—*She knew too much.* Had A really hit Hanna? And what about the things Aria had told her before Hanna's accident—could Spencer be Ali's killer? Tears dotted Emily's eyes. This was definitely the wrong time to be so far from Rosewood.

Suddenly, Allen took a sharp right off the road, veering onto a bumpy dirt path. The car wobbled over the uneven ground, crossing over several cattle guards and passing a few rickety-looking houses. Dogs ran up and down the length of the path, barking viciously at the vehicle. Finally, they pulled onto yet another dirt road and came to a gate. Helene got out and unlocked it, and Allen drove the car through. A two-story, white-shingled house loomed ahead. It was spare and modest, sort of reminiscent of the Amish houses in Lancaster, Pennsylvania, that Emily and her parents used to stop at to buy authentic shoofly pie.

"Here we are," Helene said blandly.

"It's beautiful," Emily said, trying to sound upbeat as she got out of the car.

Like the other houses they'd passed, the Weavers' property was surrounded by a chain-link fence, and there were dogs, chickens, ducks, and goats everywhere. One brave goat attached to the cattle guard by a long chain trotted right up to Emily. He butted her with his dirty-looking horns, and she screamed.

Helene looked at her sternly as the goat waddled away. "Don't scream like that. The chickens don't like it."

Perfect. The chickens' needs took precedence to Emily's. She pointed to the goat. "Why is he chained like that?"

"*She,*" Helene corrected her. "She's been a bad girl, that's why."

Emily bit her lip nervously as Helene led her into a tiny kitchen that looked like it hadn't been updated since the fifties. Emily immediately missed her mom's cheery kitchen, with its chicken collectibles, year-round Christmas towels, and refrigerator magnets shaped like Philadelphia monuments. Helene's fridge was bare and magnet-free and smelled like rotting vegetables. When they walked into a small living room, Helene pointed to a girl about Emily's age sitting on a vomit-colored chair and reading *Jane Eyre.* "You remember Abby?"

Emily's cousin Abby wore a pale khaki jumper that came to her knees and a demure eyelet blouse. She'd pulled her hair back at the nape of her neck, and she wore no makeup. In her tight LOVE AN ANIMAL, HUG A SWIMMER tee, ripped Abercrombie jeans, tinted moisturizer, and cherry-flavored lip gloss, Emily felt like a whore.

"Hello, Emily," Abby said primly.

"Abby was nice enough to offer to share her room with you," Helene said. "It's just up the stairs. We'll show you."

There were four bedrooms upstairs. The first was Helene and Allen's, and the second was for John and Matt, the seventeen-year-old twins. "And that one's for Sarah, Elizabeth, and baby Karen," Helene said, gesturing to a room that Emily had mistaken for a broom closet.

Emily gaped. She hadn't heard of any of those cousins. "How old are they?"

"Well, Karen's six months, Sarah is two, and Elizabeth is four. They're at their grandmother's right now."

Emily tried to hide a smile. For people who shunned sex, they certainly had a lot of offspring.

Helene led Emily into an almost-empty room and pointed to a twin cot in the corner. Abby settled down on her own bed, folding her hands in her lap. Emily couldn't believe the room had been lived in—the only furniture was the two beds, a plain dresser, a small round rug, and a bookshelf with hardly any books on it. At home, her room was plastered with posters and pictures; her desk was strewn with perfume bottles, cutouts from magazines, CDs, and books. Then again, the last time Emily was here, Abby had told her she was planning to become a nun, so perhaps no-frills living was part of her nunnish training. Emily glanced out the big picture window at the end of the room and saw the Weavers' enormous field, which included a large stable and a silo. Her two older boy cousins, John and Matt, were lugging bales of hay out of the stable and onto the bed of a pickup truck. There was nothing on the horizon. At all.

"So, how far away is your school?" Emily asked Abby.

Abby's face lit up. "My mom didn't tell you? We're homeschooled."

"Ohh . . ." Emily's will to live slowly seeped out the sweat glands in her feet.

"I'll give you the class schedule tomorrow." Helene plunked a few grayish towels onto Emily's bed. "You'll have to take some exams to see where I place you."

"I'm a junior in high school," Emily offered. "I'm in some AP classes."

"We'll see where I place you." Helene gave her a hard look.

Abby got up from her bed and disappeared into the hall. Emily gazed desperately out the window. *If a bird flies by in the next five seconds, I'll be back to Rosewood by next week.* Just as a delicate sparrow fluttered past, Emily remembered she wasn't playing her little superstitious games anymore. The events of the last few months—the workers finding Ali's body in the gazebo hole, Toby's suicide, A's . . . everything—had made her lose all faith in things happening for a reason.

Her cell phone chimed. Emily pulled it out and saw that Maya had sent her a text. *R U really in Iowa? Pls call me when you can.*

Help me, Emily began to type, when Helene snatched the phone from her hands.

"We don't allow cell phones in this house." Helene switched the phone off.

"But . . ." Emily protested. "What if I want to call my parents?"

"I can do that for you," Helene sang. She came close to Emily's face. "Your mother has told me a few things about you. I don't know how they do things in Rosewood, but around here, we live by my rules. Is that clear?"

Emily flinched. Helene spat when she spoke, and Emily's cheek felt moist. "It's clear," she said shakily.

"Good." Helene walked out into the hallway and dropped the phone into a large, empty jar on a wooden end table. "We'll just put this here for safekeeping." Someone had printed the words SWEAR JAR on the lid, but the jar was completely empty except for Emily's phone.

Emily's phone looked lonely in the swear jar, but she didn't dare unscrew the lid—Helene probably had it wired with an alarm. She walked back into the empty bedroom and threw herself onto the cot. There was a sharp bar in the middle of the mattress, and the pillow felt like a slab of cement. As the Iowa sky turned from russet to purple to midnight blue to black, Emily felt hot tears stream down her face. If this was the first day of the rest of her life, she'd much rather be dead.

The door opened a few hours later with a slow *creeeeaaak*. A shadow lengthened across the floor. Emily sat up on her cot, her heart pounding. She thought of A's note. *She knew too much.* And of Hanna's body, crashing down to the pavement.

But it was only Abby. She snapped on a small bedside table lamp and dropped down on her stomach next to her bed. Emily bit the inside of her cheek and pretended not to notice. Was this some freaky Iowan form of praying?

Abby sat up again, a jumble of fabric in her hands. She pulled her khaki jumper over her head, unhooked her beige bra, stepped into a denim miniskirt, and wriggled into a red tube top. Then she reached under her bed again, located a pink-and-white makeup bag, and brushed mascara over her lashes and red gloss on her lips. Finally, she pulled her hair out of its ponytail, turned her head upside down, and ran her hands through her scalp. When she flipped back up, her hair was wild and thick around her face.

Abby met Emily's eyes. She grinned broadly, as if to say, *Close your mouth. You're letting flies in.* "You're coming with us, right?"

"W-where?" Emily sputtered, once she found her voice.

"You'll see." Abby walked over to Emily and took her hand. "Emily Fields, your first night in Iowa has just begun."

4

IF YOU BELIEVE IT,
THEN IT'S TRUE

When Hanna Marin opened her eyes, she was alone in a long, white tunnel. Behind her, there was only darkness, and ahead of her, only light. Physically, she felt fantastic—not bloated from eating too many white cheddar Cheez-Its, not dry-skinned and frizzy-haired, not groggy from lack of sleep or stressed from social maneuvering. In fact, she wasn't sure when she'd last felt this . . . perfect.

This didn't feel like an ordinary dream, but something way more important. Suddenly, a pixel of light flitted in front of her eyes. And then another, and another. Her surroundings eased into view like a photo slowly loading on a Web page.

She found herself sitting with her three best friends on Alison DiLaurentis's back porch. Spencer's dirty blond hair was in a high ponytail, and Aria wore her wavy, blue-black mane in braids. Emily wore an aqua-colored T-shirt and boxers with ROSEWOOD SWIMMING written across the butt. A feeling of dread swept over Hanna, and when she looked at her reflection in the window, her seventh-grade self stared back. Her braces had green and pink rubber bands. Her poop-brown hair was twisted into a bun. Her arms looked like ham hocks and her legs were pale, flabby loaves of bread. So much for feeling wonderful.

"Uh, guys?"

Hanna turned. Ali was *here*. Right in front of her, staring at them as if they'd sprouted out of the ground. As Ali came closer, Hanna could smell her minty gum and Ralph Lauren Blue perfume. There were Ali's purple Puma flip-flops—Hanna had forgotten about them. And there were Ali's feet—she could cross her crooked second toe over her big toe, and said it was good luck. Hanna wished Ali would cross her toes right now, and do all of the other uniquely Ali things Hanna wanted so desperately to remember.

Spencer stood up. "What did she bust you for?"

"Were you getting in trouble without us?" Aria cried. "And why'd you change? That halter you had on was so cute."

"Do you want us to go?" Emily asked fearfully.

Hanna remembered this exact day. She still had some of the notes from her seventh-grade history final scribbled on the heel of her hand. She reached into her Manhattan Portage canvas messenger bag, feeling the edge of her white cotton Rosewood Day graduation beret. She had picked it up in the gym during lunch period, in preparation for tomorrow's graduation ceremony.

Graduation wasn't the only thing that would happen tomorrow, though.

"Ali," Hanna said, standing up so abruptly that she knocked over one of the patio table's citronella candles. "I need to talk to you."

But Ali ignored her, almost as if Hanna hadn't spoken at all. "I threw my hockey clothes in with my mom's delicates again," she said to the others.

"She got mad at you for *that*?" Emily looked incredulous.

"Ali." Hanna waved her hands in front of Ali's face. "You have to listen to me. Something awful is going to happen to you. And we have to stop it!"

Ali's eyes flickered over to Hanna. She shrugged and shook her hair out of its polka-dot headband. She looked at Emily again. "You know my mom, Em. She's more anal than Spencer!"

"Who cares about your mom?" Hanna shrieked. Her skin felt hot and tingly, like a zillion bees had stung her.

"Guess where we're having our end-of-seventh-grade sleepover tomorrow night?" Spencer was saying.

"Where?" Ali leaned forward on her elbows.

"Melissa's barn!" Spencer cried.

"Sweet!" Ali whooped.

"No!" Hanna cried. She climbed onto the middle of the table, to make them see her. How did they *not* see her? She was as fat as a manatee. "Guys, we *can't*. We have to have our sleepover somewhere else. Somewhere where there are people. Where it's safe."

Her mind started churning. Perhaps the universe had a kink in it, and she was really, truly back in seventh grade, right before Ali died, with knowledge of the future. She had the chance to change things. She could call the Rosewood PD and tell them she had a horrible feeling that something was going to happen to her best friend tomorrow. She could build a barbed-wire fence around the hole in the DiLaurentises' yard.

"Maybe we shouldn't have a sleepover at all," Hanna said frantically. "Maybe we should do it another night."

Finally, Ali grabbed Hanna's wrists and dragged her off the table. "Stop it," she whispered. "You're making a big deal over nothing."

"A big deal over *nothing*?" Hanna protested. "Ali, you're going to *die* tomorrow. You're going to run out of the barn during our sleepover and just . . . disappear."

"No, Hanna, listen. I'm not."

A clammy feeling washed over Hanna. Ali was staring right into her eyes. "You're . . . not?" she stammered.

Ali touched Hanna's hand. It was a comforting caress, the kind of gesture Hanna's father used to make when she was sick. "Don't worry," Ali said softly in Hanna's ear. "I'm okay."

Her voice sounded so close. So real. Hanna blinked and opened her eyes, but she wasn't in Ali's yard anymore.

She was in a white room, flat on her back. Harsh fluorescent lights hung over her. She heard beeping somewhere to her left, and the steady hiss of a machine, in and out, in and out.

A blurry figure swam over her. The girl had a heart-shaped face, bright blue eyes, and brilliant white teeth. She slowly caressed Hanna's hand. Hanna struggled to focus. It looked like . . .

"I'm okay," Ali's voice said again, her breath hot against Hanna's cheek. Hanna gasped. Her fists opened and closed. She struggled to hold on to this moment, to this realization, but then everything faded out—all sound, all smells, the feeling of Ali's hand touching hers. Then there was only darkness.

5

THIS MEANS WAR

Late Sunday afternoon, after Aria left the hospital—Hanna's condition hadn't changed—she walked up the uneven porch steps of the Old Hollis house where Ezra lived. Ezra's bottom-floor apartment was just two blocks away from the house Byron now shared with Meredith, and Aria wasn't quite ready to go there yet. She didn't expect Ezra to be home, but she'd written him a letter, telling him where she'd be living, and that she hoped they could talk. As she struggled to fit the note through Ezra's mailbox slot, she heard a creak behind her.

"Aria." Ezra emerged in the foyer, wearing faded jeans and a tomato-colored Gap T-shirt. "What are you doing?"

"I was . . ." Aria's voice was taut with emotion. She held up the note, which had crumpled a little during her attempt to shove it in the mailbox. "I was going to give this to you. It just said to call me." She took a tentative step toward Ezra, afraid to touch him. He smelled exactly as he had last night, when Aria was last here—a little like Scotch, a little like moisturizer. "I didn't think you'd be here," Aria sputtered. "Are you okay?"

"Well, I didn't have to spend the night in jail, which was good." Ezra laughed, then frowned. "But . . . I'm fired. Your boyfriend told the school staff everything—he had pictures of us to prove it. Everyone would rather keep it quiet, so unless *you* press charges, it's not going to go on my record." He hooked his thumb around one of his belt loops. "I'm supposed to go there tomorrow and clean out my office. I guess you guys are going to have a new teacher for the rest of the year."

Aria pressed her hands to her face. "I am so, *so* sorry." She grabbed Ezra's hand. At first, Ezra resisted her touch, but he slowly sighed and gave in. He brought her close to him and kissed her hard, and Aria kissed back like she'd never kissed before. Ezra slid his arms under the clasp of her bra. Aria grabbed at his shirt, tearing it off. It didn't matter that they were outside or that a group of bong-smoking college kids were staring at them from the porch next door. Aria kissed Ezra's bare neck, and Ezra circled his arms around her waist.

But when they heard a police car siren *whoop*, they shot apart, startled.

Aria ducked behind the basket-weave porch wall. Ezra crouched beside her, his face flushed. Slowly, a police car rolled past Ezra's house. The cop was on his cell phone, not paying any attention to them.

When Aria turned back to Ezra, the sexy mood had fizzled. "Come on in," Ezra said, pulling his shirt back on and walking into his apartment. Aria followed him, stepping around his front door, which still hung off its hinges from when the cops had knocked it down yesterday. The apartment smelled as it usually did, like dust and Kraft macaroni and cheese.

"I could try and find you another job," Aria suggested. "Maybe my father needs an assistant. Or he could pull some strings at Hollis."

"Aria . . ." There was a surrendering look on Ezra's face. And then, Aria noticed the U-Haul boxes behind him. The bathtub that sat in the middle of the living room had been emptied of all its books. The blobby blue candles on the mantel were gone. And Bertha, the French maid blow-up doll some friends had bought for Ezra as a joke back in college, was no longer perched on one of the kitchen chairs. In fact, most of Ezra's personal artifacts were missing. Only a few lonely, junky pieces of furniture remained.

A cold, clammy feeling washed over her. "You're leaving."

"I have a cousin who lives in Providence," Ezra mumbled into his chest. "I'm going to go up there for a while. Clear my head. Take some pottery classes at Rhode Island School of Design. I don't know."

"Take me with you," Aria blurted out. She walked up to Ezra and pulled on the hem of his shirt. "I've always wanted to go to RISD. It's my first-choice school. Maybe I could apply early." She raised her eyes to Ezra again. "I'm moving in with my father and Meredith—which is pretty much a fate worse than death. And . . . and I've never felt like I do when I'm around you. I'm not sure I ever will again."

Ezra squeezed his eyes shut, swinging Aria's hands back and forth. "I think you should look me up in a couple years. Because, I mean, I feel that way about you, too. But I have to get out of here. You know it, and I know it."

Aria dropped his hands. She felt like someone had opened up her chest and removed her heart. Just last night, for a few hours, everything had been perfect. And then Sean—and A—had ripped it all apart again.

"Hey," Ezra said, noting the tears spilling down Aria's cheeks. He pulled her into him and held her tight. "It's okay." He peered into one of his boxes, then handed her his William Shakespeare bobblehead. "I want you to have this."

Aria gave him a tiny smile. "Seriously?" The first time she'd come here, after Noel Kahn's party back in the beginning of September, Ezra had told her the bobblehead was one of his favorite possessions.

Ezra traced the line of Aria's jaw with the tip of his pointer finger, starting at her chin and ending at her earlobe. Shivers went up her spine. "Really," he whispered.

She could feel his eyes on her as she turned for the door. "Aria," he called, just as she was stepping over a big pile of old phone books to get out into the hall.

She stopped, her heart lifting. There was a wise, calm look on Ezra's face. "You're the strongest girl I've ever met," he said. "So just . . . screw 'em, you know? You'll be fine."

Ezra leaned down, sealing up boxes with clear packing tape. Aria backed out of the apartment in a daze, wondering why he'd suddenly turned all guidance counselor on her. It was like he was saying that he was the adult, with responsibilities and consequences, and she was just a kid, her whole life in front of her.

Which was *exactly* what she didn't want to hear right then.

"Aria! Welcome!" Meredith cried. She stood at the edge of the kitchen, wearing a black-and-white striped apron—which Aria was trying to imagine as a prison uniform—and a cow-shaped oven mitt covered her right hand. She was grinning like a shark about to swallow a minnow.

Aria dragged in the last of the bags Sean had dumped at her feet last night and looked around. She knew Meredith had quirky taste—she was an artist, and taught classes at Hollis College, the same place where Byron was tenured—but Meredith's living room looked like a psychopath had decorated it. There was a dentist's chair in the corner, complete with a tray for all the instruments of torture. Meredith had covered a whole wall with pictures of eyeballs. She branded messages into wood as a form of artistic expression, and there was a big wood chunk across the mantel that said, BEAUTY IS ONLY SKIN DEEP, BUT UGLY GOES CLEAN TO THE BONE. There was a large cutout of the Wicked Witch of the West pasted over the kitchen table. Aria was half tempted to point to it and say she hadn't known Meredith's mother was from Oz. Then she saw a raccoon in the corner and screamed.

"Don't worry, don't worry," Meredith said quickly. "He's stuffed. I bought him at a taxidermy store in Philly."

Aria wrinkled her nose. This place rivaled the Mütter Museum of medical oddities in Philadelphia, which Aria's brother loved almost as much as the sex museums he'd visited in Europe.

"Aria!" Byron appeared from behind a corner, wiping his hands on his jeans. Aria noted that he was wearing dark denim jeans *with a belt* and a soft gray sweater—maybe his usual uniform of a sweat-stained Sixers T-shirt and frayed plaid boxers wasn't good enough for Meredith. "Welcome!"

Aria grunted, hefting up her duffel again. When she sniffed the air, it smelled like a combination of burnt wood and Cream of Wheat. She eyed the pot on the stove suspiciously. Perhaps Meredith was cooking gruel, like an evil headmistress in a Dickens novel.

"So let me show you your room." Byron grabbed Aria's hand. He led her down the hall to a large, square room that contained a few big chunks of wood, some branding irons, an enormous band saw, and welding tools. Aria assumed this was Meredith's studio—or the room where she finished off her victims.

"This way," Byron said. He led her to a space in the corner of the studio that was separated from the rest of the room by a floral curtain. When he pushed the curtain back, he crowed, "Taa-*daaa*!"

A twin bed and a dresser missing three of its drawers occupied a space only slightly larger than a shower stall. Byron had carried in her other suitcases earlier, but because there was no room on the floor, he'd piled them on the bed. There was one flat, yellowed pillow propped up against the headboard, and someone had balanced a tiny portable TV in the windowsill. There was a sticker on the top of it that said in old, faded, seventies lettering, SAVE A HORSE, RIDE A WELDER.

Aria turned to Byron, feeling nauseated. "I have to sleep in Meredith's studio?"

"She doesn't work at night," Byron said quickly. "And look! You have your own TV and your own fireplace!" He pointed to a huge brick monstrosity that took up most of the far wall. Most Old Hollis houses had fireplaces in every room because their central heating systems sucked. "You can make it cozy in here at night!"

"Dad, I have no idea how to *light* a fireplace." Then Aria noticed a trail of cockroaches going from one corner of the ceiling to another. "Jesus!" she screamed, pointing at them and cowering behind Byron.

"They're not real," Byron reassured her. "Meredith painted them. She's really personalized this place with an artistic touch."

Aria felt like she was going to hyperventilate. "They look real to me!"

Byron looked honestly surprised. "I thought you'd like this place. It was the best we could put together on such short notice."

Aria shut her eyes. She missed Ezra's shabby little apartment, with its bathtub and thousands of books and map of the New York City subway system shower curtain. There were no roaches there, either—real *or* fake.

"Honey?" Meredith's voice rang out from the kitchen. "Dinner's ready."

Byron gave Aria a tight smile and turned for the kitchen. Aria figured she should follow. In the kitchen, Meredith was setting bowls at each of their plates. Thankfully, dinner wasn't gruel, but innocent-looking chicken soup. "I thought this would be best for my stomach," she admitted.

"Meredith's been having some stomach issues," Byron

explained. Aria turned to the window and smiled. Maybe she'd get lucky and Meredith would have somehow contracted the bubonic plague.

"It's low-salt." Meredith punched Byron in the arm. "So it's good for you, too."

Aria looked at her father curiously. Byron used to salt every single bite while it was on the fork. "Since when do you eat low-salt stuff?"

"I have high blood pressure," Byron said, pointing to his heart.

Aria wrinkled her nose. "No, you don't."

"Yes, I do." Byron tucked his napkin into his collar. "I have for a while now."

"But . . . but you've never eaten low-salt stuff before."

"I'm a slave driver," Meredith insisted, scraping back a seat and sitting down. Meredith had positioned Aria at the head of the Wicked Witch cutout. Aria slid her bowl over to cover the witch's pea-green visage. "I keep him on a regimen," Meredith went on. "I make him take vitamins, too."

Aria slumped, dread welling in her stomach. Meredith was already acting like Byron's wife, and he'd only lived with her for a month.

Meredith pointed to Aria's hand. "Whatcha got there?"

Aria stared down at her lap, realizing she was still holding the Shakespeare bobblehead Ezra had given her. "Oh. It's just . . . something from a friend."

"A friend who likes *literature,* I guess." Meredith reached out and made Shakespeare's head bob up and down. There was a tiny glint in her eye.

Aria froze. Could Meredith *know* about Ezra? She glanced at Byron. Her father slurped his soup, oblivious. He wasn't reading at the table, something he constantly did at home. Had Byron seriously been unhappy at home? Did he honestly enjoy bug-painting, taxidermy-loving Meredith more than he loved Aria's sweet, kind, loving mother, Ella? And what made Byron think Aria could just sit idly by and accept this?

"Oh, Meredith has a surprise for you," Byron piped up. "Every semester, she gets to take a class at Hollis for free. She says you can use this semester's credit to take a class instead."

"That's right." Meredith passed the Hollis College continuing education course book to Aria. "Maybe you'd like to take one of the art classes I'm teaching?"

Aria bit down hard on the inside of her cheek. She'd rather have shards of glass permanently lodged in her throat than spend a single additional moment with Meredith.

"Come on, pick a class," Byron urged. "You know you want to."

So they were forcing her to do this? Aria whipped open the book. Maybe she could take something in German filmmaking, or microbiology, or Special Topics in Neglected Children and Maladjusted Family Behavior.

Then something caught her eye. *Mindless Art: Create uniquely crafted masterpieces in tune with your soul's needs, wants, and desires. Through sculpture and touch, students learn to depend less on their eyes and more on their inner selves.*

Aria circled the class with the gray ROCKS ROCK! Hollis geology department pencil she'd found wedged in the course book. The class definitely sounded kooky. It might even end up being like one of those Icelandic yoga classes where instead of stretching, Aria and the rest of the students danced with their eyes closed, making hawk noises. But she needed a little mindlessness right now. Plus, it was one of the few art classes that Meredith *wasn't* teaching. Which pretty much made it perfect.

Byron excused himself from the table and bounded off to Meredith's minuscule bathroom. After he turned on the bathroom's overhead fan, Meredith laid down her fork and looked squarely at Aria. "I know what you're thinking," she said evenly, rubbing her thumb along the pink spiderweb tattoo on her wrist. "You hate that your father's with me. But you'd better get used to it, Aria. Byron and I are going to be married as soon as your parents' divorce goes through."

Aria accidentally swallowed an unchewed bite of noodles. She coughed up the broth, sputtering it all over the table. Meredith jumped back, her eyes wide. "Something you ate not agreeing with you?" she simpered.

Aria looked away sharply, her throat burning. Something hadn't agreed with her, all right, but it wasn't the Wicked Witch's soup.

6

EMILY'S JUST A SWEET, INNOCENT MIDWESTERN GAL

"Come on!" Abby urged, pulling Emily across the farm-yard. The sun was sinking over the flat Iowa horizon, and all sorts of long-legged Midwestern bugs were coming out to play. Apparently, Emily, Abby, and Emily's two eldest boy cousins, Matt and John, were also going out to play.

The four of them stopped at the edge of the road. John and Matt had both changed out of their plain white T-shirts and work pants into baggy jeans and T-shirts with beer slogans. Abby pulled at the bodice of her tube top and checked her lipstick in her little compact mirror. Emily, in the same jeans and swimming T-shirt she'd worn when she arrived, felt plain and underdressed—which was pretty much how she always felt back in Rosewood.

Emily gazed over her shoulder at the farmhouse. All of its lights were off, but the dogs were still running crazily around the property, and the bad goat was still chained to the cattle guard, the bell around her neck clanging back and forth. It was a wonder Helene and Allen didn't put bells on their children. "Are you sure this is a good idea?" she wondered aloud.

"It's fine," Abby answered, her hoop earrings swinging. "Mom and Dad go to bed at eight P.M. like clockwork. That's what happens when you wake up at four."

"We've been doing this for months and haven't gotten caught once," Matt assured her.

Suddenly, a silver pickup truck appeared on the horizon, dust kicking up in its wake. The truck rolled slowly up to the four of them and stopped. A hip-hop song Emily couldn't place wafted out, along with the strong smell of menthol cigarettes. A dark-haired, Noel Kahn look-alike waved to the cousins, then smiled at Emily. "Soooo . . . this is your cousin, huh?"

"That's right," Abby said. "She's from Pennsylvania. Emily, this is Dyson."

"Get in." Dyson patted the seat. Abby and Emily climbed in the front, and John and Matt climbed into the pickup bed. As they rolled off, Emily glanced once more at the farmhouse receding in the distance, an uneasy feeling gnawing at her.

"So, what brings you to glamorous Addams?" Dyson clunkily shifted gears.

Emily glanced at Abby. "My parents sent me."

"They sent you away?"

"Totally," Abby interrupted. "I heard you're a real

badass, Emily." She looked at Dyson. "Emily lives on the edge."

Emily stifled a laugh. The only rebellious thing she'd ever done in front of Abby was sneak an extra Oreo for dessert. She wondered if her cousins knew the truth of why her parents had banished her here. Probably not—*lesbian* was most likely a swear-jar word.

Within minutes, they drove up an uneven path to a large, burnt-orange silo, and parked on the grass next to a car with a bumper sticker that read, I BRAKE FOR HOOTERS. Two pale boys rolled out of a red pickup and bumped fists with a couple beefy, towheaded boys climbing out of a black Dodge Ram. Emily smirked. She'd always thought using the word *corn-fed* to describe someone from Iowa was a cliché, but right now, it was the only description that came to mind.

Abby squeezed Emily's arm. "The ratio of guys to girls here is four to one," she whispered. "So you'll totally hook up tonight. I always do."

So Abby didn't know about Emily. "Oh. Great." Emily tried to smile. Abby winked and jumped out of the truck. Emily followed the others toward the silo. The air smelled like Clinique Happy perfume; hoppy, soapy beer; and dried grass. When she walked inside, she expected to see bales of hay, a farm animal or two, and perhaps a bare, unstable ladder that led to a freaky girl's bedroom, just like in *The Ring*. Instead, the silo had been cleared out and Christmas lights hung from the ceiling. Plush, plum-colored couches lined the walls, and Emily saw a turntable in the corner and a bunch of enormous kegs near the back.

Abby, who'd already grabbed a beer, pulled a couple of guys toward Emily. Even in Rosewood, they would've been popular—they all had floppy hair, angular faces, and brilliant white teeth. "Brett, Todd, Xavi ... *this* is my cousin Emily. She's from Pennsylvania."

"Hi," Emily said, shaking the boys' hands.

"Pennsyl*va*nia." The boys nodded appreciatively, as if Abby had said Emily was from Naughty Dirty Sex Land.

As Abby wandered off with one of the boys, Emily made her way to the keg. She stood in line behind a blond couple who were grinding against each other. The DJ melted into Timbaland, whom everyone at Rosewood was into right now, too. Really, people in Iowa didn't seem that different from people at her school. The girls all wore denim skirts and wedge heels, and the guys wore oversize hoodies and baggy jeans, and seemed to be experimenting with facial hair. Emily wondered where all of them went to school, or if their parents homeschooled them as well.

"Are you the new girl?"

A tall, white-blond girl in a striped tunic and dark jeans stood behind her. She had the broad shoulders and powerful stance of a professional volleyball player, and four small earrings snaked up her left ear. But there was something very sweet and open about her round face, light blue eyes, and small, pretty lips. And unlike practically every other girl in the silo, she didn't have a guy's hands draped over her boobs. "Uh, yeah," Emily replied. "I just got here today."

"And you're from Pennsylvania, right?" The girl pivoted back on her hips and appraised Emily carefully. "I was there once. We went to Harvard Square."

"I think you mean Boston, in Massachusetts," Emily corrected her. "That's where Harvard is. Pennsylvania has Philadelphia. The Liberty Bell, Ben Franklin stuff, all that."

"Oh." The girl's face fell. "I haven't been to Pennsylvania, then." She lowered her chin at Emily. "So. If you were candy, what kind would you be?"

"Sorry?" Emily blinked.

"Come on." The girl poked her. "Me, I'd be an M&M."

"Why?" Emily asked.

The girl lowered her eyes seductively. "Because I melt in your mouth, obviously." She poked Emily. "So how about you?"

Emily shrugged. This was the strangest getting-to-know-you question anyone had ever asked her, but she kind of liked it. "I've never thought about it. A Tootsie Roll?"

The girl violently shook her head. "You wouldn't be a Tootsie Roll. That looks like a big long poop. You'd be something *way* sexier than that."

Emily breathed in very, very slowly. Was this girl *flirting* with her? "Um, I think I need to know your name before we talk about . . . sexy candy."

The girl stuck out her hand. "I'm Trista."

"Emily." As they shook, Trista spiraled her thumb around the inside of Emily's palm. She never took her eyes off Emily's face.

Maybe this was just some sort of cultural Iowan way of saying hello.

"Do you want a beer?" Emily sputtered, turning back for the keg.

"Absolutely," Trista said. "But let *me* pour it for you, Pennsylvania. You probably don't even know how to pump a keg." Emily watched as Trista pumped the keg handle a few times and let the beer filter slowly into her cup, producing almost no foam.

"Thanks," Emily answered, taking a sip.

Trista poured herself a beer and led Emily away from the line to one of the couches that lined the walls of the silo. "So, did your family just move here?"

"I'm staying with my cousins for a little while." Emily pointed to Abby, who was dancing with a tall blond boy, and to Matt and John, who were smoking cigarettes with a petite redhead wearing a skintight pink sweater and skinny jeans.

"You on a little vacation?" Trista asked, fluttering her eyelashes.

Emily couldn't be sure, but it seemed like Trista was moving closer and closer to her on the couch. She was doing everything in her power not to touch Trista's long legs, which were dangling inches from her own. "Not exactly," she blurted out. "My parents kicked me out of the house because I couldn't live by their rules."

Trista fiddled with the strap of her tan boots. "My mom's like that. She thinks I'm at a choir concert right now. Otherwise she never would've let me out."

"I used to have to lie to my parents about going to parties too," Emily said, suddenly afraid she was going to start crying again. She tried to imagine what was happening at her house right now. Her family had probably gathered around the TV after dinner. Just her mom, her dad, and Carolyn, happily chatting among themselves, *glad* that Emily, the heathen, was gone. It hurt so much it made her feel nauseated.

Trista glanced at Emily sympathetically, as if she sensed something was wrong. "So hey. Here's another one. If you were a party, what kind of party would you be?"

"A surprise party," Emily blurted out. That seemed like the story of her life lately—one big surprise after another.

"Good one." Trista smiled. "I'd be a toga party."

They smiled at each other for a long moment. There was something about Trista's heart-shaped face and wide, blue eyes that made Emily feel really...safe. Trista leaned forward, and so did Emily. It was almost like they were going to kiss, but then Trista bent down very slowly and fixed the strap on her shoe.

"So why'd they send you here, anyway?" Trista asked when she sat back up.

Emily took a huge swallow of beer. "Because they caught me kissing a girl," she blurted out.

When Trista leaned back, her eyes wide, Emily thought she'd made a horrible mistake. Perhaps Trista *was* just being Midwestern friendly, and Emily had misinterpreted. But then, Trista broke into a coy smile. She moved her lips close to Emily's ear. "You *totally* wouldn't be a Tootsie Roll. If it were up to me, you'd be a red-hot candy heart."

Emily's heart did three somersaults. Trista stood up and offered Emily her hand. Emily took it, and without a word, Trista led her to the dance floor and started dancing sexily to the music. The song changed to a fast one, and Trista squealed and started to jump around as if she were on a trampoline. Her energy was intoxicating. Emily felt like she could be goofy with Trista—not constantly poised and cool, as she always felt she had to behave around Maya.

Maya. Emily stopped, breathing in the rank, humid silo air. Last night, she and Maya had said they loved each other. Were they still together, now that Emily was possibly permanently stuck here, amid all this corn and cow manure? Did this qualify as cheating? And what did it mean that Emily hadn't thought of her once tonight, until now?

Trista's cell phone beeped. She stepped out of the

circle of dancers and pulled it out of her pocket. "My stupid mom's texting me for like the gazillionth time tonight," she yelled over the music, shaking her head.

A shock vibrated through Emily—any minute now, she'd probably be getting a text of her own. A always seemed to know when she was having naughty thoughts. Only, her cell phone . . . was in the swear jar.

Emily let out a thrilled bleat of laughter. Her phone was in the *swear jar*. She was at a party in Iowa, thousands of miles from Rosewood. Unless A was supernatural, there was no way A could know what Emily was doing.

Suddenly, Iowa wasn't quite so bad. Not. At. All.

7

BARBIE DOLL . . . OR VOODOO DOLL?

Sunday evening, Spencer swung gently on the hammock on the wraparound porch of her grandmother's vacation house. As she watched yet another hot, muscular surfer boy catch a wave at Nun's, the surfing beach just down the road that bordered a convent, a shadow fell over her.

"Your father and I are going to the yacht club for a while," her mother said, shoving her hands into her beige linen trousers.

"Oh." Spencer struggled to get out of the hammock without getting her feet tangled in the netting. The Stone Harbor yacht club was in an old sea shack that smelled a little like brine in a moldy basement. Spencer suspected her parents liked going there solely because it was a members-only establishment. "Can I come?"

Her mother caught her arm. "You and Melissa are staying here."

A breeze that smelled of surf wax and fish smacked

Spencer in the face. She tried to see things from her mother's perspective—it must have sucked to see her two children fighting so bloodthirstily. But Spencer wished her mom could understand *her* perspective, too. Melissa was an evil superbitch, and Spencer didn't want to speak to her for the rest of her life.

"Fine," Spencer said dramatically. She pulled open the sliding glass door and stalked into the grand family room. Even though Nana Hastings's Craftsman-style house had eight bedrooms, seven bathrooms, a private path to the beach, a deluxe playroom, a home theater, a gourmet chef's kitchen, and Stickley furniture throughout, Spencer's family had always affectionately called it the "taco shack." Perhaps it was because Nana's mansion in Longboat Key, Florida, had wall frescoes, marble floors, three tennis courts, and a temperature-controlled wine cellar.

Spencer haughtily passed Melissa, who was lounging on one of the tan leather couches, murmuring on her iPhone. She was probably talking to Ian Thomas. "I'll be in my room," Spencer yelled dramatically at the base of the stairs. "All. Night."

She flopped down on her sleigh bed, pleased to see that her bedroom was exactly as she'd left it five years ago. Alison had come with her the last time she visited, and the two of them had spent hours gazing at the surfers through her late Grandpa Hastings's antique mahogany spyglass on the crow's-nest deck. That had been in the early fall, when Ali and Spencer were just starting seventh grade. Things were still pretty normal between them—maybe Ali hadn't started seeing Ian yet.

Spencer shuddered. Ali had been seeing *Ian.* Did A know about that? Did A know about Spencer's argument with Ali the night Ali disappeared, too—had A *been* there? Spencer wished she could tell the police about A, but A seemed above the law. She looked around haltingly, suddenly frightened. The sun had sunk below the trees, filling the room with eerie darkness.

Her phone rang, and Spencer jumped. She pulled it out of her robe pocket and squinted at the number. Not recognizing it, she put the phone to her ear and tentatively said hello.

"Spencer?" said a girl's smooth, lilting voice. "It's Mona Vanderwaal."

"Oh." Spencer sat up too fast, and her head started to spin. There was only one reason why Mona would be calling her. "Is . . . Hanna . . . okay?"

"Well . . . no." Mona sounded surprised. "You haven't heard? She's in a coma. I'm at the hospital."

"Oh my God," Spencer whispered. "Is she going to get better?"

"The doctors don't know." Mona's voice wobbled. "She might not wake up."

Spencer began to pace around the room. "I'm in New Jersey right now with my parents, but I'll be back tomorrow morning, so—"

"I'm not calling to make you feel guilty," Mona interrupted. She sighed. "I'm sorry. I'm stressed. I called because I heard you were good at planning events."

It was cold in the bedroom and smelled a little like sand. Spencer touched the edge of the enormous conch shell that sat on top of her bureau. "Well, sure."

"Good," Mona said. "I want to plan a candlelight vigil for Hanna. I think it would be great to get everyone to, you know, band together for Hanna."

"That sounds great," Spencer said softly. "My dad was just talking about a party he was at a couple of weeks ago in this gorgeous tent on the fifteenth green. Maybe we could hold it there."

"Perfect. Let's plan for Friday—that'll give us five days to get everything ready."

"Friday it is." After Mona said she'd write out the invitations if Spencer could secure the location and the catering, Spencer hung up. She flopped back on the bed, staring at its lacy canopy. Hanna might *die*? Spencer pictured Hanna lying alone and unconscious in a hospital room. Her throat felt tight and hot.

Tap . . . tap . . . tap . . .

The wind grew still, and even the ocean was quiet. Spencer pricked up her ears. Was someone out there?

Tap . . . tap . . . tap . . .

She sat up fast. "Who's there?" The bedroom window offered a sandy view. The sun had set so quickly that all she could see was the weathered wooden lifeguard stand in the distance. She crept into the hall. Empty. She ran into one of the guest bedrooms and looked below to the front porch. No one.

Spencer slid her hands down her face. *Calm down,* she told herself. *It's not like A is here.* She stumbled out of the room and down the staircase, nearly tripping over a stack of beach towels. Melissa was still on the couch, holding a copy of *Architectural Digest* with her good hand and propping up her broken wrist on an oversize velvet pillow.

"Melissa," Spencer said, breathing hard. "I think there's someone outside."

Her sister turned around, her face pinched. "Huh?"

Tap . . . tap . . . tap . . .

"Listen!" Spencer pointed to the door. "Don't you hear that?"

Melissa stood up, frowning. "I hear *something.*" She looked at Spencer worriedly. "Let's go to the playroom. There's a good view all around the house from there."

The sisters checked and double-checked the locks before bolting up the stairs to the second-floor playroom. The room smelled closed-up and dusty, and looked as if a much-younger Melissa and Spencer had just run out for dinner and would be back at any second to resume playing. There was the Lego village that had taken them three weeks to complete. There was the make-your-own-jewelry kit, the beads and clasps still strewn all over the table. The indoor mini golf holes were still set up around the room, and the enormous chest of dolls was still open.

Melissa reached the window first. She pushed back the sailboat-printed curtain and peered into the front yard, which was landscaped with sea glass pebbles and tropical flowers. Her pink cast made a hollow sound as it tapped against the windowpane. "I don't see anyone."

"I already looked out front. Maybe they're around the side."

Suddenly, they heard it again. *Tap . . . tap.* It was growing louder. Spencer grabbed Melissa's arm. They both peered out the window again.

Then a drainpipe at the bottom of the house rattled a bit, and finally something scuttled out. It was a *seagull.* The thing had somehow gotten stuck in the pipe; the tapping sounds had probably been caused by its wings and beak as it struggled to break free. The bird waddled away, shaking its feathers.

Spencer sank down on the antique FAO Schwarz rocking horse. At first, Melissa looked angry, but then the corners of her mouth wobbled. She snorted with laughter.

Spencer laughed as well. "Stupid bird."

"Yeah." Melissa let out a huge sigh. She looked around the room, first at the Legos and then at the six oversize My Little Pony mannequin heads set up on the far table. She pointed at them. "Remember how we used to do the ponies' makeup?"

"Sure." Mrs. Hastings would give them all of last season's Chanel eye shadows and lipsticks, and they'd spend hours giving the ponies smoky eyes and plumped-up lips.

"You used to put eye shadow on their nostrils," Melissa teased.

Spencer giggled, petting the blue-and-purple mane of a pink pony. "I wanted their noses to be as pretty as the rest of their faces."

"And remember these?" Melissa walked to the oversize chest and peered inside. "I can't believe we had so many dolls."

Not only were there more than a hundred dolls, ranging from Barbies to German antiques that probably shouldn't have been carelessly tossed into a toy chest, but also tons of coordinating outfits, shoes, purses, cars, horses, and lapdogs. Spencer pulled out a Barbie in a serious-looking blue blazer and pencil skirt. "Remember how we used to make them be CEOs? Mine was the CEO of a cotton-candy factory, and yours was the CEO of a makeup company."

"We made this one president." Melissa pulled out a doll whose dirty blond hair was cut bluntly to her chin, just like her own.

"And this one had lots of boyfriends." Spencer held up a pretty doll with long, blond hair and a heart-shaped face.

The sisters sighed. Spencer felt a lump in her throat. Back in the day, they used to play for hours. Half the time they didn't even want to go down to the beach, and when it was time for bed, Spencer always sobbed and begged her parents to let her sleep in Melissa's bedroom. "I'm sorry about the Golden Orchid thing," Spencer blurted out. "I wish it had never happened."

Melissa picked up the pretty doll Spencer had been holding—the one with lots of boyfriends. "They're going to want you to go to New York, you know. And talk about your paper in front of a panel of judges. You'll have to know the material inside out."

Spencer squeezed CEO Barbie tightly around her impossibly disproportionate waist. Even if her parents wouldn't punish her for cheating, the Golden Orchid committee would.

Melissa strolled to the back of the room. "You'll do fine, though. You'll probably win. And you know Mom and Dad will get you something amazing if you do."

Spencer blinked. "And you'd be okay with that? Even though it's . . . your paper?"

Melissa shrugged. "I'm over it." She paused for a moment, then reached into a high cabinet Spencer hadn't noticed before. Her hand emerged with a tall bottle of Grey Goose vodka. She shook it, the clear liquid swishing inside the glass. "Want some?"

"S-sure," Spencer sputtered.

Melissa walked to the cabinet above the room's mini fridge and pulled out two cups from the miniature china tea set. Using only her good hand, Melissa awkwardly poured vodka into two teacups. With a nostalgic smile, she handed Spencer her old favorite pale blue teacup— Spencer used to pitch a fit if she had to drink out of any

of the others. She was astounded that Melissa remembered.

Spencer sipped, feeling the vodka burn down her
throat. "How did you know that bottle was here?"

"Ian and I snuck here for Senior Week years ago,"
Melissa explained. She sat down in a purple-and-pink-
striped child-size chair, her knees piked up to her chin.
"Cops were all over the roads, and we were terrified to
bring it back with us, so we hid it here. We thought we'd
come back for it later . . . only, we didn't."

Melissa got a faraway look on her face. She and Ian had
unexpectedly broken up shortly after Senior Week—that
same summer Ali had gone missing. Melissa had been
extra-industrious that summer, working two part-time
jobs and volunteering at the Brandywine River Museum.
Even though she never would have admitted it, Spencer
suspected she'd been trying to keep herself busy because
the breakup with Ian had really devastated her. Maybe it
was the hurt look on Melissa's face, or maybe it was that
she'd just told Spencer she'd probably win the Golden
Orchid after all, but suddenly, Spencer wanted to tell
Melissa the truth.

"There's something you should know," Spencer blurted
out. "I kissed Ian when I was in seventh grade, when you
guys were dating." She swallowed hard. "It was only one
kiss, and it didn't mean anything. I swear." Now that that
was out, Spencer couldn't stop herself. "It wasn't like the
thing Ian had with Ali."

"The thing Ian had with Ali," Melissa repeated, staring down at the Barbie she was holding.

"Yeah." Spencer's insides felt like a molten lava–filled volcano—rumbling, about to overflow. "Ali told me right before she disappeared, but I must've blocked it out."

Melissa began to brush the popular blond Barbie's hair, her lips twitching slightly.

"I blocked out some other stuff, too," Spencer continued shakily, feeling a little uneasy. "That night, Ali really teased me—she said that I liked Ian, that I was trying to steal him away. It was like she *wanted* me to get mad. And then I shoved her. I didn't mean to hurt her, but I'm afraid I . . ."

Spencer covered her hands with her face. Repeating the story to Melissa revived that awful night all over again. *Earthworms from the previous night's rain wriggled across the path. Ali's pink bra strap slid down her shoulder, and her toe ring glimmered in the moonlight.* It was *real*. It had happened.

Melissa put the Barbie down on her lap and took a slow drink of her vodka. "Actually, I knew Ian kissed you. And I knew that Ali and Ian were together."

Spencer gaped. "Ian *told* you?"

Melissa shrugged. "I guessed. Ian wasn't very good at keeping that kind of stuff a secret. Not from me."

Spencer stared at her sister, a shudder snaking down her spine. Melissa's voice was singsongy, almost like she was suppressing a giggle. Then Melissa turned to face Spencer head-on. She smiled widely, weirdly. "As for being worried that *you* were the one who killed Ali, I don't think you have it in you."

"You . . . *don't?*"

Melissa shook her head slowly, and then made the doll in her lap shake her head, too. "It takes a very unique person to kill, and that's not you."

She tipped her teacup of vodka to the ceiling, draining it. Then, with her good hand, Melissa picked the Barbie up by its neck and popped its plastic head clean off. She handed the dismembered head to Spencer, her eyes open wide. "That's not you at all."

The doll's head fit perfectly in the pit of Spencer's palm, the lips pursed in a flirtatious smile, the eyes a brilliant sapphire blue. A wave of nausea went through Spencer. She'd never noticed before, but the doll looked exactly like . . . Ali.

8

DOESN'T EVERYONE TALK ABOUT THIS STUFF IN A HOSPITAL ROOM?

Monday morning, instead of rushing to English class before the bell rang, Aria was running toward the Rosewood Day exit. She'd just received a text message on her Treo from Lucas. *Aria, come to the hospital if you can,* it said. *They're finally letting people in to see Hanna.*

She was so engrossed and focused, she didn't see her brother, Mike, until he was standing right in front of her. He wore a Playboy bunny–icon T-shirt underneath his Rosewood Day jacket and a blue Rosewood Day varsity lacrosse bracelet. Engraved in the bracelet's rubber was his team nickname, which, for whatever reason, was Buffalo. Aria didn't dare ask why—it was probably an inside joke about his penis or something. The lacrosse team was becoming more and more of a frat every day.

"Hey," Aria said, a bit distracted. "How are you?"

Mike's hands seemed welded to his hips. The sneer on his face indicated he wasn't up for small talk. "I hear you're living with Dad now."

"As a last resort," Aria said quickly. "Sean and I broke up."

Mike narrowed his ice blue eyes. "I know. I heard that too."

Aria stepped back, surprised. Mike didn't know about Ezra, did he? "I just wanted to tell you that you and Dad deserve each other," Mike snapped, whipping around and nearly colliding with a girl in a cheerleading uniform. "See ya later."

"Mike, wait!" Aria cried. "I'm going to fix this, I promise!"

But he just kept going. Last week, Mike had found out that Aria had known about their dad's affair for three years. On the surface, he'd acted all tough and cool about their parents' dissolving marriage. He played varsity lacrosse, made lewd comments to girls, and tried to give his teammates titty twisters in the hallways. But Mike was like a Björk song—all happy and giddy and fun on the surface, but bubbling with turmoil and pain underneath. She couldn't imagine what Mike would think if he found out Byron and Meredith were planning to get married.

As she heaved a huge sigh and continued toward the side door, she noticed a figure in a three-piece suit staring at her from across the hall.

"Going somewhere, Ms. Montgomery?" Principal Appleton asked.

Aria flinched, her face growing hot. She hadn't seen Appleton since Sean had told the Rosewood staff about Ezra. But Appleton didn't exactly look pissed—more like . . . nervous. Almost as if Aria was someone he had to treat very, very delicately. Aria tried to hide a smirk. Appleton probably didn't want Aria to press charges against Ezra or talk about the incident ever again. It would draw indecent attention to the school, and Rosewood Day could never have *that*.

Aria turned, fueled with power. "There's somewhere I have to be," she insisted.

It was against Rosewood Day policy to walk out of a class, but Appleton did nothing to stop her. Perhaps the Ezra mess was good for something, after all.

She reached the hospital quickly and sprinted up to the third-floor intensive care unit. Inside, patients were sprawled out in a circle, separated only by curtains. A long, U-shaped nurse's desk sat in the middle of the room. Aria passed an old black woman who looked dead, a silver-haired man in a neck brace, and a groggy-looking fortysomething who was muttering to herself. Hanna's partitioned-off area was along one of the walls. With her long, healthy auburn hair, unlined skin, and taut, young body, Hanna was definitely the thing in the ICU that didn't belong. Her cordoned-off area was full of flowers, boxes of candy, stacks of magazines, and stuffed animals. Someone had bought her a large, white teddy bear that wore a patterned wrap dress. When Aria flipped open the tag on the bear's plushy arm, she saw that the bear's name was Diane von FurstenBEAR. There was a brand-new white cast on Hanna's arm. Lucas Beattie, Mona Vanderwaal, and Hanna's parents had already signed it.

Lucas was sitting in the yellow plastic chair by Hanna's bed, a *Teen Vogue* on his lap. "'Even the pastiest legs will benefit from Lancôme Soleil Flash Browner tinted mousse, which gives skin a subtle sheen,'" he read, licking his finger to turn the page. When he noticed Aria, he stopped, a sheepish look crossing his face. "The doctors say it's good to talk to Hanna—that she can hear. But maybe fall is a stupid time to talk about self-tanners? Maybe I should read her the article on Coco Chanel instead? Or the one about *Teen Vogue*'s new interns? It says they're better than the *Hills* girls."

Aria glanced at Hanna, a lump growing in her throat. Metal guards lined the sides of her bed, as if she was a toddler at risk of rolling out. There were green bruises on her face, and her eyes seemed sealed closed. This was the first time Aria had seen a coma patient up close. A monitor recording Hanna's heartbeat and blood pressure let out a constant *beep, beep, beep* noise. It made Aria uneasy. She couldn't help but anticipate that the beeping would abruptly flatline, like it always did in the movies before someone died. "So, have the doctors said anything about her prognosis?" Aria asked shakily.

"Well, her hand's fluttering. Like that, see?" Lucas gestured to Hanna's right hand, the one with the cast on it. Her fingernails looked like someone had recently painted them a brilliant coral. "Which seems promising. But the doctors say it might not mean anything—they still aren't sure if she has any brain damage."

Aria's stomach dropped.

"But I'm trying to think positive. The fluttering means she's about to wake up." Lucas closed the magazine and set it on Hanna's bedside table. "And apparently, some of her brain activity readouts show that she might've been awake last night . . . but nobody saw it." He sighed. "I'm going to go get a soda. Want anything?"

Aria shook her head. Lucas stood up from his chair and Aria took his place. Before Lucas left, he drummed his fingers against the door frame. "Did you hear there's going to be a candlelight vigil for Hanna on Friday?"

Aria shrugged. "Don't you think it's sort of bizarre that it's at a country club?"

"Sort of," Lucas whispered. "Or fitting."

He gave Aria a smirk and padded away. As he smacked the automatic door button and walked out of the ICU ward, Aria smiled. She liked Lucas. He seemed as jaded about pretentious Rosewood bullshit as she was. And he certainly was a good friend. Aria had no idea how he was able to miss so much school to stay with Hanna, but it was nice that someone was with her.

Aria reached out and touched Hanna's hand, and Hanna's fingers curled around hers. Aria pulled away, startled, then chastised herself. It wasn't like Hanna was *dead*. It wasn't like Aria had squeezed a corpse's hand and the corpse had squeezed back.

"Okay, I can be there this afternoon, and we can go through the candids together," a voice said behind her. "Is that doable?"

Aria whirled around, nearly falling off her chair. Spencer hit the OFF button on her Sidekick and gave Aria an apologetic smile. "Sorry." She rolled her eyes. "Yearbook can't do anything without me." She looked at Hanna, paling a bit. "I came here as soon as my free period started. How's she doing?"

Aria cracked her knuckles so hard, her thumb joint made a disconcerting *pop*. It was amazing that in the middle of all this, Spencer still ran eight thousand committees and had even found time to be on the front page of yesterday's *Philadelphia Sentinel*. Even though Wilden had more or less exonerated Spencer, there was still something about her that gave Aria pause.

"Where have you been?" Aria asked sharply.

Spencer took a step back, as if Aria had shoved her. "I had to go away with my parents. To New Jersey. I came as soon as I could."

"Did you get A's note on Saturday?" Aria demanded. "*She knew too much*?"

Spencer nodded but didn't speak. She flicked the tassels of her tweed Kate Spade bag and looked warily at all of Hanna's electronic medical devices.

"Did Hanna tell you who it is?" Aria goaded.

Spencer frowned. "Who *who* is?"

"A." Spencer still looked confused, and an edgy feeling gnawed at Aria's gut. "Hanna knew who A was, Spencer." She looked at Spencer carefully. "Hanna didn't tell you why she wanted to meet?"

"No." Spencer's voice cracked. "She just said she had something important to tell me." She let out a long breath.

Aria thought of Spencer's cagey, crazy eyes peeping out from the woods behind Rosewood Day. "I saw you, you know," she blurted out. "I saw you in the woods on Saturday. You were just . . . standing there. What were you doing?"

The pigment disappeared from Spencer's face. "I was scared," she whispered. "I'd never seen anything so scary in my whole life. I couldn't believe that someone would actually *do* that to Hanna."

Spencer looked terrified. All of a sudden, Aria felt her suspicion seep out of her. She wondered what Spencer would think if she knew Aria had thought Spencer was Ali's killer, and had even shared that theory with Wilden. She recalled Wilden's judging words: *Is this what you girls do? Blame your old friends for murder?* Maybe Wilden was right: Spencer might have starred in some of the school plays, but she wasn't a good enough actress to have killed Ali, traipsed back to the barn, and convinced her remaining best friends that she was as innocent, clueless, and scared as they all were.

"I can't believe anyone would do that to Hanna either," Aria said quietly. She sighed. "So, I figured something out Saturday night. I think . . . I think Ali and Ian Thomas were dating, back when we were in seventh grade."

Spencer's mouth fell open. "I figured that out Saturday, too."

"You didn't already know?" Aria scratched her head, thrown off guard.

Spencer took another step into the room. She kept her eyes fixed on the clear liquid that filled Hanna's IV bag. "No."

"Do you think anyone else knew?"

An indescribable expression crossed Spencer's face. Talking about all this seemed to make her really uncomfortable. "I think my sister did."

"Melissa knew all this time but never said anything?" Aria ran her hands along the edge of her chin. "That's weird." She thought of A's three clues about Ali's killer: that she was close by, that she wanted something Ali had, and that she knew every inch of the DiLaurentises' yard. All three clues together only applied to a handful of people. If Melissa knew about Ali and Ian, then maybe she was one of them.

"Should we tell the cops about Ian and Ali?" Spencer suggested.

Aria wrung her hands together. "I mentioned it to Wilden."

A flush of surprise passed over Spencer's face. "Oh," she said in a small voice.

"Is that okay?" Aria asked, raising an eyebrow.

"Of course," Spencer said briskly, regaining composure. "So . . . do you think we should tell him about A?"

Aria widened her eyes. "If we do, A might . . ." She trailed off, feeling nauseated.

Spencer stared at Aria for a long time. "A's completely running our lives," she whispered.

Hanna was still immobile in her bed. Aria wondered if she really could hear them, just like Lucas said. Perhaps she'd heard everything they'd just said about A and wanted to tell them what she knew, only she was trapped inside her coma. Or maybe she'd heard everything they'd said and was disgusted that they were talking about this instead of fretting over whether Hanna would ever wake up.

Aria smoothed the sheets over Hanna's chest, tucking them up to her chin like Ella used to do when Aria had the flu. Then, a flickering reflection in the little window behind Hanna's bed caught her eye. Aria straightened, her nerves jangling. It looked like someone outside Hanna's partition was lurking next to an empty wheelchair, trying not to be seen.

She whipped around, her heart racing, and pulled back the curtain.

"What?" Spencer cried, turning around too.

Aria took a deep breath. "Nothing." Whoever it was had vanished.

9

IT'S NO FUN BEING THE SCAPEGOAT

Light streamed into Emily's eyes. She hugged her pillow and sank back into sleep. Rosewood's morning sounds were as predictable as the sunrise—the barking of the Kloses' dog as they set off on their walk around the block, the rumbling of the garbage truck, the sounds of the *Today* show, which her mother watched every morning, and the crowing of the rooster.

Her eyes sprang open. A *rooster*?

The room smelled like hay and vodka. Abby's bed was empty. Since the cousins had wanted to stay longer at last night's party than Emily did, Trista had dropped her off at the Weavers' gate. Maybe Abby hadn't come home yet—the last she'd seen of Abby at the party, she'd been all over a guy who wore a University of Iowa T-shirt that featured a big, scowling Herky the Hawk mascot on the back.

When she turned her head, she saw her aunt Helene standing in the doorway. Emily screamed and pulled the sheets around her. Helene was already dressed in a long patchwork jumper and a ruffle-edged T-shirt. Her glasses teetered precariously on the end of her nose. "I see you're up," she said. "Please come downstairs."

Emily rolled out of bed slowly, pulling on a shirt, a pair of Rosewood Day Swim Team pajama pants, and argyle socks. The rest of the previous night rushed back to her, as comforting as sinking into a long, hot bath. Emily and Trista had spent the rest of the night making up a crazy square dance, and a bunch of the boys had joined in. They'd talked nonstop on the drive back to the Weavers' house, even though both of them were exhausted. Before Emily got out of the car, Trista had touched the inside of Emily's wrist. "I'm glad I met you," Trista whispered. And Emily was glad too.

John, Matt, and Abby were at the kitchen table, staring sleepily at their bowls of Cheerios. A plate of pancakes sat in the middle of the table. "Hey, guys," Emily said cheerfully. "Is there anything for breakfast other than Cheerios or pancakes?"

"I don't think breakfast should be your main concern right now, Emily."

Emily turned, her blood running cold. Uncle Allen stood at the counter, his posture stiff, a look of disappointment on his lined, weathered face. Helene leaned against the stove, equally stern. Emily looked nervously from Matt to John to Abby, but not one of them returned her gaze.

"So." Helene started pacing around the room, her square-toed shoes clacking against the plank floor. "We know what the four of you did last night."

Emily sank into a chair, heat creeping into her cheeks. Her heart began to pound.

"I want to know whose idea this was." Helene circled the table like a hawk zeroing in on her prey. "Who wanted to hang out with those public school kids? Who thought it was okay to drink alcohol?"

Abby poked at a lone Cheerio in her bowl. John scratched his chin. Emily kept her lips pasted together. *She* certainly wasn't going to say anything. She and her cousins would form a bond of solidarity, keeping quiet for the benefit of all. It was how Emily, Ali, and the others had operated years ago, on the rare occasion that someone actually caught them doing something.

"Well?" Helene said sharply.

Abby's chin shook. "It was Emily," she exploded. "She threatened me, Mom. She knew about the public school party and demanded that I take her to it. I took John and Matt along so we'd be safe."

"*What?*" Emily gasped. She felt like Abby had smacked her in the chest with the large wooden cross that hung over the doorway. "That's not true! How would I have known about some party? I don't know anyone but you!"

Helene looked disgusted. "Boys? Was it Emily?"

Matt and John stared at their cereal bowls and nodded slowly.

Emily looked around the table, too angry and betrayed to breathe. She wanted to shout out what had really happened. Matt had done body shots from a girl's navel. John had danced to Chingy in his boxers. Abby had made out with five guys and possibly a cow. Her limbs began to shake. Why were they doing this? Weren't they her *friends*? "None of you seemed very upset to be there!"

"That's a lie!" Abby shrieked. "We were all *very* upset!"

Allen pulled at Emily's shoulder, jolting her back to her feet in a forceful, manhandling way Emily had never felt in her life. "This isn't going to work," he said in a low voice, bringing his face close to hers. He smelled like coffee and something organic, perhaps soil. "You're no longer welcome here."

Emily took a step back, her heart sinking to her feet. "What?"

"We did your parents a big favor," Helene growled. "They said you were a handful, but we never expected *this*." She pushed the ON button of the cordless phone. "I'm calling them now. We'll drive you back to the airport, but they'll have to figure out a way to pay for you to get home. And they'll have to decide what to do with you."

Emily felt all five pairs of Weaver eyes on her. She willed herself not to cry, taking big, gulping breaths of the stale farmhouse air. Her cousins had betrayed her. None of them were on her side. *No one* was.

She turned around and fled up to the little bedroom. Once there, she threw her clothes back into her swim bag. Most of her clothes still smelled like home—a mix of Snuggle fabric softener and her mom's homey cooking spices. She was glad they would never smell like this horrible place.

Just before zipping the duffel closed, she paused. Helene was probably calling her parents, telling them everything. She pictured her mother standing in her kitchen in Rosewood, holding the phone to her ear and saying, "*Please* don't send Emily back here. Our life is perfect without her."

Emily's vision blurred with tears, and her heart literally hurt. No one wanted her. And what would Helene's next option be? Would she try to ship Emily off somewhere else? Military school? A *convent*? Did those still exist?

"I have to get out of here," Emily whispered to the cold, spare room. Her cell phone was still lying at the bottom of the swear jar in the hall. The lid came off easily, and no alarm sounded. She dropped the phone into her pocket, grabbed her bags, and crept down the stairs. If she could just get off the Weaver property, she was pretty sure there was a minuscule grocery store about a mile down the road. She could plan her next move from there.

When she burst out onto the front porch, she almost didn't notice Abby curled up on the chain-link porch swing. Emily was so startled she dropped her duffel on her feet.

Abby's mouth settled into an upside-down U. "She

never catches us. So *you* must have done something to get her attention."

"I didn't do anything," Emily said helplessly. "I swear."

"And now, because of you, we're going to be stuck in lockdown for months." Abby rolled her eyes. "And for the record, Trista Taylor is a huge slut. She tries to hump anything that moves—guy *or* girl."

Emily backed up, at a loss for words. She grabbed her bag and sprinted down the front walk. When she came to the cattle gate, that same goat was still tethered to the metal post, the bell clanging softly around her neck. The rope didn't offer enough slack for her to lie down, and it looked like Helene hadn't even put out water for her. When Emily looked into the goat's yellow eyes and odd, square pupils, she felt a connection—scapegoat to "bad" goat. She knew what it was like to be cruelly, unjustly punished.

Emily took a deep breath and slid the rope off the goat's neck, then opened the cattle guard and waved her arms. "Go, girl," she whispered. "Shoo." The goat glanced at Emily, her lips pursed. She took one step forward, then another. Once she crossed the cattle guard, she broke into a trot, waddling down the road. She seemed happy to be free.

Emily slammed the cattle guard shut behind her. She was pretty damn happy to be free of this place, too.

10

ABOUT AS FAR FROM MINDLESS AS ARIA COULD GET

The clouds rolled in on Monday afternoon, darkening the sky and bringing winds that ripped through Rosewood's yellow-leafed sugar maples. Aria pulled her strawberry-colored merino wool beret down over her ears and scampered into the Frank Lloyd Wright Memorial Visual Arts Building at Hollis College for her very first Mindless Art class. The lobby walls were full of student exhibits, announcements for art sales, and want ads for housemates. Aria noticed a flyer that said, HAVE YOU SEEN THE ROSEWOOD STALKER? There was a Xeroxed photograph of a figure looming in the woods, as blurry and cryptic as the murky shots of the Loch Ness Monster. Last week, there had been all sorts of news reports on the Rosewood Stalker, who was following people around, spying on their every move. But Aria hadn't heard any stalker news for a few days now . . . about the same amount of time that A had been silent.

The elevator was out of service, so Aria climbed the cold, gray concrete stairs to the second floor. She located her Mindless Art classroom and was surprised to find it silent and dark. A jagged shape flickered against the window on the far side of the room, and as Aria's eyes adjusted, she realized the room was full.

"Come in," called a woman's husky voice.

Aria felt her way to the back wall. The old Hollis building creaked and groaned. Someone near her smelled like menthol and garlic. Someone else smelled like cigarettes. She heard a giggle.

"I believe we're all here," the voice called out. "My name is Sabrina. Welcome to Mindless Art. Now, you're all probably wondering why we're standing here with the lights off. Art is about seeing, right? Well, guess what? It isn't, not entirely. Art is also touching and smelling . . . and most definitely feeling. But mostly, it's about letting go. It's about taking everything you thought was true and throwing it out the window. It's about embracing life's unpredictability, letting go of boundaries, and starting over."

Aria stifled a yawn. Sabrina had a slow, soporific voice that made her want to curl up and close her eyes.

"The lights are off for a little exercise," Sabrina said. "We all form an image of someone in our heads, based on certain easy clues. The way one's voice sounds, maybe. The type of music someone likes. The things you know about a person's past, perhaps. But sometimes, our

412 ◆ SARA SHEPARD

judgments aren't right; in fact, sometimes they're quite wrong."

Years ago, Aria and Ali used to go to Saturday art classes together. If Ali were in this class with her now, she'd roll her eyes and say that Sabrina was a flaky granola-head with hairy armpits. But Aria thought what Sabrina was saying made sense—especially in regard to Ali. These days, everything Aria thought she'd known about Ali was wrong. Aria would never have imagined Ali was having a secret affair with her best friend's sister's boyfriend, though it certainly explained her cagey, bizarre actions before she disappeared. In those last few months, there were stretches when Ali wasn't around for weekends at a time. She'd say she had to go out of town with her parents—surely that was code for time alone with Ian. Or once, when Aria had biked over to Ali's house to surprise her, she'd found Ali sitting on one of the big boulders in her backyard, whispering into her cell phone. "I'll see you this weekend, okay?" Ali was saying. "We can talk about it then." When Aria called out her name, Ali whirled around, startled. "Who are you talking to?" Aria had asked innocently. Ali snapped her phone shut fast, narrowing her eyes. She considered her words for a while, and then said, "So, that girl your dad was kissing? I bet she's like a *Girls Gone Wild* college girl who throws herself at guys. I mean, she'd have to be pretty ballsy to hook up with her teacher." Aria had turned away, mortified. Ali had been with her the day she'd discovered Byron kissing Meredith, and she wouldn't let it go. Aria was on her bike and halfway home before she realized Ali had never answered her question.

"So this is what I want us to do," Sabrina said loudly, interrupting Aria's memories. "Find the person nearest to you, and hold hands. Try to imagine what your neighbor looks like just by the way their hands feel. Then we'll turn the lights on so you can sketch each other's portraits based on what you see in your mind."

Aria fumbled in the blue-black darkness. Someone grabbed her hand, feeling her wrist bones and the mounds in her palm.

"What sort of face do you see when you touch this person?" Sabrina called.

Aria shut her eyes, trying to think. The hand was small and a bit cold and dry. A face began to form in her mind. First the pronounced cheekbones, then the bright blue eyes. Long, blond hair, pink, bow-shaped lips.

Aria tightened her stomach. She was thinking of *Ali*.

"Turn away from your partner now," Sabrina instructed. "Get your sketch pads out, and I'm going to turn on the lights. Do not look at your partners. I want you to sketch exactly what you saw in your brain, and we'll see how close you are to the real thing."

The bright overhead lights hurt Aria's eyes as she shakily opened her sketch pad. She tentatively brushed the charcoal across her paper, but as hard as she tried, she couldn't stop from drawing Ali's face. When she stepped back, she felt a huge lump in her throat. There was a whisper of a smile across Ali's lips and a devious sparkle in her eye.

"Very nice," said Sabrina—who looked exactly like her voice, with long, knotty brown hair; big boobs; a fleshy stomach; and puny, birdlike legs. She moved on to Aria's partner. "That's *beautiful*," she murmured. Aria felt a pinch of annoyance. Why wasn't her drawing beautiful? Did someone draw better than she did? Impossible.

"Time's up," Sabrina called. "Turn around and show your partners the results."

Aria slowly turned, her eyes greedily assessing her partner's allegedly *beautiful* sketch. And actually . . . it *was* beautiful. The drawing looked nothing like Aria, but it still was a much better rendering of a person than Aria could have done. Aria's eyes floated up her partner's body. The girl wore a fitted pink Nanette Lepore top. Her hair was dark and wild, spilling down her shoulders. She had creamy, blemish-free skin. Then, Aria saw the familiar turned-up button nose. And the giant Gucci sunglasses. There was a sleeping dog in a blue canvas vest at the girl's feet. Aria's entire body turned to ice.

"I can't see what you drew of me," her partner said in a soft, sweet voice. She pointed to her Seeing Eye dog in explanation. "But I'm sure it's great."

Aria's tongue felt leaden in her mouth. Her partner was Jenna Cavanaugh.

11

WELCOME BACK . . . SORT OF

After what seemed like days of spinning through the stars, Hanna suddenly found herself thrust into the light again. Once more, she was sitting on Ali's back porch. Once more, she could feel herself busting out of her American Apparel T-shirt and Seven jeans.

"We get to have our sleepover in Melissa's barn!" Spencer was saying.

"Nice." Ali grinned. Hanna recoiled. Maybe she was stuck revisiting this day over and over again, sort of like that guy in that old movie *Groundhog Day*. Maybe Hanna would have to keep reliving this one day until she got it right and convinced Ali that she was in grave danger. But . . . the last time Hanna had been in this memory, Ali had loomed close by, telling Hanna that she was okay. But she *wasn't* okay. *Nothing was okay.*

"Ali," Hanna urged. "What do you mean, you're okay?"

Ali wasn't paying attention. She watched Melissa as she strode through the Hastingses' bordering yard, her graduation gown slung over her arm. "Hey, Melissa!" Ali cooed. "Excited to go to Prague?"

"Who cares about her?" Hanna shouted. "Answer my question!"

"Is Hanna . . . *talking*?" a far-off voice gasped. Hanna cocked her head. That didn't sound like any of her old friends.

Across the yard, Melissa put her hand on her hip. "Of course I'm excited."

"Is *Ian* going?" Ali asked.

Hanna grabbed the sides of Ali's face. "Ian doesn't matter," she said forcefully. "Just listen to me, Ali!"

"Who's Ian?" The far-off voice sounded like it was coming from the other end of a very long tunnel. Mona Vanderwaal's voice. Hanna looked around Ali's backyard, but didn't see Mona anywhere.

Ali turned to Hanna, heaving an exasperated sigh. "Give it a rest, Hanna."

"But you're in danger," Hanna sputtered.

"Things aren't always what they seem," Ali whispered.

"What do you mean?" Hanna urged desperately. When she reached out for Ali, her hand went right through Ali's arm, like Ali was just an image projected onto a screen.

"What does *who* mean?" Mona's voice called.

Hanna's eyes popped open. A bright, painful light

practically blinded her. She was lying on her back on an uncomfortable mattress. Several figures stood around her—Mona, Lucas Beattie, her mother, and her father.

Her *father*? Hanna tried to frown, but her face muscles were in excruciating pain.

"Hanna." Mona's chin wobbled. "Oh my God. You're . . . *awake*."

"Are you okay, honey?" her mother asked. "Can you talk?"

Hanna glanced down at her arms. At least they were thin and not ham hocks. Then, she saw the IV tube sticking out of the crook in her elbow and the clunky cast on her arm. "What's going on?" she croaked, looking around. The scene in front of her eyes seemed staged. Where she'd just been—on Ali's back porch, with her old best friends—seemed far more real. "Where's Ali?" she asked.

Hanna's parents exchanged uneasy looks. "Ali's dead," Hanna's mother said quietly.

"Go easy on her." A white-haired, hawk-nosed man in a white coat swept around a curtain to the foot of Hanna's bed. "Hanna? My name's Dr. Geist. How do you feel?"

"Where the hell am I?" Hanna demanded, her voice rising with panic.

Hanna's father took her hand. "You had an accident. We were really worried."

Hanna looked fitfully at the faces around her, then at the various contraptions that fed into different parts of her body. In addition to the IV drip, there was a machine that measured her heartbeat and a tube that sent oxygen into her nose. Her body felt hot, then cold, and her skin prickled with fear and confusion. "Accident?" she whispered.

"A car hit you," Hanna's mother said. "At Rosewood Day. Can you remember?"

Her hospital sheets felt sticky, like someone had drizzled nacho cheese all over them. Hanna searched her memory, but nothing about an accident was there. The last thing she remembered, before sitting in Ali's backyard, was receiving the champagne-colored Zac Posen dress for Mona's birthday party. That had been Friday night, the day before Mona's celebration. Hanna turned to Mona, who looked both distraught and relieved. Her eyes had huge, kind of ugly purple circles under them, too, as if she hadn't slept in days. "I didn't miss your party, did I?"

Lucas made a sniffing noise. Mona's shoulders tensed. "No . . ."

"The accident happened afterward," Lucas said. "You don't remember?"

Hanna tried to pull the oxygen tube out of her nose— no one looked attractive with something dangling from a nostril—and found that it had been taped down. She closed her eyes and grappled for something, *anything*, to explain all this. But the only thing she saw was Ali's face looming over her and whispering *something* before dissipating into black nothingness.

"No," Hanna whispered. "I don't remember any of that at all."

12

ON THE LAM

Late Monday evening, Emily sat on a faded blue bar stool at the counter of the M&J diner across from the Greyhound station in Akron, Ohio. She hadn't eaten anything all day and contemplated ordering a piece of nasty-looking cherry pie to go with her metallic-tasting coffee. Next to her, an old man slowly slurped a spoonful of tapioca pudding, and a bowling pin–shaped man and his knitting needle–shaped friend were shoveling down greasy burgers and fries. The jukebox was playing some twangy country song, and the hostess leaned heavily against the register, polishing dust off the Ohio-shaped magnets that were on sale for ninety-nine cents.

"Where you headed?" a voice asked.

Emily looked into the eyes of the diner's fry cook, a sturdy man who looked like he did a lot of bow hunting when he wasn't making grilled cheese. Emily searched for a name tag, but he wasn't wearing one. His red ball cap had a big, singular letter *A* stitched in the center. She licked her lips, shivering a little. "How do you know I'm headed somewhere?"

He gave her a knowing look. "You're not from here. And Greyhound's across the street. And you have a big duffel bag. Clever, aren't I?"

Emily sighed, staring into her cup of coffee. It had taken her less than twenty minutes to power-walk the mile from Helene's to the mini mart down the road, even with her heavy duffel in tow. Once there, she'd found a ride to the bus station, and had bought a ticket for the first bus out of Iowa. Unfortunately it had been going to Akron, a place where Emily knew absolutely no one. Worse, the bus smelled like someone had bad gas, and the guy sitting next to her had his iPod cranked up to maximum volume while he sang along to Fall Out Boy, a band she detested. Then, weirdly, when the bus pulled into the Akron station, Emily had discovered a crab scuttling around under her seat. A *crab*, even though they were nowhere near an ocean. When she'd stumbled into the terminal and noticed that the big departures board said there was a 10 P.M. bus to Philadelphia, an ache had welled up inside her. She'd never missed Pennsylvania as much as she did now.

Emily shut her eyes, finding it hard to believe that she was really, truly running away. There were many times she'd imagined running away before—Ali used to say she'd go with her. Hawaii was one of their top five choices. So was Paris. Ali said they could assume different identities. When Emily protested, saying that sounded difficult, Ali shrugged and said, "Nah. Becoming someone else is probably really easy." Wherever they chose, they promised to spend tons of uninterrupted time together, and Emily had always secretly hoped that maybe, just maybe, Ali would have realized she loved Emily as much as Emily loved her. But in the end, Emily always felt bad and said, "Ali, you have no reason to run away. Your life is perfect here." And Ali would shrug in response, saying Emily was right, her life *was* pretty perfect.

Until someone killed her.

The fry cook turned up the volume on the tiny TV sitting next to the eight-slice toaster and an open package of Wonder Bread. When Emily looked up, she saw a CNN reporter standing in front of the familiar Rosewood Memorial Hospital. Emily knew it well—she passed it every morning on her drive to Rosewood Day.

"We have reports that Hanna Marin, seventeen-year-old resident of Rosewood and friend to Alison DiLaurentis, the girl whose body mysteriously turned up in her old backyard about a month ago, has just awakened from the coma she'd been in since Saturday night's tragic accident," the reporter said into her microphone.

Emily's coffee cup clattered against her saucer. *Coma?* Hanna's parents swam onto the screen, saying that, yes, Hanna was awake and seemed okay. There were no leads as to who had hit Hanna, or why.

Emily covered her mouth with her hand, which smelled like the fake-leather Greyhound bus seat. She whipped her Nokia out of her jean jacket pocket and turned it on. She'd been trying to conserve the battery because she'd accidentally left her charger behind in Iowa. Her fingers shook as she dialed Aria's number. It went to voice mail. "Aria, it's Emily," she said after the beep. "I just found out about Hanna, and . . ."

She trailed off, her eyes returning to the screen. There, in the upper right-hand corner, was her *own* face, staring back at her from the photo she'd had taken for last year's yearbook. "In other Rosewood news, another one of Ms. DiLaurentis's friends, Emily Fields, has gone missing," the anchor said. "She was visiting relatives in Iowa this week, but vanished from the property this morning."

The fry cook turned from flipping a grilled cheese and glanced at the screen. A look of disbelief crossed his face. He looked at Emily, then back at the screen again. His metal spatula fell to the floor with a hollow clatter.

Emily hit END without finishing her message to Aria. On the TV screen, her parents were standing in front of Emily's blue-shingled house. Her father wore his best plaid polo shirt, and her mom had a cashmere sweater cardigan draped over her shoulders. Carolyn stood off to the side, holding Emily's swim team portrait for the camera. Emily was too stunned to be embarrassed that a picture of her in a high-cut Speedo tank suit was on national television.

"We're very worried," Emily's mother said. "We want

Emily to know that we love her and just want her to come home."

Tears bloomed at the corners of Emily's eyes. Words couldn't describe what it felt like to hear her mother say those three little words: *we love her.* She slid off the stool, pushing her arms into her jacket sleeves.

The word PHILADELPHIA was plastered on top of a red, blue, and silver Greyhound bus across the street. The big 7-Up clock over the diner's counter said 9:53. *Please don't let the 10 P.M. bus be sold out,* Emily prayed.

She glanced at the scribble-covered bill next to her coffee. "I'll be back," she said to the cook, grabbing her bags. "I just have to get a bus ticket."

The fry cook still looked like a tornado had picked him up and dropped him onto a different planet. "Don't worry about it," he said faintly. "Coffee's on the house."

"Thanks!" The sleigh bells on the diner's door jingled together as Emily left. She ran across the empty highway and skidded into the bus station, thanking the various forces of the universe that had prevented a line from forming at the ticket window. Finally, she had a destination: home.

13

ONLY LOSERS GET HIT BY CARS

Tuesday morning, when she *should* have been strolling into her Pilates II class at Body Tonic gym, Hanna was instead lying flat on her back as two fat female nurses cleaned her off with a sponge. After they left, her physician, Dr. Geist, strode into the room and flipped on the light.

"Turn it off!" Hanna demanded sharply, quickly covering her face.

Dr. Geist left it on. Hanna had put in a request for a different doctor—if she was spending all this time here, couldn't she at least have an M.D. who was a little bit hotter?—but it seemed like nobody in this hospital was listening.

Hanna slid halfway under the covers and peeked into her Chanel compact. Yep, her monster face was still there, complete with the stitches on her chin, the two black eyes, the fat, purplish bottom lip, and the enormous bruises on her collarbone—it was going to be ages before she could

wear low-cut tops again. She sighed and snapped the compact closed. She couldn't wait to go to Bill Beach to fix
all the damage.

Dr. Geist inspected Hanna's vital signs on a computer
that looked like it had been built in the sixties. "You're
recovering very well. Now that the swelling's gone down,
we don't see any residual brain injury. Your internal
organs look fairly good. It's a miracle."

"Ha," Hanna grumbled.

"It *is* a miracle," Hanna's father butted in, walking in to
stand behind Dr. Geist. "We were sick with worry, Hanna.
It makes me sick that someone did this to you. And that
they're still out there."

Hanna sneaked a peek at him. Her dad wore a
charcoal gray suit and sleek black shiny loafers. In the
twelve hours since she'd awakened, he'd been incredibly patient, succumbing to Hanna's every whim . . .
and Hanna had lots of whims. First, she demanded that
they move her into her own private room—the last thing
she needed was to hear the old lady on the other side of
the curtain in intensive care talk about her bowel hab-
its and imminent hip replacement. Next, Hanna had
made her dad get her a portable DVD player and some
DVDs from the nearby Target. The hospital rent-a-TVs
only got six lame-ass network channels. She'd begged
her dad to make the nurses give her more painkillers,
and she'd deemed the mattress on the hospital bed
completely uncomfortable, forcing him to go out to the

Tempur-Pedic store an hour ago to get her a space-age foam topper. From the looks of the mammoth Tempur-Pedic plastic bag he was holding, it appeared that his trip had been successful.

Dr. Geist dropped Hanna's clipboard back into the slot at the foot of her bed. "We should be able to let you out in a few more days. Any questions?"

"Yes," Hanna said, her voice still croaky from the ventilator they'd had her on since her accident. She pointed to the IV in her arm. "How many calories is this thing giving me?" By the way her hip bones felt, it seemed as if she'd lost weight while being in the hospital—*bonus!*—but she just wanted to make sure.

Dr. Geist looked at her crazily, probably wishing *he* could switch patients too. "It's antibiotics and stuff to hydrate you," Hanna's father quickly interjected. He patted Hanna's arm. "It's all going to make you feel much better." As he and her dad left the room, Dr. Geist snapped off the light again.

Hanna glowered for a moment at the empty doorway, then fell back onto her bed. The only thing that could make her feel better right now was a six-hour massage by some hot, shirtless Italian male model. And, oh yeah, a brand-new face.

She was completely weirded out that this had happened to her. She kept wondering if, after falling asleep again, she'd wake up in her own bed with its six-hundred thread-count pima cotton sheets, beautiful as before, ready for a day of shopping with Mona. Who gets hit by a car? She wasn't even in the hospital for something cool, like a high-stakes kidnapping or Petra Nemcova's tsunami tragedy.

But something that scared her far more—and something that she didn't want to think about—was that the whole night was a huge, gaping hole in Hanna's memory. She couldn't even remember Mona's party.

Just then, two figures in familiar blue blazers appeared at the door. When they saw Hanna was awake and decent, Aria and Spencer rushed in quickly, their faces pinched with worry. "We tried to see you last night," Spencer said, "but the nurses wouldn't let us in."

Hanna noticed that Aria was sneaking a peek at Hanna's greenish bruises, a grossed-out look on her face. *"What?"* Hanna snapped, smoothing out her long, auburn hair, which she'd just spritzed with Bumble & Bumble Surf Spray. "You should try to be a little more Florence Nightingale, Aria. Sean's really into that."

It still rankled Hanna that her ex, Sean Ackard, had broken up with *her* to be with Aria. Today, Aria's hair hung in chunks around her face, and she wore a red-and-white-checkered tent dress under her Rosewood Day blazer. She looked like a cross between that freaky drummer girl in the White Stripes and a tablecloth. Besides, didn't she know that if she got caught without the plaid pleated skirt part of the school's uniform, Appleton would just send her home and make her change?

"Sean and I broke up," Aria mumbled.

Hanna raised a curious eyebrow. "Oh *really*? And why is that?"

Aria sat down in the little orange plastic chair next to Hanna's bed. "That doesn't matter right now. What matters is . . . this. You." Her eyes welled with tears. "I wish we would've gotten to the playground sooner. I keep thinking about it. We could've stopped that car, somehow. We could've pulled you out of the way."

Hanna stared at her, her throat constricting. "You were *there*?"

Aria nodded, then glanced at Spencer. "We were all there. Emily too. You wanted to meet us."

Hanna's heart quickened. "I did?"

Aria leaned closer. Her breath smelled like Orbit Mint Mojito gum, a flavor Hanna hated. "You said you knew who A was."

"*What?*" Hanna whispered.

"You don't *remember*?" Spencer shrieked. "Hanna, that's who hit you!" She whipped out her Sidekick and brought up a text. "Look!"

Hanna stared at the screen. *She knew too much.* —A

"A sent us this right after you were hit by the car," Spencer whispered.

Hanna blinked hard, stunned. Her mind was like a big, deep Gucci purse, and when Hanna rooted around in the bottom, she couldn't come up with the memory she needed. "A tried to *kill* me?" Her stomach began to churn.

All day, she'd had this awful feeling, deep down, that this hadn't been an accident. But she'd tried to quell it, telling herself that was nonsense.

"Maybe A had spoken to you?" Spencer tried. "Or maybe you saw A doing something. Can you think? We're afraid that if you don't remember who A is, A might . . ." She trailed off, gulping.

". . . strike again," Aria whispered.

Hanna shivered spastically, breaking out in a cold, horrified sweat. "Th-the last thing I remember was the night before Mona's party," she stammered. "The next thing I know, we're all sitting in Ali's backyard. We're in seventh grade again. It's the day before Ali disappeared, and we're talking about how we're going to have the sleepover in the barn. Remember that?"

Spencer squinted. "Uh . . . sure. I guess."

"I kept trying to warn Ali that she was going to die the next day," Hanna explained, her voice rising. "But Ali wouldn't pay attention to me. And then she looked at me and said I should stop making a big deal out of it. She said she was fine."

Spencer and Aria exchanged a glance. "Hanna, it was a dream," Aria said softly.

"Well, *yeah*, obviously." Hanna rolled her eyes. "I'm just saying. It was like Ali was right *there*." She pointed at a pink GET WELL SOON balloon at the end of the bed. It had a round face and accordion-style arms and legs, and it could walk on its own.

Before either of Hanna's old friends could respond, a loud voice interrupted them. "Where's the sexiest patient in this hospital?"

Mona stood in the doorway, her arms outstretched. She, too, wore her Rosewood Day blazer and skirt along with an amazing pair of Marc Jacobs boots Hanna had never seen. Mona glanced at Aria and Spencer suspiciously, then dumped a pile of *Vogue, Elle, Lucky,* and *Us Weekly* magazines on the nightstand. "*Pour vous,* Hanna. A lot has happened to Lindsay Lohan that you and I need to discuss."

"I *so* love you," Hanna cried, quickly trying to switch gears. She couldn't dwell on this A thing. She just *couldn't.* She was relieved that she hadn't been hallucinating yesterday when she woke up and saw Mona standing over her bed. Things with Mona had been rocky last week, but Hanna's last memory was receiving a court dress for Mona's birthday party in the mail. It was obviously an olive branch, but it was weird that she couldn't remember their makeup conversation—usually, when Hanna and Mona made up, they gave each other gifts, like a new iPod case or a pair of Coach kidskin gloves.

Spencer looked at Mona. "Well, now that Hanna's awake, I guess we don't have to do that thing on Friday."

Hanna perked up. "What thing?"

Mona perched on Hanna's bed. "We were going to have a little vigil for you at the Rosewood Country Club," she admitted. "Everyone at school was invited."

Hanna put her IV-rigged hand to her mouth, touched. "You guys were going to do that . . . for me?" She caught Mona's eye. It seemed unusual that Mona would be planning a party with Spencer—Mona had a lot of issues with Hanna's old friends—but Mona actually looked excited. Hanna's heart lifted.

"Since the club's already booked . . . maybe we could have a welcome-back party instead?" Hanna suggested in a small, tentative voice. She crossed her other hand's fingers under her sheets for luck, hoping Mona wouldn't think it was a stupid idea.

Mona pursed her perfectly lined lips. "I can't say no to a party. Especially a party for you, Han."

Hanna's insides sparkled. This was the best news she'd gotten all day—even better than when the nurses had permitted her to use the bathroom unattended. She wanted to leap up and give Mona an enormous, thankful, I'm-so-happy-we're-friends-again hug, but she was attached to too many tubes. "Especially since I can't remember your birthday party," Hanna pointed out, pouting. "Was it awesome?"

Mona lowered her eyes, picking a fuzz ball off her sweater.

"It's cool," Hanna said quickly. "You can tell me it rocked. I can handle it." She thought for a moment. "And I have a fantastic idea. Since it's kind of close to Halloween, and since I don't look my absolute best right now . . ."

She waved her hands around her face. "Let's make it a masquerade!"

"*Perfect,*" Mona gushed. "Oh, Han, it'll be amazing!"

She grabbed Mona's hands and they started squealing together. Aria and Spencer stood there awkwardly, left out. But Hanna wasn't about to squeal with them, too. This was something only BFFs did, and there was only one of those in Hanna's world.

14

INTERROGATION, WITH A SIDE
OF SPYING

Tuesday afternoon, after a quick yearbook meeting and an hour of field hockey drills, Spencer pulled up to her blue slate circular driveway. There was a Rosewood PD squad car sitting in her driveway next to her mother's battleship gray Range Rover.

Spencer's heart catapulted into her throat, as it had been doing a lot the past few days. Had it been a huge mistake to confess her guilt about Ali to Melissa? What if Melissa only said that Spencer didn't have the killer instinct to throw her off track? What if she'd called up Wilden and told him that Spencer had done it?

Spencer thought of that night again. Her sister had had such an eerie smile on her face when she said Spencer couldn't have murdered Ali. The words she'd chosen were odd, too—she'd said it took a very *unique* person to kill. Why hadn't she said *crazy* or *heartless*? *Unique* made it sound special. Spencer had been so freaked out, she'd avoided Melissa ever since, feeling awkward and uncertain in her presence.

As Spencer slipped inside her front door and hung her Burberry trench coat in the hall closet, she noticed that Melissa and Ian were sitting very rigidly on the Hastingses' living room couch, as if they were being berated in the principal's office. Officer Wilden sat across from them, on the leather club chair. "H-hi," Spencer sputtered, surprised.

"Oh, Spencer." Wilden gave Spencer a nod. "I'm just talking to your sister and Ian for a moment, if you'll excuse us."

Spencer took a big step back. "W-what are you talking about?"

"Just a few questions about the night Alison DiLaurentis went missing," Wilden said, his eyes on his notepad. "I'm trying to get everyone's perspective."

The room was silent except for the sound of the ionizer Spencer's mother had bought after her allergist told her that dust mites gave women wrinkles. Spencer backed out of the room slowly.

"There's a letter for you on the hall table," Melissa called out just as Spencer rounded the corner. "Mom left it for you."

There was indeed a stack of mail on the hall table, next to a hive-shaped terra-cotta vase that had allegedly been a gift to Spencer's great-grandmother from Howard Hughes. Spencer's letter was right on top, in an already-opened creamy envelope with her name handwritten across the front. Inside was an invitation on heavy cream card stock. Gold, scrolling script read, *The Golden Orchid committee invites you to a finalists' breakfast and interview at Daniel Restaurant in New York City on Friday, October 15.*

There was a pink Post-it note affixed to the corner. Her mother had written, *Spencer, we already cleared this with your teachers. We have rooms reserved at the W for Thursday night.*

Spencer pressed the paper to her face. It smelled a little like Polo cologne, or maybe that was Wilden. Her parents were actually *encouraging* her to compete, knowing what they knew? It seemed so surreal. And *wrong.*

Or . . . was it? She ran her finger along the invite's embossed letters. Spencer had longed to win a Golden Orchid since third grade, and perhaps her parents recognized that. And if she hadn't been so freaked out about Ali and A, she definitely would have been able to write her own Golden Orchid–worthy essay. So why not really go for it? She thought about what Melissa had said—her parents would reward her handsomely for winning. She *needed* a reward right now.

The living room's grandfather clock bonged six times. Spencer guessed that Wilden was waiting to make sure she'd gone upstairs before he began his discussion. She stomped loudly up the first few stairs, then stopped halfway and marched in place to make it sound like she'd climbed the rest of the way up. She had a perfect view of

Ian and Melissa through the banister spindles, but no one could see her.

"Okay." Wilden cleared his throat. "So, back to Alison DiLaurentis."

Melissa wrinkled her nose. "I'm still not sure what this has to do with us. You'd be better off talking to my sister."

Spencer squeezed her eyes shut. *Here it comes.*

"Just bear with me," Wilden said slowly. "You two *do* want to help me find Alison's killer, don't you?"

"Of course," Melissa said haughtily, her face turning red.

"Good," Wilden said. As he pulled out a black spiral-bound notebook, Spencer slowly let out her breath.

"So," Wilden continued. "You guys were in the barn with Alison and her friends shortly before she disappeared, right?"

Melissa nodded. "They walked in on us. Spencer had asked our parents to use the barn for her sleepover. She thought I was going to Prague that night, but I was actually going the next day. We left, though. We let them have the barn." She smiled proudly, as if she'd been oh-so charitable.

"Okay . . ." Wilden scribbled in his notepad. "And you didn't see anything strange in your yard that night? Anyone lurking around, nothing like that?"

"Nothing," Melissa said quietly. Again, Spencer felt grateful but also confused. Why wasn't heart-of-ice Melissa ratting her out?

"And where did you go after that?" Wilden asked.

Melissa and Ian looked surprised. "We went to Melissa's den. Right in there." Ian pointed down the hall. "We were just . . . hanging out. Watching TV. I don't know."

"And you were together the whole night?"

Ian glanced at Melissa. "I mean, it was over four years ago, so it's kind of hard to remember, but yeah, I'm pretty sure."

"Melissa?" Wilden asked.

Melissa flicked a tassel on one of the couch pillows. For a shimmering second, Spencer saw a look of terror cross her face. In a blink, it was gone. "We were together."

"Okay." Wilden looked back and forth at them, as if something bothered him. "And . . . Ian. Was there something going on with you and Alison?"

Ian's face went slack. He cleared his throat. "Ali had a crush on me. I flirted with her a little, that's all."

Spencer rolled her jaw around, surprised. Ian, lying . . . to a cop? She peeked at her sister, but Melissa was staring straight ahead, a small smirk on her face. *I kind of knew Ian and Ali were together,* she'd said.

Spencer thought about the memory Hanna had brought up at the hospital earlier about the four of them going over to Ali's house the day before she went missing. The details of the day were foggy, but Spencer remembered that they'd seen Melissa walking back to the Hastingses' barn. Ali had yelled out to her, asking if Melissa was worried that Ian might find another girl-friend while Melissa was in Prague. Spencer had smacked Ali for the remark, warning her to shut up. Since she'd admitted to Ali and only Ali that she'd kissed Ian, Ali had been threatening to tell Melissa what Spencer had done if Spencer didn't confess to it herself. So Spencer thought Ali's comments were meant to mess with her, not Melissa.

That *was* what Ali was doing, wasn't it? She wasn't so sure anymore.

After that, Melissa had shrugged, muttered under her breath, and stormed toward the Hastingses' barn. On her way, though, Spencer remembered her sister pausing to look at the hole the workers were digging in Ali's back-yard. It was as if she were trying to commit its dimensions to memory.

Spencer clapped a hand over her mouth. She'd received a text from A last week when she was sitting in front of her vanity mirror. It had said, *Ali's murderer is right in front of you,* and right after Spencer read it, Melissa had appeared in her doorway to announce that the *Philadelphia Sentinel* reporter was downstairs. Melissa had been as much in front of Spencer as her own reflec-tion had.

As Wilden shook hands with Ian and Melissa and rose to leave, Spencer scampered quietly the rest of the way up the stairs, her mind spinning. The day before she went missing, Ali had said, "You know what, guys?

I think this is going to be the summer of Ali." She had seemed so certain of it, so confident that everything would work out the way she wanted. But although Ali could boss the four of them into doing everything she said, no one, absolutely *no one,* played those kinds of games with Spencer's sister. Because in the end, Melissa. Always. Won.

15

GUESS WHO'S BA-A-ACK?

Early Wednesday morning, Emily's mother silently steered the minivan out of the Philadelphia Greyhound bus station parking lot, down Route 76 in the middle of morning rush hour, past the Schuylkill River's charming row houses, and straight to Rosewood Memorial Hospital. Even though Emily was badly in need of a shower after her grueling, ten-hour bus trip, she really wanted to see how Hanna was doing.

By the time they reached the hospital, Emily began to worry that she'd made a grave mistake. She'd called her parents before getting on the bus to Philadelphia at 10 P.M. last night, saying she'd seen them on TV, that she was okay, and that she was coming home. Her parents had *sounded* happy . . . but then her cell phone's battery had died, so she didn't really know for sure. Since Emily had gotten in the car, all her mom had said to her was, "Are you okay?"

After Emily said yes, her mom told her that Hanna had woken up, and then she went mute.

Her mother pulled under the awning of the hospital's main entrance and put the car into park. She let out a long, whinnying sigh, resting her head briefly against the steering wheel. "It scares me to death, driving in Philly."

Emily stared at her mom, with her stiff gray hair, emerald-green cardigan, and prized pearl necklace that she wore every single day, kind of like Marge on *The Simpsons*. Emily suddenly realized that she had never seen her mother drive anywhere remotely near Philadelphia. And her mom had always been terrified about merging, even if no cars were coming. "Thanks for picking me up," she said in a small voice.

Mrs. Fields studied Emily carefully, her lips wobbling. "We were so worried about you. The idea that we might have lost you forever really made us rethink some things. That wasn't right, sending you to Helene's the way we did. Emily, we might not accept the decisions you've made for . . . for your life, but we're going to try and live with it as best we can. That's what Dr. Phil says. Your father and I have been reading his books."

Outside the car, a young couple wheeled a Silver Cross pram to their Porsche Cayenne. Two attractive, twenty-something black doctors shoved each other jokingly. Emily breathed in the honeysuckle air and noticed a Wawa market across the street. She was definitely in Rosewood. She hadn't crash-landed in some other girl's life.

"Okay," Emily croaked. Her whole body felt itchy, especially her palms. "Well . . . thank you. That makes me really happy."

Mrs. Fields reached into her purse and took out a plastic Barnes & Noble bag. She handed it to Emily. "This is for you."

Inside was a DVD of *Finding Nemo*. Emily looked up, confused.

"Ellen DeGeneres is the voice of the funny fish," Emily's mother explained in a slightly *uh-duh* voice. "We thought you might like her." Emily suddenly got it. Ellen DeGeneres was a fish—a lesbian swimmer, just like Emily.

"Thanks," she said, clutching the DVD to her chest, oddly touched.

She tumbled out of the car and walked through the hospital's automatic front door in a daze. As she passed by the check-in, the coffee bar, and the high-end gift shop, her mother's words slowly sank in. Her family had *accepted her*? She wondered if she should call Maya and tell her she was back. But what would she say? *I'm home! My parents are cool now! We can date now!* It seemed so . . . cheesy.

Hanna's room was on the fifth floor. When Emily pushed open the door, Aria and Spencer were already sitting next to her bed, their hands wrapped around Venti Starbucks coffees. A row of ragged black stitches stood out on Hanna's chin, and she wore a hulking cast on her arm. There was an enormous bouquet of flowers next to her bed, and the whole room smelled like rosemary aromatherapy oil. "Hey, Hanna," Emily said, shutting the door softly. "How are you?"

Hanna sighed, almost annoyed. "Are you here to ask me about A too?"

Emily looked at Aria, then at Spencer, who was picking nervously at her coffee cup's cardboard sleeve. It was strange to see Aria and Spencer together—didn't Aria suspect that Spencer had killed Ali? She raised an eyebrow at Aria, indicating as much, but Aria shook her head, mouthing, *I'll explain later.*

Emily looked back at Hanna. "Well, I wanted to see how you were, but yeah . . ." she started.

"Save it," Hanna said haughtily, winding a tendril of hair around her finger. "I don't remember what happened. So we might as well talk about something else." Her voice wobbled with distress.

Emily stepped back. She looked beseechingly at Aria, her eyes saying, *She really doesn't remember?* Aria shook her head no.

"Hanna, if we don't keep asking, you're never going to remember," Spencer urged. "Did you get a text? A note? Maybe A put something in your pocket?"

Hanna glowered at Spencer, her lips smushed closed.

"You found out sometime during or after Mona's party," Aria encouraged. "Does it have something to do with that?"

"Maybe A said something incriminating," Spencer said. "Or maybe you saw the person behind the wheel of the SUV that hit you?"

"Would you just stop?" Tears brimmed at the corners of Hanna's eyes. "The doctor said pushing me like this isn't good for my recovery." After a pause, she ran her hands along her soft cashmere blanket and took a deep breath. "If you guys could go back to the time before Ali died, do you think you could prevent it from happening?"

Emily looked around. Her friends seemed as stunned by the question as she was. "Well, sure," Aria murmured quietly.

"Of course," Emily said.

"And you'd still want to?" Hanna goaded. "Would we really want Ali around? Now that we know Ali kept the secret about Toby from us and had been seeing Ian behind our backs? Now that we've grown up a little and realized that Ali was basically a bitch?"

"Of course I'd want her here," Emily said sharply. But when she looked around, her friends were staring at the floor, saying nothing.

"Well, we certainly didn't want her dead," Spencer finally mumbled. Aria nodded and scratched at her purple nail polish.

Hanna had wrapped a Hermès scarf around part of her cast in what Emily imagined was an attempt to make it look prettier. The rest of the cast, Emily noticed, was filled with signatures. Everyone from Rosewood had signed already—there was a sweeping signature from Noel Kahn; a tidy one from Spencer's sister, Melissa; a spiky one from Mr. Jennings, Hanna's math teacher. Someone had signed the cast only with the word KISSES!, the dot in the exclamation point a smiley face. Emily ran her fingers over the word, as if it were Braille.

After a few more minutes of not saying much at all, Aria, Emily, and Spencer gloomily filed out of the room. They were silent until they reached the elevator bank. "What brought on all that stuff she was saying about Ali?" Emily whispered.

"Hanna had a dream about Ali while she was in the coma." Spencer shrugged and punched the down button for the elevator.

"We have to get Hanna to remember," Aria whispered. "She *knows* who A is."

It was barely 8 A.M. when they emerged into the parking lot. As an ambulance raced past them, Spencer's cell phone began to play Vivaldi's *Four Seasons*. She checked her pocket, irritated. "Who could be calling me this early in the morning?"

Then Aria's cell phone buzzed too. And Emily's.

A cold wind swept over all the girls. The hospital-logo flags that hung from the main awning billowed in the breeze. "No," Spencer gasped.

Emily peeked at the text's subject line. It said, KISSES!, just like on Hanna's cast.

Miss me, bitches? Stop digging for answers, or I'll have to erase your memories too. —A

16

A NEW VICTIM

That Wednesday afternoon, Spencer waited on Rosewood Country Club's outdoor patio to begin planning Hanna's welcome-back masquerade with Mona Vanderwaal. She absentmindedly flipped through the AP econ essay that had been nominated for a Golden Orchid. When she'd stolen the essay from Melissa's arsenal of old high school papers, Spencer hadn't understood half of it . . . and she still didn't. But since the Golden Orchid judges were going to grill her at Friday's breakfast, she'd decided to learn it word for word. How hard could it be? She memorized entire monologues for drama club all the time. Plus, she was hoping it would get her mind off A.

She closed her eyes and mouthed the first few paragraphs perfectly. Then she imagined the outfit she'd wear for her Golden Orchid interview—definitely something Calvin or Chanel, maybe with some clear-framed, academic-looking glasses. Maybe she'd even bring in the article the *Philadelphia Sentinel* had done about her and leave it sticking just slightly out of her bag. Then the interviewers would see it and think, *My, she's already been on the front page of a major newspaper!*

"Hey." Mona stood above her in a pretty olive-green dress and tall black boots. She had an oversize dark purple bag slung over her right shoulder, and she carried a Jamba Juice smoothie in her hand. "Am I too early?"

"Nope, you're perfect." Spencer moved her books off the seat across from her and stuffed Melissa's essay into her purse. Her hand grazed against her cell phone. She fought against the masochistic urge to pull it out and look at A's message again. *Stop digging for answers.* After everything that had happened, after three days of radio silence, A was still after them. Spencer was dying to talk to Wilden about it, but she was terrified about what A might do if she did.

"You okay?" Mona sat down and stared at Spencer worriedly.

"Sure." Spencer rattled the straw in her empty Diet Coke glass, trying to push A from her mind. She gestured to her books. "I just have this interview for an essay competition on Friday. It's in New York. So I'm sort of freaking out."

Mona smiled. "That's right, that Golden Orchid thing? You've been all over the announcements."

Spencer ducked her head faux-bashfully. She loved

hearing her name on the morning announcements, except when she had to read them herself—then it just seemed boastful. She inspected Mona carefully. Mona had really done a fantastic job transforming from Razor scooter–loving dork to fabulous diva, but Spencer had never really gotten past seeing Mona as one of the many girls Ali liked to tease. This was possibly the first time she'd ever spoken to Mona one-on-one.

Mona cocked her head. "I saw your sister outside your house when I left for school this morning. She said your picture was in Sunday's paper."

"*Melissa* told you that?" Spencer's eyes widened, feeling a glimmer of uneasiness. She recalled the fearful look that had crossed Melissa's face yesterday when Wilden asked her where she'd been the night Ali vanished. What was Melissa so afraid of? What was Melissa hiding?

Mona blinked, lost. "Yeah. Why? Is it not true?"

Spencer shook her head slowly. "No, it's true. I'm just surprised Melissa said something nice about me, is all."

"What do you mean?" Mona asked.

"We're not the best of friends." Spencer glanced furtively around the country club patio, filled with a horrible feeling that Melissa was here, *listening.* "Anyway," she said. "About the party. I just talked to the club manager, and they're all ready for Friday."

"Perfect." Mona pulled out a stack of cards and slid them across the table. "These are the invites I came up with.

They're in the shape of a mask, see? But then there's foil on the front, so when you look into it, you see yourself."

Spencer looked at her slightly fuzzy reflection in the invite. Her skin was clear and glowing and her newly touched-up buttery highlights brightened her face.

Mona flipped through her Gucci wallet diary, consulting her notes. "I also think, to make Hanna feel *really* special, we should bring her into the room in a grand princess–style entrance. I'm thinking four hot, shirtless guys could carry her in on a canopied pedestal. Or something like that. I've arranged for a bunch of models to come over to Hanna's tomorrow so she can choose them for herself."

"That's *awesome*." Spencer folded her hands over her Kate Spade diary. "Hanna's lucky to have you as a friend."

Mona looked ruefully out at the golf course and let out a long sigh. "The way things have been between us lately, it's a miracle that Hanna doesn't hate me."

"What are you talking about?" Spencer had heard something about Mona and Hanna getting in a fight at Mona's birthday party, but she'd been so busy and distracted, she hadn't really paid attention to the rumors.

Mona sighed and tucked a strand of white-blond hair behind her ear. "Hanna and I haven't been on the best of terms," she admitted. "It's just that, she'd been acting so *weird*. We used to do everything together, but suddenly she started keeping all these secrets, blowing off plans we made, and acting like she hated me." Mona's eyes welled with tears.

A lump formed in Spencer's throat. She knew just how that felt. Before she disappeared, Ali had done the same thing to her.

"She was spending a lot of time with you guys—and that made me a little jealous." Mona traced her pointer finger around the perimeter of an empty bread plate on the table. "Truthfully, I was stunned when Hanna wanted to be friends with me in eighth grade. She was part of Ali's clique, and you guys were *legend*. I always thought our friendship was too good to be true. Maybe I still kind of feel that way from time to time."

Spencer stared at her. It was incredible how similar Mona and Hanna's friendship was to Spencer and Ali's—Spencer had been astonished when Ali chose her to be part of her inner circle, too. "Well, Hanna's been hanging out with us because we've been dealing with some . . . issues," she said. "I'm sure she'd rather be with you."

Mona bit her lip. "I was terrible to her. I thought she was trying to ditch me, so I just . . . went on the defensive. But when she got hit by the car . . . and when I realized she might die . . . it was awful. She's been my best friend for years." She covered her face with her hands. "I just want to forget about all of it. I just want things to be *normal* again."

The charms dangling off Mona's Tiffany bracelet

tinkled together prettily. Her mouth puckered, as if she were about to start sobbing. Spencer suddenly felt guilty about the way they used to tease Mona. Ali had taunted her about her vampire tan, and even her height—Ali always said Mona was short enough to be the girl version of Mini Me from *Austin Powers*. Ali also claimed that Mona had cellulite on her gut—she'd seen Mona changing in the country club locker room and had nearly thrown up it was so ugly. Spencer didn't believe her, so once, when Ali was spending the night at Spencer's, they sneaked over to Mona's house down the street and spied on Mona as she was dancing to videos on VH1 in the den. "I hope her shirt flutters up," Ali whispered. "Then you'll see her in all her nastiness."

Mona's shirt stayed put. She'd continued to dance around crazily, the way Spencer danced when she thought no one was watching. Then Ali knocked on the window. Mona's face reddened and she fled out of the room.

"I'm sure everything will be fine between you and Hanna," Spencer said gently, touching Mona's thin arm. "And the last thing you should do is blame yourself."

"I hope so." Mona gave Spencer a vulnerable smile. "Thanks for listening."

The waitress interrupted them, setting the leather booklet containing Spencer's bill on the table. Spencer opened it up and signed her two Diet Cokes to her father's account. She was surprised that her watch said it was almost five. She stood up, feeling a twinge of sadness, not wanting the conversation to end. When had she last talked to anyone about anything *real*? "I'm late for rehearsal." She let out a long, stressed sigh.

Mona inspected her for a moment, then glanced across the room. "Actually, you might not want to leave quite yet." She nodded toward the double French doors, color returning to her face. "That guy over there just checked you out."

Spencer glanced over her shoulder. Two college-age guys in Lacoste polos sat at a corner table, nursing Bombay Sapphires and sodas. "Which one?" Spencer murmured.

"Mr. Hugo Boss model." Mona pointed to a dark-haired guy with a chiseled jaw. A devious look came over her face. "Want to make him lose his mind?"

"How?" Spencer asked.

"Flash him," Mona whispered, nudging her chin at Spencer's skirt.

Spencer demurely covered her lap. "They'll kick us out!"

"No, they won't." Mona smirked. "I bet it'll make you feel better about all your Golden Orchid stress. It's like an instant spa treatment."

Spencer considered it for a moment. "I'll do it if you do it."

Mona nodded, standing up. "On three."

Spencer stood too. Mona cleared her throat to get their attention. Both boys' heads swiveled over. "One . . . two . . ." Mona counted.

"Three!" Spencer cried. They pulled up their skirts fast. Spencer revealed green silk Eres boy shorts, and Mona showed off sexy, lacy black panties—definitely not the kind of thing worn by a girl who loves Razor scooters. They only held up their skirts for a moment, but it was enough. The dark-haired guy in the corner sputtered up a swallow of beer. Hugo Boss Model looked like he was going to faint. Spencer and Mona let their skirts drop and doubled over with laughter.

"Holy shit." Mona giggled, her chest heaving. "That was awesome."

Spencer's heart continued to rocket in her chest. Both of the guys were still staring, slack-jawed. "Do you think anyone else saw?" she whispered.

"Who the hell cares? Like they'd really kick *us* out of here."

Spencer's cheeks warmed, flattered that Mona considered her as traffic-stopping as she was. "Now I'm *really* late," she murmured. "But it was worth it."

"Of course it was." Mona blew her a kiss. "Promise me we'll do this again?"

Spencer nodded and blew her a kiss back, then breezed through the main dining room. She felt better than she had in days. With Mona's help, she'd managed to forget about A, the Golden Orchid, and Melissa for three whole minutes.

But as she walked through the parking lot, she felt a hand on her arm. "Wait."

When Spencer turned around, she found Mona nervously spinning her diamond necklace around her neck. Her expression had morphed from one of gleeful naughtiness to something much more guarded and uncertain.

"I know you're super-late," Mona blurted out, "and I don't want to bother you, but something's happening to me, and I really need to talk to someone about it. I know we don't know each other well, but I can't talk to Hanna— she's got enough problems. And everyone else would spread it around the school."

Spencer perched on the edge of a large ceramic planter, concerned. "What is it?"

Mona looked around cautiously, as if to make sure there were no Ralph Lauren–clad golfers nearby. "I've been getting these . . . text messages," she whispered.

Spencer lost hearing for a moment. *"What did you say?"*

"Text messages," Mona repeated. "I've only gotten two, but they're not really signed, so I don't know who they're from. They say these . . . these *horrible* things about me." Mona bit her lip. "I'm kind of scared."

A sparrow fluttered past and landed on a barren crab apple tree. A lawn mower rumbled to life in the distance. Spencer gaped at Mona. "Are they from . . . A?" she whispered.

Mona went so pale, even her freckles vanished. "H-how did you know that?"

"Because." Spencer breathed in. *This wasn't happening. This* couldn't *be happening.* "Hanna and I—and Aria and Emily—we've all been getting them too."

17

CATS CAN FIGHT NICE, CAN'T THEY?

Wednesday afternoon, just as Hanna flopped over in her hospital bed—apparently, lying too still caused bedsores, which sounded even nastier than acne—she heard a knock at her door. She almost didn't want to answer it. She was a little sick of all her nosy visitors, especially Spencer, Aria, and Emily.

"Let's get ready to par-*tay!*" someone yelled. Four boys swept inside: Noel Kahn; Mason Byers; Aria's younger brother, Mike; and, surprise of all surprises, Sean Ackard, Hanna's—and Aria's, it seemed—ex-boyfriend.

"Hey, boys." Hanna lifted the oatmeal-colored cashmere blanket Mona had brought her from home over the bottom half of her face, revealing only her eyes. Seconds later, Lucas Beattie arrived, carrying a big bouquet of flowers.

Noel glanced at Lucas, then rolled his eyes. "Overcompensating for something?"

"Huh?" Lucas's face was nearly swallowed up by the bouquet.

Hanna didn't get why Lucas was always visiting her. Sure, they'd been friends for like a *minute* last week, when Lucas took her up in his dad's hot-air balloon and let her vent about all of her troubles. Hanna knew how much he liked her—he'd pretty much reached in, pulled out his heart, and handed it to her during their balloon ride together, but after she'd received Mona's court dress in the mail, Hanna clearly remembered sending Lucas a nasty text confirming that she was out of his league. She considered reminding him of that now, only . . . Lucas had been pretty useful. He'd gone to Sephora to buy Hanna a whole bunch of new makeup, read *Teen Vogue* to her line by line, and cajoled the doctors into allowing him to douse the room with Bliss aromatherapy oil, just as Hanna had asked him to. She kind of liked having him around. If she weren't so popular and fabulous, he'd probably make a great boyfriend. He was definitely cute enough—way cuter than Sean, even.

Hanna glanced at Sean now. He was sitting stiffly in a plastic visitor's chair, peeking at Hanna's various get-well cards. Visiting Hanna in the hospital was *so* him. She wanted to ask him why he and Aria had broken up, but all of a sudden, she realized that she didn't care.

Noel looked at Hanna curiously. "What's with the veil?"

"The doctors told me to do this." Hanna pulled the

blanket tight around her nose. "To, like, keep away germs. And besides, you get to focus on my beautiful eyes."

"So, what was it like being in a coma?" Noel perched on the side of Hanna's bed, squeezing a stuffed turtle that her aunt and uncle had given her yesterday. "Was it, like, a really long acid trip?"

"And are they giving you medicinal marijuana now?" Mike asked hopefully, his blue eyes glinting. "I bet the hospital stash *rocks*."

"Nah, I bet they're giving her painkillers." Mason's parents were doctors, so he always busted out his medical knowledge. "Hospital patients have such a sweet setup."

"Are the nurses hot?" Mike burbled. "Do they strip for you?"

"Are you naked under there?" Noel asked. "Give us a peek!"

"Guys!" Lucas said in a horrified voice. The boys looked at him and rolled their eyes—except for Sean, who looked almost as uncomfortable as Lucas did. Sean was probably still in Virginity Club, Hanna thought with a smirk.

"It's fine," Hanna chirped. "I can handle it." It was actually refreshing to have the boys here, making inappropriate comments. Everyone else who visited had been so damn serious. As the boys gathered around to sign Hanna's cast, Hanna remembered something and sat up. "You guys are coming to my welcome-back party on Friday, right? Spencer and Mona are planning it, so I'm sure it's going to rock."

"Wouldn't miss it." Noel glanced at Mason and Mike, who were looking out the window, chatting about what limbs they'd break if they jumped from Hanna's fifth-floor balcony. "What's up with you and Mona, anyway?" Noel asked.

"Nothing." Hanna flinched. "Why?"

Noel capped the pen. "You guys had quite a catfight at her party. *Rrow!*"

"We did?" Hanna asked blankly. Lucas coughed uncomfortably.

"Noel, it was so not *rrow!*" Mona breezed into the room. She blew air-kisses at Noel, Mason, and Mike, shot a frosty smile at Sean, and dropped an enormous binder at the bottom of Hanna's bed. She ignored Lucas completely. "It was just a little BFF bitchiness."

Noel shrugged. He joined the other boys at the window and proceeded to get into a noogie fight with Mason.

Mona rolled her eyes. "So listen, Han, I was just talking to Spencer, and we made a must-have party list. I want to run the details by you." She opened her Tiffany-blue binder. "You, of course, have the final say before I talk to the venue." She licked her finger and turned a page. "Okay. Bisque or ivory napkins?"

Hanna tried to focus, but Noel's words were still fresh in Hanna's mind. *Rrow?* "What were we fighting about?" Hanna blurted out.

Mona paused, lowering her list to her lap. "Seriously,

Han, nothing. You remember we were fighting the week before? About the skywriter? Naomi and Riley?"

Hanna nodded. Mona had asked Naomi Zeigler and Riley Wolfe, their biggest rivals, to be part of her Sweet Seventeen party court. Hanna suspected it was in retaliation to Hanna blowing off their Frenniversary celebration.

"Well, you were totally right," Mona went on. "Those two are enormous bitches. I don't want us to hang out with them anymore. I'm sorry I let them in the inner circle for a little bit, Han."

"It's okay," Hanna said in a small voice, feeling a tiny lift.

"So, anyway." Mona pulled out two magazine cutouts. One was a longish, white, pleated bubble dress with a silk rosette on the back, and the other was a wild-print dress that hit high on the thigh. "Phillip Lim gathered gown or flirty Nieves Lavi minidress?"

"Nieves Lavi," Hanna answered. "It's boatneck and short, so it'll show lots of leg but detract from my collarbone and face." She pulled the sheet up to her eyes again.

"Speaking of that," Mona chirped, "look what I got for you!"

She reached into her butter-colored Cynthia Rowley tote and pulled out a delicate porcelain mask. It was in the shape of a pretty girl's face, with prominent cheekbones, pretty, pouty lips, and a nose that would definitely be on a plastic surgeon's most-requested list. It was so beautiful and intricate, it looked *almost* real.

"These exact masks were used in last year's Dior haute couture show," Mona breathed. "My mom knows someone at Dior's PR company in New York, and we had someone drive it down from New York City this morning."

"Oh my God." Hanna reached out and touched the edge of the mask. It felt like a mix between baby-soft skin and satin.

Mona held the mask up to Hanna's face, which was still half-covered by the blanket. "It will cover all your bruises. You'll be the most gorgeous girl at your party."

"Hanna's already gorgeous," Lucas piped up, whirling around from all the medical machines. "Even without a mask."

Mona's nose wrinkled as if Lucas had just told her he was going to take her temperature in her butt. "Oh, Lucas," she said frostily. "I didn't see you standing there."

"I've been here the whole time," Lucas pointed out tersely.

The two of them glowered at each other. Hanna noticed something almost apprehensive about Mona's expression. But in a blink, it was gone.

Mona placed Hanna's mask against her vase of flowers, positioning it so that it was staring at her. "This is going to be *the* party of the year, Han. I can't wait."

With that, Mona blew her a kiss and danced out of the room. Noel, Mason, Sean, and Mike followed, telling Hanna they'd be back tomorrow and she'd *better* share some of her medicinal marijuana with them. Only Lucas remained, leaning against the far wall next to a soothing Monet-esque poster of a field of dandelions. There was a disturbed expression on his face.

"So that cop, Wilden? He asked me some questions about the hit-and-run while we were waiting for you to wake up from your coma a couple days ago," Lucas said quietly, sitting down on the orange chair next to Hanna's bed. "Like, if I'd seen you the night it happened. If you were acting weird or worried. It kind of sounded like he thought the hit-and-run wasn't an accident."

Lucas swallowed hard and raised his eyes to Hanna. "You don't think it was the same person who was sending you those weird text messages, do you?"

Hanna shot up. She'd forgotten that she'd told Lucas about A when they'd gone up in the hot-air balloon together. Her heart started to pound. "Tell me you didn't say anything about that to Wilden."

"Of course not," Lucas assured her. "It's just . . . I'm worried about you. It's so scary that someone *hit* you, is all."

"Don't worry about it," Hanna interrupted, crossing her arms over her chest. "And please, *please* don't say a word to Wilden about it. Okay?"

"Okay," Lucas said. "Sure."

"Good," Hanna barked. She took a long sip from the glass of water that was next to her bed. Whenever she dared to consider the truth—that A had *hit her*—her mind closed off, refusing to let her ponder it any further.

"So. Isn't it nice that Mona's throwing a party for me?" Hanna asked pointedly, wanting to change the subject. "She's been such a wonderful friend. Everyone's saying so."

Lucas fiddled with the buttons on his Nike watch. "I'm not sure if you should trust her," he mumbled.

Hanna wrinkled her brow. "What are you talking about?"

Lucas hesitated for a few long seconds.

"Come on," Hanna said, annoyed. "What?"

Lucas reached over and tugged Hanna's sheet down, exposing her face. He took her cheeks in his hands and kissed her. Lucas's mouth was soft and warm and fit perfectly with hers. Tingles scampered up Hanna's spine.

When Lucas broke away, they stared at each other for seven long beeps on Hanna's EKG machine, breathing hard. Hanna was pretty sure the look on her face was one of pure astonishment.

"Do you remember?" Lucas asked, his eyes wide.

Hanna frowned. "Remember . . . what?"

Lucas stared at her for a long time, his eyes flickering back and forth. And then he turned away. "I–I should go," Lucas mumbled awkwardly, and pushed out of the room.

Hanna stared after him, her bruised lips still sparking from his kiss. What had just happened?

18

NOW, INTRODUCING, FOR THE FIRST TIME EVER IN ROSEWOOD, JESSICA MONTGOMERY

That same afternoon, Aria stood outside the Hollis art building, staring at a group of kids doing capoeira on the lawn. Aria had never understood capoeira. Her brother described it best, saying it looked less like a Brazilian fight dance and more like the people were trying to smell one another's butts or pee on each other like dogs.

She felt a cold, thin hand on her shoulder. "Are you on campus for your art class?" a voice whispered in Aria's ear.

Aria stiffened. "Meredith." Today, Meredith wore a green pin-striped blazer and ripped jeans, and had an army green knapsack slung over her shoulder. The way she was staring at Aria, Aria felt like a little ant beneath a Meredith-shaped magnifying glass.

"You're taking Mindless Art, right?" Meredith said. When Aria nodded dumbly, Meredith looked at her watch. "You'd better get up there. It starts in five minutes."

Aria felt trapped. She'd been considering bagging this class completely—the last thing she wanted to do was spend two hours with Jenna Cavanaugh. Just seeing her the other day had brought back all sorts of uncomfortable memories. But Aria knew Meredith would relay everything to Byron, and Byron would give her a lecture on how it wasn't very nice to throw Meredith's charitable gift away. Aria pulled her pink cardigan around her shoulders. "Are you going to walk me up?" she snapped.

Meredith looked surprised. "Actually . . . I can't. I have to go do something. Something . . . important."

Aria rolled her eyes. She wasn't being serious, but Meredith was looking back and forth shiftily, as if concealing a big secret. A horrible thought occurred to Aria: What if she was doing something *wedding* related? Even though Aria really, really didn't want to imagine Meredith and her father standing at the front of a church altar, repeating their vows, the horrible image popped into her head anyway.

Without saying good-bye, Aria walked over to the building and took the stairs two at a time. Upstairs, Sabrina was about to start her lecture, instructing all the artists to find workstations. It was like a big game of musical chairs, and when the dust settled, Aria still didn't have a seat. There was only one art table left . . . next to the girl with the white cane and the big golden retriever guide dog. Naturally.

It felt like Jenna's eyes were following her as Aria's thin-soled Chinese slippers slapped against the wood floor toward the empty workstation. Jenna's dog panted amiably at Aria as she passed. Today, Jenna wore a low-cut black blouse with a tiny bit of a lacy black bra peeking through. If Mike were here, he would probably adore Jenna because he could stare at her boobs without her ever knowing. When Aria sat down, Jenna cocked her head closer to her. "What's your name?"

"It's . . . Jessica," Aria blurted, before she could stop herself. She glanced at Sabrina at the front of the room; half the time, art teachers for the continuing-ed classes didn't bother to learn people's names, and hopefully Meredith hadn't told Sabrina to look out for her in class.

"I'm Jenna." She stuck out her hand, and Aria shook it. Afterward, Aria turned away quickly, wondering how on earth she would get through the rest of the class. A new Jenna memory had come to mind that morning when Aria was eating breakfast in Meredith's freak show of a kitchen, probably brought on by the looming dwarves on top of Meredith's refrigerator. Ali, Aria, and the others used to call Jenna Snow, after Snow White in the Disney movie. Once, when their class went to the Longwood Orchards for apple-picking, Ali had suggested they give Jenna an apple they'd dunked in the orchard's filthy women's toilet, just like the wicked witch gave Snow White a poisoned apple in the movie.

Ali suggested that Aria give Jenna the apple—she always made the others do her dirty work. "This apple is special," Aria had said to Jenna, holding the fruit outstretched, listening as Ali snickered behind her. "The farmer told me it was from the sweetest tree. And I wanted to give it to you." Jenna's face had been so surprised and touched. As soon as she took a big, juicy bite, though, Ali crowed, "You ate an apple that's been peed on! Toilet breath!" Jenna had stopped mid-chew, letting the apple chunk fall out of her mouth.

Aria shook the memory from her head and noticed a bunch of oil paintings stacked at the edge of Jenna's workstation. They were portraits of people, all done in vibrant colors and energetic strokes. "Did you paint those?" she asked Jenna.

"The stuff on my desk?" Jenna asked, laying her hands on her lap. "Yeah. I was talking to Sabrina about my work, and she wanted to see them. I might be in one of her gallery shows."

Aria balled up her fists. Could this day get *any* worse? How the hell had Jenna gotten a gallery show? How on earth did Jenna even know how to paint if she couldn't see?

At the front of the room, Sabrina told the students to pick up a pouch of flour, strips of newspaper, and an empty bucket. Jenna tried to retrieve the things herself, but in the end, Sabrina carried them back for her. Aria noticed how all of the students were looking at Jenna out of the corners of their eyes, afraid that if they looked too pointedly, someone would chastise them for staring.

When they all returned to their desks, Sabrina cleared her throat. "Okay. Last time, we talked about seeing things by touch. We're going to do something similar today by making masks of one another's faces. We all wear masks in our own ways, don't we? We all pretend. What you might find, when you look at a mold of your face, is that you don't really look the way you thought you did at all."

"I've done this before," Jenna whispered in Aria's ear. "It's fun. Do you want to work together? I'll show you how to do it."

Aria wanted to dive out the classroom window. But she found herself nodding, and then, realizing Jenna couldn't *see* she was nodding, she said, "Sure."

"I'll do you first." As Jenna turned, something in her jeans pocket beeped. She pulled out a slim LG phone with a foldout keypad, and held it up to Aria, as if she knew Aria had been staring. "This has a voice-activated keyboard, so I can finally text people."

"Aren't you worried about getting flour all over it?" Aria asked.

"It'll wash off. I love it so much I keep it with me always."

Aria cut up strips of newspaper for Jenna, since she didn't really trust her with scissors. "So, where do you go to school?" Jenna asked.

"Um, Rosewood High," Aria said, naming the local public school.

"That's cool," Jenna said. "Is this your first art class?"

Aria stiffened. She had taken art classes before she'd even learned to read, but she had to swallow her pride. She wasn't Aria—she was *Jessica*. Whoever Jessica was. "Um, yeah," she said, quickly conjuring up a character. "It's a big jump for me—I'm usually more into sports, like field hockey."

Jenna poured water into her bowl. "What position do you play?"

"Um, all of them," Aria mumbled. Once, Ali had tried to teach her field hockey, but she'd stopped the lesson about five minutes in because she said Aria ran like a pregnant gorilla. Aria wondered why on earth she'd conjured up a Typical Rosewood Girl—the exact type of girl she tried her hardest *not* to be—as her alter ego.

"Well, it's nice that you're trying something new," Jenna murmured, mixing the flour and water together. "The only time the field hockey–playing girls at my old school tried something new was when they took a chance on some emerging designer they read about in *Vogue*." She snorted sarcastically.

"There were field hockey girls at your school in Philly?" Aria blurted out, thinking of the school for the blind Jenna's parents had sent her to.

Jenna straightened. "Uh . . . no. How did you know I went to a school in Philly?"

Aria pinched the inside of her palm. What was she going to say next, that Aria had given her a toilet-poisoned apple in sixth grade? That she'd kind of been involved in her stepbrother's death a couple weeks back? That she'd blinded her and ruined her life? "Just a guess."

"Well, I meant my old school before that. It's around here, actually. Rosewood Day? Do you know it?"

"I've heard of it," Aria mumbled.

"I'm going back there next year." Jenna dunked a strip of paper into the flour-and-water mixture. "But I don't know how I feel about it. Everyone at that school is so perfect. If you aren't into the right kinds of things, you're nothing." She shook her head. "Sorry. I'm sure you have no idea what I'm talking about."

"No! I totally agree!" Aria protested. She couldn't have put it more succinctly herself. A nagging feeling prodded at her. Jenna was beautiful—tall, graceful, cool, and artistic. *Really* artistic, in fact—if she really did go to Rosewood Day, Aria probably wouldn't be the school's best artist anymore. Who knew what Jenna could've been if her accident hadn't happened. Suddenly, the desire to tell Jenna who Aria really was and how sorry she felt about what they'd done was so nauseatingly overpowering, it took all of Aria's strength to keep her mouth shut.

Jenna came close to her. She smelled like cupcake icing. "Hold still," Jenna instructed Aria as she located Aria's head and laid the goopy strips over her face. They were wet and cool now, but soon they would harden over her face's contours.

"So, do you think you'll use your mask for anything?" Jenna asked. "Halloween?"

"My friend is having a masquerade," Aria said, then immediately wondered if she was again giving up too much information. "I'll probably wear it there."

"That's great," Jenna cooed. "I'm going to take mine with me to Venice. My parents are taking me there next month, and I hear it's the mask capital of the world."

"I love Venice!" Aria squeaked. "I've been there with my family four times!"

"Wow." Jenna layered newspaper strips over Aria's forehead. "Four times? Your family must like to travel together."

"Well, they *used* to," Aria said, trying to keep her face still for Jenna.

"What do you mean, used to?" Jenna began to cover Aria's cheeks.

Aria twitched—the strips were beginning to harden and get itchy. She could tell Jenna this, right? It wasn't like Jenna knew anything about her family. "Well, my parents are . . . I don't know. Getting divorced, I guess. My dad has a new girlfriend, this young girl who teaches art classes at Hollis. And I'm living with them right now. She hates me."

"And do you hate her?" Jenna asked.

"Totally," Aria said. "She's running my dad's life. She

makes him take vitamins and do yoga. And she's convinced she has the stomach flu, but she seems fine to me." Aria bit down hard on the inside of her cheek. She wished Meredith's supposed stomach flu would just kill her already. Then she wouldn't have to spend the next few months trying to figure out ways to stop Meredith and Byron from getting married.

"Well, at least she cares about him." Jenna paused, then smiled halfway. "I can feel you frowning, but all families have issues. Mine certainly does."

Aria tried not to make any more facial movements that would give anything away.

"But maybe you should give this girlfriend a chance," Jenna went on. "At least she's artistic, right?"

Aria's stomach dropped. She couldn't control the muscles around her mouth. "How did you know she's artistic?"

Jenna stopped. Some of the floury goop on her hands plopped to the scuffed wood floor. "You just said it, right?"

Aria felt dizzy. *Had* she? Jenna squished more newspaper strips to Aria's cheeks. As she moved from Aria's cheeks to chin to forehead to nose, Aria realized something. If Jenna could feel her frowning, she could probably tell other things about her face, too. She might be able to *feel* what Aria looked like. Just then, when she looked up, a startled, uncomfortable look settled on Jenna's face, as if she'd figured it all out, too.

The room felt sticky and hot. "I have to . . ." Aria

fumbled around her workstation, nearly tipping over her large unused bucket of water.

"Where are you going?" Jenna called.

All Aria needed was to get out of here for a few minutes. But as she stumbled toward the door, the mask tightening and suctioning to her face, Aria's Treo let out a bleep. She reached into her bag for it, careful not to get flour all over the keypad. She had one new text message.

> Sucks to be in the dark, huh? Imagine how the blind must feel! If you tell ANYONE what I did, I'll put you in the dark for good. Mwah! —A

Aria glanced back at Jenna. She was sitting at her workstation, fiddling with her cell phone, oblivious to the flour all over her fingers. Another beep from her own phone startled her. She glanced down at the screen again. Another text had come in.

> P.S. Your stepmommy-to-be has a secret identity, just like you! Want an eyeful? Go to Hooters tomorrow. —A

19

WANDERING MINDS WANT TO KNOW

Thursday morning, as Emily emerged from one of the bathroom stalls in the gym locker room dressed in her regulation Rosewood Day white T-shirt, hoodie, and royal blue gym shorts, an announcement blared over the PA system.

"Hey, everyone!" a chirpy, way-too-enthusiastic boy's voice called out. "This is Andrew Campbell, your class president, and I just want to remind you that Hanna Marin's welcome-back party is tomorrow night at the Rosewood Country Club! Please come out and bring your mask—it's costumes only! And also, I want everyone to wish Spencer Hastings a great big good luck—she's off to New York City tonight for her Golden Orchid finalist interview! Best wishes, Spencer!"

Several girls in the locker room groaned. There was *always* at least one announcement about Spencer. Emily found it strange, though, that Spencer hadn't mentioned the Golden Orchid trip yesterday at the hospital when they were visiting Hanna. Spencer usually overtalked about her achievements.

As Emily passed the giant cardboard cutout of Rosewood's shark mascot and emerged into the gym, she heard hooting and clapping, like she'd just walked into her own surprise party.

"Our favorite girl is back!" Mike Montgomery whooped, standing underneath the basketball hoop. It seemed like every freshman boy in Emily's mixed-grade gym class had gathered behind him. "So, you were on a sex vacation, right?"

"*What?*" Emily looked back and forth. Mike was talking kind of loudly.

"You know," Mike goaded, his elfin face a near mirror of Aria's. "To Thailand or whatever." He got a dreamy smile on his face.

Emily wrinkled her nose. "I was in Iowa."

"Oh." Mike looked confused. "Well, Iowa's hot, too. There are lots of milkmaids there, right?" He winked knowingly, as if milkmaids equaled instant porn.

Emily wanted to say something nasty, but then shrugged. She was pretty sure Mike wasn't teasing her in a mean way. The other gangly freshman boys gaped, as if Emily were Angelina Jolie, and Mike had been brave enough to ask for her e-mail address.

Mr. Draznowsky, their gym teacher, blew his whistle. All the students sat down cross-legged on the gym floor in their squads, which was basically gym-speak for rows. Mr. Draznowsky took roll and led them through stretches, and then everyone started to file out to the tennis courts. As Emily selected a Wilson racket from the equipment bin, she heard someone behind her whisper. *"Psssst."*

Maya stood by a box of Bosu balls, Pilates magic circles, and other equipment that exercise-aholic girls used during their free periods. "Hi," she squealed, her face bright pink with pleasure.

Emily tentatively walked into Maya's arms, inhaling her familiar banana gum smell. "What are you doing here?" she gasped.

"I skipped out of Algebra III to find you," Maya whispered. She held up a wooden hall pass carved into *pi*'s squiggly shape. "When did you get back? What happened? Are you here for good?"

Emily hesitated. She'd been in Rosewood for a whole day, but yesterday had been such a blur—there was her visit to the hospital, then A's note, then classes and swimming and time spent with her parents—she hadn't had time to talk to Maya yet. Emily had noticed Maya in the halls once yesterday, but she'd ducked into an empty classroom and waited for Maya to pass. She couldn't exactly explain why. It wasn't as if she was *hiding* from Maya or anything.

"I didn't get back that long ago," she managed. "And I'm back for good. I hope."

The door to the tennis courts banged shut. Emily looked at the exit longingly. By the time she got outside, everyone in her gym class would've already found a tennis partner. She'd have to hit balls with Mr. Draznowsky, who, because he was also a health teacher, liked to give his students on-the-fly contraception lectures. Then, Emily blinked hard, as if startled out of a dream. What was her *problem*? Why did she care about stupid gym class when Maya was here?

She whipped back around. "My parents have done a one-eighty. They were so worried that something had happened to me after I left my aunt and uncle's farm, they've decided to accept me for who I am."

Maya widened her eyes. "That's awesome!" She grabbed Emily's hands. "So what happened at your aunt and uncle's? Were they mean to you?"

"Sort of." Emily shut her eyes, picturing Helene and Allen's stern faces. Then, she imagined do-si-do'ing with Trista at the party. Trista had told Emily that if she were a dance, she'd most definitely be the Virginia reel. Maybe she should confess to Maya what happened with Trista . . . only, what *had* happened? Nothing, really. It would be better to just forget the whole thing. "It's a long story."

"You'll have to give me all the details later, now that we can actually hang out in *public*." Maya jiggled up and down, then glanced at the enormous clock on the scoreboard. "I should probably get back," she whispered. "Can we meet up tonight?"

Emily hesitated, realizing this was the first time she could say yes without sneaking around behind her parents' backs. Then she remembered. "I can't. I'm having dinner out with my family."

Maya's face fell. "Tomorrow, then? We could go to Hanna's party together."

"S-sure," Emily stammered. "That would be great."

"And, oh! I have a huge surprise for you." Maya hopped from foot to foot. "Scott Chin, the yearbook photographer? He's in my history class, and he told me that you and I were voted this year's best couple! Isn't that fun?"

"Best *couple*?" Emily repeated. Her mouth felt gummy.

Maya took Emily's hands and swung them back and forth. "We have a photo shoot in the yearbook room tomorrow. Won't that be so cute?"

"Sure." Emily picked up the hem of her T-shirt and squeezed it in her palm.

Maya cocked her head. "You sure you're okay? You don't sound so enthused."

"No. I am. Totally." Just as Emily took a breath to go on, her cell phone vibrated in her hoodie pocket, jolting straight through to her waist. She jumped and pulled it out, her heart pounding. *One new text message,* the screen said.

When she hit READ and saw the signature, her stomach turned for a different reason. She snapped the phone shut without reading the message. "Get anything good?" Maya asked, a little nosily, Emily thought.

"Nah." Emily slid the phone back into her pocket.

Maya tossed the *pi* hall pass from one hand to the other. She gave Emily a quick kiss on the cheek, then sauntered out of the gym, her tall, sandstone-colored Frye boots clunking heavily against the wood floor. As Maya rounded the corner into the hall, Emily pulled out her cell phone, took a deep breath, and looked at the screen again.

Hey, Emily! I just heard the news that you're GONE! I'm really going to miss you! Where do you live in PA? If you were a famous Philadelphia historical figure, who would you be? I'd be that guy on the Quaker Oats box. . . . He counts, right?

Maybe I could visit sometime? xxx, Trista

The gym's central heater came on with a clank. Emily snapped her phone shut, and, after a pause, turned it off completely. Years ago, right before Emily had kissed Ali up in the DiLaurentises' old tree house, Ali had confessed that she was secretly seeing an older guy. She'd never said what his name was, but Emily realized now that she must have been talking about Ian Thomas. Ali had grabbed Emily's hands, full of giddy emotion. "Whenever I think about him, my stomach swoops around like I'm on a roller coaster," she'd swooned. "Being in love is the best feeling in the world."

Emily zipped up her hoodie to her chin. She thought she was in love, too, but it certainly didn't make her feel like she was on a roller coaster. Inside the fun house was more like it—with surprises at every turn, and absolutely no idea what would happen next.

20

NO SECRETS BETWEEN FRIENDS

Thursday afternoon, Hanna stared at her reflection in the downstairs powder room mirror. She dabbed a bit of foundation on the stitches in her chin and winced. Why did stitches have to *hurt* so much? And why did Dr. Geist have to sew up her face with Frankenstein black thread? Couldn't he have used a nice flesh-tone color?

She picked up her brand-new BlackBerry, considering. The phone had been waiting for her on the kitchen island when her father brought her home from the hospital earlier today. There was a card on the BlackBerry's box that said, WELCOME HOME! LOVE, MOM. Now that Hanna wasn't on the brink of death, her mother had returned to her round-the-clock hours at work, business as usual.

Hanna sighed, then dialed the number on the back of her foundation bottle. "Hello, Bobbi Brown hotline!" a cheerful voice on the other end chirped.

"This is Hanna Marin," Hanna said briskly, trying to

channel her inner Anna Wintour. "Can I book Bobbi for a makeup job?"

The hotline girl paused. "You'd have to go through Bobbi's booking agent for something like that. But I think she's really busy—"

"Can you get me her agent's number anyway?"

"I don't think I'm allowed to—"

"Sure you can," Hanna cooed. "I won't tell."

After a bit of hemming and hawing, the girl put Hanna on hold, and someone else picked up the line and gave Hanna a 212 phone number. She wrote it down in lipstick on the bathroom mirror and hung up, feeling ambivalent. On one hand, it rocked that she could still push people to do exactly what she wanted. Only queen-of-the-school divas could do that. On the other hand, what if even *Bobbi* couldn't fix Hanna's mess of a face?

The doorbell rang. Hanna dabbed more foundation on her stitches and headed into the hall. That was probably Mona, coming over to help audition male models for her party. She'd told Hanna she wanted to book her the best hotties money could buy.

Hanna paused in the foyer next to her mother's giant raku ceramic pot. What had Lucas meant at the hospital yesterday, when he said that Hanna shouldn't trust Mona? And more than that, what had that kiss been about? Hanna had thought of little else since it happened. She'd expected to see Lucas at the hospital this morning, greeting her with magazines and a Starbucks latte. When

484 ◆ SARA SHEPARD

he wasn't there, she'd felt . . . disappointed. And this afternoon, after her father dropped her off, Hanna had lingered on *All My Children* on TV for three whole minutes before changing the channel. Two characters on the soap were passionately kissing, and she'd watched them, wide-eyed, with tingles running up and down her back again, suddenly able to relate.

Not that she *liked* Lucas or anything. He wasn't in her stratosphere. And just to make sure, she'd asked Mona last night what she thought of Lucas, when Mona dropped off the coming-home-from-the-hospital outfit she'd selected from Hanna's closet—skinny Seven jeans, a cropped plaid Moschino jacket, and an ultrasoft tee. Mona had said, "Lucas *Beattie*? Huge loser, Han. Always has been."

So there you had it. No more Lucas. She would tell no one about the kiss, ever.

Hanna reached the front door, noticing the way Mona's white-blond hair glowed through the frosted panels. She nearly fell over when she opened the door and saw Spencer standing there behind Mona. And Emily and Aria were walking up the front path. Hanna wondered if she'd accidentally told all of them to visit at the same time.

"Well, this is a surprise," Hanna said nervously.

But it was Spencer who pushed around Mona and walked into Hanna's house first. "We need to talk to you," she said. Mona, Emily, and Aria followed, and the girls assembled on Hanna's toffee-colored leather couches, sitting in the exact same seats they used to sit in when they used to be friends: Spencer in the big leather chair in the corner, and Emily and Aria on the couch. Mona had taken Ali's seat, on the chaise by the window. When Hanna squinted, she could almost mistake Mona for Ali. Hanna snuck a look at Mona to see if she was pissed, but Mona looked sort of . . . okay.

Hanna sat down on the leather chair's ottoman. "Um, we need to talk about *what*?" she asked Spencer. Aria and Emily looked a little confused too.

"We got another note from A after we left your hospital room," Spencer blurted.

"*Spencer,*" Hanna hissed. Emily and Aria gaped at her too. Since when did they talk about A around other people?

"It's okay," Spencer said. "Mona knows. She's been getting notes from A too."

Hanna suddenly felt faint. She looked at Mona for confirmation, and Mona's mouth was taut and serious. "*No,*" Hanna whispered.

"You?" Aria gasped.

"How many?" Emily stammered.

"Two," Mona admitted, staring at the outline of her knobby knees through her burnt orange C&C California jersey dress. "I got them this week. When I told Spencer about it yesterday, I never would have imagined that you guys were getting them too."

"But that doesn't make sense," Aria whispered, looking

around at the others. "I thought A was only sending messages to Ali's old friends."

"Maybe everything we thought was wrong," Spencer said.

Hanna's stomach spun. "Did Spencer tell you about the SUV that hit me?"

"That it was A. And that you knew who A was." Mona's face was pale.

Spencer crossed her legs. "Anyway, we got a new note. A obviously doesn't want you to remember, Hanna. If we keep pushing you on it, A's going to hurt us next."

Emily let out a small whimper.

"This is really scary," Mona whispered. She hadn't stopped jiggling her foot, something she did only when she was very tense. "We should go to the police."

"Maybe we should," Emily agreed. "They could help us. This is serious."

"No!" Aria nearly shrieked. "A will *know*. It's like . . . A can see us, at all times."

Emily clamped her mouth shut, staring down at her hands.

Mona swallowed hard. "I guess I know what you mean, Aria. Ever since I've gotten the notes, I've felt like someone has been watching me." She looked around at them, her eyes wide and scared. "Who knows? A could be watching us right now."

Hanna shivered. Aria looked around frantically, canvassing Hanna's stuffy living room. Emily peeked behind

Hanna's baby grand piano, as if A might be crouching in the corner. Then Mona's Sidekick buzzed, and everyone let out startled little yelps. When Mona pulled it out, her face paled. "Oh my God. It's another one."

Everyone gathered around Mona's phone. Her newest message was a belated birthday e-card. Below the images of happy balloons and a frosted white cake that Mona would *never* eat in real life, the message read,

> Happy belated b-day, Mona! So when are you going to tell Hanna what you did? I say wait until AFTER she finally gives you your birthday present. You might lose the friendship, but at least you'll get to keep the gift! —A

Hanna's blood turned to ice. "What you *did*? What's A talking about?"

Mona's face went white. "Hanna . . . okay. We did get into a fight the night of my party. But it was just a little one. Honestly. We should just forget about it."

Hanna's heart thrummed as loud as a car engine. Her mouth instantly went dry.

"I didn't want to bring up the fight after your accident because I didn't think it mattered," Mona went on, her voice high-pitched and desperate. "I didn't want to upset you. And I felt terrible about us fighting last week, Hanna, especially when I thought I'd lost you forever. I just wanted to forget about it. I wanted to make it up to you by throwing you this amazing party, and—"

A few aching seconds passed. The heat switched on, making them all jump. Spencer cleared her throat. "You guys shouldn't fight," she said gently. "A's just trying to distract you from figuring out who's sending these awful notes in the first place."

Mona shot Spencer a grateful look. Hanna lowered her shoulders, feeling all eyes on her. The last thing she wanted to do was talk about this with the others around. She wasn't sure she wanted to talk about it at all. "Spencer's right. This *is* what A does."

The girls fell into silence, staring at the square-shaped, paper Noguchi lamp that sat on the coffee table. Spencer grabbed Mona's hand and squeezed. Emily grabbed Hanna's.

"What else have your notes been about?" Aria asked Mona quietly.

Mona ducked her head. "Just some stuff from the past."

Hanna bristled, focusing on the bluebird-shaped hair clip in Aria's hair. She had a feeling she knew just what A was taunting Mona about—the time before Hanna and Mona were friends, when Mona was dorky and uncool. What secret had A focused on most? When Mona had tagged along behind Ali, wanting to be just like her? When Mona was the butt of everyone's jokes? She and Mona never discussed the past, but sometimes Hanna felt like the painful memories loomed close behind, bubbling just below the surface of their friendship like an underground geyser.

"You don't have to tell us if you don't want to," Hanna said quickly. "A lot of our A notes have been about the past, too. There's lots of stuff we *all* want to forget."

She met her best friend's eyes, hoping Mona understood. Mona squeezed Hanna's hand. Hanna noticed that Mona was wearing the silver-and-turquoise ring Hanna had made for her in Jewelry II, even though it looked more like one of the clunky Rosewood Day class rings that only nerds wore than a pretty bauble from Tiffany. A small spot in Hanna's pounding heart warmed. A was right about one thing: Best friends shared everything. And now she and Mona could too.

The doorbell rang, three short Asian-inspired *bongs*. The girls shot up. "Who's that?" Aria whispered fearfully.

Mona stood, shaking out her long blond hair. She broke into a big smile and pranced toward Hanna's front door. "Something to make us forget about our problems."

"What, like pizza?" Emily asked.

"No, ten male models from the Philly branch of the Wilhelmina modeling agency, of course," Mona said simply.

As if it were preposterous to think it could be anyone else.

21

HOW DO YOU SOLVE A PROBLEM LIKE EMILY?

Thursday night, after leaving Hanna's, Emily skirted her way around all of the shopping bag–laden, expensive perfume–wearing King James Mall consumers. She was meeting her parents at All That Jazz!, the Broadway musical–themed restaurant next to Nordstrom. It had been Emily's favorite restaurant when she was younger, and Emily guessed that her parents assumed it still was. The restaurant looked the same as always, with a fake Broadway marquee facade, a giant Phantom of the Opera statue next to the hostess podium, and photos of Broadway stars all over the walls.

Emily was the first to arrive, so she slid into a seat at the long, granite-topped bar. For a while, she stared at the collectible *Little Mermaid* dolls in a glass case near the hostess stand. When she was younger, Emily wished she could switch places with Ariel the Mermaid Princess—Ariel could have Emily's human legs, and Emily would take

Ariel's mermaid fins. She used to make her old friends watch the movie, up until Ali told her it was lame and babyish and she should just stop.

A familiar image on the TV screen above the bar caught her eye. There was a blond, busty reporter in the foreground, and Ali's seventh-grade school picture in the corner. "For the past year, Alison DiLaurentis's parents have been living in a small Pennsylvania town not far from Rosewood while their son, Jason, finishes up his degree at Yale University. They've all been leading quiet lives . . . until now. While Alison's murder investigation rolls on with no new leads, how is the rest of the family holding up?"

A stately, ivy-covered building flashed on the screen over a caption that read, NEW HAVEN, CONNECTICUT. Another blond reporter chased after a group of students. "Jason!" she called. "Do you think the police are doing enough to find your sister's killer?"

"Is this bringing your family closer together?" someone else shouted.

A boy in a Phillies ball cap turned around. Emily's eyes widened—she'd only seen Jason DiLaurentis a couple of times since Ali had gone missing. His eyes were cold and hard, and the corners of his mouth turned down.

"I don't speak to my family much," Jason said. "They're too messed up."

Emily hooked her feet under her stool. Ali's family . . . messed up? In Emily's eyes, the DiLaurentises seemed perfect. Ali's father had a good job but was able to come home on the weekends and barbecue with his kids. Mrs. DiLaurentis used to take Ali, Emily, and the others shopping and made them great oatmeal raisin cookies. Their house was spotless, and whenever Emily ate dinners at the DiLaurentises', there was always lots of laughing.

Emily thought of the memory Hanna had mentioned earlier, the one from the day before Ali went missing. After Ali had emerged on the back patio, Emily had excused herself to go to the bathroom. As she passed through the kitchen and skirted around Charlotte, Ali's Himalayan cat, she'd heard Jason whispering to someone on the stairs. He sounded angry.

"You better stop it," Jason hissed. "You know how that pisses them off."

"I'm not hurting anything," another voice whispered back.

Emily had pressed her body against the foyer wall, befuddled. The second voice sounded a little like Ali's.

"I'm just trying to help you," Jason went on, getting more and more agitated.

Just then, Mrs. DiLaurentis whirled in through the side door, running to the sink to wash dirt off her hands. "Oh, hi, Emily," she chirped. Emily stepped away from the stairs. She heard footsteps climbing to the second floor.

Emily glanced again at the TV screen. The news anchor was now issuing an advisory to Rosewood Country Club members because the Rosewood Stalker had been spotted sneaking around the club's grounds. Emily's throat itched. It was easy to draw parallels between the Rosewood Stalker and A . . . and the country club? Hanna's party was going to be there. Emily had been very careful not to ask Hanna any questions ever since she received A's last note, but she still wondered if they *should* go to the police—this had gone far enough. And what if A had not only hit Hanna but killed Ali, too, as Aria suggested the other day? But maybe Mona was right: A was close by, watching their every move. A would know if they told.

As if on cue, her cell phone trumpeted. Emily jumped, nearly teetering off her chair. She had a new text, but thankfully, it was only from Trista. Again.

Hey, Em! What are you doing this weekend? xxx, Trista

Emily wished Rita Moreno wouldn't sing "America" so loudly, and she wished she weren't sitting so close to a picture of the cast of *Cats*—all the felines leered at her like they wanted to use her as a scratching post. She ran her hand along her Nokia's bumpy keys. It would be rude not to reply, right? She typed, *Hi! I'm going to a masquerade party for my friend this Friday. Should be fun! —Em*

Almost immediately, Trista sent back a reply. *OMG! Wish I could come!*

Me too, Emily texted back. *C ya!* She wondered what Trista really planned to do this weekend—go to another silo party? Meet another girl?

"Emily?" Two ice-cold hands curled around her shoulders. Emily whirled around, dropping her phone on the floor. Maya stood behind her. Emily's mother and father and her sister Carolyn and her boyfriend, Topher, stood behind Maya. Everyone grinned madly.

"Surprise!" Maya crowed. "Your mom called me this afternoon to ask if I wanted to come to your dinner!"

"O-ohh," Emily stammered. "That's . . . great." She rescued her phone from the floor and held it between her hands, covering the screen as if Maya could see what Emily had just written. It felt like there was a hot, beaming spotlight on her. She looked at her parents, who were standing next to a big photo of the *Les Misérables* actors storming the barricades. Both of them were nervously smiling, acting the same way they had when they'd met Emily's old boyfriend, Ben.

"Our table's ready," Emily's mother said. Maya took Emily's hand and followed the rest of her family. They all slid into an enormous royal purple banquette. An effeminate waiter, who Emily was pretty sure was wearing mascara, asked if they wanted any cocktails.

"It's so nice to finally meet you, Mr. and Mrs. Fields," Maya said once the waiter left. She grinned across the booth at Emily's parents.

Emily's mom smiled back. "It's nice to meet you too."

There was nothing but warmth in her voice. Emily's father smiled too.

Maya pointed at Carolyn's bracelet. "That is *so* pretty. Did you make it?"

Carolyn blushed. "Yeah. In Jewelry III."

Maya's burnt-umber eyes widened. "I wanted to take jewelry, but I have no sense for color. Everything on that bracelet goes so well together."

Carolyn looked down at her gold-flecked dinner plate. "It's not really that hard." Emily could tell she was flattered.

They eased into small talk, about school, the Rosewood Stalker, Hanna's hit-and-run, and then California—Carolyn wanted to know if Maya knew any kids who went to Stanford, where she'd be attending next year. Topher laughed at a story Maya told about her old neighbor in San Francisco who had had eight pet parakeets and made Maya parakeet-sit for her. Emily looked at all of them, annoyed. If Maya was so easily likable, then why hadn't they given her a chance before? What was all that talk about how Emily should stay away from Maya? Did she really have to run away for them to take her life seriously?

"Oh, I forgot to mention," Emily's father said as everyone received their dinners. "I reserved the house in Duck for Thanksgiving again."

"Oh, wonderful." Mrs. Fields beamed. "Same house?"

"Same one." Mr. Fields stabbed at a baby carrot.

"Where's Duck?" Maya asked.

Emily raked her fork through her mashed potatoes. "It's this little beach town in the Outer Banks of North Carolina. We rent a house there every Thanksgiving. The water's still warm enough to swim if you have a wet suit."

"Perhaps Maya would like to come," Mrs. Fields said, primly wiping her mouth with a napkin. "You always bring a friend, after all."

Emily gaped. She always brought a *boyfriend*, more like it—last year, she'd brought Ben. Carolyn had brought Topher.

Maya pressed her palm to her chest. "Well . . . yeah! That sounds great!"

It felt like the restaurant's faux stage-set walls were closing in around her. Emily pulled at the collar of her shirt, then stood up. Without explaining, she wound her way around a pack of waiters and waitresses dressed up as the characters from *Rent*. Fumbling into a bathroom stall, she leaned against the mosaic-tiled wall and shut her eyes.

The door to the bathroom opened. Emily saw Maya's square-toed Mary Janes under her stall door. "Emily?" Maya called softly.

Emily peeked through the crack in the metallic door. Maya had her crocheted bag slung across her chest, her lips pressed together in worry. "Are you okay?" Maya asked.

"I just felt a little faint," Emily stammered, awkwardly flushing and then walking to the sink. She stood with her back to Maya, her body rigid and tense. If Maya touched her right now, Emily was pretty sure she would explode.

Maya reached out, then recoiled, as if sensing Emily's vibe. "Isn't it so sweet your parents invited me to Duck with you? It'll be so fun!"

Emily pumped a huge pile of foamy soap into her hands. When they went to Duck, Emily and Carolyn always spent at least three hours in the ocean every day bodysurfing. Afterward, they watched marathons on the Cartoon Network, refueled, and went into the water again. She knew Maya wouldn't be into that.

Emily turned around to face her. "This is all kind of . . . weird. I mean, my parents *hated* me last week. And now they like me. They're trying to win me over, having you surprise me at dinner, and then inviting you to the Outer Banks."

Maya frowned. "And that's a *bad* thing?"

"Well, yes," Emily blurted out. "Or, no. Of course not." This was coming out all wrong. She cleared her throat and met Maya's eyes in the mirror. "Maya, if you could be any kind of candy, what kind would you be?"

Maya touched the edge of a gilded tissue box that sat in the middle of the bathroom's vanity counter. "Huh?"

"Like . . . would you be Mike and Ike? Laffy Taffy? A Snickers bar? What?"

Maya stared at her. "Are you drunk?"

Emily studied Maya in the mirror. Maya had glowing, honey-colored skin. Her boysenberry-flavored lip gloss gleamed. Emily had fallen for Maya as soon as she'd laid eyes on her, and her parents were making a huge effort to accept Maya. What was her problem, then? Why, whenever Emily tried to think about kissing Maya, did she imagine kissing Trista instead?

Maya leaned back against the counter. "Emily, I think I know what's going on."

Emily looked away quickly, trying not to blush. "No, you don't."

Maya's eyes softened. "It's about your friend Hanna, isn't it? Her accident? You were there, right? I heard that the person who hit her had been stalking her."

Emily's canvas Banana Republic purse slipped out of her hands and fell to the tiled floor with a clunk. "Where did you hear that?" she whispered.

Maya stepped back, startled. "I . . . I don't know. I can't remember." She squinted, confused. "You can talk to me, Em. We can tell each other anything, right?"

Three long measures of the Gershwin song that was twinkling out of the speakers passed. Emily thought about the note A had sent when she and her three old friends met with Officer Wilden last week: *If you tell ANYONE about me, you'll be sorry.* "No one is stalking

Hanna," she whispered. "It was an accident. End of story."

Maya ran her hands along the ceramic sink basin. "I think I'm going to go back to the table now. I'll . . . I'll see you out there." She backed out of the bathroom slowly. Emily listened to the main door waft shut.

The song over the speakers switched to something from *Aida*. Emily sat down at the vanity mirrors, clunking her purse in her lap. *No one said anything,* she told herself. *No one knows except for us. And no one is going to tell A.*

Suddenly, Emily noticed a folded-up note sitting in her open purse. It said EMILY on the front, in round pink letters. Emily opened it up. It was a membership form for PFLAG—Parents and Friends of Lesbians and Gays. Someone had filled in Emily's parents' information. At the bottom was familiar spiky handwriting.

Happy coming-out day, Em—your folks must be so proud! Now that the Fields are alive with the sound of love and acceptance, it would be such a shame if something happened to their little lesbian. So you keep quiet . . . and they'll get to keep you! —A

The bathroom door was still swinging from Maya's exit. Emily stared back at the note, her hands trembling. All at once, a familiar scent filled the air. It smelled like . . .

Emily frowned and sniffed again. Finally, she put A's note right up to her nose. When she breathed in, her insides turned to stone. Emily would recognize this smell anywhere. It was the seductive scent of Maya's banana gum.

22

IF THE W'S WALLS COULD TALK . . .

Thursday evening, after a dinner at Smith & Wollensky, an upscale Manhattan steak house Spencer's father frequented, Spencer followed her family down the W Hotel's gray-carpeted hallway. Sleek black-and-white Annie Leibovitz photographs lined the halls, and the air smelled like a mix between vanilla and fresh towels.

Her mother was on her cell phone. "No, she's sure to win," she murmured. "Why don't we just book it now?" She paused, as if the person on the other end was saying something very important. "Good. I'll talk to you tomorrow." She clapped her phone closed.

Spencer tugged at the lapel of her dove-gray Armani Exchange suit—she'd worn a professional outfit to dinner to get into award-winning essayist mode. She wondered who her mom was talking to on the phone. Perhaps she was planning something amazing for Spencer if she won the Golden Orchid. A fabulous trip? A day with a Barneys personal shopper? A meeting with the family friend who worked at the *New York Times*? Spencer had begged her parents to let her be a summer intern at the *Times,* but her mother had never allowed it.

"Nervous, Spence?" Melissa and Ian appeared behind her, pulling matching plaid suitcases. Unfortunately, Spencer's parents insisted that Melissa come along to Spencer's interview for moral support, and Melissa had brought Ian. Melissa held up a little bottle labeled MARTINI TO GO! "Do you want one of these? I could get one for you, if you need something to calm you down."

"I'm fine," Spencer snapped. Her sister's presence made Spencer feel like roaches were crawling under her Malizia bra. Whenever Spencer shut her eyes, she saw Melissa fidgeting as Wilden asked her and Ian where they'd been the night of Ali's disappearance and heard Melissa's voice saying, *It takes a very unique person to kill. And that's not you.*

Melissa paused, shaking the mini martini bottle. "Yeah, it's probably best you don't drink. You might forget the gist of your Golden Orchid essay."

"That's very true," Mrs. Hastings murmured. Spencer bristled and turned away.

Ian and Melissa's room was right next to Spencer's, and they slipped inside, giggling. As her mother reached for Spencer's room key, a pretty girl about Spencer's age swept past. Her head was down, and she was studying a cream-colored card that looked suspiciously similar to the

Golden Orchid breakfast invite Spencer had tucked into her tweed Kate Spade bag.

The girl noticed Spencer staring and broke into a glimmering smile. "Hi!" she called brightly. She had the look of a CNN newscaster: poised, perky, congenial. Spencer's mouth fell open and her tongue lolled clumsily in her mouth. Before she could respond, the girl shrugged and looked away.

The single glass of wine Spencer's parents had allowed her to drink at dinner gurgled in her stomach. She turned to her mom.

"There are a lot of *really* smart applicants up for the Golden Orchid," Spencer whispered, after the girl rounded the corner. "I'm not a shoo-in or anything."

"Nonsense." Mrs. Hastings's voice was clipped. "You are going to win." She handed her a room key. "This one's yours. We got you a suite." With that, she patted Spencer's arm and continued down the hall to her own room.

Spencer bit her lip, unlocked the door to her suite, and snapped on the light. The room smelled like cinnamon and new carpet, and her king-size bed was loaded with a dozen pillows. She squared her shoulders and wheeled her bag to the dark mahogany wardrobe. Immediately, she hung up her black Armani interview suit and placed her lucky pink Wolford bra and panty set in the top drawer of the adjacent bureau. After changing into her pajamas, she went around the suite and made sure all of the chunky picture frames were straight and the enormous cerulean bed pillows were fluffed symmetrically. In the bathroom, she fixed the towels so they hung evenly on the racks. She positioned the Bliss body wash, the shampoo, and the conditioner in a diamond pattern around the sink. When she returned to her bedroom, she stared blankly at a copy of *Time Out New York* magazine. On the cover was a confident-looking Donald Trump standing in front of Trump Tower.

Spencer did yoga fire breaths, but she still didn't feel any better. Finally, she pulled out her five economics books and a marked-up copy of Melissa's paper and spread everything on her bed. *You are going to win,* her mother's voice rang in her ear.

After a mind-numbing hour of rehearsing parts of Melissa's paper in front of the mirror, Spencer heard a knock at the little adjoining door that led to the next suite. She sat up, confused. That door led to Melissa's room.

Another knock. Spencer slid out of bed and crept toward the door. She glanced at her cell phone, but it was impassive and blank. "Hello?" Spencer called softly.

"Spencer?" Ian called hoarsely. "Hey. I think our rooms connect. Can I come in?"

"Um," Spencer stammered. The adjoining door made a few clanking noises, then opened. Ian had changed out of his dress shirt and khakis into a T-shirt and Ksubi jeans. Spencer curled up her fingers, afraid and excited.

Ian looked around Spencer's suite. "Your room is *huge* compared to ours."

Spencer clasped her hands behind her back, trying not to beam. This was probably the first time ever she'd gotten a better room than Melissa. Ian gazed at the books splayed out on Spencer's bed, then shoved them aside and sat down. "Studying, huh?"

"Sort of." Spencer stayed glued to the table, afraid to move.

"Too bad. I thought we could take a walk or something. Melissa's sleeping, after just one of those to-go cocktails. She's such a lightweight." Ian winked.

Outside, a series of cabs honked their horns, and a neon light blinked on and off. The look on Ian's face was the same one Spencer remembered from years ago, when he'd stood in her driveway, about to kiss her. Spencer poured a glass of ice water from the pitcher on the table and took a long gulp, an idea forming in her mind. She actually had questions for Ian . . . about Melissa, about Ali, about the missing pieces of her memory, and about the dangerous, almost taboo suspicion that had been growing in her mind since Sunday.

Spencer set down her glass, her heart thumping hard. She tugged at her oversize University of Pennsylvania T-shirt so that it fell off one of her shoulders. "So, I know a secret about you," she murmured.

"About me?" Ian thumbed his chest. "What is it?"

Spencer pushed some of her books aside and sat next

to Ian. When she inhaled his Kiehl's Pineapple Papaya facial scrub smell—Spencer knew the whole Kiehl's skincare line by heart, she loved it so much—her head felt faint. "I know that you and a certain little blond girl used to be more than just friends."

Ian smiled lazily. "And would that little blond girl be . . . you?"

"No . . ." Spencer pursed her lips. "Ali."

Ian's mouth twitched. "Ali and I hooked up once or twice, that's it." He poked Spencer's bare knee. Tingles shot up Spencer's back. "I liked kissing *you* more."

Spencer leaned back, perplexed. In their last fight, Ali had told Spencer that she and Ian were *together,* and that Ian only kissed Spencer because Ali made him. Why, then, did Ian always seem so flirty with Spencer? "Did my sister know you hooked up with Ali?"

Ian scoffed. "Of course not. You know how jealous she gets."

Spencer stared out over Lexington Avenue, counting ten yellow taxis in a row. "So were you and Melissa really together the whole night Ali went missing?"

Ian leaned back on his elbows, letting out an exaggerated sigh. "You Hastings girls are something. Melissa's been talking about that night too. I think she's nervous that cop is going to find out that we were drinking, since we were underage. But so what? It was over four years ago. No one's going to bust us for it now."

"She's been . . . nervous?" Spencer whispered, her eyes widening.

Ian lowered his eyes seductively. "Why don't you forget about all that Rosewood stuff for a little while?" He brushed Spencer's hair off her forehead. "Let's just make out instead."

Desire teemed through her. Ian's face came closer and closer, blocking out Spencer's view of the buildings across the street. His hand kneaded her knee. "We shouldn't do this," she whispered. "It's not right."

"Sure it is," Ian whispered back.

And then, there was another knock on her adjoining door.

"Spencer?" Melissa's voice was thick. "Are you there?"

Spencer sprang out of bed, knocking her books and notes to the floor. "Y-yeah."

"Do you know where Ian went?" her sister called.

When she heard Melissa turning the adjoining door's knob, Spencer frantically gestured Ian toward the front door. He leaped off the bed, straightened his clothes, and slipped out of the room, just as Melissa pushed the door open.

Her sister had shoved her black silk sleeping mask onto her forehead and wore striped Kate Spade pajama pants and bottoms. She raised her nose slightly to the air, almost as if she was sniffing for Kiehl's Pineapple Papaya. "Why your room so much *bigger* than mine?" Melissa finally said.

They both heard the mechanical sound of Ian's key card sliding into his door. Melissa turned around, her hair swinging. "Oh, *there* you are. Where'd you go?"

"To the vending machines." Ian's voice was buttery and smooth. Melissa shut the adjoining door without even saying good-bye.

Spencer flopped back on the bed. "*So* close," she groaned loudly, although, she hoped, not loud enough for Melissa and Ian to hear.

23

BEHIND CLOSED DOORS

When Hanna opened her eyes, she was behind the wheel of her Toyota Prius. But hadn't the doctors told her she shouldn't drive with a broken arm? Shouldn't she be in bed, with her miniature Doberman, Dot, by her side?

"Hanna." A blurry figure sat next to her in the passenger seat. Hanna could only tell that it was a girl with blond hair—her vision was way too blurry to see anything else. "Hey, Hanna," the voice said again. It sounded like . . .

"Ali?" Hanna croaked.

"That's right." Ali leaned close to Hanna's face. The tips of her hair grazed Hanna's cheek. *I'm A,* she whispered.

"What?" Hanna cried, her eyes wide.

Ali sat up straight. "I said, *I'm okay.*" Then she opened the door and fled into the night.

Hanna's vision snapped into focus. She was sitting in the parking lot of the Hollis Planetarium. A big poster that said THE BIG BANG flapped in the wind.

Hanna shot up, panting. She was in her cavernous bedroom, snuggled under her cashmere blanket. Dot was curled up in a ball on his little Gucci dog bed. To her right was her closet, with its racks and racks of beautiful, expensive clothes. She took deep breaths, trying to get her bearings. "Jesus," she said out loud.

The doorbell rang. Hanna groaned and sat up, feeling like her head was stuffed with straw. What had she just *dreamed* about? Ali? The Big Bang? A?

The doorbell rang again. Dot was now out of his dog bed, jiggling up and down at Hanna's closed door. It was Friday morning, and when Hanna checked her bedside clock, she realized it was after ten. Her mom was long gone, if she'd even come home last night at all. Hanna had fallen asleep on the couch, and Mona had helped her upstairs to bed.

"Coming," Hanna said, pulling on her navy blue silk robe, sweeping her hair into a quick ponytail, and checking her face in the mirror. She winced. The stitches on her chin were still jagged and black. They reminded her of the crisscrossed laces on a football.

When she peeped through the panels of her front door, she saw Lucas standing on the porch. Hanna's heart immediately sped up. She checked her reflection in the hallway mirror and pushed back a few strands of hair. Feeling like a circus fat lady in her billowing silk robe, she considered running back upstairs and putting on real clothes.

Then she stopped herself, letting out a haughty laugh.

What was she *doing*? She couldn't like Lucas. He was . . . *Lucas.*

Hanna wriggled her shoulders, let out a breath, and flung open the door. "Hi," she said, trying to act bored.

"Hi," Lucas said back.

They stared at each other for what seemed like ages. Hanna was certain Lucas could hear her heart beating. She wanted to muzzle it. Dot danced around their legs, but Hanna was too transfixed to reach down and shoo him away.

"Is this a bad time?" Lucas asked cautiously.

"Um, no," Hanna said quickly. "Come in."

When she backed up, she nearly tripped over a carved Buddha doorstop that had been in her hallway for at least ten years. She wheeled her arms around, trying to keep herself from falling. Suddenly, she felt Lucas's strong arms wrap around her waist. When he pulled Hanna upright again, they stared at each other. The corner of Lucas's mouth curled into a smile. He leaned to her, and his mouth was on hers. Hanna melted into him. They danced over to the couch and fell down onto the cushions, Lucas carefully maneuvering around her sling. After minutes of nothing but smacking and slurping noises, Hanna rolled over, catching her breath. She let out a whimper and covered her face in her hands.

"I'm sorry." Lucas sat back up. "Should I not have done that?"

Hanna shook her head. She certainly couldn't tell him

that for the past two days, she'd been fantasizing that this would happen again. Or that she had an eerie feeling that she'd kissed Lucas before their kiss on Wednesday—only, how was that possible?

She pulled her hands away from her face. "I thought you said you were in the ESP club at school," she said quietly, remembering something Lucas had told her on their balloon ride. "Shouldn't you telepathically *know* if you should've done that or not?"

Lucas smirked and poked her bare knee. "Well, then, I would guess that you did want me to. And that you want me to do it again."

Hanna licked her lips, feeling as though the thousands of wild butterflies she'd seen at the Museum of Natural History a few years ago were fluttering around in her stomach. When Lucas reached out and lightly touched the inside of her elbow, where all the IVs had been, Hanna thought she was going to dissolve into goo. She ducked her head and let out a groan. "Lucas . . . I just don't know."

He sat back. "What don't you know?"

"I just . . . I mean . . . Mona . . ." She waved her hands futilely. This wasn't coming out right at all, not that she had any idea what she was trying to say.

Lucas raised an eyebrow. "What about Mona?"

Hanna picked up the stuffed dog her father had given her in the hospital. It was supposed to be Cornelius Max-imillian, a character they'd made up when Hanna was younger. "We just became friends again," she said in a small eggshell of a voice, hoping that Lucas knew what that meant without her having to explain.

Lucas leaned back. "Hanna . . . I think you should watch out for Mona."

Hanna dropped Cornelius Maximillian to her lap. "What do you mean?"

"I just mean . . . I don't think she wants the best for you."

Hanna's mouth fell open. "Mona's been by my side at the hospital this whole time! And you know, if this has something to do with the fight at her party, she *told* me about it. I'm over it. It's fine."

Lucas studied Hanna carefully. "It's fine?"

"Yes," Hanna snapped.

"So . . . you're okay with what she did to you?" Lucas sounded shocked.

Hanna looked away. Yesterday, after they'd finished talking about A and interviewed the male models and the other girls had left, Hanna found a bottle of Stoli Vanil in the same cabinet where her mother hid her wedding china. She and Mona had flopped down in the den, turned on *A Walk to Remember,* and played their Mandy Moore drinking game. Whenever Mandy looked fat, they drank. Whenever Mandy pouted, they drank. Whenever Mandy sounded robotic, they drank. They didn't talk about the note A had sent Mona—the one about their fight. Hanna was certain they'd just bickered about something stupid, like party pictures or whether Justin Timberlake was an idiot. Mona always said he was, and Hanna always said he wasn't.

Lucas blinked furiously. "She *didn't* tell you, did she?"

Hanna breathed forcefully out of her nose. "It doesn't *matter*, okay?"

"Okay," Lucas said, holding up his hands in surrender.

"Okay," Hanna stated again, squaring her shoulders. But when she closed her eyes, she saw herself in her Prius again. The Hollis Planetarium flag flapped behind her. Her eyes stung from crying. Something—maybe her BlackBerry—beeped at the bottom of her bag. Hanna tried to grab hold of the memory, but it was useless.

She could feel warmth radiating off Lucas's body, he was sitting so close. He didn't smell like cologne or fancy deodorant or other weird things boys sprayed on themselves, but just kind of like skin and toothpaste. If only they lived in a world where Hanna could have both things—Lucas *and* Mona. But she knew that if she wanted to stay who she was, that wasn't possible.

Hanna reached out and grabbed Lucas's hand. A sob welled up in her throat, for reasons she couldn't explain or even understand completely. As she moved forward to kiss him, she tried yet again to access her memory of what was surely the night of her accident. But, as usual, there was nothing there.

24

SPENCER GETS THE GUILLOTINE

Friday morning, Spencer stepped into Daniel on Sixty-fifth Street between Madison and Park, a quiet, well-maintained block somewhere between Midtown Manhattan and the Upper East Side. It looked like she'd stepped onto the set of *Marie Antoinette*. The restaurant's walls were made of carved marble, which reminded Spencer of creamy white chocolate. Luxurious dark red curtains billowed, and small, elegantly sculpted topiaries lined the entrance to the main dining room. Spencer decided that when she earned her millions, she would design her house to look exactly like this.

Her entire family was right behind her, Melissa and Ian included. "Do you have all your notes?" her mother murmured, fiddling with one of the buttons on her pink houndstooth Chanel suit—she was dressed as if *she* were going to be interviewed. Spencer nodded. Not only did she have them, she'd *alphabetized* them.

Spencer tried to quell the churning feelings in her stomach, although the smell of scrambled eggs and truffle oil wafting in from the dining room wasn't helping. There was a sign that said GOLDEN ORCHID INTERVIEW CHECK-IN over the hostess station. "Spencer Hastings," she said to a shiny-haired Parker Posey look-alike who was taking names.

The girl found Spencer on the list, smiled, and handed her a laminated name tag. "You're at table six," she said, gesturing toward the dining room entrance. Spencer saw bustling waiters, giant flower arrangements, and a few adults milling about, chatting and drinking coffee. "We'll call you when we're ready," the check-in girl assured her.

Melissa and Ian examined a marble statuette near the bar. Spencer's father had migrated out to the street and was talking to someone on his cell phone. Her mom was on her cell phone, too, half-concealed behind one of Daniel's bloodred curtains. Spencer heard her say, "So we're booked? Well, fantastic. She'll love it."

I'll love what? Spencer wanted to ask. But she wondered if her mom wanted to keep it a surprise until after Spencer won.

Melissa slipped off to the bathroom, and Ian plopped down on the chaise beside Spencer. "Excited?" He grinned. "You should be. This is huge."

Spencer wished that just *once,* Ian would smell like rotting vegetables or dog breath—it would make it much easier to be near him. "You didn't tell Melissa you were in my room last night, did you?" she whispered.

Ian's face became businesslike. "Of course not."

"And she didn't seem suspicious or anything?"

Ian put on aviator sunglasses, concealing his eyes. "Melissa isn't *that* scary, you know. She's not going to bite you."

Spencer clamped her mouth shut. These days, it seemed that Melissa wasn't *just* going to bite her—she was going to give Spencer rabies. "Just don't say anything," she growled.

"Spencer Hastings?" the girl at the desk called. "They're ready for you."

When Spencer stood up, her parents gathered around her like bees swarming a hive. "Don't forget about the time you played Eliza Doolittle in *My Fair Lady* with the raging stomach flu," Mrs. Hastings whispered.

"Don't forget to mention that I know Donald Trump," her father added.

Spencer frowned. "You do?"

Her father nodded. "We sat next to each other at Cipriani once and exchanged business cards."

Spencer breathed yoga fire breaths as covertly as she could.

Table six was a small, intimate nook at the back of the restaurant. Three adults had already gathered there, sipping coffee and picking at croissants. When they saw Spencer, they all stood. "Welcome," a balding, baby-faced man said.

"Jeffrey Love. Golden Orchid '87. I have a seat on the New York Stock Exchange."

"Amanda Reed." A tall, wispy woman shook Spencer's hand. "Golden Orchid 1984. I'm editor in chief at *Barron's*."

"Quentin Hughes." A black man in a beautiful Turnbull & Asser button-down nodded at her. "Nineteen-ninety. I'm a managing director at Goldman Sachs."

"Spencer Hastings." Spencer tried to sit down as daintily as possible.

"You're the one who wrote the 'Invisible Hand' essay." Amanda Reed beamed, settling back down in her chair.

"We were all very impressed with it," Quentin Hughes murmured.

Spencer folded and unfolded her white cloth napkin. Naturally, everyone at this table worked in finance. If only they could've thrown her an art historian, or a biologist, or a documentary filmmaker, someone she could talk to about something else. She tried to picture her interviewers in their underwear. She tried to picture her labradoodles, Rufus and Beatrice, humping their legs. Then she imagined telling them the truth about all this: that she didn't understand economics, that she really *hated* it, and that she'd stolen her sister's paper for fear of messing up her 4.0 average.

At first, the interviewers asked Spencer basic questions—about where she went to school, what she liked to do, and what her volunteering and leadership experiences were.

Spencer breezed through the questions, the interviewers smiling, nodding, and jotting notes down in their little leather Golden Orchid notebooks. She told them about her part in *The Tempest,* how she was the yearbook editor, and how she'd organized an ecology trip to Costa Rica her sophomore year. After a few minutes, she sat back and thought, *This is okay. This is really okay.*

And then her cell phone beeped.

The interviewers looked up, their stride broken. "You were supposed to turn off your phone before you came in here," Amanda said sternly.

"I'm sorry, I thought I did." Spencer fumbled in her bag, reaching to turn the phone to silent. Then, the preview screen caught her eye. She had received an IM from someone called AAAAAA.

> AAAAAA: Helpful hint to the not-so-wise: You're not fooling anyone. The judges can see you're faker than a knockoff Vuitton.
>
> P.S. She did it, you know. And she won't think twice about doing it to you.

Spencer quickly shut off her phone, biting hard on her lip. *She did it, you know.* Was A suggesting what Spencer *thought* A was suggesting?

When she looked again at her interviewers, they seemed like completely different people—hunched and serious, ready to get down to the *real* questions. Spencer started folding the napkin again. *They don't know I'm fake,* she told herself.

Quentin folded his hands next to his plate. "Have you always been interested in economics, Miss Hastings?"

"Um, of course." Spencer's voice came out scratchy and dry. "I've always found . . . um . . . economics, money, all that, very fascinating."

"And whom do you consider to be your philosophical mentors?" Amanda asked.

Spencer's brain felt hollowed out. *Philosophical mentors?* What the hell did that mean? Only one person came to mind. "Donald Trump?"

The interviewers sat stunned for a moment. Then Quentin began to laugh. Then Jeffrey, then Amanda. They were all smiling, so Spencer smiled, too. Until Jeffrey said, "You're kidding, right?"

Spencer blinked. "Of *course* I'm kidding." The interviewers laughed again. Spencer wanted so badly to rearrange the croissants in the middle of the table into a neater pyramid. She shut her eyes, trying to focus, but all she saw was the image of a plane falling from the sky, its nose and tail in flames. "But as far as inspirations . . . well, I have so many. It's hard to name just one," she sputtered.

The interviewers didn't look particularly impressed. "After college, what's your ideal first job?" Jeffrey asked.

Spencer spoke before thinking. "Working as a reporter at the *New York Times.*"

The interviewers looked confused. "A reporter in the economics section, right?" Amanda qualified.

Spencer blinked. "I don't know. Maybe?"

She hadn't felt this awkward and nervous since . . . well, ever. Her interview notes remained in a neatly stacked pile in her hands. Her mind felt like a chalkboard erased clean. A peal of laughter floated over from table ten. Spencer looked over and saw the brunette girl from the W smiling easily, her interviewers happily smiling back. Beyond her was a wall of windows; outside, on the street, Spencer saw a girl looking in. It was . . . Melissa. She was just *standing* there, staring blankly at her.

And she won't think twice about doing it to you.

"So." Amanda added more milk to her coffee. "What would you say is the most significant thing that's happened to you during your high school career?"

"Well . . ." Spencer's eyes flicked back to the window, but Melissa was gone. She took a nervous breath and tried to get a grip. Quentin's Rolex gleamed in the light of the chandelier. Someone had put on too much musky cologne. A French-looking waitress poured another round of coffee at table three. Spencer knew what the right answer was: competing in the econ math bowl in ninth grade. Summer interning on the options trading desk at the Philly branch of J. P. Morgan. Only, those weren't *her* accomplishments, they were Melissa's, this award's rightful winner. The words swelled on the tip of her tongue, but suddenly, something unexpected spilled out of her mouth instead.

"My best friend went missing in seventh grade," Spencer blurted out. "Alison DiLaurentis? You may have heard about it. For years, I had to live with the question of what happened to her, where she'd gone. This September, they found her body. She'd been murdered. I think my greatest achievement is that I've held it together. I don't know how any of us have done it, how we've gone to school and lived our lives and just kept *going*. She and I may have hated each other sometimes, but she meant everything to me."

Spencer shut her eyes, returning to the night Ali went missing, to when she had shoved Ali hard, and Ali slid backward. A horrible *crack* rang through the air. And suddenly, her memory opened an inch or two wider. She saw something else . . . something new. Just after she shoved Ali, she heard a small, almost girlish gasp. The gasp sounded close, as if whoever it was had been standing right behind her, breathing on her neck.

She did it, you know.

Spencer's eyes sprang open. Her judges seemed to be on pause. Quentin held a croissant an inch from his face. Amanda's head was cocked at an awkward angle. Jeffrey kept his napkin at his lips. Spencer wondered, suddenly, if she'd just voiced her newly recalled memory out loud.

"Well," Jeffrey said finally. "Thank you, Spencer."

Amanda stood, tossing her napkin on her plate. "This

has been very interesting." Spencer was pretty sure that was shorthand for *You have no chance of winning.*

The other interviewers snaked away, as did most of the rest of the candidates. Quentin was the only one who remained sitting. He studied her carefully, a proud smile on his face. "You're a breath of fresh air, giving us an honest answer like that," he said in a low, confidential voice. "I've followed your friend's story for a while now. It's just awful. Do the police have any suspects?"

The air-conditioning vent far above Spencer's head showered cold air on her full force, and the image of Melissa beheading a Barbie doll popped into her mind. "They don't," she whispered.

But I might.

25

WHEN IT RAINS, IT POURS

After school on Friday, Emily wrung out her still-wet-from-swim-practice hair and walked into the yearbook room, which was plastered with snapshots of Rosewood Day's finest. There was Spencer from last year's graduation-pin ceremony, accepting the Math Student of the Year award. And there was Hanna, emceeing last year's Rosewood Day charity fashion show, when she really should've been a model herself.

Two hands clapped over Emily's eyes. "Hey there," Maya whispered in her ear. "How was swimming?" She said it teasingly, sort of like a nursery rhyme.

"Fine." Emily felt Maya's lips brush against hers, but she couldn't quite kiss back.

Scott Chin, a closeted-but-not-really yearbook photographer, swept into the room. "Guys! Congratulations!" He air-kissed both of them, then reached out to turn Emily's collar out and sweep a stray kinky hair out of Maya's face.

"Perfect," he said.

Scott pointed Maya and Emily toward the white backdrop on the far wall. "We're taking all the Most Likely To photos there. Personally, I would *love* to see the two of you against a rainbow background. Wouldn't that be awesome? But we have to be consistent."

Emily frowned. "Most likely to . . . what? I thought we were voted best couple."

Scott's houndstooth newsboy cap slipped over one of his eyes as he bent over the camera tripod. "No, you were voted most likely to be together at the five-year reunion."

Emily's mouth fell open. At the *five-year reunion*? Wasn't that a tad extreme?

She massaged the back of her neck, trying to calm down. But she hadn't felt calm since she found A's note in the restaurant bathroom. Not knowing what else to do with it, she'd stashed it in the front pocket of her bag. She'd been taking it out periodically through her classes, each time pressing it to her nose to smell the sweet scent of banana gum.

"Say gouda!" Scott cried, and Emily moved toward Maya and tried to smile. The flash from Scott's camera left spots in front of her eyes, and she suddenly noticed that the yearbook room smelled like burning electronics. In the next shot, Maya kissed Emily on the cheek. And in the next, Emily willed herself to kiss Maya on the lips.

"Hot!" Scott encouraged.

Scott peeked into his camera's preview windowpane.

"You're free to go," he said. Then, he paused, looking curiously at Emily. "Actually, before you do, there's something you might want to see."

He led Emily to a large drafting table and pointed to a bunch of pictures arranged in a two-page layout. *Missing You Terribly,* said the headline across the top of the mockup. A familiar seventh-grade portrait stared at Emily—not only did she have a copy in the top drawer of her nightstand, but she'd also seen it nearly every night on the news for months now.

"The school never did a page for Alison when she went missing," Scott explained. "And now that she . . . well . . . we thought we should. We might even have a commemorative event to show off all these old Ali photos. Sort of an Ali retrospective, if you will."

Emily touched the edge of one of the photos. It was of Emily, Ali, Spencer, Aria, and Hanna at a lunch table. In the photo, they all clutched Diet Cokes, their heads thrown back in hysterical laughter.

Next to it was a photo of just Ali and Emily, walking down the hall with their books clutched to their chests. Emily towered over the petite Ali, and Ali was leaning up to her, whispering something in her ear. Emily bit down on her knuckles. Even though she'd found out lots of things about Ali, things that she wished Ali had shared with her years ago, she still missed her so much that it ached.

There was someone else in the background of the

photo that Emily hadn't noticed at first. She had long, dark hair and a familiar apple-cheeked face. Her eyes were round and green, and her lips were pink and bow-shaped. Jenna Cavanaugh.

Jenna's head was turned toward someone beside her, but Emily could only see the edge of the other girl's thin, pale arm. It was strange to see Jenna . . . sighted. Emily glanced at Maya, who had moved on to the next photo, obviously not seeing this one's significance. There was so much Emily hadn't told her.

"Is that Ali?" Maya said. She pointed to a shot of Ali and her brother, Jason, embracing on the Rosewood Day commons.

"Uh, *yeah.*" Emily couldn't control the annoyance in her voice.

"Oh." Maya stood back. "It just doesn't look like her, is all."

"It looks like every *other* picture of Ali here." Emily fought the urge to roll her eyes as she glanced at the picture. Ali looked impossibly young, maybe only ten or eleven. It had been taken before they'd become friends. It was hard to believe that once upon a time, Ali had been the leader of a completely different clique—Naomi Zeigler and Riley Wolfe had been her underlings. They'd even teased Emily and the other girls from time to time, making fun of Emily's hair, which was tinged green from hours spent in chlorinated water.

Emily studied Jason's face. He seemed so delighted to be

giving Ali a bear hug. What in the world had he meant in that news interview yesterday, when he said his family was messed up?

"What's this?" Maya pointed to the photos on the next desk.

"Oh, that's Brenna's project." Scott stuck his tongue out, and Emily couldn't help but giggle. The bitter rivalry between Scott and Brenna Richardson, another yearbook photographer, was the stuff of reality TV. "But for once, I think it's a good idea. She took pictures of the insides of people's bags to show what a typical Rosewood student carries around each day. Spencer hasn't seen it yet, though, so she might not approve."

Emily leaned over the next desk. The yearbook committee had written each bag's owner's name next to each photo. Inside Noel Kahn's lacrosse duffel bag were a bacteria-laden towel, the lucky squirrel stuffed animal he always talked about, and Axe body spray. Ick. Naomi Zeigler's elephant-gray quilted tote held an iPod Nano, a Dolce & Gabbana glasses case, and a square object that was either a tiny camera or a jeweler's loupe. Mona Vanderwaal carried around M.A.C. lip gloss, a pack of Snif tissues, and three different organizers. Part of a photo showing a slim arm with a frayed sleeve cuff poked out of the blue one. Andrew Campbell's backpack contained eight textbooks, a leather day planner, and the same Nokia Emily had. The photo showed the start of a text message he had either written or received, but Emily couldn't tell what it said.

When Emily looked up, she saw Scott fiddling with his camera, but she didn't see Maya anywhere in the room. Just then, her cell phone started vibrating. She had one new text message.

Tsk tsk, Emily! Does your girlfriend know about your weakness for blondes? I'll keep your secret . . . if you keep mine. Kisses! —A

Emily's heart hammered. Weakness for blondes? And . . . where had Maya gone?

"Emily?"

A girl stood in the yearbook doorway, wearing a gauzy pink baby-doll top, as if she were impervious to the mid-October chill. Her blond hair whipped around like she was a bikini model standing in front of a wind machine.

"Trista?" Emily blurted out.

Maya reemerged from the hallway, frowning, then smiling. "Em! Who's this?"

Emily whipped her head around at Maya. "Where were you just now?"

Maya cocked her head. "I was . . . in the hall."

"What were you doing?" Emily demanded.

Maya shot her a look that seemed to say, *What does it matter?* Emily blinked hard. She felt like she was losing her mind, suspecting Maya. She looked back at Trista, who was striding across the room.

"It's so good to see you!" Trista crowed. She gave Emily a huge hug. "I hopped a plane! Surprise!"

"Yeah," Emily croaked, her voice barely more than a whisper. Over Trista's shoulder, Emily could see Maya glaring at her. "Surprise."

26

DELIGHTFULLY TACKY,
YET UNREFINED

After school on Friday, Aria drove down Lancaster Avenue past the strip malls, Fresh Fields, A Pea in the Pod, and Home Depot. The afternoon was overcast, making the normally colorful trees that lined the road look faded and flat.

Mike sat next to her, sullenly screwing and unscrewing his Nalgene bottle cap over and over again. "I'm missing lacrosse," he grumbled. "When are you going to tell me what we're doing?"

"We're going somewhere that's going to make everything right," Aria said stiffly. "And don't worry, you're going to love it."

As she paused at a stop sign, a shimmer of pleasure ran through her. A's hint about Meredith—that she had a dirty little Hooters secret—made perfect sense. Meredith had acted so funny when Aria saw her at Hollis the other day, saying she had to be somewhere but not telling where that somewhere was. And just two nights ago, Meredith had commented that because the rent on the Hollis house was going up and she hadn't made much on her artwork lately, she might have to get a second job to make ends meet. Hooters girls probably got great tips.

Hooters. Aria clamped her mouth shut to keep from laughing. She couldn't wait to reveal this to Byron. Every time they'd driven by the place in years past, Byron had said that only puerile philistines went to Hooters, men who were more closely related to monkeys than humans. Last night, Aria had given Meredith a chance to admit her sins to Byron on her own, sidling up to her and saying, "I know what you're hiding. And you know what? I'm going to tell Byron if you don't."

Meredith had stepped back, dropping the dish towel from her hands. So she *did* feel guilty about something! Still, Meredith clearly hadn't said a word about it to Byron. Just this morning they'd peacefully crunched on bowls of Kashi GoLean at the table, getting along as happily as before. So Aria had decided to take matters into her own hands.

Even though it was midafternoon, the Hooters parking lot was nearly full. Aria noticed four cop cars lined up—the place was a notorious cop hangout, as it was right next to the police station. The Hooters owl on the sign grinned at them, and Aria could just make out girls in skintight shirts and orange mini shorts through the restaurant's tinted windows. But when she looked over to

Mike, he wasn't frothing at the mouth or getting a hard-on or whatever normal boys did when they pulled up to this place. Instead, he looked annoyed. "What the hell are we doing here?" he sputtered.

"Meredith works here," Aria explained. "I wanted you to be here with me so we could confront her together."

Mike's mouth dropped open so wide, Aria could see the bright green gum lodged behind his molars. "You mean . . . Dad's . . . ?"

"That's right." Aria reached into her yak-fur bag for her Treo—she wanted to take pictures of Meredith, for evidence—but it wasn't in its usual place. Aria's stomach churned. Had she lost it? She'd dropped her phone on a table after she'd gotten A's note in art class, fleeing the room and peeling off her mask in Hollis's lobby bathroom. Had she forgotten to pick it up? She made a mental note to stop by class later to look for it.

When Aria and Mike swept through the double doors, they were greeted by a blaring Rolling Stones song. Aria was overcome by the stench of hot wings. A blond, super-tan girl stood at the hostess station. "Hi!" she said happily. "Welcome to Hooters!"

Aria gave their name and the girl turned around to check on available tables, shaking her ass as she walked away. Aria nudged Mike. "Did you see the boobs on her? Gi*nor*mous!"

She couldn't believe the things that were spilling out of her mouth. Mike, however, didn't even crack a smile.

He was acting like Aria had dragged him to a poetry read-ing instead of hooter heaven. The hostess returned and led them to their booth. When she bent to place their silverware on the table, Aria could see right down the girl's T-shirt to her bright fuchsia bra. Mike's eyes remained fixed on the orange carpet, as if this sort of thing was against his religion.

After the hostess left, Aria looked around. She noticed a group of cops across the room, shoveling in enormous plates of ribs and french fries, staring alternately at a football game on TV and the waitresses that passed by their table. Among them was Officer Wilden. Aria slid down in her seat. It wasn't as if she couldn't be here—Hooters always stressed that it was a *family place*—but she didn't really feel like seeing Wilden right now, either.

Mike stared sourly at the menu as six more waitresses passed by, each one more jiggly than the last. Aria won-dered if somehow, instantly, Mike had turned gay. She turned away—if he was going to be like that, fine. She'd search for Meredith herself.

All the girls were dressed alike, their shirts and shorts eight sizes too small and their sneakers the kind the cheerleading squad wore on game day. They all sort of had the same face, too, which would make it easy to pick out Meredith among them. Only, she didn't see a single dark-haired girl here, much less one with a spi-derweb tattoo. By the time the waitress set down their

enormous plate of fries, Aria finally got up the courage to ask. "Do you know if someone named Meredith
Gates works here?"

The waitress blinked. "I don't recognize that name.
Although sometimes the girls here go by different names.
You know, stuff that's more . . ." She paused, searching for
an adjective.

"Hooters-y?" Aria suggested jokily.

"Yes!" The girl smiled. When she sashayed away again,
Aria snorted and poked Mike with a fry. "What do you
think Meredith goes by here. Randi? Fifi? Oh! What
about Caitlin? That's really perky, right?"

"Would you stop?" Mike exploded. "I don't want to
hear anything about . . . about *her*, okay?"

Aria blinked, sitting back.

Mike's face flushed. "You think this is the big thing
that's going to make things right? Shoving the fact that
Dad is with someone else in my face *yet again*?" He stuffed
a bunch of fries in his mouth and looked away. "It doesn't
matter. I'm over it."

"I wanted to make everything up to you," Aria
squeaked. "I wanted to make this all better."

Mike let out a guffaw. "There's nothing you can do,
Aria. You've ruined my life."

"I didn't ruin anything!" Aria gasped.

Mike's ice-blue eyes narrowed. He threw his napkin on
the table, stood up, and shoved his arm into his anorak
sleeve. "I have to get to lacrosse."

"Wait!" Aria grabbed his belt loop. Suddenly, she felt like she was going to cry. "Don't go," Aria wailed. "Mike, please. My life is ruined too. And not just because of Dad and Meredith. Because of . . . of something else."

Mike glanced at her over his shoulder. "What are you talking about?"

"Sit back down," Aria said desperately. A long second passed. Mike grunted, then sat. Aria stared at their plate of fries, working up the courage to speak. She overheard two men discussing the Eagles' defensive tactics. A used-car-dealership commercial on the flat-screen TV above the bar featured a man in a chicken suit babbling about deals that were more cluck for your buck.

"I've been getting these threats from someone," Aria whispered. "Someone who knows *everything* about me. The person who's been threatening me even tipped off Ella about Byron and Meredith's relationship. Some of my friends have been getting messages, too, and we think the person writing them is behind Hanna's hit-and-run accident. I even got a message about Meredith working here. I don't know how this person knows all of this stuff, but they just . . . do." She shrugged, trailing off.

Two more commercials passed before Mike spoke. "You have a *stalker*?"

Aria nodded miserably.

Mike blinked, confounded. He gestured to the booth of cops. "Have you told any of *them*?"

Aria shook her head. "I can't."

"Of course you can. We can tell them right now."

"I have it under control," Aria said through her teeth. She pressed her fingers to her temples. "Maybe I shouldn't have told you."

Mike leaned forward. "Don't you remember all the freaky shit that's happened in this town? You have to tell someone."

"Why do you care?" Aria snapped, her body filling with anger. "I thought you hated me. I thought I ruined your life."

Mike's face went slack. His Adam's apple bobbed as he swallowed. When he stood up, he seemed taller than Aria remembered. Stronger, too. Maybe it was from all of the lacrosse he'd been playing, or maybe it was because he was the man of the house these days. He snatched Aria's wrist and pulled her to her feet. "You're telling them."

Aria's lip wobbled. "But what if it's not safe?"

"What's unsafe is *not* telling," Mike urged. "And . . . and I'll keep you safe. Okay?"

Aria's heart felt like a brownie, straight out of the oven—all gooey and warm and a little melted. She smiled unsteadily, then glanced at the blinking neon sign above the Hooters' dining room. It said, DELIGHTFULLY TACKY, YET UNREFINED. But the sign was broken; all the letters were dark except for *tacky*'s lowercase *A*, which flickered menacingly. When Aria shut her eyes, the *A* still remained, glowing like the sun.

She took a deep breath. "Okay," she whispered.

Just as she moved away from Mike toward the cops, the waitress returned with their check. As the girl turned to leave, Mike got a sneaky look on his face, reached both his hands out, and squeezed the air, mimicking squeezing the girl's tight, orange satin–clad butt. He caught Aria's eye and winked.

It looked like the real Mike Montgomery was back. Aria had missed him.

27

BIZARRE LOVE TRIANGLE

Friday night, just before the limo was supposed to arrive to escort Hanna to her party, Hanna stood in her bedroom, twirling around in her brightly printed Nieves Lavi dress. She was finally a perfect size two, thanks to a diet of IV fluids and facial stitches that made it too painful to chew solid foods.

"That looks great on you," a voice called. "Except I think you're a tad too thin."

Hanna whirled around. In his black wool suit, dark purple tie, and purple-striped button-down, her father looked like George Clooney circa *Ocean's Eleven*. "I'm *so* not too thin," she answered quickly, trying to hide her thrill. "Kate's way thinner than me."

Her father's face clouded over, perhaps at the mention of his perfect, poised, yet incredibly evil quasi-stepdaughter. "What are you doing here, anyway?" Hanna demanded.

"Your mom let me in." He walked into Hanna's room and sat down on her bed. Hanna's stomach flipped. Her dad hadn't been in her bedroom since she was twelve, right before he moved out. "She said I could change here for your big party."

"*You're* coming?" Hanna squawked.

"Am I allowed?" her father asked.

"I . . . I guess so." Spencer's parents were coming, as well as some Rosewood Day faculty and staff. "But, I mean, I thought you'd want to get back to Annapolis . . . and Kate and Isabel. You've been away from them for almost a *week*, after all." She couldn't hide the bitterness in her voice.

"Hanna . . ." her father started. Hanna turned away. She suddenly felt so angry that her dad had left her family, that he was here now, that maybe he loved Kate more than he loved her—not to mention that she had scars all over her face and that her memory about Saturday night still hadn't returned. She felt tears in her eyes, which made her even angrier.

"Come here." Her father put his strong arms around her, and when she pressed her head to his chest, she could hear his heart beating.

"You okay?" he asked her.

A horn honked outside. Hanna pulled back her bamboo blinds and saw the limo Mona had arranged waiting in her driveway, its wipers moving furiously over the windshield to keep off the rain. "I'm great," she said suddenly, the whole world tipping up again. She slid her Dior mask over her face. "I'm Hanna Marin, and I'm fabulous."

Her father handed Hanna a huge black golf umbrella. "You definitely are," he said. And for the first time ever, Hanna thought she just might believe him.

What seemed like only seconds later, Hanna was perched atop a pillow-laden platform, trying to keep the balcony's tassels from knocking off her Dior mask. Four gorgeous man-slaves had hoisted her up, and they were now beginning their slow parade into the party tent on the fifteenth green of the Rosewood Country Club.

"Presenting . . . in her big return to Rosewood . . . the fabulous Hanna Marin!" Mona screamed into a microphone. As the crowd erupted, Hanna waved her arms around excitedly. All of her guests were wearing masks, and Mona and Spencer had transformed the tent into the Salon de l'Europe at Le Casino in Monte-Carlo, Monaco. It had faux-marble walls, dramatic frescoes, and roulette and card tables. Sleek, gorgeous boys roamed the room with trays of canapés, manned the tents' two bars, and acted as croupiers at the gambling tables. Hanna had demanded that none of her party's staff be female.

The DJ switched to a new White Stripes song and everyone began to dance. A thin, pale hand caught Hanna's arm, and Mona dragged her through the crowd and gave her a huge hug.

"Do you love it?" Mona cried from behind her expressionless mask, which looked similar to Hanna's Dior masterpiece.

"Naturally." Hanna bumped her hip. "And I *love* the gambling tables. Does anyone win anything?"

"They win a hot night with a hot girl—you, Hanna!" Spencer cried, prancing up behind them. Mona grabbed her hand, too, and the three jiggled with glee. Spencer looked like a blond Audrey Hepburn in her black satin trapeze dress and adorable round-toe flats. When Spencer put her arm around Mona's shoulders, Hanna's heart leaped. As much as she didn't want to give A credit for anything, A's notes to Mona had made Mona accept Hanna's old friends. Yesterday, in between rounds of their Mandy Moore drinking game, Mona had told Hanna, "You know, Spencer's really cool. I think she could be part of our posse." Hanna had waited *years* for Mona to say something like that.

"You look great," a voice said in Hanna's ear. A boy stood behind her, dressed in fitted pin-striped pants, a white long-sleeved button-down, a matching pin-striped vest, and a long-nosed bird mask. Lucas's telltale white-blond hair peeked out from the mask's top. When he reached out and clasped her hand, Hanna's heart started racing. She held it for a second, squeezed, and let it drop before anyone could see. "This party is awesome," Lucas said.

"Thanks, it was nothing," Mona piped in. She nudged

Hanna. "Although, I don't know, Han. Do you think that hideous thing Lucas is wearing qualifies as a mask?"

Hanna glanced at Mona, wishing she could see her face. She looked over Lucas's shoulder, pretending she'd been distracted by something that was going on over at the blackjack table.

"So, Hanna, can I talk to you for a sec?" Lucas asked. "Alone?"

Mona was now chatting with one of the waiters. "Um, okay," Hanna mumbled.

Lucas led her to a secluded nook and pulled off his mask. Hanna tried to thwart the tornado of nerves rumbling inside her stomach, avoiding looking anywhere near Lucas's super-pink, super-kissable lips. "Can I take yours off, too?" he asked.

Hanna made sure they were truly alone, and that no one else would be able to see her bare, scarred face, and then she let him lift off her mask. Lucas kissed her softly on her stitches. "I missed you," he whispered.

"You only saw me a couple hours ago." Hanna giggled.

Lucas smiled crookedly. "That seems like a long time."

They kissed for a few more minutes, snuggled together on a single couch cushion, oblivious to the cacophony of party noises. Then Hanna heard her name through the tent's gauzy curtains. "Hanna?" Mona's voice called. "Han? Where are you?"

Hanna freaked. "I should go back out." She picked up

Lucas's mask by its long bird beak and shoved it at him. "And you should put this back on."

Lucas shrugged. "It's hot under that thing. I think I'll leave it off."

Hanna tied her own mask's strings tight. "It's a masquer*ade*, Lucas. If Mona sees that you've taken yours off, she'll kick you out for real."

Lucas's eyes were hard. "Do you always do everything Mona says?"

Hanna tensed. *"No."*

"Good. You shouldn't."

Hanna flicked a tassel on one of the pillows. She looked at Lucas again. "What do you want me to say, Lucas? She's my best friend."

"Has Mona told you what she did to you yet?" Lucas goaded. "I mean, at her party."

Hanna stood up, annoyed. "I told you, it doesn't matter."

He lowered his eyes. "I care about you, Hanna. I don't think she does. I don't think she cares about anyone. Don't let it drop, okay? Ask her to tell you the truth. I think you deserve to know."

Hanna stared at him long and hard. Lucas's eyes were shiny and his lip quivered a little. There was a purple welt on his neck from their earlier make-out session. She wanted to reach out and touch it with her thumb.

Without another word, she whipped the curtain open and stormed back onto the dance floor. Aria's brother,

Mike, was demonstrating his best stripper pole dance to a girl from the Quaker school. Andrew Campbell and his nerdy Knowledge Bowl friends were talking about counting cards in blackjack. Hanna smiled when she saw her father chatting with her old cheerleading coach, a woman whom she and Mona had privately called The Rock, because she bore a resemblance to the professional wrestler.

She finally found Mona sitting in another one of the pillow-laden enclaves. Eric Kahn, Noel's older brother, dangled next to her, whispering in her ear. Mona noticed Hanna and sat up. "Thank *God* you got away from Loser Lucas," she groaned. "Why has he been hanging around you so much, anyway?"

Hanna scratched at her stitches underneath her mask, her heart suddenly racing. All at once, she needed to ask Mona. She needed to know for sure. "Lucas says I shouldn't trust you." She forced a laugh. "He says there's something you're not telling me, as if there would *ever* be something you wouldn't tell me." She rolled her eyes. "I mean, he's totally bullshitting me. It's so lame."

Mona crossed her legs and sighed. "I think I know what he's talking about."

Hanna swallowed hard. The room suddenly smelled too strongly of incense and freshly cut Bermuda grass. There was a burst of applause at the blackjack table; someone had won. Mona moved closer to her, talking right in Hanna's ear. "I never told you this, but Lucas and I dated the summer between seventh and eighth grade. I was his first kiss. I dumped him when you and I became friends. He called me for, like, six months afterward. I'm not sure he's ever gotten over it."

Hanna sat back, stunned. She felt like she was on one of those amusement park swings that abruptly changed directions halfway through the ride. "You and Lucas . . . dated?"

Mona lowered her eyes and pushed a stray lock of golden hair off her mask. "I'm sorry I never said anything about it before. It's just that . . . Lucas is a loser, Han. I didn't want you to think *I* was a loser too."

Hanna ran her hands through her hair, thinking about her conversation with Lucas in the hot-air balloon. She had told him *everything*, and his face had been so innocent and open. She thought about how intensely they'd kissed, and the little moaning noises he'd made when she ran her fingers up and down his neck.

"So, he was trying to be my friend and saying nasty things about you to . . . to get back at you for dumping him?" Hanna stammered.

"I think so," Mona said sadly. "*He's* the one you shouldn't trust, Hanna."

Hanna stood up. She remembered how Lucas had said she was so pretty, and how *good* that had felt. How he'd read her DailyCandy blog entries while the nurses changed her IV fluids. How, after he'd kissed her in the hospital bed, Hanna's heart rate had stayed elevated for a full half hour—she'd watched it on the heart monitor.

Hanna had told Lucas about her eating issues. About Kate. About her friendship with Ali. About *A*! Why had he never told her about Mona?

Lucas was now sitting on another couch, talking to Andrew Campbell. Hanna made a beeline right for him, and Mona followed close behind, grabbing her arm. "Deal with this later. Why don't I just throw him out? You should be enjoying your big night."

Hanna waved Mona away. She poked Lucas in the back of his pin-striped vest. When Lucas turned around, he looked genuinely happy to see her, giving her a sweet, ecstatic smile.

"Mona told me the truth about you," Hanna hissed, placing her hands on her hips. "You guys used to date."

Lucas's lip twitched. He blinked hard, opened his mouth, then shut it again. "Oh."

"*That's* what this is all about, isn't it?" she demanded. "It's why you want me to hate her."

"Of course not." Lucas looked at her, his brows furrowed. "We weren't serious."

"*Right,*" Hanna scoffed.

"Hanna doesn't like boys who lie," Mona added, appearing behind Hanna.

Lucas's mouth dropped open. A bloom of redness crawled from his neck to his cheeks. "But I suppose she likes *girls* who lie, huh?"

Mona crossed her arms over her chest. "I'm not lying about anything, Lucas."

"No? So then you told Hanna what really happened at your party?"

"It doesn't *matter*," Hanna screeched.

"Of course I told her," Mona said at the same time.

Lucas looked at Hanna, his face growing more and more crimson. "She did something awful to you."

Mona inserted herself in front of him. "He's just *jealous*."

"She *humiliated* you," Lucas added. "*I* was the one who came and saved you."

"What?" Hanna squeaked in a small voice.

"Hanna." Mona grabbed Hanna's hands. "It's all a misunderstanding."

The DJ switched to a Lexi song. It was a song Hanna didn't hear often, and at first she wasn't sure when she'd heard it last. Then, all at once, she remembered. Lexi had been the special musical guest at Mona's party.

A memory suddenly caught fire in Hanna's mind. She saw herself wearing a skin-tight champagne-colored dress, struggling to walk into the planetarium without her outfit bursting at the seams. She saw Mona laughing at her, and then she felt her knee and elbow hitting the hard marble floor. There was a long, painful *riiiip* noise as her dress gave way, and everyone stood around her, laughing. Mona laughed the hardest of all.

Underneath her mask, Hanna's mouth dropped open and her eyes widened. *No.* It couldn't be true. Her memory was scrambled from the accident. And even if it was true, did it matter now? She looked down at her brand-new Paul & Joe bracelet, a delicate gold chain with a pretty butterfly charm clasp. Mona had bought it for her as a welcome-back-from-the-hospital present, giving it to Hanna right after A sent Mona that taunting e-card. "I don't want us ever to be mad at each other again," Mona had said as Hanna lifted the jewelry box lid.

Lucas stared at her expectantly. Mona had her hands on her hips, waiting. Hanna tied the mask's ribbon closure in a tighter knot. "You're just jealous," she said to Lucas, putting her arm around Mona. "We're best friends. Always will be."

Lucas's face crumpled. "Fine." He wheeled around and ran out the door.

"*What* a lame-ass," Mona said, sliding her arm in the crook of Hanna's elbow.

"Yeah," Hanna said, but her voice was so quiet, she doubted Mona heard.

28

POOR LITTLE DEAD GIRL

The sky was darkening on Friday night as Mrs. Fields dropped Emily and Trista off at the country club's main entrance. "Now, you know the rules," Mrs. Fields said sternly, draping her arm over Emily's seat. "No drinking. Be home by midnight. Carolyn will give you girls a ride home. Got it?"

Emily nodded. It was kind of a relief that her mom was enforcing some rules. Her parents had been so lenient since she'd come home, she was beginning to think that they both had brain tumors or had been replaced by clones.

As Emily's mom sped away, Emily straightened the black jersey dress she'd borrowed from Carolyn's closet and tried not to wobble in her red leather kitten heels. In the distance, she could see the huge, glowing party tent. A Fergie song blared out of the speakers, and Emily heard Noel Kahn's unmistakable voice cry, "That's so *hot*!"

"I am so excited for tonight," Trista said, grabbing Emily's arm.

"Me too." Emily pulled her jacket closer around her, watching the skeleton wind sock twist from the country club's main entrance. "If you could be any Halloween character in the world, what would you be?" she asked. Lately, Emily had been thinking of everything in Trista-isms, trying to figure out which sort of spaghetti noodle she was most like, which Great Adventure roller coaster, which kind of deciduous Rosewood tree.

"Catwoman," Trista answered promptly. "You?"

Emily looked away. Right now, she kind of felt like a witch. After Trista surprised Emily in the yearbook room, she'd explained that since her father was a pilot with US Air, she got big discounts even on last-minute flights. After Emily's text yesterday, she'd decided to hop on a flight, accompany Emily to Hanna's masquerade party, and camp out on Emily's bedroom floor. Emily didn't quite know how to say, "You shouldn't have come" . . . and didn't quite want to, either.

"When's your friend meeting us?" Trista asked.

"Um, she's probably already here." Emily started across the parking lot, passing eight BMW 7 Series cars in a row.

"Cool." Trista spread ChapStick over her lips. She passed it to Emily, and their fingers lightly touched. Emily felt tingles run through her, and when she met Trista's eyes, the amorous look on Trista's face indicated she was thinking equally tingly thoughts.

Emily stopped short next to the valet stand. "Listen. I have a confession to make. Maya is sort of my girlfriend."

Trista stared at her blankly.

"And I kind of told her—and my parents—that you're my pen pal," Emily went on. "That we've been writing for a few years."

"Oh, *really*?" Trista nudged her playfully. "Why didn't you just tell her the truth?"

Emily swallowed, crushing a few dried, fallen leaves under her toe. "Well . . . I mean, if I told her what really happened . . . in Iowa . . . she might not get it."

Trista smoothed down her hair with her hands. "But nothing *did* happen. We just danced." She poked Emily in the arm. "Geez, is she *that* possessive?"

"No." Emily stared at the Halloween scarecrow display on the country club's front lawn. It was one of three scarecrows around the grounds, and yet a crow was perched on a nearby flagpole, not one bit frightened. "Not exactly."

"Is it a problem that I'm here?" Trista asked pointedly.

Trista's lips were the exact same pink as Emily's favorite tutu back when she'd taken ballet. Her pale blue shift dress pulled against her shapely chest and showed the flatness of her stomach and the roundness of her butt. She was like a ripe, juicy fruit, and Emily sort of wanted to bite her. "Of course it's not a problem you're here," Emily breathed.

"Good." Trista pulled her mask over her face. "Then I'll keep your secret."

Once they entered the tent, Maya found Emily immediately, untied her rabbit-shaped mask, and pulled Emily close for an extra-passionate kiss. Emily opened her eyes in the middle of it, and noticed that Maya was staring directly at Trista, seemingly flaunting what she and Emily were doing. "When are you going to ditch her?" Maya whispered in Emily's ear. Emily looked away, pretending she hadn't heard.

As they moved through the party tent, Trista kept grabbing Emily's arm and gasping, "It's so beautiful! Look at all the pillows!" And, "There are so many hot *guys* in Pennsylvania!" And, "So many girls here wear diamonds!" Her mouth fell open like a little kid's on her first trip to Disney World. When a crowd of kids at the bar separated them, Maya pulled off her mask.

"Was that girl raised in a hermetically sealed terrarium?" Maya's eyes bugged out. "Honestly, why does she find *everything* so amazing?"

Emily glanced at Trista as she leaned up against the bar. Noel Kahn had approached her and was now seductively running his hand up and down Trista's arm. "She's just excited to be here," she mumbled. "Things are pretty boring in Iowa."

Maya cocked her head and stood back. "It's quite a coincidence that you have a pen pal in the *exact same* Iowa town you were banished to last week."

"Not really," Emily croaked, staring at the shimmering disco ball in the middle of the tent. "She's from the same town as my cousins, so Rosewood Day did an exchange with her school. We started writing a couple years ago."

Maya mushed her lips together, her jaw tense. "She's awfully *pretty*. Did you pick pen pals by their pictures?"

"It wasn't, like, Match.com." Emily shrugged, trying to act oblivious.

Maya gave her a knowing look. "It would make sense if you did. You loved Alison DiLaurentis, and Trista looks a lot like her."

Emily tensed up, her eyes flicking back and forth. "No, she doesn't."

Maya looked away. "Whatever."

Emily considered her next words very carefully. "That banana gum you chew, Maya. Where do you get it?"

Maya looked confused. "My father brought me a carton from London."

"Can you get it in the States? Do you know anyone else who chews it?" Emily's heart pounded.

Maya stared at her. "Why the hell are you asking me about banana gum?" Before Emily could answer, Maya turned away. "Look, I'm going to go to the bathroom, okay? Don't go anywhere without me. We can talk when I get back."

Emily watched Maya snake through the baccarat tables, feeling like she had hot coals in her stomach. Almost immediately, Trista emerged from the crowd, holding three plastic cups. "They're spiked," she whispered excitedly, pointing to Noel, who was still standing by the bar. "That boy had a flask of something and gave me some." She looked around. "Where's Maya?"

Emily shrugged. "Off being pissy."

Trista had removed her mask, and her skin glowed in the flashing dance floor lights. With her pursed, pink lips, her wide, blue eyes, and high cheekbones, maybe she did look a little like Ali. Emily shook her head and reached for one of the cups—she would drink this first, figure out everything else later. Trista's finger ran seductively down Emily's wrist. Emily tried to keep her face impassive, even though she felt like she was about to melt.

"So, if you were a color right now, what color would you be?" Trista whispered.

Emily looked away.

"I'd be red," Trista whispered. "But . . . not a mad red. Like a deep, dark, beautiful sexy red. A lusty red."

"I think I'd be that color, too," Emily admitted.

The music thumped like a pulse. Emily took a long, needy drink, her nose tickling with the spicy flavor of rum. When Trista curled her hand around Emily's, Emily's heart jumped. They moved closer, then closer still, until their lips were nearly touching. "Maybe we shouldn't do this," Trista whispered.

But Emily moved closer anyway, her body rippling with excitement.

A hand smacked Emily on the back. "What the *hell*?"

Maya stood behind them, her nostrils flaring. Emily

took a giant step away from Trista, opening and closing her mouth like a goldfish. "I thought you were going to the bathroom" was all Emily could think to say.

Maya blinked, her face purple with fury. Then, she turned and stormed out of the tent, pushing people out of her way.

"Maya!" Emily followed her through the doors. But just before she was about to exit, she felt a hand on her arm. It was a man she didn't recognize in a police uniform. He had short spiky hair and a lanky build. His badge said SIMMONS.

"Are you Emily Fields?" the cop asked.

Emily nodded slowly, her heart suddenly quickening.

"I need to ask you a couple questions." The cop placed his hand gently on Emily's shoulder. "Have you . . . have you been getting some threatening messages?"

Emily's mouth fell open. The flickering strobe lights made her woozy. "W-why?"

"Your friend Aria Montgomery told us about them this afternoon," the cop said.

"What?" Emily shrieked.

"It'll be okay," the cop reassured her. "I just want to know what you know, all right? It's probably someone you know, someone right under your nose. If you talk to us, maybe we can figure it out together."

Emily looked out the tent's filmy opening. Maya was darting across the grass, her heels sinking into the dirt. A horrible feeling washed over Emily. She thought of how Maya had looked at her when she said, *I heard that the person who hit Hanna was stalking her.* How could Maya have known that?

"I can't talk right now," Emily whispered, a lump growing in her throat. "I have to take care of something first."

"I'll be here," the cop said, stepping aside so Emily could pass. "Take your time. I have a few other people to find anyway."

Emily could just make out Maya's shape running into the country club's main building. She sprinted after her, through two glass French doors and down a long hallway. She looked through the last door at the end of the hall, which led to the indoor pool. The window had fogged up with condensation, and Emily could just make out Maya's tiny body walking to the pool's edge, looking at her reflection.

She pushed her way in and walked around a small tiled wall separating the entryway from the pool. The pool's water was flat and dead, and the air was thick and humid. Even though Maya had surely heard Emily come in, she didn't turn around. If things had been different, Emily might jokingly have pushed her in the water, then jumped in too. She cleared her throat. "Maya, the Trista thing isn't what it looks like."

"No?" Maya peeked over her shoulder. "It looked pretty obvious to me."

"It's just . . . she's fun," Emily admitted. "She doesn't put any pressure on me."

"And I do?" Maya shrieked, whirling around. Tears streamed down her face.

Emily swallowed hard, gathering her strength. "Maya . . . have you been sending me . . . text messages? Notes? Have you been . . . spying on me?"

Maya's brow crinkled. "Why would I spy on you?"

"Well, I don't know," Emily started. "But if you are . . . the police know."

Maya slowly shook her head. "You're not making any sense."

"I won't tell if it's you," Emily pleaded. "I just want to know *why*."

Maya shrugged, then let out a little whimper of frustration. "I have no idea what you're talking about." A tear streaked down her face. She shook her head, disgusted. "I love you," she spat. "And I thought you loved me." She turned around, yanked the pool's glass door open, then slammed it shut.

The pool's overhead lights dimmed, turning the reflections coming off the pool from whitish-gold to orangish-yellow. Beads of humid sweat gathered on the top of the diving board. All of a sudden, the realization hit Emily, like the shock of diving into ice-cold water on an already cold day. Of course Maya wasn't A. A had set all this up for Maya to look suspicious, so things would be ruined between the two of them forever.

Her cell phone buzzed. Emily grabbed for it, her hands shaking.

Emmykins:

There's a girl waiting for you in the hot tub. Enjoy! —A

Emily let her phone drop to her side, her heart pounding. The hot tub was separated from the rest of the room by a partition, and it had its own door that led back out to the hall. Emily crept slowly to the hot tub. It bubbled like a cauldron, and mist rose off the water's surface. Suddenly, she noticed a flash of red in the bubbly water and jumped back in terror. Looking again, she realized it was only a doll floating facedown, its long red hair fanned out around it.

She reached in and pulled the doll out. It was an Ariel doll from *The Little Mermaid*. The doll had scaly green and purple fins, but instead of a clamshell bikini, Ariel wore a sleek racing suit that said ROSEWOOD DAY SHARKS across the boobs. There were X's over her eyes, as if she'd drowned, and there was something written in thick marker across her forehead.

Tell and die. —A

Emily's hands started to shake, and she dropped the doll on the slick, tiled floor. As she stepped away from the hot tub's edge, a door slammed.

Emily shot up, her eyes wide. "Who's there?" she whispered.

Silence.

She stepped out from the hot tub partition and looked around. There was no one in the pool area. She couldn't see around the tiled wall that hid the front door, but she saw a distinct shadow on the far wall. Someone was here with her.

Emily heard a giggle and jumped. Then a hand flew out from behind the tiled wall. A blond ponytail appeared, then another pair of hands, larger and masculine, with a silver Rolex dangling from one wrist.

Noel Kahn emerged first, darting from behind the wall to one of the nearby chaises. "Come on," he whispered. Then the blonde scampered to him. It was Trista. They lay down on the chaise together and resumed kissing.

Emily was so stunned, she burst out laughing. Trista and Noel glanced at her. Trista's mouth fell open, but then she shrugged, as if to say, *Hey, you weren't around.* Emily suddenly thought of Abby's warning—*Trista Taylor tries to hump anything that moves, girl or guy.* She had a feeling Trista wouldn't be camping out on Emily's bedroom floor tonight after all.

Noel's lips spread into an easy smile. Then they went back to what they were doing, as if Emily didn't exist at all. Emily looked back at the drowned Ariel splayed out on the ground and shivered. Of course if she told anyone about A, A would make sure that Emily *really* didn't exist.

29

NO ONE CAN HEAR YOU SCREAM

Aria dashed from her dented Subaru to the Hollis art building. A storm was building on the horizon, and the rain had already begun to fall. She had finished telling the cops about A only a little while ago, and although she'd tried to call her old friends on Wilden's phone, none of them had picked up—probably because they didn't recognize his number. She was now going into the Hollis art building to see if she had left her Treo here; without it, she had no concrete proof of what A was doing to her. Mike had offered to go into the building with her, but Aria had told him she'd see him later, at Hanna's party.

As Aria pushed the call button for the elevator, she pulled her Rosewood Day blazer around her—she hadn't had time to change yet. Mike's insistence that she tell Wilden about A had been a wake-up call, but had she done the right thing? Wilden had wanted to know the

details of every last text, IM, e-mail, and note that A had
sent. He had asked over and over again, "Is there anyone
the four of you hurt? Is there anyone who might want to
harm you?"

Aria had paused and shaken her head, not wanting to answer. Who *hadn't* they hurt, back in the day,
with Ali at the helm? There was one clear front-runner,
though . . . Jenna.

She thought of A's notes: *I know EVERYTHING. I'm
closer than you think.* She thought of Jenna fiddling with
her cell phone, saying, *I'm so psyched I can send texts!* But
was Jenna truly capable of something like this? She was
blind—A obviously wasn't.

The elevator doors slid open, and Aria got in. As it
pulled her to the third floor, she thought about the memory Hanna had mentioned when she first woke up from her
coma—the one about the afternoon before Ali went missing. Ali had been acting so strangely that day, first reading
some notebook she wouldn't show the others, then appearing downstairs moments later, seeming so disoriented. Aria
had lingered on Ali's porch by herself for a few minutes
after the others left, knitting the last few rows of one of
the cuff bracelets she planned to give to each of them as
a first-full-day-of-summer present. As she went around the
house to retrieve her bike, she saw Ali standing in the middle of her front yard, transfixed. Ali's eyes flickered from
the DiLaurentises' curtained dining room window to the
Cavanaughs' house across the street.

"Ali?" Aria had whispered. "Are you okay?"

Ali didn't move. "Sometimes," she said in an entranced voice, "I just wish she was out of my life forever."

"What?" Aria whispered. "Who?"

Ali seemed stunned, as if Aria had snuck up on her. There was a flash of something in the DiLaurentises' window—or perhaps it was just a reflection. And when Aria looked at the Cavanaughs' yard, she saw someone lurking behind the large shrub by Toby's old tree house. It reminded Aria of the figure she swore she'd seen standing in the Cavanaughs' yard the night they blinded Jenna.

The elevator let out a *ding*, and Aria jumped. Who had Ali been talking about when she said, *I just wish she was out of my life forever*? At the time, she'd thought Ali meant Spencer—they were constantly fighting. Now she wasn't sure at all. There were just so many things she hadn't known about Ali.

The hallway leading to the Mindless Art studio was dark, save for a brief moment when a zigzag of lightning came dangerously close to the window. When Aria reached the open door of her classroom, she flipped on the light and blinked in the sudden brightness. Her class's cubbies were along the back wall, and amazingly, Aria's Treo was in an empty cubby, seemingly untouched. She ran to it and cradled it in her arms, letting out a sigh of relief.

Then, she noticed the masks her class had completed,

one drying in each cubby. The alcove with Aria's name written in Scotch tape on the bottom was empty, but Jenna's wasn't. Someone else must have helped Jenna make her mask, because there it was, faceup and perfectly formed, the blank, hollowed-out eyes staring at the cubby's ceiling. Aria lifted it slowly. Jenna had painted her mask to look like an enchanted forest. Vines swirled around the nose, a flower bloomed above her left eye, and there was a gorgeous butterfly on her right cheek. The detailed brushwork was impeccable—perhaps *too* impeccable. It didn't seem possible for someone who couldn't see.

A crack of thunder sounded like it was splitting open the earth. Aria yelped, dropping the mask to the table. When she looked to the window, she saw the silhouette of something swinging from the window's top crank. It looked like a tiny . . . person.

Aria stepped closer. It was a plush doll of the Wicked Queen from *Snow White*. She wore a long black robe and a gold crown on her head, and her frowning face was ghostly pale. She hung from a rope around her neck, and someone had drawn big, black *X*'s over her eyes. There was a note pinned to the doll's long gown.

Mirror, mirror on the wall, who's the naughtiest of them all?
You told. So you're next. —A

Tree branches scraped violently against the window. More lightning set fire to the sky. As another crack of thunder sounded, the studio's lights died. Aria shrieked.

The streetlights just outside the window had gone off, too, and somewhere, far away, Aria heard a fire alarm screaming. *Stay calm,* Aria told herself. She grabbed her Treo and dialed the number for the police dispatch. Just as someone picked up, a knife-shaped bolt of lightning flickered outside the window. Aria's phone slipped from her fingers and clattered to the floor. She reached for it, then tried to dial again. But her phone no longer had service.

Lightning lit up the room again, illuminating the shapes of the desks, the cabinets, the swinging Wicked Queen from the window, and, finally, the door. Aria widened her eyes, a scream frozen in her throat. *There was someone there.*

"H-hello?" she cried out.

With another zing of lightning, the stranger was gone. Aria bit into her knuckles, her teeth chattering. "Hello?" she called. Lightning flashed again. A girl was standing just inches from her face. Aria felt dizzy with fear. It was . . .

"Hello," the girl said.

It was Jenna.

30

THREE LITTLE WORDS CAN CHANGE
EVERYTHING

Spencer sat at the roulette table, moving her shiny plastic casino chips from one palm to the other. As she placed a few chips on numbers 4, 5, 6, and 7, she felt the push of the crowd now gathered thickly behind her. It seemed like all of Rosewood was here tonight—everyone from Rosewood Day, plus the people from rival private schools who were staples at Noel Kahn's parties. There was even a cop here, wandering the perimeter. Spencer wondered why.

When the wheel stopped, the ball landed on the number 6. This was the third time in a row she'd won. "Nice job," someone said in her ear. Spencer looked around, but she couldn't locate who'd spoken to her. It sounded like her sister's voice. Only, why would Melissa be here? No other college kids had come, and before Spencer's Golden Orchid interview, Melissa had said Hanna's party sounded ridiculous.

She did it, you know. Spencer couldn't get A's text out of her head.

She scanned the tent. Someone with chin-length blond hair was slinking toward the stage, but when Spencer stood up, the person seemed to have evaporated into the crowd. She rubbed her eyes. Maybe she was going crazy.

Suddenly, Mona Vanderwaal grabbed her arm. "Hey, sweetie. You have a sec? I have a surprise."

She led Spencer through the crowd to a more secluded spot, snapped her fingers, and a waiter magically appeared, handing each of them a tall, fluted glass filled with bubbly liquid. "It's real champagne," Mona said. "I wanted to propose a toast to thank you, Spencer. For planning this fantastic party with me . . . and also for being there for me. About . . . you know. The notes."

"Of course," Spencer said faintly.

They clinked glasses and sipped. "This party is really awesome," Mona went on. "I couldn't have done it without you."

Spencer waved her hand humbly. "Nah. You put it all together. I just made a couple of calls. You're a natural at this."

"We're *both* naturals at this," Mona said, belting back her champagne. "We should start a party-planning business together."

"And we'll flash country club boys on the side," Spencer joked.

"Of course!" Mona chirped, bumping Spencer's hip.

Spencer ran her finger up and down the length of the champagne flute. She wanted to tell Mona about her newest text from A—the one about Melissa. Mona would understand. Only, the DJ switched songs to a fast one by OK Go, and before Spencer could say a word, Mona squealed and made a run for the dance floor. She glanced over her shoulder at Spencer, as if to say, *Are you coming?* Spencer shook her head.

The few sips of champagne had made her dizzy. After a couple minutes of wading through the crowd, she walked out of the tent into the clear night air. Except for the spotlights that surrounded the tent, the golf course was very dark. The man-made grassy knolls and sand traps weren't visible, and Spencer could only see the bare outlines of the trees in the distance. Their branches waved like bony fingers. Somewhere, a bunch of crickets screamed.

A doesn't know anything about Ali's killer, Spencer assured herself, looking back at the fuzzy shapes of the partygoers inside. And anyway, it made no sense—Melissa wouldn't ruin her whole future by killing someone over a guy. This was just another one of A's tactics to make Spencer believe something that wasn't true.

She sighed and headed off for the bathrooms, which were outside the tent in a bubble-shaped trailer. Spencer climbed the wheelchair ramp and pushed through the flimsy plastic door. Of the three stalls, one was occupied, and two were empty. As she flushed and wriggled her dress back into position, the bathroom's main door slammed shut. Pale silver Loeffler Randall shoes made their way over to the trailer's minuscule sink. Spencer clapped her hand over her mouth. She'd seen those shoes plenty of times before—they were Melissa's favorite pair.

"Uh, hi?" Spencer said when she stepped out of her stall. Melissa was leaning against the sink, her hands on her hips, a small smile on her face. She wore a long, narrow black dress with a slit up the side. Spencer tried to breathe calmly. "What are you doing here?"

Her sister didn't say anything, just kept staring. A droplet of water struck the sink basin, making Spencer jump.

"What?" Spencer sputtered. "Why are you looking at me like that?"

"Why did you lie to me again?" Melissa growled.

Spencer pressed her back against one of the stall doors. She looked back and forth for something she could use as a weapon. The only thing she could think of was her shoe's kitten heel, and she slowly slid her foot out of the toe box. "Lie?"

"Ian told me he was in your hotel room last night," Melissa whispered, her nostrils flaring in and out. "I told you he wasn't good at keeping a secret."

Spencer's eyes widened. "We didn't do anything. I swear."

Melissa took a step toward her. Spencer covered her face with one hand and pulled her shoe off her foot with the other. *"Please,"* she begged, holding out her shoe like a shield.

Melissa hovered just inches from her face. "After all you admitted to me at the beach, I thought we had an understanding. But I guess not." She whirled around and stormed out of the bathroom. Spencer heard her clonk down the ramp and stamp across the grass.

Spencer leaned over the sink and rested her forehead on the mirror's cool surface. Suddenly, a toilet flushed. After a pause, the third stall door swung open. Mona Vanderwaal strode out. There was a horrified look on her face.

"Was that your *sister*?" Mona whispered.

"Yeah," Spencer sputtered, turning around.

Mona grabbed Spencer's wrists. "What's going on? Are you okay?"

"I think so." Spencer stood back up. "I just need a second alone is all."

"Of course." Mona's eyes widened. "I'll be outside if you need me."

Spencer smiled gratefully at Mona's back. After a pause, she heard the flick of a lighter, and the sparkly, burning sound of Mona taking a drag of a cigarette. Spencer faced the mirror and smoothed down her hair. Her hands shook wildly as she reached for her sequined clutch, hoping there was a tube of aspirin inside. Her hands bumped against her wallet, her lip gloss, her poker chips . . . and then something else, something square and glossy. Spencer pulled it out slowly.

It was a photograph. Ali and Ian stood close together, their arms entwined. Behind them was a round, stone building, and behind that was a line of yellow school buses. By the looks of Ali's shaggy haircut and her tropical-shade long-sleeve J. Crew polo, Spencer was pretty sure this photo had been taken during their class trip to see *Romeo and Juliet* at the People's Light playhouse a few towns away. A bunch of Rosewood Day students had gone along—Spencer, Ali, her other friends, and a slew of juniors and seniors like Ian and Melissa. Someone had written something in big, jagged letters over Ali's smiling face.

You're dead, bitch.

Spencer stared at the handwriting, immediately identifying it. Not too many people made their lowercase *a*'s look like a curly number 2. Cursive was practically the only thing Melissa had gotten a B in, ever. Her second-grade penmanship teacher had chastised her, but making funny-looking *a*'s was a habit Melissa had never been able to break.

Spencer let the picture slip from her hands and let out a small, pained yelp of disbelief. "Spencer?" Mona called from outside. "You okay?"

"Fine," Spencer said after a long pause. Then, she looked down at the floor. The photo had landed face-down. There was more writing on the back.

Better watch your back . . . or you'll be a dead bitch too. —A

31

SOME SECRETS GO EVEN DEEPER

As Aria opened her eyes, something wet and smelly scraped its tongue up and down her face. She reached out, her hand sinking into soft, warm fur. For some reason, she was now on the art studio floor. A lightning bolt lit up the room, and she saw Jenna Cavanaugh and her dog sitting on the floor next to her.

Aria shot up, screaming.

"It's okay!" Jenna cried, catching her arm. "Don't worry! It's okay!"

Aria scuttled backward, away from Jenna, knocking her head on a nearby table leg. "Don't hurt me," she whispered. "Please."

"You're safe," Jenna reassured her. "I think you had a panic attack. I was coming here to pick up my sketchbook, but then I heard you—and when I came close, you fell." Aria could hear herself swallowing hard in the darkness. "A woman in my service-dog-training class gets panic attacks, so I know a little about them. I tried to call for help, but my cell phone wasn't working, so I just stayed with you."

A breeze blew through the room, bringing in the smell of wet, rained-on asphalt, a scent Aria usually found calming. Aria certainly *felt* like she'd just had a panic attack—she was sweaty and disoriented, and her heart was beating like mad. "How long was I out?" she croaked, smoothing out her pleated uniform skirt so that it covered her thighs.

"About a half hour," Jenna said. "You might've hit your head, too."

"Or I might've really needed the sleep," Aria joked, and then felt like she was going to cry. Jenna didn't want to hurt her. Jenna had *sat* with her, a stranger, while she'd lain like a lump on the floor. For all Aria knew, she'd drooled on Jenna's lap and talked in her sleep. She suddenly felt sick with guilt and shame.

"I have to tell you something," Aria blurted out. "My name's not Jessica. It's Aria. Aria Montgomery."

Jenna's dog sneezed. "I know," Jenna admitted.

"You . . . *do*?"

"I could just . . . tell. By your voice." Jenna sounded almost apologetic. "But why didn't you just say it was you?"

Aria closed her eyes tight and pressed her hands hard into her cheeks. Another streak of lightning illuminated the room, and Aria saw Jenna sitting cross-legged on the floor, her hands wrapped around her ankles. Aria took a huge breath, perhaps the biggest one of her life. "I didn't tell you because . . . there's something else you should know about me." She pressed her hands to the rough wood floor, gathering strength. "You should know something about the night of your accident. Something no one ever told you. I guess you don't remember much of what happened that night, but—"

"That's a lie," Jenna interrupted. "I remember everything."

Thunder rumbled in the distance. Somewhere close by, a car alarm went off, starting a cycle of harsh, piercingly loud buzzes and *ee-oo*s. Aria could hardly breathe. "What do you mean?" she whispered, stunned.

"I remember everything," Jenna repeated. She traced the sole of her shoe with a finger. "Alison and I set it up together."

Every muscle in Aria's body went limp. "*What?*"

"My stepbrother used to set off fireworks from his tree house roof all the time," Jenna explained, frowning. "My parents kept warning him that it was dangerous—he might mess up, send a firework right into our house, and cause a fire. They said the next time he set one off, they were going to send him to boarding school. And that was final.

"So Ali agreed to steal fireworks out of Toby's stash and make it look like Toby had launched it off the tree house roof. I wanted her to do it that night because my parents were home, and they were already mad at Toby for something anyway. I wanted him out of my life as soon as possible." Her voice caught. "He . . . he wasn't a good stepbrother."

Aria clenched and unclenched her fist. "Oh my God." She tried to comprehend everything Jenna was telling her.

"Only . . . things went wrong," Jenna explained, her voice teetering. "I was with Toby in his tree house that night. And just before it happened, he looked down and said angrily, 'There's someone on our lawn.' I looked down, too, pretending to be surprised . . . and then there was a flash of light, and then . . . this horrible pain. My eyes . . . my face . . . it felt like they just melted away. I think I passed out. Afterward, Ali told me that she'd forced Toby to take the blame."

"That's right." Aria's voice was barely more than a whisper.

"Ali thought fast." Jenna shifted her weight, making the floor beneath her creak. "I'm glad she did. I didn't want her to get in trouble. And it kind of worked out the way I wanted. Toby left. He was out of my life."

Aria slowly rolled her jaw around. *But . . . you're blind!* she wanted to scream. *Was it really worth* that? Her head hurt, trying to process everything Jenna had just told her. Her whole world felt smashed open. It felt like someone had proclaimed that animals could talk, and dogs and spiders now ruled the world. Then something else hit her: Ali had set things up like it was a prank *they* pulled on Toby, but Ali and Jenna had been the ones who planned it out . . . *together*. Not only had Ali set up Toby, she'd set up her friends, too. Aria felt sick.

"So you and Ali were . . . friends." Aria's voice was faint with disbelief.

"Not exactly," Jenna said. "Not until this . . . not until I told her about what Toby was doing. I knew Ali would understand. She had sibling problems, too."

A flash of light streaked across Jenna's face, revealing a calm, matter-of-fact expression. Before Aria could ask what Jenna meant, Jenna added, "There's something else you should know. There was someone else there that night. Someone else saw."

Aria gasped. The image of that night scissored through her head. The firework burst inside the tree house, lighting up the surrounding yard. Aria always thought she'd seen a dark figure crouching near the Cavanaughs' side porch—but Ali insisted, over and over again, that she'd imagined the whole thing.

Aria wanted to smack her forehead. It was so obvious who'd seen. How could she have not realized till now?

I'm still here, bitches. And I know everything. —A.

"Do you know who it was?" Aria whispered, her heart hammering fast.

Jenna turned sharply away. "I can't tell."

"Jenna!" Aria shrieked. "Please! You have to! I need to know!"

All of a sudden, the power snapped back on. The room flooded with light so bright, it hurt Aria's eyes. The fluorescent bulbs hummed. Aria saw a streak of blood on her hands and felt a cut on her forehead. The contents of her bag had spilled out onto the floor, and Jenna's dog had eaten half of one of Aria's Balance bars.

Jenna had taken her sunglasses off. Her eyes stared out blankly at nothing, and there were wrinkled, puckered burn scars on the bridge of her nose and the bottom of her forehead. Aria winced and looked away.

"Please, Jenna, you don't understand," Aria said quietly. "Something horrible is happening. You have to tell me who else was there!"

Jenna stood up, grabbing hold of her dog's back for balance. "I've said too much already," she croaked, her voice shaky. "I should go."

"Jenna, please!" Aria pleaded. *"Who else was there?"*

Jenna paused, sliding her sunglasses back on. "I'm sorry," she whispered, pulling on her dog's harness. She tapped her cane once, twice, three times, fumbling clumsily for the door. And then she was gone.

32

HELL HATH NO FURY . . .

After Emily caught Trista hooking up with Noel, she ran out of the pool room, searching frantically for Spencer or Hanna. She needed to tell them that Aria had told the police about A . . . and show them the doll she'd just found. As she rounded the craps table for the second time, Emily felt a cold hand on her shoulder and yelped. Spencer and Mona stood behind her. Spencer was clutching a small, square photograph tightly in her hands. "Emily, we need to talk."

"I need to talk to you, too," Emily gasped.

Spencer wordlessly pulled her across the dance floor. Mason Byers was in the middle, making a jackass out of himself. Hanna was talking to her father and Mrs. Cho, her photography teacher. Hanna looked up as Spencer, Mona, and Emily approached, her face clouding over. "Do you have a sec?" Spencer asked.

They found an empty booth and piled in. Without a

word, Spencer reached into her beaded purse and pulled out a photograph of Ali and Ian Thomas. Someone had drawn an *X* over Ali's face and had written, *You're dead, bitch,* in spiky letters at the bottom.

Emily clapped a hand over her mouth. Something was very familiar about the photograph. Where had she seen it before?

"I found this in my purse when I was in the bathroom." Spencer turned the photo over. *Better watch your back . . . or you'll be a dead bitch too.* Emily recognized the spiky handwriting immediately. She'd seen it scrawled on a PFLAG application just the other day.

"It was in your bag?" Hanna gasped. "So does that mean A is *here?*"

"A's definitely here," Emily said, looking around. The male model cocktail waiters swirled. A bunch of girls in minidresses flounced by, whispering that Noel Kahn had smuggled in alcohol. "I just got a . . . a message, sort of, saying so," Emily went on. "And . . . you guys. *Aria* told the cops about A. Some cop came up to me saying he wanted to ask me questions. I think A knows about that too."

"Oh my God," Mona whispered, her eyes wide. She looked from one girl to the other. "That's bad, right?"

"It could be *really* bad," Emily said. Someone elbowed her in the back of the head, and she rubbed her skull, annoyed. This party wasn't exactly the right venue to be talking about this.

Spencer ran her hands along the velvet couch cushion. "Okay. Let's not panic. The cops are here, right? So we're safe. We'll just find them and stick by them. But this . . ." She tapped the big *X* over Ali's face, then *You're dead, bitch.* "I know who wrote this part of it." She looked around at them, taking a deep breath. "Melissa."

"Your sister?" Hanna squeaked.

Spencer nodded gravely, the party's strobe lights flickering against her face. "I think . . . I think Melissa killed Ali. It makes sense. She knew that Ali and Ian were together. And she couldn't take it."

"Rewind." Mona put down her can of Red Bull. "Alison and . . . Ian Thomas? They were together?" She stuck out her tongue, disgusted. "Ew. Did you guys know?"

"We only figured it out a few days ago," Emily mumbled. She wrapped her coat around her body. Suddenly, she was freezing.

Hanna examined Melissa's signature on her cast against the writing on the photo. "The writing *is* similar."

Mona stared at Spencer fearfully. "And she was acting so weird in the bathroom just now."

"Is she still here?" Hanna craned her neck to look around the room. Behind them, a waiter dropped a tray of glasses. A crowd of kids clapped.

"I've looked all over for her," Spencer said. "I couldn't find her anywhere."

"So what are you going to do?" Emily asked, her heart pounding faster and faster.

"I'm going to tell Wilden about Melissa," Spencer said matter-of-factly.

"But, Spencer," Emily argued. "A knows what we're doing. And A knows Aria told. What if this is just some sort of big mind game?"

"She's right," Mona agreed, crossing her legs. "It could be a trap."

Spencer shook her head. "It's Melissa. I'm sure of it. I have to turn her in. We have to do it for Ali." She reached into her sequined bag and found her phone. "I'll call the station. Wilden's probably there." She dialed and pressed her phone to her ear.

Behind them, the DJ shouted out, "Is everyone having a good time tonight?!" The crowd on the dance floor screamed, "Yeah!"

Emily shut her eyes. *Melissa.* Ever since the police had deemed Ali's death a murder, Emily hadn't been able to stop herself from imagining just how the murderer had done it. She'd envisioned Toby Cavanaugh grabbing Ali from behind, hitting her on the head, and throwing her into the DiLaurentises' half-dug gazebo hole. She'd tried to picture Spencer doing the same thing to Ali, distraught over Ali's relationship with Ian Thomas. Now she saw Melissa Hastings grabbing Ali's waist and dragging her toward the hole. Only . . . Melissa was so thin Emily couldn't quite believe she'd had the strength to coerce Ali into doing what she wanted. Perhaps she'd had a weapon, like a kitchen knife or a box cutter. Emily winced, imagining a box cutter at Ali's delicate throat.

"Wilden's not answering." Spencer threw her phone back into her bag. "I'm just going to go down to the station." She paused, smacking herself on the forehead. "*Shit.* My parents drove me here. We came straight from New York. I don't have a car."

"I'll take you." Mona leaped up.

Emily stood up. "I'll go too."

"We'll all go," Hanna said.

Spencer shook her head. "Hanna, this is *your* party. You should stay."

"Seriously," Mona said.

Hanna adjusted her sling. "This party's been great, but this is more important."

Mona bit the edge of her lip awkwardly. "I think you should stay for a little while longer."

Hanna raised an eyebrow. "Why?"

Mona rocked back and forth on her heels. "We got Justin Timberlake to come."

Hanna clutched her chest as if Mona had shot her. "*What?*"

"He was my dad's client when he was just starting out, so he owed him a favor. Only, he's kind of late. I'm sure he'll be here soon, but I wouldn't want you to miss him." She smiled sheepishly.

"Whoa." Spencer widened her eyes. "Seriously? You didn't even tell *me* that."

"And you *hate* him, Mon," Hanna breathed.

Mona shrugged. "Well, it's not my party, is it? It's yours. He's going to call you up to the stage to dance with him, Han. I wouldn't want you to miss it."

Hanna had liked Justin Timberlake as long as Emily had known her. Whenever Hanna used to talk about how Justin should be with *her* instead of Cameron Diaz, Ali would always cackle and say, "Well, with you, he'd sort of get *two* Camerons for the price of one—you're twice her size!" Hanna would turn away, hurt, until Ali insisted that she shouldn't be so sensitive.

"I'll stay with you, Hanna," Emily said, grabbing Hanna's arm. "We'll stay for Justin. We'll stick really close together, next to that cop over there. Okay?"

"I don't know," Hanna said uncertainly, even though Emily could tell she wanted to stay. "Maybe we should go."

"*Stay,*" Spencer urged. "Meet us there. You'll be okay here. A can't hurt you with a cop nearby. Just don't go to the bathroom or anywhere else alone."

Mona took Spencer's arm, and they slid through the crowd toward the tent's main opening. Emily shot Hanna a brave smile, her stomach churning. "Don't leave me," Hanna said in a small, terrified voice.

"I won't," Emily assured her. She took Hanna's hand and squeezed hard, but she couldn't help scanning the crowd nervously. Spencer had said she'd run into Melissa in the bathroom. That meant Ali's murderer was here with them *right now*.

33

THE MOMENT OF CLARITY

Standing up on stage with the *real* Justin Timberlake—not a wax figurine at Madame Tussauds or an imposter at the Trump Taj Mahal in Atlantic City—was going to be surreal. It would be Justin's real mouth giving Hanna a big smile, Justin's real eyes canvassing Hanna's body as she danced around, and Justin's real hands as he gave her a round of applause for having the strength to pull through such a devastating accident.

Unfortunately, Justin hadn't shown up yet. Hanna and Emily peeked out one of the tent's openings, keeping their eyes peeled for a convoy of limos. "This is going to be so exciting," Emily murmured.

"Yeah," Hanna said. But she wondered if she'd even be able to enjoy it. She felt like there was something really, really wrong. Something inside her wanted to break through, like a moth struggling inside a cocoon.

Suddenly, Aria emerged from the crowd. Her dark hair was tangled and there was a bruise on her cheek. She still wore her Rosewood Day blazer and pleated skirt, and looked very out of place amid the other dressed-up people at the party. "You guys," she said breathlessly. "I need to talk to you."

"And we need to talk to *you*," Emily shrieked. "You told Wilden about A!"

Aria's eyelid twitched. "I . . . I did. Yes. I thought it was the right thing to do."

"It *wasn't*," Hanna snapped, her body filling with rage. "A knows, Aria. A's after us. What the hell is wrong with you?"

"I know A knows," Aria said, seeming distracted. "I have to tell you guys something else. Where's Spencer?"

"Spencer went to the police station," Emily said. The disco lights came back on, turning her face from pink to blue. "We tried to call you, but you didn't pick up."

Aria sank down into a nearby couch, looking a little shaken and confused. She picked up a carafe of sparkling water and poured herself a huge glass. "Did she go to the police station because of . . . A? The cops want to ask all of us more questions."

"She didn't," Hanna said. "She went because she knows who killed Ali."

Aria's eyes were glassy. She seemed to be ignoring what Hanna just said altogether. "Something really weird just happened to me." She drained her water glass. "I just had a long conversation with Jenna Cavanaugh. And . . . she knows about that night."

"What were you doing talking to Jenna?" Hanna barked. Then the rest of what Aria had said finally registered, the same way, her physics teacher had explained, it takes radio waves years to reach outer space. Hanna's mouth fell open, and all the blood drained from her head. *"What did you just say?"*

Aria pressed her hands to her forehead. "I've been taking these art classes, and Jenna's in my class too. Tonight, I went up to the art studio and . . . and Jenna was there. I had this horrible fear that she was A . . . and that she was going to hurt me. I had a panic attack . . . but when I woke up, Jenna was still with me. She had *helped* me. I felt terrible, and I just started to blurt out what we did. Only, before I could really say anything, Jenna interrupted. She said that she remembered everything about that night, after all." Aria looked at Hanna and Emily. "She and Ali set up the whole thing together."

There was a long pause. Hanna could feel her pulse at her temples. "That's not possible," Emily finally said, abruptly standing up. "It *can't* be."

"It can't be," Hanna echoed weakly. What was Aria saying?

Aria pushed a stray strand of hair behind her ears. "Jenna said that she came to Ali with the plan to hurt Toby. She wanted him gone—I'm sure because he was . . .

you know. Touching her. Ali said she'd help. Only, things went wrong. But Jenna kept the secret anyway—she said that things worked out the way she wanted. Her brother was gone. But . . . she also said that someone else was there that night. Besides Ali, and besides us. Someone else saw."

Emily gaped. *"No."*

"Who?" Hanna demanded, feeling her knees go weak.

Aria shook her head. "She wouldn't tell me."

A long pause followed. A bass line from a Ciara song throbbed in the background. Hanna looked around the party, amazed at how blissfully unaware everyone was. Mike Montgomery was grinding against some girl from the Quaker school; the adults were all hovering around the bar, getting drunk; and a bunch of girls in her grade were whispering cattily about how pudgy everyone else looked in their dresses. Hanna almost wanted to tell everyone to go home, that the universe had tipped upside down and right now, having fun was out of the question.

"Why did Jenna go to *Ali*, of all people?" Emily sounded out. "Ali hated her."

Aria ran her fingers through her hair, which was wet from the rain. "She said that Ali would understand. That Ali had sibling problems, too."

Hanna frowned, confused. *"Sibling* problems? You mean like Jason?"

"I . . . I guess," Aria mused. "Maybe Jason was doing what Toby did."

Hanna wrinkled her nose, recalling Ali's handsome-but-sullen older brother. "Jason *was* always kind of . . . weird."

"You guys, *no*." Emily's hands fell to her lap. "Jason was moody, but he wasn't a molester. He and Ali always seemed really happy around each other."

"Toby and Jenna seemed happy around each other, too," Aria reminded her.

"I heard, like, one in four boys is abusive to his sister," Hanna seconded.

"That's ridiculous," Emily snorted. "Don't believe everything you hear."

Hanna froze. She whipped her head around to Emily. "What did you just say?"

Emily's lip trembled. "I said . . . don't believe everything you hear."

The words fanned out in sonarlike concentric circles. Hanna heard them again and again, banging back and forth inside her head.

The foundations of her brain started to crumble. *Don't believe everything you hear.* She had seen those words before. It was her last text. From A. From the night she couldn't remember.

Hanna must have made some sort of noise because Aria turned. "Hanna . . . what?"

Memories began to flood back to her, like a line of dominoes falling down one after another. Hanna saw herself wobbling into Mona's party in the court dress, freaked because it didn't fit. Mona had laughed in her face and called her a whale. It wasn't Mona who had sent her that dress, Hanna realized—A had.

She saw herself taking a step back, her ankle buckling, and collapsing to the ground. The devastating *riiipppp* of seams. The sounds of laughter above her, Mona's loudest of all. And then, Hanna saw herself much later, sitting alone in her Toyota Prius in the Hollis Planetarium parking lot, wearing a sweatshirt and gym shorts, her eyes puffy from crying. She heard her BlackBerry chime and she saw herself reaching for her phone. *Oops, guess it wasn't lipo!* the text said. *Don't believe everything you hear! —A*

Except the text wasn't from A. It had been from a regular cell phone number—a number Hanna knew well.

Hanna let out a muffled shriek. The faces looking down at her blurred and shimmered, as if they were holograms. "Hanna . . . what is it?" Emily shrieked.

"Oh. My. God," Hanna whispered, her head reeling. "It's . . . Mona."

Emily frowned. "What's Mona?"

Hanna pulled off her mask. The air felt cool and liberating. Her scar pulsed, as if it was a separate entity from her chin. She didn't even look around to see how many people were staring at her bruised, ugly face, because right now, it didn't matter. "I remember what I was going to tell you guys that night, when I wanted to meet you at Rosewood Day," Hanna said, tears brimming in her eyes. "A is Mona."

Emily and Aria stared at her so blankly that Hanna wondered if they'd even heard her. Finally, Aria said, "Are you *sure*?"

Hanna nodded.

"But Mona's with . . . Spencer," Emily said slowly.

"I know," Hanna whispered. She tossed her mask on the couch and stood up. "We have to find her. Now."

34

I'LL GET YOU, MY PRETTIES . . .

It had taken Spencer and Mona almost ten minutes to cross the country club lawn to the parking lot, climb into Mona's enormous taxicab-yellow Hummer, and roar out of the parking lot. Spencer glanced at Hanna's receding party tent. It was lit up like a birthday cake, and the vibrations from the music were almost visible.

"That was a really awesome thing you did, setting up Justin Timberlake for Hanna," Spencer murmured.

"Hanna's my best friend," Mona answered. "She's been through a lot. I wanted to make it really special."

"She used to talk about Justin all the time when we were younger," Spencer went on, gazing out the window as an old farmhouse, which used to belong to one of the DuPonts but was now a restaurant, flew past. A few people who had finished dinner were standing out on the porch, happily chatting. "I didn't know she still liked him so much."

Mona smiled halfway. "I know lots of things about Hanna. Sometimes I think I know Hanna better than Hanna knows herself." She glanced at Spencer briefly. "You have to do good things for people you care about, you know?"

Spencer nodded faintly, biting at her cuticles. Mona slowed for a stop sign and rooted around in her purse, pulling out a pack of gum. The car immediately smelled like artificial bananas. "Want a piece?" she asked Spencer, unwrapping a stick and pushing it into her mouth. "I'm obsessed with this stuff. Apparently you can only get it in Europe, but this girl in my history class gave me a whole pack." She chewed thoughtfully. Spencer waved the open pack away. She wasn't much in a gum-chewing mood right now.

As Mona passed the Fairview Riding Academy, Spencer smacked her thighs hard. "I can't do this," she wailed. "We should turn around, Mona. I can't turn Melissa in."

Mona glanced at her, then turned into the riding academy's parking lot. They pulled into the handicapped space and Mona shifted the Hummer into park. "Okay . . ."

"She's my *sister*." Spencer stared blankly forward. It was pitch-black out, and the air smelled like hay. She heard a whinnying in the distance. "If Melissa did it, shouldn't I be trying to protect her?"

Mona reached into her clutch and pulled out a Marlboro Light. She offered one to Spencer, but Spencer shook her head. As Mona lit up, Spencer watched the orange butt glow and the smoke curl, first around the Hummer's cabin, then out the slight crack at the top of the driver's side window.

"What did Melissa mean in the bathroom?" Mona asked quietly. "She said, after what you told her at the beach, she thought you guys had an understanding. What did you tell her?"

Spencer dug her nails into the heels of her hands. "This memory had come back to me about the night Ali went missing," she admitted. "Ali and I had this fight . . . and I shoved her. Her head smacked against the stone wall. But I'd blocked it out for years." She glanced at Mona, gauging her reaction, but Mona's face was blank. "I blurted it out to Melissa the other day. I had to tell *someone.*"

"Whoa," Mona whispered, glancing at Spencer carefully. "You think *you* did it?"

Spencer pressed her palms into her forehead. "I was definitely mad at her."

Mona twisted in her seat, breathing smoke out her nose. "A put that photo of Ali and Ian in your purse, right? What if A fed Melissa some sort of clue, too, convincing *her* to tell on *you*? Melissa could be going to the cops right now."

Spencer's eyes widened. She remembered what Melissa said about them no longer having an "understanding." "Shit," she whispered. "Do you think?"

"I don't know." Mona grabbed Spencer's hand. "I think you're doing the right thing. But if you want me to turn around and go back to the party, I will."

Spencer ran her fingers against the rough beads on her clutch. *Was* it the right thing? She wished she hadn't been the one to discover Melissa was the killer. She wished someone else could've found out instead. Then, she thought about how she'd torn around the country club tent, looking frantically for Melissa. Where had she gone? What was she doing right now?

"You're right," she whispered in a dry voice. "This is the right thing."

Mona nodded, then shifted gears again and backed out of the riding school lot. She tossed her cigarette butt out the window, and Spencer watched it as they drove away, a tiny flicker of light among the dry blades of grass.

When they were farther down the road, Spencer's Sidekick beeped. Spencer unzipped her bag. "Maybe that's Wilden," she murmured. Only, it was a text from Emily.

Hanna remembered. Mona is A! Reply if you get this.

Spencer's phone slipped from her hands to her lap. She read the text again. And again. The words might as well have been written in Arabic—Spencer couldn't process them at all. *R U sure?* she texted back. *Yes,* Emily wrote. *Get out of there. NOW.*

Spencer stared at a billboard for Wawa coffee, a stone sign for a housing development, then an enormous, triangular-shaped church. She tried to breathe as steadily as possible, counting from one to one hundred by fives, hoping it would calm her down. Mona was watching the road carefully and dutifully. Her halter dress didn't quite fit her in the chest. She had a scar on her right shoulder, probably from the chicken pox. It didn't seem possible that she could have done this.

"So was it Wilden?" Mona chirped.

"Um, no." Spencer's voice came out squawky and muffled, like she was talking through a can. "It was . . . it was my mom."

Mona nodded slightly, keeping the same speed. Spencer's phone lit up again. Another text had come in. Then another, then another, then another. *Spencer, what's going on? Spencer, pls txt us back. Spencer, yr in DANGER. Pls tell us if yr okay.*

Mona smiled, her canine teeth glowing in the dim light shining off the Hummer's dashboard console. "You're certainly popular. What's going on?"

Spencer tried to laugh. "Um, nothing."

Mona glanced at Spencer's main text message window. "Emily, huh? Did Justin show up?"

"Um . . ." Spencer swallowed audibly, her throat catching.

Mona's smile evaporated. "Why won't you tell me what's going on?"

"N-nothing's going on," Spencer stammered.

Mona scoffed, tossing a lock of hair behind her shoulders. Her pale skin glowed in the darkness. "What, is it a secret? Am I not good enough to know or something?"

"Of course not," Spencer squeaked. "It's just . . . I . . ."

They rolled to a red light. Spencer looked back and forth, then slowly pressed the Hummer's UNLOCK button. As she curled her fingers around the door handle, Mona grabbed her other wrist.

"What are you *doing*?" Mona's eyes glowed in the traffic light's red glare. Her head swiveled from Spencer's phone back to Spencer's panicked face. Spencer could see the realization flooding over Mona—it was like watching black and white turn to color in *The Wizard of Oz*. Mona's expression went from confusion to shock to . . . glee. She pressed the car door's LOCK button again. When the light turned green, she gunned the engine and made a stomach-churning left through the intersection and veered off onto a bumpy, two-lane country road.

Spencer watched as the odometer climbed from fifty to sixty to seventy. She clutched her door handle tightly. "Where are we going?" she asked in a small, terrified voice.

Mona glanced at Spencer sideways, a sinister smile pasted on her face. "You were never one for patience." She winked and blew Spencer a kiss. "But this time you'll just have to wait and see."

35

THE CHASE IS ON

Since Hanna had arrived at the party in a limo and Emily's mother had driven her, their only vehicle option was Aria's clunky, unpredictable Subaru. Aria led the others through the parking lot, her green suede flats slapping against the pavement. She manually unlocked the door and threw herself into the driver's seat. Hanna sat in the front passenger seat, and Emily pushed aside all of Aria's books, empty coffee cups, spare clothes, skeins of yarn, and a pair of stacked-heel boots, and climbed into the back. Aria had her cell phone wedged between her chin and her shoulder—she'd called Wilden to see if Spencer and Mona had shown up at the police station. But after the eighth unanswered ring, she hung up in frustration.

"Wilden isn't at his desk," she said. "And he's not answering his cell, either." They were quiet for a moment, all lost in their own thoughts. *How could Mona be A?* Aria thought. *How could Mona know so much about us?* Aria went over everything Mona had done to her—threatened her with that Wicked Queen doll, sent Sean the pictures that got Ezra arrested, sent Ella the letter that splintered her family apart. Mona had hit Hanna with a car, outed Emily to the school, and made them think that Spencer had killed Ali. Mona had had a hand in Toby Cavanaugh's death . . . and maybe Ali's, too.

Hanna was staring straight ahead, her eyes wide and unblinking, as if she was possessed. Aria touched her hand. "Are you *sure* about this?"

Hanna nodded fitfully. "Yes." Her face was pale and her lips looked dry.

"Do you think it was a good idea that we texted Spencer?" Emily asked, checking her phone for the billionth time. "She hasn't written back again."

"Maybe they're in the police station now," Aria answered, trying to stay calm. "Maybe Spencer turned off her phone. And maybe that's why Wilden isn't answering."

Aria looked at Hanna. There was a big, glistening tear rolling down her cheek, past her bruises and her stitches. "It's my fault if Spencer is hurt," Hanna whispered. "I should have remembered sooner."

"It's absolutely not your fault," Aria said sternly. "You can't *control* when you remember things." She placed a hand on Hanna's arm, but Hanna wrenched it away, using her hands to cover her face. Aria had no idea how to console her. What must that feel like, to realize that your best friend was also your worst enemy? Hanna's best friend had tried to *kill* her.

Suddenly, Emily gasped too. "That picture," she whispered.

"What picture?" Aria asked, starting the car and speeding out of the lot.

"That . . . that picture Spencer showed us of Ali and Ian. The one with the writing on it? I *knew* I'd seen it before. Now I know where." Emily let out a laugh of disbelief. "I was in the yearbook room a couple days ago. And there were these pictures of the insides of people's bags. That's where I saw that picture." She raised her eyes, looking around at the others. "In *Mona's* bag. But I only saw Ali's arm. The pink sleeve was frayed and had a tiny rip."

The police station was only a mile or so away, right next to Hooters. It was amazing that Aria and Mike had been there just hours before. When they pulled into the lot, all three of them leaned forward over the dash. *"Shit."* There were eight squad cars in the parking lot, and that was it. "They're not here!"

"Calm down." Aria turned off the car's headlights. They all jumped out quickly, sprinting for the police station entrance. The fluorescent light inside was greenish and harsh. Several cops stopped and stared at them, their mouths hanging open. The little green waiting benches were all empty except for a few random pamphlets about what you should do if you were the victim of a car theft.

Wilden appeared from around a corner, his cell phone in one hand, a mug of coffee in another. When he saw Hanna and Emily in their party dresses with their masks dangling from their wrists, and Aria in her Rosewood Day uniform with a big bruise on her head, he squinted in confusion. "Hi, girls," he said slowly. "What's going on?"

"You have to help us," Aria said. "Spencer is in trouble."

Wilden stepped forward, gesturing for them to sit on the benches. "How so?"

"The texts we've been getting," Aria explained. "What I was telling you about earlier today. We know who they're from."

Wilden stood up, alarmed. "You *do*?"

"It's Mona Vanderwaal," Hanna said, her voice breaking into a sob. "That's what I remembered. It's my best frickin' *friend*."

"Mona . . . Vanderwaal?" Wilden's eyes traveled from one girl to another. "The girl who planned your party?"

"Spencer Hastings is in the car with Mona now," Emily said. "They were supposed to be coming here—Spencer had something to tell you. But then I sent her a text, warning her about Mona . . . and now we don't know where they are. Spencer's phone is shut off."

"Have you tried to reach Mona?" Wilden asked.

Hanna stared at the linoleum floor. Off in the police bullpen, a phone rang, and then another. "I did. She didn't pick up either."

Suddenly, Wilden's cell phone lit up in his hand. Aria

caught a glimpse of the number in the preview screen. "That's Spencer!" she cried.

Wilden flipped it open but didn't say hello. He pressed the speakerphone button, then looked around at the girls, a finger to his lips. *Shhh*, he mouthed.

Aria and her old best friends crowded around the little phone. At first, there was only white noise. Then they heard Spencer's voice. It sounded far away. "I always thought Swedesford Road was so pretty," she said. "So many trees, especially in this secluded part of town."

Aria and Emily exchanged a confused glance. And then, Aria understood—she'd seen this once in a TV show she'd watched with her brother. Mona *must* have figured it out—and Spencer must have managed to secretly call Wilden to give him clues about where Mona was taking her.

"So . . . why are we turning down Brainard Road?" Spencer asked very loudly and brightly. "This isn't the way to the police station."

"*Duh*, Spencer," they heard Mona say back.

Wilden flipped open his pad and wrote down *Brainard Road*. A few other cops had gathered around them. Emily quietly explained what was going on, and one of the cops brought out a large, foldout map of Rosewood, highlighting the intersection of Swedesford and Brainard with a yellow marker.

"Are we going to the stream?" Spencer's voice rang out again.

"Maybe," Mona singsonged.

Aria's eyes widened. The Morrell Stream was more of a gushing river.

"I just love the stream," Spencer said loudly.

Then there was a gasp and a shriek. They heard a few bumping noises, a squeal of tires, the dissonant tone of a bunch of phone buttons being pressed at once . . . and then nothing. Wilden's cell phone screen blinked. *Call Lost.*

Aria sneaked a look at the others. Hanna had her head buried in her hands. Emily looked like she was going to faint. Wilden stood up, put his phone back in its holster, and pulled his car keys out of his pocket. "We'll try all the stream entrances in that area." He pointed to a big burly cop sitting behind a desk. "See if you can do a GPS trace on this phone call." Then he turned and headed for his car.

"Wait," Aria said, running after him. Wilden turned. "We're coming."

Wilden's shoulders dropped. "This isn't—"

"We're *coming*," Hanna said behind Aria, her voice strong and steely.

Wilden raised one shoulder and sighed. He gestured to the back of the squad car. "Fine. Get in."

36

AN OFFER SPENCER CAN'T REFUSE

Mona grabbed Spencer's phone out of her hands, hit END, and tossed it out the window, all without changing the Hummer's speed. She then made an abrupt U-turn, back-tracked down bumpy, narrow Brainard Road, and got on the highway heading south. They drove for about five miles and got off the exit near the Bill Beach burn clinic. More horse farms and housing developments flew past, and the road devolved into woods. It wasn't until they swept by the old, dilapidated Quaker church that Spencer realized where they were really going—the Floating Man Quarry.

Spencer used to play in the big lake at the base of Floating Man Quarry. Kids used to cliff-dive off the upper rocks, but last year, during a drought-filled sum-mer, a public-school boy had dived off the rocks and died, making Floating Man's name seem eerie and prophetic. These days, there were rumors that the boy's ghost lived at the quarry's perimeter, guarding the lake. Spencer had even heard whispers that the Rosewood Stalker had his lair here. She glanced at Mona, feeling a shiver run up her spine. She had a feeling the Rosewood Stalker was driving this Hummer.

Spencer had her fingernails pressed so deeply into the center armrest that she was certain they would leave permanent marks. Calling Wilden and giving her location had been her only plan, and now she was completely trapped.

Mona glanced at Spencer out of the corner of her eye. "So, I guess Hanna remembered, huh?"

Spencer's nod was barely perceptible.

"She shouldn't have remembered," Mona chanted. "She knew remembering would put all of you in danger. Just like Aria shouldn't have told the cops. I sent her to Hooters as a test to see if she'd really listen to my warnings—the Hooters is so close to the police station, after all. The cops are always there—so it would be tempting to tell them everything. And obviously, she did." Mona threw her hands up in the air. "Why do you girls continue to do such stupid things?"

Spencer shut her eyes, wishing she could just pass out from fear.

Mona sighed dramatically. "Then again, you've been doing stupid things for years, haven't you? Starting with good old Jenna Cavanaugh." She winked.

Spencer's mouth dropped open. Mona . . . *knew?*

Of course she knew. She was A.

Mona stole a quick glance at Spencer's horrified face and made a faux-surprised face in return. Then Mona pulled down the side zipper of her halter dress, revealing a black silky bra and a good portion of her stomach. There was a huge, wrinkled laceration circling the bottom of her rib cage. Spencer stared at it for a few seconds until she had to look away.

"I was there the night you hurt Jenna," Mona whispered, her voice rough-edged. "Jenna and I were friends, which you might have known if you hadn't been so effing self-absorbed. I went over to Jenna's to surprise her that night. I saw Ali . . . I saw everything . . . and I even got a little souvenir from it." She stroked her burn scars. "I tried to tell people it was Ali, but no one believed me. Toby took the blame so fast, my parents thought I was blaming Ali because I was *jealous* of her." Mona shook her head, her blond hair swinging back and forth. As soon as she finished her cigarette and tossed it out the window, she lit another one, sucking hard on the filter. "I even tried to talk to Jenna about it, but Jenna refused to listen. She kept saying, 'You're wrong. It was my stepbrother.'" Mona mimicked Jenna's voice at a higher octave.

"Jenna and I weren't friends after that," Mona went on. "But every time I'm in front of my mirror at home and look at my otherwise perfect self, I'm reminded of what you bitches did. I know what I saw. And I. Will. Never. Forget."

Her mouth dripped into an eerie smile. "This summer, I found a way to get you bitches back. I found Ali's diary among all that crap the new people were throwing away. I knew it was Ali's instantly—and she wrote tons of secrets about all of *you*. Really damaging ones, actually. It's like she wanted the diary to fall into enemy hands."

A flash came to Spencer—the day before Ali went missing, discovering Ali in her bedroom, hungrily reading a notebook, an amused, greedy smile on her face. "Why didn't the cops find her diary when she went missing?" she sputtered.

Mona pulled the car under a thicket of trees and stopped. There was only darkness ahead of them, but Spencer could hear rushing water and smell moss and wet grass.

"Who the hell knows? But I'm glad they didn't and I did." Mona rezipped her dress, then turned to face Spencer, her eyes bright. "Ali wrote down every horrible thing you guys did. How you guys tortured Jenna Cavanaugh, that Emily kissed her in her tree house, that *you*, Spencer, kissed your sister's boyfriend. It made it so easy for me to just . . . I don't know, *become* her. All it took was for me to get a second phone with a blocked number. And I really had you going that it was Ali contacting you at first, didn't I?" Mona grabbed Spencer's hand and laughed.

Spencer recoiled from her touch. "I can't believe it was you the whole time."

"I know, right? It must have been so annoying not knowing!" Mona clapped happily. "It was *so fun* watching you guys go crazy . . . and then Ali's body showed up and you *really* went crazy. Sending *myself* notes, though, was pure brilliance. . . ." She reached around and patted her left shoulder blade. "I had to do a lot of running around, anticipating your moves before even *you* knew what they'd be. But the whole thing was so elegantly done, almost like a couture dress, don't you think?"

Mona's eyes canvassed Spencer for a reaction. Then, slowly, she reached out and punched Spencer jokily on the arm. "You look so freaked right now. Like I'm going to hurt you or something. It doesn't have to be this way, though."

"Be . . . what way?" Spencer whispered.

"I mean, at first, I hated you, Spencer. You most of all. You were always closest to Ali, and you had *everything*." Mona lit another cigarette. "But then . . . we became friends. It was so fun, planning Hanna's party, spending time together. Didn't you have fun flashing those boys? Wasn't it nice, *really talking*? So I thought . . . maybe I could be a philanthropist. Like Angelina Jolie."

Spencer blinked, dumbstruck.

"I decided to help you," Mona explained. "The Golden Orchid thing—that was a fluke. But this—I honestly want to make your life better, Spencer. Because I truly, honestly *care* about you."

Spencer knitted her brow. "W-what are you talking about?"

"Melissa, silly!" Mona exclaimed. "Setting her up as the killer. It's so *perfect*. Isn't it what you always wanted? Your sister in jail for murder and out of your life, for good. You'll look so perfect in comparison!"

Spencer stared at her. "But . . . Melissa had a motive."

"Did she?" Mona grinned. "Or is that just what you want to believe?"

Spencer opened her mouth, but no sound came out. Mona had sent the text that said, *Ali's murderer is right in front of you*. And the IM that said, *She did it, you know*. Mona had planted the photo in Spencer's purse.

Mona gave Spencer a devious look. "We can turn this around. We can go back to the police station and tell Hanna it's a huge misunderstanding–that she's not remembering things properly. We can pin A on someone else, someone you don't like. How about Andrew Campbell? You've always hated him, haven't you?"

"I . . ." Spencer sputtered.

"We can put your sister in jail," Mona whispered. "And we can *both* be A. We can control everyone. You're just as conniving as Ali was, Spence. And you're prettier, smarter, and richer. *You* should've been the leader of the group, not her. I'm giving you the chance, now, to be the leader you're meant to be. Your life at home would be perfect. Your life at school would be perfect." Her lips spread into a smile. "And I know how badly you want to be perfect."

"But you hurt my friends," Spencer whispered.

"Are you sure they're your friends?" Mona's eyes glittered. "You know who I set up as the killer before Melissa? *You*, Spencer. I fed your good friend Aria all kinds of clues that *you* did it—I heard you fighting with Ali that night she went missing, over your wall. And Aria, your BFF? She totally bought it. She was all ready to turn you in."

"Aria wouldn't do that," Spencer shrieked.

"No?" Mona raised an eyebrow. "Then why did I hear her telling Wilden exactly that in the hospital on Sunday morning, the day after Hanna's accident?" She put *accident* in air quotes. "She wasted no time, Spence. Lucky for you, Wilden didn't buy it. Now, why would you call someone who did *that* to you your friend?"

Spencer took a few deep breaths, not knowing what to believe. A thought spiraled into her head. "Wait . . . if Melissa didn't kill Ali, then *you* did."

Mona leaned back in her seat, the leather crinkling underneath her. "No." She shook her head. "I do know who *did*, though. Ali wrote about it on the last page of her diary—poor widdle girl, the last thing she ever wrote before she died." Mona stuck out her lip in a pout. "She said, *Ian and I are having a supersecret meeting tonight.*" Mona did a fake Ali voice, too, but the voice sounded more like a diabolical doll in a horror movie. *"And I gave him an ultimatum. I told him that he better break up with Melissa before she goes to Prague—or I'd tell her and everyone else about us."* Mona sighed, sounding bored. "It's pretty obvious what happened—she pushed Ian to his breaking point. And he killed her."

The wind picked up the edges of Mona's hair. "I modeled myself after Ali—she was *the* perfect bitch. No one was safe from her blackmail. And if you want, no one will be safe from yours, either."

Spencer shook her head slowly. "But . . . but you hit Hanna with your car."

Mona shrugged. "Had to do it. She knew too much."

"I'm . . . I'm sorry," Spencer whispered. "There's no way I want to . . . to *be* A with you. To rule the school with you. Or whatever it is you're offering. That's nuts."

Mona's disappointed expression morphed into something darker. She knitted her eyebrows together. "Fine. Have it your way, then."

Mona's voice felt like a knife cutting into Spencer's skin. The crickets chirped hysterically. The rushing water beneath sounded like blood gushing through a vein. In one swift movement, Mona burst forward and wrapped her hands around Spencer's neck. Spencer screamed and jerked back, flailing to hit the UNLOCK button again. She kicked Mona's chest. As Mona squealed and recoiled, Spencer yanked at the door handle and shoved it open, tumbling out of the car to the spiny grass. Immediately, she pushed herself up and sprinted into the darkness. She felt the grass under her feet, then gravel, then dirt, then mud. The noise of the water grew louder and louder. Spencer could tell she was nearing the quarry's rocky edge.

Mona's footsteps rang out behind her, and Spencer felt Mona's arms wrap around her waist. She fell heavily to the ground. Mona climbed on top of her and wrapped her hands around her neck. Spencer kicked and struggled and choked. Mona giggled, as if this were all a game.

"I thought we were friends, Spencer." Mona grimaced, trying to keep Spencer still.

Spencer struggled to breathe. "I guess not!" she screamed. Using all her might, Spencer pressed her legs onto Mona's body, throwing her backward. Mona landed on her butt a few feet away, her bright yellow gum spewing out of her mouth. Spencer scrambled quickly to her feet. Mona got up, too, her eyes flashing and her teeth clenched. Time seemed to spread out as Mona advanced on her, her mouth a triangle of fury. Spencer shut her eyes and just . . . reacted. She grabbed Mona around her legs. Mona's feet went out from under her, and she started to fall. Spencer felt her arms pressing against Mona's stomach, pushing as hard as she could. She saw the whites of Mona's eyes as they widened, and heard Mona's screams in her ears. Mona fell backward, and in a blink, she disappeared.

Spencer didn't realize it at first, but she was falling, too. Then she hit the ground. She heard a scream echo through the gulch, and thought for a moment that it was her own. Her head hit the ground with a crack . . . and her eyes fluttered shut.

37

SEEING IS BELIEVING

Hanna crammed into the back of Wilden's squad car next to Aria and Emily. It was where criminals—not that Rosewood had many—typically sat. Even though she could barely see Wilden through the metal grates connected to the front seat, she could tell by his tone of CB radio voice that he was as worried and tense as she was.

"Has anyone found anything yet?" he said into the walkie-talkie. They were idling at a stop sign as Wilden decided which way to go next. They had just driven around the main mouth of Morrell Stream, but they'd only found a couple of public-school kids lying on the grass getting stoned. There weren't signs of Mona's Hummer anywhere.

"Nothing," said the voice on the CB radio.

Aria grabbed Hanna's hand and squeezed hard. Emily quietly sobbed into her collar. "Maybe she meant another stream," Hanna volunteered. "Maybe she meant the stream at the Marwyn Trail." And while she was at it, maybe Spencer and Mona were just hanging out and talking. Maybe Hanna had it wrong, maybe Mona wasn't A.

Another voice crackled through the CB radio. "We got a call about a disturbance at Floating Man Quarry."

Hanna dug her nails into Aria's hand. Emily gasped. "On it," Wilden said.

"Floating Man . . . Quarry?" Hanna repeated. But Floating Man was a happy place—not long after their makeovers, Hanna and Mona had met boys from Drury Academy there. They'd performed a swimsuit fashion show for them along the rocks, reasoning that it was much more alluring to *tease* a boy than to actually make out with him. Right after that, they'd painted *HM + MV= BBBBBFF* on the roof of Mona's garage, swearing they would be close forever.

So was that all a lie? Had Mona planned this from the beginning? Had Mona been waiting for the day she could hit Hanna with her car? Hanna felt an overwhelming urge to ask Wilden to pull over so she could throw up.

When they arrived at the Floating Man Quarry's entrance, Mona's bright yellow Hummer glowed like the beacon on top of a lighthouse. Hanna grabbed the door handle, even though the car was still moving. The door lurched open, and she tumbled out. Hanna started running toward the Hummer, her ankles twisting on the uneven gravel.

"Hanna, no!" Wilden cried. "It's not safe!"

Hanna heard Wilden stop his car, then more doors slammed. Leaves crunched behind her. As she reached the car, she noticed someone curled up in a ball near the front left tire. Hanna saw a flash of blond hair, and her heart lifted. *Mona.*

Only, it was Spencer. Dirt and tears streaked her face and hands, and there were gashes up and down her arms. Her silky dress was torn and she wasn't wearing any shoes. "Hanna!" Spencer cried raggedly, reaching out for her.

"Are you okay?" Hanna gasped, crouching down and touching Spencer's shoulder. She felt cold and wet.

Spencer could barely get the words out, she was sobbing so hard. "I'm so sorry, Hanna. I'm so sorry."

"Why?" Hanna asked, clutching Spencer's hands.

"Because . . ." Spencer gestured to the edge of the quarry. "I think she fell."

Almost instantly, an ambulance screamed behind them, followed by another police car. The rescue team and more cops surrounded Spencer.

Hanna backed away numbly as the paramedics began to ask Spencer if she could move everything, what hurt, and what happened. "Mona was threatening me," Spencer said over and over. "She was strangling me. I tried to run away from her, but we fought. And then she . . ." She gestured again toward the quarry's edge.

Mona was threatening me. Hanna's knees buckled. This was *real.*

The cops had fanned out around the quarry with Ger-man shepherds, flashlights, and guns. Within minutes, one of them yelled, "We got something!"

Hanna leaped to her feet and sprinted over to the cop. Wilden, who was closer, caught her from behind. "Hanna," he said into her ear. "No. You shouldn't."

"But I have to see!" Hanna screamed.

Wilden wrapped his arms around her. "Just stay here, okay? Just stay with me."

Hanna watched as a team of cops disappeared over the lip of the quarry, down toward the rushing water. "We need a stretcher!" one of them screamed. More EMS workers emerged with supplies. Wilden kept petting Han-na's hair, using part of his body to shield her from what was happening. But Hanna could *hear* it. She heard them saying that Mona was caught between two rocks. And that it looked like Mona's neck was broken. And that they needed to be very, very careful pulling her out. She heard their grunts of encouragement as they lifted Mona to the surface, loaded her onto a stretcher, and tucked her into the ambulance. As they passed, Hanna saw a shock of Mona's white-blond hair. She twisted free of Wilden and started to run.

"Hanna!" Wilden screamed. "No!"

But Hanna didn't run toward the ambulance. She ran to the other side of Mona's Hummer, crouched down, and threw up. She wiped her palms on the grass and curled up into a tiny ball. The ambulance doors shut and the engine roared, but they didn't turn on the siren. Hanna wondered if that was because Mona was already dead.

She sobbed until it felt like there were no more tears left in her body. Drained, she rolled over on her back. Something hard and square pressed into her thigh. Hanna sat up and wrapped her hands around it. It was a tan suede phone case, one Hanna didn't recognize. She brought it to her face and breathed in. It smelled like Jean Patou Joy, which had been Mona's favorite perfume for years.

Only, the phone nestled inside wasn't the Chanel limited edition Sidekick Mona had begged her father to bring back from Japan, nor did it have *MV* embossed in Swarovski crystals on the back. This phone was a plain and generic BlackBerry, giving nothing away.

Hanna's heart sank, realizing what this second phone signified. All she needed to do to prove to herself that Mona had really done this to them was turn the phone on and look. The scent of the quarry's raspberry bushes drifted past her nose, and she suddenly felt like she was back three years ago, she in her Missoni string bikini and Mona in her one-piece Calvin tank. They had made their fashion show a game—if the Drury boys looked only mildly amused, they lost. If the boys salivated like starved dogs, they would buy each other a spa treatment. Afterward, Hanna chose the jasmine seaweed scrub, and Mona had a jasmine, carrot, and sesame body buff.

Hanna heard footsteps approaching behind her. She

touched her thumb to the BlackBerry's blank, innocent screen, then dropped it into her silk purse, stumbling to find the others. People were talking all around her, but all she could hear was a voice in her head screaming, "Mona's dead."

38

THE FINAL PIECE

Spencer limped to the back of the squad car with Aria and Wilden's help. They asked her again and again if she needed an ambulance. Spencer said she was pretty sure she didn't—nothing felt broken, and luckily, she'd fallen on the grass, knocking herself out for a moment, but not damaging anything. She dangled her legs out the squad car's back door and Wilden crouched in front of her, holding a notepad and a tape recorder. "Are you sure you want to do this right now?"

Spencer nodded forcefully.

Emily, Aria, and Hanna gathered behind Wilden as he pressed the RECORD button. The headlights of another squad car made a halo around him, backlighting his body in red. It reminded Spencer of the way bonfires used to silhouette her friends' bodies at summer camp. If only she were really at summer camp, right now.

Wilden took a deep breath. "So. You're *sure* she told you Ian Thomas killed Ali."

Spencer nodded. "Ali had given him an ultimatum the night she went missing. She wanted them to meet . . . and she said that if Ian didn't break up with Melissa by the time she went to Prague, Ali would tell everyone what was going on." She pushed her greasy, mud-caked hair off her face. "It's written in Ali's diary. Mona has it. I don't know where, but—"

"We're going to search Mona's house," Wilden interrupted, placing a hand on Spencer's knee. "Don't worry." He turned away and spoke into his walkie-talkie, radioing other cops to locate Ian to bring him in for questioning. Spencer listened, staring numbly at the dirt caked under her fingernails.

Her friends stood around for a long time, stunned. "God," Emily whispered. "Ian *Thomas*? That just sounds . . . crazy. But I guess it makes sense. He was so much older, and if she ever told anyone, well . . ."

Spencer pulled her arms around herself, feeling goose bumps rising on her skin. To her, Ian *didn't* make sense. Spencer believed that Ali had threatened him, and she believed that Ian might've gotten angry, but angry enough to *kill* her? It was eerie, too, that in all the time Spencer had spent with him, she hadn't suspected Ian one bit. He hadn't seemed nervous or remorseful or pensive whenever Ali's murder came up.

But perhaps she'd misinterpreted the signs—she'd

missed plenty of others. She'd gotten into the car with Mona, after all. Who knew what else was right in front of her face that she didn't see?

A beep came over Wilden's walkie-talkie. "The suspect isn't at his residence," a female cop's voice called. "What do you want us to do?"

"Shit." Wilden looked at Spencer. "Can you think where else Ian might be?"

Spencer shook her head, her brain feeling like it was plodding through a swamp. Wilden threw himself in the front seat. "I'll drive you home," he said. "Your parents are on their way home from the country club, too."

"We want to go to Spencer's with you." Aria indicated for Spencer to move over, then she, Hanna, and Emily all crammed into the backseat. "We don't want to leave her alone."

"You guys, you don't have to," Spencer said softly. "And anyway, Aria, your car." She motioned to Aria's Subaru, which looked like it was sinking into the mud.

"I can leave it overnight." Aria smirked. "Maybe I'll get lucky and someone will steal it."

Spencer folded her hands in her lap, too weak to protest. The car was silent as Wilden rolled past the Floating Man Quarry sign, then along the narrow trail that led to the main road. It was hard to believe that just an hour and a half had passed since Spencer left the party. Things were so different now.

"Mona was there the night we hurt Jenna," Spencer

mumbled absently.

Aria nodded. "It's a long story, but I actually talked to Jenna tonight. Jenna knows what we did. Only, get this—she and Ali set it up together."

Spencer sat up straighter. For a moment, she couldn't breathe. "*What? Why?*"

"She said that she and Ali both had sibling issues or something," Aria explained, not sounding very confident in the answer.

"I just don't understand that," Emily whispered. "I saw Jason DiLaurentis on the news the other day. He said he doesn't even speak to his parents anymore, and that his family was really messed up. Why would he say that?"

"There's a lot you can't tell about people, looking in from the outside," Hanna murmured tearfully.

Spencer covered her face with her hands. There was so much she didn't understand, so much that didn't make sense. She knew that things should at least feel resolved now—A was really gone, Ali's killer would soon be apprehended—but she felt more lost than ever. She took her hands away, staring at the sliver of moon in the sky. "You guys," Spencer broke the silence, "there's something I need to tell you."

"Something *else*?" Hanna wailed.

"Something . . . about the night Ali went missing." Spencer slid her silver charm bracelet up and down her arm, keeping her voice to a whisper. "You know how I ran out of the barn after Ali? And how I said I didn't see

where she was going? Well . . . I did see. She went right
down the path. I went up to her and . . . and we fought. It
was about Ian. I . . . I'd kissed Ian not long before, and Ali
had told me that he only kissed me because *she* told him
to. And she said that she and Ian were really in love, and
she teased me for caring."

Spencer felt her friends' eyes on her. She gathered up
strength to go on.

"I got so mad . . . I shoved her. She fell against the
rocks. There was this awful *crack* noise." A tear wobbled
out of the corner of her eye and spilled down her cheek.
She hung her head. "I'm sorry, guys. I should've told you.
I just . . . I didn't remember. And then when I did, I was
so scared."

When she looked up, her friends were aghast. Even
Wilden's head tilted toward the back, as if he were trying to listen. If they wanted to, they could throw the
Ian theory out the window. They could make Wilden
stop the car and make Spencer repeat exactly what
she'd said. Things could go in a horrible direction
from here.

Emily was the first to take Spencer's hand. Then Hanna
placed hers on top of Emily's, and then Aria laid hers on top
of Hanna's. It reminded Spencer of when they used to all
touch the photo of the five of them that hung in Ali's foyer.
"We know it wasn't you," Emily whispered.

"It was Ian. It all makes sense," Aria said forcefully,
gazing into Spencer's eyes. It seemed like she believed

Spencer wholly and completely.

They reached Spencer's street, and Wilden pulled into her family's long, circular driveway. Spencer's parents weren't home yet, and the house was dark. "Do you want me to stay with you guys until your folks get home?" Wilden asked as the girls got out.

"It's okay." Spencer glanced around at the others, suddenly relieved that they were here.

Wilden backed out of the driveway and turned slowly around the cul-de-sac, first passing the DiLaurentises' old house, then the Cavanaughs', and then the Vanderwaals', the big monstrosity with the detached garage down the street. There was no one home at Mona's, obviously. Spencer shuddered.

A flash of light in the backyard caught her eye. Spencer cocked her head, her heart speeding up. She walked down the stone path that led to her backyard and curled her hands along the stone wall surrounding their property. There, past the deck, the rock-lined pool, the burbling hot tub, the expansive yard, and even the renovated barn, at the very back of the property near where Ali had fallen, Spencer saw two figures, lit only by moonlight. They reminded her of something.

The wind picked up, tiptoeing up and down Spencer's back. Even though it wasn't the right season, the air briefly smelled like honeysuckle, just as it had that horrible night four and a half years ago. All at once, her memory broke free. She saw Ali fall backward into the stone wall. A *crack* rang out through the air, as loud as church bells. When Spencer heard the girlish gasp in her ear, she turned. No one was behind her. No one was anywhere. And when she turned back, Ali was still slumped against the stone wall, but her eyes were open. And then, Ali grunted and pushed herself to her feet.

She was fine.

Ali glared at Spencer, about to speak, but something down the path distracted her. She took off fast, disappearing into a thicket of trees. In seconds, Spencer heard Ali's signature giggle. There was rustling, and then two distinct shapes. One was Ali's. Spencer couldn't tell who the other person was, but it didn't look like Melissa. It was hard to believe that, only moments after this, Ian would push Ali into the DiLaurentises' half-dug gazebo hole. Ali might've been a bitch, but she didn't deserve anything like that.

"Spencer?" Hanna said softly, her voice sounding far away. "What's wrong?"

Spencer opened her eyes and shuddered. "I didn't do it," she whispered.

The figures near the barn stepped into the light. Melissa's posture was stiff and Ian's fists clenched. The wind carried their voices to the front yard, and it sounded like they were fighting.

Spencer's nerves felt ignited. She wheeled around and looked down her street. Wilden's car was gone. Frantically, she fumbled in her pocket for her phone, but remembered—Mona had thrown it out the window.

"I got it," Hanna said, pulling out her own BlackBerry and dialing a number. She handed the phone to Spencer. *Calling WILDEN,* the screen said.

Spencer had to hold the phone with two hands, her fingers were trembling so badly. Wilden answered after two rings. "Hanna?" He sounded confused. "What is it?"

"It's Spencer," Spencer bleated. "You have to turn around. Ian's here."

39

THE ALL-NEW MONTGOMERYS,
DISTURBING AS EVER

The following afternoon, Aria sat on Meredith's living room futon, absently flicking the William Shakespeare bobblehead Ezra had given her. Byron and Meredith sat next to her, and they were all staring at Meredith's television. There was a press conference about Ali's murder on TV. *Ian Thomas arrested*, said a big banner at the bottom of the screen.

"Mr. Thomas's arraignment is set for Tuesday," a newscaster said, standing in front of the grand stone steps of the Rosewood County Courthouse. "No one in this community ever expected that a quiet, polite boy like Ian Thomas could be behind this."

Aria pulled her knees into her chest. The cops had gone to the Vanderwaal residence this morning and had found Ali's diary underneath Mona's bed. Mona had been telling Spencer the truth about the last entry—it was about how

Ali had given Ian an ultimatum that he either break up with Melissa Hastings or she would tell the world about them. The news showed the police leading Ian to the station in handcuffs. When asked to make a statement, all Ian said was "I'm innocent. This is a mistake."

Byron scoffed in disbelief. He reached over and grabbed Aria's hand. Then, predictably, the news flashed to the next story—Mona's death. The screen showed the string of yellow police tape around the Floating Man Quarry, then a shot of the Vanderwaal house. A random BlackBerry phone icon appeared in the corner. "Miss Vanderwaal had been stalking four Rosewood Day girls for over a month now, and the threats had turned deadly," the newscaster said. "There was a scuffle between Miss Vanderwaal and an unnamed minor last night at the edge of the quarry, which is notoriously dangerous. Miss Vanderwaal slipped off the edge, breaking her neck in the fall. Police found Miss Vanderwaal's personal BlackBerry in her purse at the bottom of the Quarry, but they're still looking for a second phone—the one she used to send most of the troubling messages."

Aria gave Shakespeare's head another bobble. Her head felt like an overstuffed suitcase. Too much had happened in the last day for her to process things. And her emotions were all mixed up. She felt terrible that Mona had died. She felt freaked out and weirdly wounded that Jenna's accident hadn't really been an accident—that Jenna and Ali had set it up all along. And after all this time, the killer was Ian. . . . The newscaster made a sympathetic, relieved face and said, "Finally, the whole community of Rosewood can put this horrible story behind them"– something everyone had been saying all morning. Aria burst into tears. She didn't feel resolved at all.

Byron looked over at her. "What is it?"

Aria shook her head, unable to explain. She cupped the bobblehead in her hands, letting the tears drip on top of Shakespeare's plastic head.

Byron let out a frustrated sigh. "I realize this is overwhelming. You had a stalker. And you never talked about it to us. You *should* have. We should talk about it now."

"I'm sorry." Aria shook her head. "I can't."

"But we *need* to," Byron urged. "It's important you get this out."

"Byron!" Meredith hissed sharply. "Jesus!"

"What?" Byron asked, raising his arms in surrender.

Meredith jumped up, placing herself between Aria and her father. "You and your discussions," Meredith scolded. "Hasn't Aria been through enough these last few weeks? Just give her some space!"

Byron shrugged, looking cowed. Aria's mouth fell open. She met Meredith's eyes, and Meredith smiled. There was an understanding glimmer in her eye that seemed to say, *I get what you're going through. And I know it's not easy.* Aria stared at the pink spiderweb tattoo on Meredith's wrist. She thought about how eager she had been to find out something damaging about Meredith, and here Meredith was, sticking up for her.

Byron's cell phone vibrated, scooting across the scuffed coffee table. He stared at the screen, frowning, then picked it up. "Ella?" His voice cracked.

Aria tensed. Byron's eyebrows knitted together. "Yes . . . she's here." He passed the phone to Aria. "Your mother wants to talk to you."

Meredith cleared her throat awkwardly, standing up and drifting toward the bathroom. Aria stared at the phone as if it were a piece of putrefied shark, which some- one in Iceland had once dared her to eat. After all, the Vikings used to eat it. She put the phone tentatively to her ear. "Ella?"

"Aria, are you all right?" Ella's voice cried from the other end.

"I'm . . . fine," Aria said. "I don't know. I guess. I'm not hurt or anything."

There was a long silence. Aria pulled out her father's little antenna and pushed it back in again.

"I'm so sorry, honey," Ella gushed. "I had no idea you were going through this. Why didn't you tell us someone was threatening you?"

"Because . . ." Aria wandered into her tiny bedroom off Meredith's studio and picked up Pigtunia, her pig pup- pet. Explaining A to Mike had been hard. But now that it was over, and Aria didn't have to worry about A's retalia- tion, she realized the real reason didn't matter. "Because you guys were caught up in your own stuff." She sank onto her lumpy twin bed, and the bedsprings let out a mooing groan. "But . . . *I'm* sorry, Ella. For everything. It was terrible of me not to say anything about Byron for all that time."

Ella paused. Aria snapped on the tiny TV that sat in the windowsill. The same press conference images emerged on the screen. "I get why you didn't," Ella finally said. "I should've understood that. I was just angry, that's all." She sighed. "My relationship with your dad hadn't been good for a long time. Iceland stalled the inevitable—we both knew this was coming."

"Okay," Aria said softly, running her hands up and down Pigtunia's pink fur.

Ella sighed. "I'm sorry, sweetie, and I miss you."

An enormous, egg-shaped lump formed in Aria's throat. She stared up at the cockroaches Meredith had painted on the ceiling. "I miss you too."

"Your room is here if you want it," her mother said.

Aria hugged Pigtunia to her chest. "Thanks," she whispered, and clapped the phone shut. How long had she been waiting to hear that? What a relief it would be to sleep in her own bed again, with its normal mattress and soft, downy pillows. To be among all her knitting projects and books and her brother and Ella. But what about Byron? Aria listened to him coughing in the other room. "Do you need a Kleenex?" Meredith called from the bathroom, sounding concerned. She thought about the card Meredith had made for Byron and pinned up on the fridge. It was a cartoon elephant saying, *Just stamping by to say I hope you have a great day!* It seemed the kind of thing that Byron—or Aria—would do.

Maybe Aria had been overreacting. Maybe Aria could convince Byron to buy a comfier bed for this little room. Maybe she could sleep here every once in a while.

Maybe.

Aria glanced at the TV screen. The press conference on Ian had just ended, and everyone stood to leave. As the camera swung wide, Aria noticed a blond girl with a familiar heart-shaped face. *Ali?* Aria sat up. She rubbed her eyes until they hurt. The camera panned over the crowd again, and she realized the blond woman was at least thirty. Aria was obviously hallucinating from lack of sleep.

She wandered back into the living room, Pigtunia still in her hand. Byron opened his arms and Aria slid into them. Her dad patted Pigtunia absentmindedly on the head as they sat there, watching the press conference aftermath on TV.

Meredith emerged from the bathroom, her face a bit green. Byron slid his arm from Aria's shoulders. "You still feeling sick?"

Meredith nodded. "I am." There was an anxious look on her face, as if she had a secret she needed to spill. She raised her eyes to both of them, the corners of her lips spreading into a tiny smile. "But it's okay. Because . . . I'm pregnant."

40

ALL THAT GLITTERS IS NOT A GOLDEN ORCHID

Later that evening, after the police had finished raiding the Vanderwaal mansion, Wilden arrived at the Hastingses' house to ask Melissa a few final questions. He was sitting on their leather living room couch now, his eyes puffy and tired. Everyone looked tired, actually—except for Spencer's mother, who wore a crisp Marc Jacobs shirtdress. She and Spencer's father were standing on the far side of the room, as if their daughters were covered in bacteria.

Melissa's voice was monotone. "I didn't tell you the truth about that night," she admitted. "Ian and I had been drinking, and I fell asleep. When I woke up, he wasn't there. Then I fell asleep again and he was there when I woke."

"Why didn't you say anything about this before?" Spencer's father demanded.

Melissa shook her head. "I went to Prague that next

morning. At that point, I'm not sure anyone really knew Alison was missing. When I got back and everyone was frantic . . . well, I just never thought Ian would be capable of something like that." She picked at the hem on her pale yellow Juicy hoodie. "I suspected they'd hooked up all those years ago, but I didn't think it was serious. I didn't think Alison had given him an *ultimatum*." Like everyone else, Melissa had learned of Ian's motives. "I mean, she was in *seventh grade*."

Melissa glanced at Wilden. "When you started asking questions this week about where Ian and I were, I started to wonder if maybe I should've said something years ago. But I still didn't think it was possible. And I didn't say anything then because . . . because I thought I'd somehow get in trouble for concealing the truth. And, I mean, I couldn't have that. What would people think of me?"

Her sister's face crumpled. Spencer tried hard not to gape. She'd seen her sister cry plenty of times, but usually out of frustration, anger, rage, or a ploy to get her own way. Never out of fear or shame.

Spencer waited for her parents to rush over to console Melissa. But they sat stock-still, judgmental looks on their faces. She wondered if she and Melissa had been dealing with the exact same issues all this time. Melissa had made impressing their parents look so effortless that Spencer never realized that she agonized about it, too.

Spencer plopped down at her sister's side and threw her arms around Melissa's shoulders. "It's okay," she whispered in her ear. Melissa raised her head for a moment, noted Spencer confusedly, then set her head on Spencer's shoulder and sobbed.

Wilden handed Melissa a tissue and stood up, thanking them for their cooperation throughout this ordeal. As he was leaving, the house phone rang. Mrs. Hastings walked primly to the phone in the den and answered. Within seconds, she poked her head into the living room. "Spencer," she whispered, her face still sober but her eyes bright with excitement. "It's for you. It's Mr. Edwards."

A hot, sick feeling washed over Spencer. Mr. Edwards was the head of the Golden Orchid committee. A personal phone call from him could mean only one thing.

Spencer licked her lips, then stood. The other side of the room, where her mom was standing, seemed a mile away. She wondered what her mom's secret phone calls were about—what big gift she'd bought for Spencer because she'd been so certain Spencer would win the Golden Orchid. Even if it was the most wonderful thing in the world, Spencer wasn't sure she'd be able to enjoy it.

"Mom?" Spencer approached her mother and leaned against the antique Chippendale desk next to the phone. "Don't you think it's wrong that I cheated?"

Mrs. Hastings quickly covered the phone's mouthpiece. "Well, of course. But we discussed this." She shoved the phone to Spencer's ear. "Say hello," she hissed.

Spencer swallowed hard. "Hello?" she finally croaked into the phone.

"Miss Hastings?" a man's voice chirped. "This is Mr. Edwards, the head of the Golden Orchid committee. I know it's late, but I have some very exciting news for you. It was a tough decision, given our two hundred outstanding nominees, and I am pleased to announce that . . ."

It sounded as if Mr. Edwards were talking underwater—Spencer barely heard the rest. She glanced at her sister, sitting all alone on the couch. It had taken so much courage for Melissa to admit she'd lied. She could've said she didn't remember, and no one would've been the wiser, but instead, she'd done the right thing. Spencer thought, too, of Mona's offer to her—*I know how badly you want to be perfect.* The thing was, being perfect didn't mean anything if it wasn't real.

Spencer put her mouth back up to the phone. Mr. Edwards paused, waiting for Spencer to reply. She took a deep breath, rehearsing in her head what she would say: *Mr. Edwards, I have a confession to make.*

It was a confession no one was going to like. But she could do this. She really could.

41

PRESENTING, IN HER RETURN TO ROSEWOOD, HANNA MARIN

Tuesday morning, Hanna sat on her bed, slowly stroking Dot's muzzle and staring at herself in her handheld mirror. She'd finally found the right foundation that covered her bruises and stitches and wanted to share the good news. Her first instinct, of course, was to call Mona.

She watched in the mirror as her bottom lip twitched. It still wasn't real.

She supposed she could call her old friends, whom she'd seen a lot of the last few days. They'd taken yesterday off school and hung out in Spencer's hot tub, reading *Us Weekly* articles about Justin Timberlake, who had shown up at Hanna's party *just* after she left. He and his posse had been stuck in two hours of turnpike traffic. When the girls moved on to reading beauty and style tips, Hanna was reminded of how Lucas had read her an entire issue of *Teen Vogue* while she was in the hospital. She felt a pang of sadness, wondering if Lucas knew what had happened to her in the past few days. He hadn't called her. Maybe he never wanted to speak to her again.

Hanna put down the mirror. All at once, as easily as recalling a random fact, like the name of Lindsay Lohan's lawyer or Zac Efron's latest girlfriend, Hanna suddenly saw something else from the night of her accident. After she'd ripped her dress, Lucas had appeared over her, handing her his jacket to cover herself. He'd led her to the Hollis College Reading Room and held her as she sobbed. One thing led to another . . . and they were kissing, just as greedily as they'd kissed this past week.

Hanna sat on her bed for a long time, feeling numb. Finally, she reached for her phone and dialed Lucas's number. It went straight to voice mail. "Hey," she said when it beeped. "It's Hanna. I wanted to see if . . . if we could talk. Call me."

When she hung up, Hanna patted Dot on top of his argyle-sweatered back. "Maybe I should forget him," she whispered. "There's probably a cooler boy out there for me, don't you think?" Dot cocked his head uncertainly, like he didn't believe her.

"Hanna?" Ms. Marin's voice floated upstairs. "Can you come down?"

Hanna stood, rolling back her shoulders. Perhaps it was inappropriate to wear a bright red Erin Fetherston trapeze dress to Ian's arraignment—like wearing color to a funeral—but Hanna needed a little color pick-me-up. She snapped a gold cuff bracelet on her wrist, picked up her red Longchamp hobo bag, and shook her hair down her back. In the kitchen, her father sat at the table, doing a *Philadelphia Inquirer* crossword. Her mother sat next to him, checking her e-mail on her laptop. Hanna gulped. She hadn't seen them sitting together like this since they were married.

"I thought you'd be back in Annapolis by now," she muttered.

Mr. Marin laid down his ballpoint pen, and Hanna's mother pushed her laptop aside. "Hanna, we wanted to talk to you about something important," her dad said.

Hanna's heart leaped. *They're getting back together. Kate and Isabel are gone.*

Her mother cleared her throat. "I've been offered a new job . . . and I've accepted." She tapped her long, red nails against the table. "Only . . . it's in Singapore."

"Singapore?" Hanna squawked, sinking into a chair.

"I don't expect you to come," her mother went on. "Plus, with the amount of traveling I'll have to do, I'm not sure you *should* come. So these are the options." She held out one hand. "You could go to boarding school. Even around here, if you like." Then, she held out the other hand. "Or you could move in with your father."

Mr. Marin was nervously twiddling his pen in his fingers. "Seeing you in the hospital . . . it really made me realize a few things," he said quietly. "I want to be close to you, Hanna. I need to be a bigger part of your life."

"I'm not moving to Annapolis," Hanna blurted out.

"You don't have to," her father said gently. "I can transfer to my firm's office here. Your mother has offered to let me move into this house, in fact."

Hanna gaped. This sounded like a reality TV show gone wrong. "Kate and Isabel are staying in Annapolis, right?"

Her father shook his head no. "It's a lot to think about. We'll give you some time to decide. I only want to transfer here if you'll live here too. Okay?"

Hanna looked around her sleek, modern kitchen, trying to picture her father and Isabel standing at the counter preparing dinner. Her father would sit in his old seat at the dinner table, Isabel in her mother's. Kate could have the chair that they normally piled with magazines and junk mail.

Hanna would miss her mom, but she wasn't around that much anyway. And Hanna had longed for her father to come back—only, she wasn't sure if she wanted it like *this*. If she allowed Kate to move in, it would be war. Kate was skinny and blond and beautiful. Kate would try to march into Rosewood Day and take over.

But Kate would be the new girl. And Hanna . . . Hanna would be the popular girl.

"Um, okay. I'll think about it." Hanna stood up from the table, scooped up her bag, and walked to the downstairs powder room. Truthfully, she felt kind of . . . pumped. Maybe this would be awesome. *She* had the advantage. Over the next few weeks, she would have to make sure that she was *the* most popular girl in school. With Mona gone, it would be easy.

Hanna felt around in her purse's silk-lined pocket. Inside, two BlackBerries were nestled side by side—hers and Mona's. She knew the cops were looking for Mona's second phone, but she couldn't hand it over yet. She had one thing to do first.

She took a deep breath, pulled out the phone in the tan suede holder, and pressed the ON button. The device sprang to life. There was no greeting, no personalized wallpaper. Mona had used this phone strictly for business.

Mona had saved every text message she'd sent to them, each note with a crisp, singular letter *A*. Hanna scrolled slowly through each of hers, chewing feverishly on her bottom lip. There was the first one she'd ever received, when she was at the police station for stealing the Tiffany bracelet and necklace—*Hey, Hanna, since prison food makes you fat, you know what Sean's gonna say? Not it!* And there was the last text Mona had sent from this phone, which included the chilling lines, *And Mona? She's not your friend, either. So watch your back.*

The only one of Hanna's texts that hadn't been sent from this phone was the one that said, *Don't believe everything you hear.* Mona had accidentally sent that text from her regular phone. Hanna shivered. She'd just gotten a new phone that night and hadn't programmed everyone's numbers in yet. Mona had messed up, and Hanna had recognized her number. If she hadn't, who knew how long this would have gone on.

Hanna squeezed Mona's BlackBerry, wanting to crush it flat. *Why?* she wanted to scream. She knew she should despise Mona right now—the cops had found the SUV Mona used to hit Hanna stashed in the Vanderwaals' detached garage. The car had a tarp over it, but the front fender was bashed in, and blood—Hanna's blood—was spattered on the headlights.

But Hanna couldn't hate her. She just *couldn't*. If only she could erase every good memory she had of Mona instead—their shopping sprees, their triumphant popularity coups, their Frenniversaries. Who would she consult in a wardrobe crisis? Who would she go shopping with? Who would fake-friend for her?

She pressed the bathroom's peppermint-scented guest soap to her nose, willing herself not to cry and smear all her carefully applied makeup. After she took a few cleansing, calming breaths, Hanna looked at Mona's sent-message box again. She highlighted each of the texts Mona had sent to her as A, and then hit DELETE ALL. *Are you sure you want to delete?* a screen asked. Hanna clicked YES. A garbage can lid opened and closed. If she couldn't delete their friendship, at least she could delete her secrets.

Wilden stood waiting in the foyer—he had offered to drive Hanna to the arraignment. Hanna noticed that his eyes were heavy and his mouth turned down. She wondered if he was exhausted from the weekend's activity, or if her mom had just told him about her Singapore job too. "Ready?" he asked Hanna quietly.

Hanna nodded. "But hang on." She reached into her bag and held out Mona's BlackBerry. "Present for you."

Wilden took it from her, confused. Hanna didn't bother to explain. He was a cop. He'd figure it out soon enough.

Wilden opened the squad car's passenger side and Hanna slipped in. Before they drove away, Hanna rolled back her shoulders, took a deep breath, and checked out her reflection in the visor mirror. Her dark eyes shone, her auburn hair was full of body, and the creamy foundation was still covering all of her bruises. Her face was thin, her teeth were straight, and she didn't have a single zit. The ugly, chubby seventh-grade Hanna who had haunted her reflection for weeks now was banished forever. Starting now.

She was Hanna Marin, after all. And she was fabulous.

42

DREAMS—AND NIGHTMARES— CAN COME TRUE

Tuesday morning, Emily scratched at the back of the polka-dotted cap-sleeve dress she'd borrowed from Hanna, wishing she could've just worn pants. Next to her, Hanna was all dolled up in a red retro swing dress, and Spencer wore a sleek, savvy pin-striped suit. Aria was wearing one of her usual layered getups—a short-sleeved black bubble dress over a green thermal shirt, with thick white cable-knit tights and chic ankle boots that she said she'd bought in Spain. They all stood outside in the cold morning air in an empty lot next to the courthouse, away from the media flurry on the grand front steps.

"Are we ready?" Spencer asked, gazing around at everyone.

"Ready," Emily chanted along with the others. Slowly, Spencer stretched out a large Hefty trash bag, and the girls dropped things in, one by one. Aria threw in a *Snow White* Wicked Queen doll with *X*'s over her eyes. Hanna tossed in a crumpled-up piece of paper that said, *Feel sorry for me.* Spencer threw in the photo of Ali and Ian. They took turns pitching in all the physical things A had sent them. Their first instinct had been to burn it all, but Wilden needed it as evidence.

When it was Emily's final turn, she stared down at the last thing she held in her hands. It was the letter she had written to Ali not long after she'd kissed her in the tree house, not long before she died. In it, Emily had professed her undying love for Ali, pouring out every possible shred of emotion that existed in her body. A had written over some of the words, *Thought you might want this back. Love, A.*

"I kind of want to keep this," Emily said softly, folding up the letter. The others nodded. Emily wasn't certain that they knew what it was, but she was pretty sure they had a good idea. She let out a long, tortured sigh. All this time, a little light had been burning inside of her. She had hoped that somehow, A was Ali, and that Ali somehow wasn't dead. She knew she wasn't being rational, she knew Ali's body had been found in the DiLaurentises' backyard along with her one-of-a-kind Tiffany initial ring on her finger. Emily knew she had to let Ali go . . . but as she curled her hands around her love note, she wished she didn't have to.

"We should go in." Spencer tossed the bag in her Mercedes, and Emily followed her and the others through one of the courthouse's side doors. As they entered the wood-paneled, high-ceilinged courtroom, Emily's stomach flipped. All of Rosewood was here—her peers and teachers, her swim coach, Jenna Cavanaugh and her parents, all of Ali's old hockey friends—and they were all staring. The only person Emily didn't immediately see was Maya. In fact, she hadn't heard a word from Maya since Hanna's party on Friday night.

Emily put her head down as Wilden emerged from a group of police officers and led them to an empty bench. The air was taut with tension and smelled like various expensive colognes and perfumes. After a few more minutes, the doors slammed shut. Then the room fell into dead silence as the bailiffs brought Ian down the center aisle. Emily clasped Aria's hand. Hanna put her arm around Spencer. Ian wore an orange prison jumpsuit. His hair was uncombed and there were enormous purple circles under his eyes.

Ian walked up to the bench. The judge, a stern, balding man who wore an enormous class ring, glowered at him. "Mr. Thomas, how do you wish to plead?"

"Not guilty," Ian said in a very small voice.

A murmur went through the crowd. Emily bit down on the inside of her cheek. As she shut her eyes, she saw the horrible images again—this time with a new killer, a killer that made sense: Ian. Emily remembered seeing Ian that summer when she was Spencer's guest at the Rosewood Country Club, where Ian used to lifeguard. He'd sat atop his lifeguard stand, twirling his whistle like he didn't have a care in the world.

The judge leaned over his high perch and glared at Ian. "Because of the seriousness of this crime, and because we have deemed you a flight risk, you are to remain in jail until your pretrial hearing, Mr. Thomas." He banged his gavel and then folded his hands. Ian's head slumped down, and his attorney patted him comfortingly on the shoulder. Within seconds, he was marching out again, his hands cuffed. It was all over.

The members of the Rosewood community rose to leave. Then Emily noticed a family down front that she hadn't seen earlier. The bailiffs and cameras had blocked them. She recognized Mrs. DiLaurentis's short, chic haircut and Mr. DiLaurentis's handsome, aging leading-man looks. Jason DiLaurentis stood next to them, dressed in a crisp black suit and a dark checked tie. As the family embraced, they all looked incredibly relieved . . . and maybe the slightest bit repentant, too. Emily thought about what Jason had said on the news: *I don't talk to my family much. They're too messed up.* Maybe they all felt guilty for going so long without speaking. Or maybe Emily was just imagining things.

Everyone lingered outside the courthouse. The weather was nothing like that sublime, cloudless fall day of Ali's memorial service just weeks earlier. Today, the sky was blurred with dark clouds, making the whole world dull and shadowless. Emily felt a hand on her arm. Spencer wrapped her arms around Emily's shoulders.

"It's all over," Spencer whispered.

"I know," Emily said, hugging back.

The other girls joined in on the hug. Out of the corner of her eye, Emily saw a camera flash. She could already imagine the newspaper caption: *Alison's Friends Distraught but at Peace*. At that moment, a black Lincoln idling near the curb caught her eye. A chauffeur sat in the passenger seat, waiting. The tinted back window was rolled down the tiniest crack, and Emily saw a pair of eyes staring straight at her. Emily's mouth fell open. She'd only seen blue eyes like that one other time in her life.

"Guys," she whispered, clamping down hard on Spencer's arm.

The others broke out of their hug. "What?" Spencer asked, concerned.

Emily pointed to the sedan. The back window was now closed, and the chauffeur was shifting the car into gear. "I swear I just saw . . ." she stammered, but then paused. They'd think she was crazy—fantasizing that Ali was alive was just another way to cope with her death. Emily swallowed hard, standing up straighter. "Never mind," she said.

The girls turned away, drifting back to their own families, promising to call one another later. But Emily remained where she was, her heart pounding as the sedan pulled away from the curb. She watched as it cruised down the street, turned right at the light, and disappeared. Her blood chilled. *It couldn't have been her,* she told herself.

Could it have?

WHAT HAPPENS NEXT . . .

So after big bad Mona departed this dear world and Ian was sent away to a cold prison cell, our Pretty Little Liars were finally able to live in peace. Emily found true love at Smith College; Hanna ruled as queen bee of Rosewood Day and married a billionaire; Spencer graduated first in her class at Columbia School of Journalism and went on to be managing editor of the *New York Times*; Aria got her MFA from Rhode Island School of Design and moved to Europe with Ezra. We're talking sunsets, fat babies, and blissful happiness. Nice, huh? Oh, and none of them ever told a lie again.

Are you effing kidding me? Wake up, Sleeping Beauty. There's no happily ever after in Rosewood.

I mean, have you learned *nothing*? Once a pretty little liar, *always* a pretty little liar. Emily, Hanna, Spencer, and Aria just can't *help* but be bad. That's what I love best about them. So who am I? Well, let's just say there's a new A in town, and this time our girlies aren't getting off so easily.

See ya soon. And until then, try not to be *too* good. Life's always more fun with a few pretty little secrets.

Mwah!
—A

ACKNOWLEDGMENTS

First and foremost, I want to thank those I've mentioned in the dedication—the people who encouraged Spencer to kiss her sister's boyfriends, Aria to kiss her English teacher, Emily to kiss a girl (or two), and Hanna to kiss the dorky boy in school. The people who aided and abetted in Alison's murder first laughed at the phrase "pussies who ride small, gay horses," and were excited about this project from the very beginning . . . which was, wow, three whole years ago. I'm talking, of course, about my friends at Alloy—Lanie Davis, Josh Bank, Les Morgenstein, and Sara Shandler. Being a working writer is something of an oxymoron for most, and I am immensely appreciative for all you've done for me. I'm lucky to work with all of you, and I seriously doubt these books would be half as good without your wonderfully creative minds . . . and humor . . . and, of course, baked goods. Here's to more fabulous twists and turns in the future!

I'm grateful also to all those at Harper who champion these books—Farrin Jacobs, for your careful reading, and Kristin Marang, for all your dedication, attention, and friendship. And a big thanks to Jennifer Rudolph Walsh at William Morris for your belief in this series' future. You are truly magical.

Love to the slew of people I mention in every book: Joel, my husband, for your ability to predict the future—strangely, it always involves tickling. To my father, Shep, because you like to impersonate French travel agents, because we thought you got lost in the desert this December, and because you once threatened to leave a restaurant because they had run out of red wine. To my sister, Ali, for creating the greatest team ever (Team Alison) and for taking pictures of Squee the stuffed lamb with a cigarette hanging out of his mouth. And to my mom, Mindy—I hope you never take a vaccine for silliness. Thank you so much for your support of all of my writing.

I also want to thank all of the Pretty Little Liars readers out there. I absolutely adore hearing from you guys, and I'm so glad you care as much about the characters as I do. Keep your amazing letters coming!

Finally, much love to my grandma, Gloria Shepard. I'm touched that you read the Pretty Little Liars series—and I'm so happy you think the books are funny! I'll try to include more jokes about nose hair in the future.

SARA SHEPARD is the author of two *New York Times* bestselling series, Pretty Little Liars and The Lying Game. She graduated from New York University and has an MFA from Brooklyn College. Sara's Pretty Little Liars novels were inspired by her upbringing in Philadelphia's Main Line.

FOLLOW SARA SHEPARD ON

For exclusive information
on your favorite authors and artists,
visit www.authortracker.com.

You don't have to be *good* to be perfect.

Read on for a sneak peek at Sara Shepard's next series

The Perfectionists

IN MANY WAYS, BEACON HEIGHTS, Washington, looks like any affluent suburb: Porch swings creak gently in the evening breeze, the lawns are green and well kept, and all the neighbors know one another. But this satellite of Seattle is anything but average. In Beacon, it's not enough to be good; you have to be the *best*.

With perfection comes pressure. Students here are some of the best in the country, and sometimes they have to let off a little steam. What five girls don't know, though, is that steam can scald just as badly as an open flame.

And someone's about to get burned.

On Friday night, just as the sun was setting, cars began to pull up to Nolan Hotchkiss's huge, faux-Italian villa on a peninsula overlooking Lake Washington. The house had wrought iron gates, a circular driveway with a marble fountain, multiple balconies, and a three-tiered, crystal chandelier visible through the front two-story window. All the lights were on, loud bass thumped from inside, a cheer rose up from the backyard. Kids with liquor spirited from their parents' cabinets or bottles of wine shoved into their purses sauntered up to the front steps and walked right inside. No need to ring the bell—Mr. and Mrs. Hotchkiss weren't home.

Too bad. They were missing the biggest party of the year.

Caitlin Martell-Lewis, dressed in her best pair of straight-leg jeans, a green polo that brought out the amber flecks in her eyes, and TOMS houndstooth sneakers, climbed out of an Escalade with her boyfriend, Josh Friday, and his soccer friends Asher Collins and Timothy Burgess. Josh, whose breath already smelled yeasty from the beer he'd drunk at the pregame party, shaded his brown eyes and gaped at the mansion. "This place is freaking sick."

Ursula Winters, who desperately wanted to be Timothy's girlfriend—she was also Caitlin's biggest soccer rival—stepped out of the backseat and adjusted her oversize, dolman-sleeve shirt. "The kid has it all."

"Except a soul," Caitlin muttered, limping up the lawn on her still-sore-from-a-soccer-injury ankle. Silence fell over the group as they stepped inside the grand foyer, with its checkerboard floor and a sweeping double staircase. Josh cast her a sideways glance. "What? I was kidding," Caitlin said with a laugh.

Because if you spoke out against Nolan—if you so much as boycotted his party—you'd be off the Beacon Heights High A-list. But Nolan had as many enemies as friends, and Caitlin hated him most of all. Her heart pounded, thinking about the secret thing she was about to do. She wondered whether the others were there yet.

The den was filled with candles and fat red cushions. Julie Redding held court in the middle of the room. Her auburn hair hung straight and shiny down her back. She wore a strapless Kate Spade dress and bone-colored high heels that showed off her long, lithe legs. One after another, classmates walked up to her and complimented her outfit, her white teeth, her amazing jewelry, that funny thing she'd said in English class the other day. It was par for the course, naturally—everyone *always* loved Julie. She was the most popular girl in school.

Then Ashley Ferguson, a junior who'd just dyed her hair the same auburn shade as Julie's, stopped and gave a reverent smile. "You look amazing," she gushed, same as the others.

"Thank you," Julie said modestly.

"Where'd you get the dress?" Ashley asked.

3

Julie's friend Nyssa Frankel inserted herself between the two. "Why, Ashley?" she snapped. "Are you going to buy the exact same one?"

Julie laughed as Nyssa and Natalie Houma, another of Julie's friends, high-fived. Ashley set her jaw and stomped away. Julie bit her lip, wondering if she'd been too mean. There was only one person she wanted to be mean to deliberately tonight.

And that was Nolan.

Meanwhile, Ava Jalali stood with her boyfriend, Alex Cohen, in the Hotchkisses' reclaimed oak and marble kitchen, nibbling on a carrot stick. She eyed a tower of cupcakes next to the veggie tray longingly. "Remind me why I decided to do a cleanse again?"

"Because you're insane?" Alex raised his eyebrows mischievously.

Ava gave him an *uh-duh* look and pushed her smooth, straight, perfect dark hair out of her eyes. She was the type of girl who hated even looking at cross sections of the human body in biology class; she couldn't stand the idea that *she* was that ugly and messy inside.

Alex swiped his thumb on the icing and brought his hand toward Ava's face. "Yummy . . ."

Ava drew back. "Get that away!" But then she giggled. Alex had moved here in ninth grade. He wasn't as popular or as rich as some of the other guys, but he always made her laugh. But then the sight of someone in the doorway wiped the smile off her face. Nolan Hotchkiss, the party's host, stared at her with an almost territorial grin.

He deserves what he's going to get, she thought darkly.

In the backyard—which had high, swooping arcades that connected one patio to another; huge potted plants; and a long slate walkway that practically ended in the water—Mackenzie Wright rolled up her jeans, removed her toe rings, and plunked her feet into the infinity-edge pool. A lot of people were swimming, including her best friend, Claire Coldwell, and Claire's boyfriend, Blake Strustek.

Blake spun Claire around and laced his fingers through hers. "Hey, watch the digits," Claire warned. "They're my ticket to Juilliard."

Blake glanced at Mac and rolled his eyes. Mac looked away, almost as if she didn't like Blake at all.

Or perhaps because she liked him *too* much.

Then the patio door opened, and Nolan Hotchkiss, the man of the hour, sauntered onto the lawn with a smug, *I'm-the-lord-of-this-party* look on his face. He strolled to two boys and bumped fists. After a beat, they glanced Mac's way and started whispering.

Mac sucked in her stomach, feeling their gazes canvass her snub nose, her glasses with their dark hipster frames, and her large, chunky knit scarf. She knew what they were talking about. Her hatred for Nolan flared up all over again.

Beep.

Her phone, which sat next to her on the tiled ground, lit up. Mac glanced at the text from her new friend Caitlin Martell-Lewis.

It's time.

Julie and Ava received the same missives. Like robots, they all stood, excused themselves, and walked to the rendezvous point. Empty cups lay on the ground in the hall. There was a cupcake smashed on the kitchen wall, and the den smelled distinctly of pot. The girls convened by the stairs and exchanged long, nervous glances.

Caitlin cleared her throat. "So."

Ava pursed her full lips and glanced at her reflection in the enormous mirror. Caitlin rolled back her shoulders and felt for something in her purse. It rattled slightly. Mac checked her own bag to make sure the camera she'd swiped from her mom's desk was still inside.

Then Julie's gaze fixed on a figure hovering in the doorway. It was Parker Duvall, her best friend in the world. She'd *come*, just as Julie hoped she would. As usual, Parker wore a short denim skirt, black lace tights, and an oversize black sweatshirt. When she saw Julie, she poked her face out from the hood, a wide grin spreading across her cheeks and illuminating her scars. Julie tried not to gasp, but it was so rare that Parker allowed anyone to see her face. Parker rushed up to the girls, pulling the hoodie around her face once more.

All five of them glanced around to see if anyone was watching. "I can't believe we're doing this," Mackenzie admitted.

Caitlin's eyebrows made a V. "You're not backing out, are you?"

Mac shook her head quickly. "Of course not."

"Good." Caitlin glanced at the others. "Are we all still in?"

Parker nodded. After a moment, Julie said yes, too. And Ava, who was touching up her lip gloss, gave a single, decisive nod.

Their gazes turned to Nolan as he wove through the living room. He greeted kids heartily. Slapped friends on the back. Shot a winning smile to a girl who looked like a freshman, and the girl's eyes widened with shock. Whispered something to a different girl, and her face fell just as quickly.

That was the kind of power Nolan Hotchkiss had over people. He was *the* most popular guy at school—handsome, athletic, charming, the head of every committee and club he joined. His family was the wealthiest, too—you couldn't go a mile without seeing the name *Hotchkiss* on one of the new developments popping up or turn a page in the newspaper without seeing Nolan's state senator mother cutting a ribbon at a new bakery, day care facility, community park, or library. More than that, there was something about him that basically . . . *hypnotized* you. One look, one suggestion, one command, one snarky remark, one blow-off, one public embarrassment, and you were under his thumb for life. Nolan controlled Beacon, whether you liked it or not. But what's that saying? "Absolute power corrupts absolutely." And for all the people who worshipped Nolan, there were those who couldn't stand him, too. Who wanted him . . . *gone*, in fact.

The girls looked at one another and smiled. "All right, then," Ava said, stepping out into the crowd, toward Nolan. "Let's do this."

Like any good party, the bash at the Hotchkiss house lingered into the wee hours of the morning. Leave it to Nolan to have an in with the cops, because no one raided the place for booze or even told them to cut the noise. Shortly after midnight, some party pics were posted online: two girls kissing in the powder room; the school's biggest prude doing a body shot off the star running back's chest; one of the stoners grinning sloppily, holding several cupcakes aloft; and the party's host passed out on a Lovesac beanbag upstairs with something Sharpied on his face. Partying hard was Nolan's specialty, after all.

Revelers passed out on the outdoor couch, on the hammock that hung between two big birch trees at the back of the property, and in zigzag shapes on the floor. For several hours, the house was still, the cupcake icing slowly hardening, a tipped-over bottle of wine pooling in the sink, a raccoon digging through some of the trash bags that had been left out in the backyard. Not everyone awoke when the boy screamed. Not even when that same someone—a junior named Miro—ran down the stairs and screamed what had happened to the 911 dispatcher did all the kids stir.

It was only when the ambulances screeched into the driveway, sirens blaring, lights flashing, walkie-talkies crackling, that all eyes opened. The first thing everyone saw were EMT workers in their reflective jackets busting inside. Miro pointed them to the upper floor. There were boots on the stairs, and then . . . those same EMT people carrying someone back down. Someone who had Sharpie marker on his face. Someone who was limp and gray.

The EMT worker spoke into his radio. "We have an eighteen-year-old male DOA."

Was that Nolan? everyone would whisper in horror as they staggered out of the house, horrifically hungover. *And . . . DOA? Dead on arrival?*

By Saturday afternoon, the news was everywhere. The Hotchkiss parents returned from their business meeting in Los Angeles that evening to do damage control, but it was too late—the whole town knew that Nolan Hotchkiss had dropped dead at his party, probably from too much fun.

Darker rumors posited that perhaps he'd *meant* to do it. Beacon was notoriously hard on its offspring, after all, and maybe even golden boy Nolan Hotchkiss had felt the heat.

When Julie woke up Saturday morning and heard the news, her throat closed. Ava picked up the phone three times before talking herself down. Mac stared into space for a long, long time, then burst into hot, quiet tears. And Caitlin, who'd wanted Nolan dead for so long, couldn't help but feel sorry for his family, even though he had destroyed hers. And Parker? She went to the dock and stared at the water, her face hidden under her hoodie. Her head pounded with an oncoming migraine.

They called one another and spoke in heated whispers. They felt terrible, but they were smart girls. Logical girls. Nolan Hotchkiss was gone; the dictator of Beacon Heights High was no more. That meant no more tears. No more bullying. No more living in fear that he'd expose everyone's awful secrets—somehow, he'd known so many. And anyway, not a single person had seen them go upstairs with Nolan that night—they'd made sure of it. No one would ever connect them to him.

The problem, though, was that someone had seen. Someone knew what they'd done that night, and so much more.

And someone was going to make them pay.

Don't miss a single scandal!